"十三五"江苏省高等学校重点教材
（编号：2019-2-074）

U0653206

非裔美国文学作品选读

Selected Readings in African American Literature

主　编　王玉括
副主编　尤　蕾　朱　莉
编　者　徐在中　却　俊　黄成林
　　　　胡慧勇　柏云彩　高鸣敏
　　　　王娜娜

南京大学出版社

前　言

经过几个世纪的发展,非裔美国文学不断壮大,涌现出许多杰出的诗人、剧作家、小说家、传记家,以及享誉世界的学者与社会活动家,许多名篇佳作也成为美国文学的重要组成部分,入选《诺顿美国文学选集》与《诺顿文学理论与批评选集》等。20 世纪 70 年代以来,美国许多高校开始设置"黑人研究"项目,进一步推动了非裔美国文学与文化研究的深入。

20 世纪以来,我国始终关注非裔美国文化及文学的发展。20 世纪初,林纾翻译的《黑奴吁天录》在中国社会产生非常大的影响,黑奴汤姆叔叔成为处于半封建半殖民地社会的中国人反观自身的一面镜子。长期以来,美国黑人文学是中国学术界关注、借鉴的重要对象。20 世纪30 年代,休斯访华推动了中国社会对非裔美国文学作家作品的介绍与翻译。40 年代,我国几乎与美国同步介绍赖特的新作,可谓新的例证。1949 年至 1979 年间,我国学术界始终关注美国黑人文学的战斗功能及其对揭露美国资本主义社会的各种问题所发挥的作用,翻译、介绍了休斯、赖特等进步作家或具有左翼倾向的非裔美国文学作品。

改革开放以来,我国学术界继续重视非裔美国文学的现实主义特征及其认知功能,也越来越重视非裔美国文学的美学价值与文化意义,许多硕士、博士论文以非裔美国文学为研究对象;国内许多重要的外国文学研究期刊也以相当大的篇幅介绍非裔美国文学研究动态与趋势;许多著名高校开设非裔美国文学或非裔美国重要作家专题研讨课,并向全校的素质类拓展课方向发展。

为更好地建设特色鲜明的英语专业,更好地服务于全校的综合素质类课程,南京邮电大学外国语学院集中文学方向的精锐力量,结合兄弟高校优秀师资,编写国内第一部非裔美国文学作品选读教材。

本教材涵盖非裔美国文学的主要文类:小说、自传、戏剧与诗歌,积极借鉴美国高校同类课程选材的原则与方法,重点选取非裔美国文学代表作家与作品,并结合中国学生的实际需要,配以作家简介、作品简介与选读赏析等,辅之以注释与思考题,注重培养学生的文本细读能力与批判性思维能力,为丰富中华文化建设提供他山之石与借鉴之镜。

王玉括
2020 年 10 月于南京仙林

目 录

Contents

非裔美国文学简介

　　非裔美国文学（African American Literature）是指由非洲人后裔在美国以英语创作的文学作品。作为美国文学的重要组成部分，非裔美国文学已经取得令人瞩目的成就，产生了一批具有世界影响力的作品，在书写自身文化传统的过程中，秉承对自由、公正、平等、独立等美国主流价值观的追求、质疑与坚守，为美国文化的多样性乃至世界流散文学与文化研究做出了自己的独特贡献。

　　据记载，1619 年，第一批非洲黑人踏上美国的土地，之后的非洲奴隶贸易为北美大陆输送了大量黑奴，19 世纪上半叶，美国南方种植园扩大再生产的需要引发大规模的奴隶买卖，并制定了许多限制奴隶人身自由、剥夺他们受教育机会的法令法规。远离故土的非洲黑人不仅失去与自己文化传统的联系，被黑色大西洋无情地隔开，而且在文化传统方面被连根拔起，因此，黑人的书面文学创作与作品出版相对较晚。目前能够确定的由非裔美国人创作的散文作品最早发表于 1760 年，最早的诗歌作品是露西·泰莉（Lucy Terry）于 1746 年创作的《巴尔斯之战》（"Bars Fight"），哈蒙（Jupiter Hammon）的第一首诗歌《夜思》（"An Evening Thought：Salvation by Christ With Penitential Cries"）出版于 1760 年。但是学术界普遍认为，惠特莉（Phillis Wheatley）创作出版的《关于宗教、道德诸主题的诗歌》（*Poems on Various Subjects, Religious and Moral*，1773）是非裔美国文学的开始，开创了非裔美国文学（与批评）传统，也开启了黑人女性文学传统。

　　18 世纪下半叶至 19 世纪末出现的大量奴隶叙事作品为非裔美国文学传统的形成奠定了重要的基础。1865 年内战结束前的奴隶叙事作品大致可以分为两个阶段和两种主要类型，以 19 世纪 30 年代为分界点。第一部美国奴隶叙事《布里顿·哈蒙：一位黑人的惊世苦难与离奇拯救》（*Narrative of the Uncommon Sufferings, and Surprising Deliverance of Briton Hammon, a Negro Man*）于 1760 年在波士顿出版，之后出版的奴隶叙事作品分别由葛洛尼韶（James Gronniosaw）、马兰特（John Marrant）、库高诺（Ottobah Cugoano）、艾奎亚诺（Olaudah Equiano）及杰伊（John Jea）所撰写。其中尤以《艾奎亚诺的传奇人生》（*The Interesting Narrative of the Life of Olaudah Equiano*）最具代表性，是 19 世纪美国奴隶叙事的原型，为后来的奴隶叙事奠定了重要基础。1845 年出版的道格拉斯的《弗里德里克·道格拉斯：一个美国黑人奴隶的生平自述》（*Narrative of the Life of Frederick Douglass, an American Slave*）是奴隶叙事的典型代表，成为衡量其他奴隶叙事的标准文本，作品以"我出生于某地"开始，描写残酷的男主人、女主人或监工经常鞭打奴隶；此外，也记录了奴隶学习读写过程中遇到的困难，遭遇的挫折与障碍，揭露号称"基督徒"的奴隶主的伪善；奴隶叙事中不可或缺的是描绘奴隶的逃亡，以及猎奴队与猎狗紧追其后的追捕等；最后叙述奴隶成功逃往北方的喜悦，取个新的姓氏，作为自由人获得一种合适的新的社会身份，然后对奴隶制进行反思等。其中最突出的特征是：学习读写，掌握读写能力；敢于反抗奴役，并成功逃亡；特别强调个体的自我再现。

　　19 世纪 30 年代之前以艾奎亚诺为代表的奴隶叙事并非仅仅局限于美国本土，而是在更加广阔的大西洋区域的历史背景下进行，叙述者在非洲、欧洲与美洲活动；以道格拉斯为代表的第二阶段的奴隶叙事作品,主要揭露美国南方奴隶制的罪恶,配合废奴运动,呼吁白人读者的同情与支持。1865 年内战结束前,美国出版了 87 部奴隶叙事的书或小册子,平均每年1.3 部;1866 至 1901 间,出版了 54 部前奴隶的叙事作品,平均每年 1.5 部。

非裔美国女性也积极参与奴隶叙事的书写,发展、丰富了奴隶叙事创作与研究中的性别维度。普林斯(Mary Prince)是第一位发表奴隶叙事的女性,于 1831 年出版《玛丽·普林斯的生平》(*The History of Mary Prince*),彻底改变了奴隶叙事这一文类中的男性视角,不仅揭露黑人女奴遭受的性虐待与性剥削,而且强调黑人女性对待孩子与家庭的自然情感。雅各布斯(Harriet Jacobs)的《女奴生平》(*Incident in the Life of a Slave Girl*,1861)借鉴感伤小说模式,修改了艾奎亚诺与道格拉斯这两位著名黑人男性作家的奴隶叙事模式,直接面向女性(包括白人女性)读者进行创作,与她所继承的男性文学传统拉开距离,把奴隶叙事推向高潮。

除奴隶叙事之外,19 世纪的其他重要非裔美国作家与作品还包括内战前沃克(David Walker)鼓励读者反对奴役、反对奴隶制的小册子《呼吁》(*An Appeal to the Coloured Citizens of the World*,1829),较早体现了黑人民族主义的思想,布朗(William Wells Brown)的第一部非裔美国小说《科洛泰尔》(*Clotel;or,The President's Daughter*,1853)和第一部非裔美国戏剧《逃往自由》(*The Escape;or,A Leap for Freedom*,1858),1859 年,德莱尼(Martin R. Delany)发表《美国小屋》(*Blake;or The Huts of America*),同年出现非裔美国女作家哈珀(Frances Ellen Watkins Harper)的短篇小说和威尔逊(Harriet E. Wilson)的长篇小说《我们的黑鬼》(*Our Nig;or,Sketches from the Life of a Free Black*)。19 世纪末的重要非裔美国作家有获得全国认可与国际声誉的邓巴(Paul Dunbar),他以方言诗为时人所知,以及探索内战后美国南方复杂的种族与社会身份的切斯纳特(Charles Chesnutt)等,邓巴对非裔美国民俗与方言的使用,对后来的非裔美国作家产生了重要影响。

20 世纪 20—30 年代的哈莱姆文艺复兴不仅推动了文艺创作,而且深化了对种族问题的思考,重点探索种族与艺术、历史、性别、阶级、性、政治、社会学、哲学等之间的关系。学术界普遍认为,哈莱姆文艺复兴指 20 年代发生于纽约的哈莱姆黑人居住区的黑人文艺运动(也被称为新黑人文艺复兴),有几位公认的重要代表人物,如杜波伊斯(W. E. B. Du Bois)、洛克(Alain Locke)、约翰逊(James Weldon Johnson),几处重要的诗歌与小说发表园地,如《危机》(*The Crisis*)、《机遇》(*Opportunity*)、《信使》(*Messenger*)等杂志,由于一些白人与黑人赞助人的热心帮助,许多年轻的黑人作家得以进行创作,陆续发表、出版许多诗歌与小说作品。华盛顿(Booker T. Washington)的自传《从奴役中奋起》(*Up from Slavery*,1901)重视黑人的技能教育与经济条件的改善,忽略黑人的政治平等诉求,杜波伊斯的《黑人的灵魂》(*The Souls of Black Folk*,1903)发人深省,影响深远,不仅提出非裔美国人的双重意识问题,而且预言般地指出美国 20 世纪的最大问题是种族问题,约翰逊的《前有色人自传》(*The Autobiography of an Ex-Colored Man*,1912)率先关注黑人混为白人的问题,洛克的《新黑人》(*The New Negro*,1925)为一个时代命名,提出黑人的自信与自我表达问题;此外,图默(Jean Toomer)的《甘蔗》(*Cane*,1923)极具实验性特点,诗人休斯(Langston Hughes)积极借鉴黑人爵士乐的主题与节奏进行创作。费希尔(Rudolph Fisher)的《术师死去》(*The Conjure Man Dies*,1932)通常被视为第一部非裔美国侦探小说,瑟曼(Wallace Thurman)的《莓子愈黑》(*The Blacker the Berry*,1929)是第一部涉及同性恋的非裔美国小说。戏剧方面有第一部在百老汇上演的非裔美国非音乐剧——理查森(Willis Richardson)的《拾荒老妪的财产》(*The Chip Woman's Fortune*,1923)。民俗学家和小说家赫斯顿(Zora Neale Hurston)是哈莱姆文艺复兴的杰出代表,融南方黑人民俗于小说创作,《他们眼望上苍》(1937)成功地塑造了新黑人时代的女性人物珍妮。

美国民权运动之前的非裔美国代表性作家主要有关注黑人的不公正遭遇、强调文学的社会批判功能、更加青睐现实主义与自然主义风格的赖特（Richard Wright）、佩特里（Ann Petry）和海姆斯（Chester Himes）等，赖特的小说《土生子》（*Native Son*，1940）塑造了暴力特征明显的主人公别格，彻底颠覆了温顺的"汤姆叔叔"形象，自传作品《黑孩子》（*Black Boy*，1945）借鉴了 19 世纪奴隶叙事追求自由的主题与形式。佩特里的《大街》（*The Street*，1946）和海姆斯的《他要是抱怨就让他走》（*If He Hollers Let Him Go*，1945）与赖特的抗议小说一脉相传，海姆斯也是著名非裔美国侦探小说家，其哈莱姆侦探小说系列广受好评。此外，关注黑人社区普通黑人喜怒哀乐的布鲁克斯（Gwendolyn Brooks），因诗集《安妮·艾伦》（*Annie Allen*，1949）成为第一位获得普利策诗歌奖的非裔美国诗人；埃里森（Ralph Ellison）探索黑人主人公寻找自我人生旅程的小说《看不见的人》（*Invisible Man*，1952）获得国家图书奖；以批评赖特的抗议小说为学术界瞩目的鲍德温（James Baldwin）不仅出版多部文集如《土生子札记》（*Notes of a Native Son*，1955），《下次是火》（*The Fire Next Time*，1963）等，也创作了多部小说，如《向苍天呼吁》（*Go Tell It on the Mountain*，1953），《乔万尼的房间》（*Giovanni's Room*，1956）是第一部公开处理同性恋主题的非裔美国小说，《另一国度》（*Another Country*，1962）则探讨了双性恋、黑人与白人之间的性行为等主题；年轻剧作家汉丝贝利（Lorraine Hansberry）描写黑人家庭反对种族隔离、挑战限制性条款的作品《阳光下的干葡萄》（*A Raisin in the Sun*，1959）获得纽约剧评人奖。

美国民权运动催生的黑人艺术运动与黑人权力运动明确提出追求黑人的团结、黑人的民族身份等主张，渴望创造一种新的历史、象征、神话与传说，创立自己的黑人美学等。黑人艺术家们创办黑人剧院，发表充满火药味的诗作。著名代表人物有诗人兼剧作家琼斯/巴拉卡（LeRoi Jones/Amiri Baraka），其《荷兰人》（*Dutchman*，1964）获得奥比奖，布林斯（Ed Bullins）三获奥比奖；其他重要诗人有桑切斯（Sonia Sanchez）、科特斯（Jayne Cortez）、奈特（Etheridge Knight）、罗杰斯（Carolyn M. Rodgers）和乔万尼（Nikki Giovanni）等；自传作品有《马尔科姆·艾克斯自传》（*The Autobiography of Malcolm X*，1965）及穆迪（Anne Moody）的《成年于密西西比》（*Coming of Age in Mississippi*，1968）；重要小说有里德（Ishmael Reed）以戏仿方式调侃黑人文化民族主义的《胡言乱语》（*Mumbo Jumbo*，1972），盖恩斯（Ernest J. Gaines）的小说《简·皮特曼小姐自传》（*The Autobiography of Miss Jane Pittman*，1971）等。

20 世纪 70 年代兴起的黑人女性主义，进一步推动了非裔美国文学的繁荣，重要代表作家作品主要有玛雅·安吉洛（Maya Angelou）及其自传《我知道笼中鸟为何歌唱》（*I Know Why the Caged Bird Sings*，1970），沃克（Alice Walker）的代表作《紫色》（*The Color Purple*，1982）描绘了非裔美国社区内部的问题，特别是黑人男性对女性的压迫问题，她对赫斯顿的关注与考古，推动了黑人女性主义的发展；1993 年获得诺贝尔文学奖的托妮·莫里森（Toni Morrison）始终关注黑人社区内部的矛盾与问题，重视对普通黑人生活的再现与描绘，陆续发表多部作品，其代表作《宠儿》（*Beloved*，1987）获得多项大奖，不仅深化了对非裔美国历史与记忆的思考与再现，而且成功地激励其他年轻非裔美国女作家创作出更多更好的作品。此外，还有著名女性主义诗人洛德（Audre Lorde），普利策诗歌奖获得者、美国桂冠诗人达夫（Rita Dove），小说家马歇尔（Paule Marshall），金凯德（Jamaica Kincaid），剧作家尚格（Ntozake Shange），第一位获得雨果奖和星云奖的非裔美国女性科幻小说家巴特勒（Octavia E. Butler）等，她们的创作不仅关注白人与黑人之间的种族问题，而且反思黑人族群内部男性至上的观念对黑人女性的压迫与伤害，丰富了非裔美国文学的性别维度。

非裔美国男性作家也取得了不俗的成绩,小说家怀德曼(John Wideman)获得多种奖项,其自传《兄弟与看护人》(*Brothers and Keepers*,1984)是 20 世纪晚期最具创意的作品之一,约翰逊(Charles R. Johnson)的《中间航道》(*Middle Passage*,1990)获得美国国家图书奖;戏剧方面的代表人物主要有因《无处成名》(*No Place to be Somebody*,1969)获得 1970 年普利策戏剧奖的第一位非裔美国剧作家戈登(Charles Gordone),1973 年获得托尼奖的沃克(Joseph A. Walker),因《士兵的报酬》(*A Soldier's Pay*,1981)获得普利策奖和纽约戏剧批评界奖的富勒(Charles H. Fuller, Jr.),而最具代表性的剧作家当属威尔逊(August Wilson),他以 10 部作品涵盖 20 世纪 10 个不同的时段,探讨了不同时期非裔美国人的个体、家庭与社区生活及其与历史的联系,分别以《栅栏》(*Fences*,1985)与《钢琴课》(*The Piano Lesson*,1987)两次获得普利策戏剧奖。

进入 21 世纪,非裔美国文学继续保持良好的发展势头,不仅创作主题多样,而且创作手法与风格多变。既有许多作家继续关注奴隶制及种族隔离制度等历史问题,也有许多作家关心大迁徙运动对黑人的影响,以及城市化过程中黑人面临的新的身份认同与种族歧视问题,既有现实主义的杰作,也有许多现代主义和后现代主义风格的作品,在小说、诗歌和戏剧领域都有非常突出的表现,多次获得大奖,成为美国族裔文学中最靓丽的一道风景线,如琼斯(Edward Jones)探讨奴隶制时期黑人奴隶主问题的小说《已知世界》(*The Known World*,2003)获得普利策奖;怀特黑德(Colson Whitehead)的小说《地下铁道》(*The Underground Railroad*,2016)获得美国国家图书奖与普利策小说奖;美国桂冠诗人特雷塞韦(Natasha Trethewey)的诗集《黑人卫士》(*Native Guard*,2006)获得 2007 年普利策诗歌奖;帕克斯(Suzan-Lori Parks)因探讨黑人男性兄弟家庭关系的剧作《赢家/输家》(*Topdog/Underdog*,2001)成为第一位获得普利策戏剧奖的非裔美国女剧作家;杰西(Tyehimba Jess)以《奥利奥》(*Olio*,2016)获得 2017 年普利策诗歌奖;诺塔奇(Lynn Nottage)以《劳役》(*Sweat*,2016)于 2017 年第二次获得普利策戏剧奖等,再次证明当代非裔美国文学的繁荣与生命力。读者有理由期待,非裔美国文学在反思种族、性别与阶级的时代背景下,在质疑种族的社会建构特征的进程中,会涌现出越来越多的杰作,为美国乃至世界读者深入了解族裔的多元性特征提供更多更好的优秀文本。

African American Poetry
非裔美国诗歌简介

与很多民族的文学发展进程类似的是,非裔美国文学也以诗歌开始,注重反映非裔美国民族的社会生活与个体境遇。美国两个多世纪的奴隶制进一步强化了非裔美国诗歌对社会内容的重点关注,揭示了美国制度性的种族歧视给美国黑人个体造成的身体与心理伤害。1865 年内战结束以后,杰出的非裔美国诗人不断涌现,著名代表人物有 19 世纪末赢得广泛赞誉的邓巴,以及 20 世纪 20 年代哈莱姆文艺复兴时期的代表人物休斯、麦凯、卡伦、布朗等人;第二次世界大战后,布鲁克斯成为第一位获得普利策奖的非裔美国诗人,这一殊荣进一步扩大了非裔美国文学特别是非裔美国诗歌的影响。20 世纪 70 年代以来,伴随着民权运动的深入,争取非裔美国民族的合法权益,提倡文学的宣传甚至战斗功能,成为很长一段时间内许多非裔美国诗人的共同追求。

作为非裔美国文学的缩影,非裔美国诗歌在内容与形式两个方面的发展预示了非裔美国文学其他文类的大致走向,其内容方面的多样与形式方面的创新为非裔美国文学注入了新的活力。本单元选取非裔美国诗歌发展不同时段的 10 首代表性诗歌,旨在引导学生领略非裔美国诗歌的艺术魅力及其在不同时代的发展。

1. "Bars Fight" by Lucy Terry[①]

August，'twas the twenty-fifth,
Seventeen hundred forty-six,
The Indians did in ambush lay,
Some very valiant men to slay,

The names of whom I'll not leave out：
Samuel Allen like a hero fout，
And though he was so brave and bold，
His face no more shall we behold.

Eleazor Hawks was killed outright，

---

① 这首诗歌是露西·泰莉 16 岁(1746 年)时创作的,是目前能够确认的美国黑人创作的第一首诗歌,但是直到 1855年才发表。

Before he had time to fight—
Before he did the Indians see,
Was shot and killed immediately.

Oliver Armsden he was slain,
Which caused his friends much grief and pain.
Simeon Arsden they found dead
Not many rods distant from his head.

Adonijah Gillet, we do hear,
Did lose his life which was so dear.
John Sadler fled across the water,
And thus escaped the dreadful slaughter.

Eunice Allen see the Indians coming,
And hopes to save herself by running;
And had not her petticoats stopped her,
The awful creatures had not catched her,

Nor tommy hawked her on the head,
And left her on the ground for dead.
Young Samuel Allen, Oh, lack-a-day!
Was taken and carried to Canada.

2. "To the University of Cambridge, in New-England" by Phillis Wheatley[①]

From Poems on Various Subjects, Religious and Moral

WHILE an intrinsic ardor prompts to write,
The muses promise to assist my pen;
'Twas not long since I left my native shore
The land of errors, and *Egyptian* gloom:
Father of mercy, 'twas thy gracious hand
Brought me in safety from those dark abodes.

---

① 菲丽丝·惠特莉(1753—1784)是从非洲劫掠卖到美国的奴隶,她聪慧好学,借鉴英国诗人亚历山大·蒲柏等人的风格与创作技巧,出版诗集《关于宗教、道德诸主题的诗歌》(1773),开启非裔美国文学传统(及非裔美国女性文学传统)。

Students, to you 'tis giv'n to scan the heights
Above, to traverse the ethereal space,
And mark the systems of revolving worlds.
Still more, ye sons of science ye receive
The blissful news by messengers from heav'n,
How *Jesus'* blood for your redemption flows.
See him with hands out-stretcht upon the cross;
Immense compassion in his bosom glows;
He hears revilers, nor resents their scorn:
What matchless mercy in the Son of God!
When the whole human race by sin had fall'n,
He deign'd to die that they might rise again,
And share with him in the sublimest skies,
Life without death, and glory without end.

Improve your privileges while they stay,
Ye pupils, and each hour redeem, that bears
Or good or bad report of you to heav'n.
Let sin, that baneful evil to the soul,
By you be shunn'd, nor once remit your guard;
Suppress the deadly serpent in its egg.
Ye blooming plants of human race divine,
An *Ethiop* tells you 'tis your greatest foe;
Its transient sweetness turns to endless pain,
And in immense perdition sinks the soul.

[1773]

3. "We Wear the Mask" by Paul Laurence Dunbar[①]

From *Lyrics of Lowly Life*

We wear the mask that grins and lies,
It hides our cheeks and shades our eyes—
This debt we pay to human guile;
With torn and bleeding hearts we smile,
And mouth with myriad subtleties.

---

① 保罗·劳伦斯·邓巴(1872—1906)是以黑人方言入诗而为美国读者所熟悉的"种族"诗人。他引以为憾的是,自己很多以标准英语创作的诗歌无人问津。本诗中的"面具"(mask)道尽美国黑人不为人知的辛酸。

Why should the world be overwise,
In counting all our tears and sighs?
Nay, let them only see us, while
We wear the mask.

We smile, but, O great Christ, our cries
To thee from tortured souls arise.
We sing, but oh the clay is vile
Beneath our feet, and long the mile;
But let the world dream otherwise,
We wear the mask!

4. "If We Must Die" by Claude McKay^①

From *Harlem Shadows*

If we must die, let it not be like hogs
Hunted and penned in an inglorious spot,
While round us bark the mad and hungry dogs,
Making their mock at our accursèd lot.
If we must die, O let us nobly die,
So that our precious blood may not be shed
In vain; then even the monsters we defy
Shall be constrained to honor us though dead!
O kinsmen! we must meet the common foe!
Though far outnumbered let us show us brave,
And for their thousand blows deal one deathblow!
What though before us lies the open grave?
Like men we'll face the murderous, cowardly pack,
Pressed to the wall, dying, but fighting back!

[1922]

---

① 克劳德·麦凯(1889—1948)出生于牙买加,是哈莱姆文艺复兴时期的重要作家,主要作品包括《回到哈莱姆》(1928)、《班卓》(1929)、《香蕉谷》(1933)和自传《远离故土》(1937)等。这首小诗不仅揭示了美国的种族问题,也成为鼓舞人们以昂扬的斗志、不懈的努力,争取自由的名篇。

5. "The Negro Speaks of Rivers" by Langston Hughes[①]

I've known rivers:
I've known rivers ancient as the world and older than the
flow of human blood in human veins.

My soul has grown deep like the rivers.

I bathed in the Euphrates when dawns were young.
I built my hut near the Congo and it lulled me to sleep.
I looked upon the Nile and raised the pyramids above it.
I heard the singing of the Mississippi when Abe Lincoln
went down to New Orleans, and I've seen its
muddy bosom turn all golden in the sunset

I've known rivers:
Ancient, dusky rivers.

My soul has grown deep like the rivers.

[1921, 1926]

6. "We Real Cool" by Gwendolyn Brooks[②]

THE POOL PLAYERS.
SEVEN AT THE GOLDEN SHOVEL.

We real cool. We
Left school. We

Lurk late. We
Strike straight. We

Sing sin. We

---

① 兰斯顿·休斯(1902—1967)是位多产作家,哈莱姆文艺复兴时期最杰出的非裔美国诗人。

② 格温多林·布鲁克斯(1917—2000)是第一位获得普利策诗歌奖(1949年)的非裔美国抒情诗人,也是伊利诺伊州的桂冠诗人;20世纪60年代的民权运动期间,她的诗歌创作趋向激进,风格大变。

Thin gin. We

Jazz June. We
Die soon.

〔1960〕

7. "Black Art" by Amiri Baraka[①]

Poems are bullshit unless they are
teeth or trees or lemons pilled
on a step. Or black ladies dying
of men leaving nickel hearts
beating them down. Fuck poems
and they are useful, wd they shoot
come at you, love what you are,
breathe like wrestlers, or shudder
strangely after pissing. We want live
words of the hip world live flesh &
coursing blood. Hearts Brains
Souls splintering fire. We want poems
like fists beating niggers out of Jocks
or dagger poems in the slimy bellies
of the owner-jews. Black poems to
smear on girdlemamma mulatto bitches
whose brains are red jelly stuck
between 'lizabeth taylor's toes. Stinking
Whores! We want "poems that kill."
Assassin poems, Poems that shoot
guns. Poems that wrestle cops into alleys
and take their weapons leaving them dead
with tongues pulled out and sent to Ireland. Knockoff
pomes for dope selling wops or slick halfwhite
politicians Airplane poems, rrrrrrrrrrrrrr
rrrrrrrrrrrrrr … tuhtuhtuhtuhtuhtuhtuhtuh
… rrrrrrrrrrrrrrrr … Setting fire and death to

① 阿米利·巴拉卡(1934—2014)是位与时俱进的诗人,20 世纪 50 年代,他是先锋派诗人;60 年代,他转向黑人民族主义;70 年代,成为马克思主义者。"9·11"之后,因发表反犹诗歌,他被剥夺了新泽西州桂冠诗人的称号。作为 60 年代美国民权运动时期的代表性诗人,他主张以诗歌为武器,奋起抗争。

whities ass. Look at the Liberal
Spokesman for the jews clutch his throat
& puke himself into eternity ... rrrrrrr
There's a negroleader pinned to
a bar stool in Sardi's eyeballs melting
in hot flame Another negroleader
on the steps of the white house one
kneeling between the sheriff's thighs
negotiating cooly for his people.
Agggh ... stumbles across the room ...
Put it on him，poem. Strip him naked
to the world! Another bad poem cracking
steel knuckles in a jewlady's mouth
Poem scream poison gas on beasts in green berets
Clean out the world for virtue and love，
Let there be no love poems written
until love can exist freely and
cleanly. Let Black People understand
that they are the lovers and the sons
of lovers and warriors and sons
of warriors Are poems & poems &
all the loveliness here in the world

We want a black poem. And a
Black World.
Let the world be a Black Poem
And Let All Black People Speak This Poem
Silently
or LOUD

$\lbrack 1969 \rbrack$

8. "David Walker" by Rita Dove①

Free to travel，he still couldn't be shown how lucky
he was：*They strip and beat and drag us about*
like rattlesnakes. Home on Brattle Street，he took in the sign

① 丽塔·达夫(1952—)是当代著名非裔美国诗人,1986 年获得普利策奖,40 岁时成为美国桂冠诗人(第一位获此殊荣的非裔美国诗人)。

on the door of the slop shop. All day at the counter—
white caps, ale-stained pea coats. Compass: needles,
eloquent as tuning forks, shivered, pointing north.
Evenings, the ceiling fan sputtered like a second pulse.
Oh Heaven! I am full!! I can hardly move my pen!!!

On the faith of an eve-wink, pamphlets were stuffed
into trouser pockets. Pamphlets transported
in the coat linings of itinerant seamen, jackets
ringwormed with salt traded drunkenly to pursers
in the Carolinas, pamphlets ripped out, read aloud:
Men of colour, who are also of sense.
Outrage. Incredulity. Uproar in the state legislatures.

We are the most wretched, degraded and abject set
Of beings that ever lived since the world began.
The jeweled canaries in the lecture halls tittered,
pressed his dark hand between their gloves.
Every half-step was n step at all.
Every morning, the man on the corner strung a fresh
bunch of boots from his shoulders. "I'm happy!" he said.
"I never want to live any better or happier than
when I can get a-plenty of boots and shoes to clean!"

a second edition. A third.
The abolitionist press is *perfectly appalled.*
Humanity, kindness and the fear of the Lord
does not consist in protecting devils. A month—
his person (is that all?) found face-down
in the doorway at Brattle Street,
his frame slighter than friends remembered.

[1980]

9. "Sleeping with the Dictionary" by Harryette Mullen[①]

From *Sleeping with the Dictionary*

I beg to dicker with my silver-tongued companion, whose lips are ready to read my shining gloss. A versatile partner, conversant and well-versed in the verbal art, the dictionary is not averse to the solitary habits of the curiously wide-awake reader. In the dark night's insomnia, the book is a stimulating sedative, awakening my tired imagination to the hypnagogic trance of language. Retiring to the canopy of the bedroom, turning on the bedside light, taking the big dictionary to bed, clutching the unabridged bulk, heavy with the weight of all the meanings between these covers, smoothing the thin sheets, thick with accented syllables—all are exercises in the conscious regimen of dreamers, who toss words on their tongues while turning illuminated pages. To go through all these motions and procedures, groping in the dark for an alluring word, is the poet's nocturnal mission. Aroused by myriad possibilities, we try out the most perverse positions in the practice of our nightly act, the penetration of the denotative body of the work. Any exit from the logic of language might be an entry in a symptomatic dictionary. The alphabetical order of this ample block of knowledge might render a dense lexicon of lucid hallucinations. Beside the bed, a pad lies open to record the meandering of migratory words. In the rapid eye movement of the poet's night vision, this dictum can be decoded, like the secret acrostic of a lover's name.

[2002]

10. "Miscegenation" by Natasha Trethewey[②]

In 1965 my parents broke two laws of Mississippi;
they went to Ohio to marry, returned to Mississippi.

They crossed the river into Cincinnati, a city whose name
begins with a sound like sin, the sound of wrong—mis in Mississippi.

A year later they moved to Canada, followed a route the same
as slaves, the train slicing the white glaze of winter, leaving Mississippi.

---

① 哈里叶特·马伦(1953—)是美国当代最著名的实验性诗人之一,目前任加州大学洛杉矶分校英语系教授。

② 娜塔莎·特雷塞韦(1966—)是诗人、历史学家、埃默里大学创意写作教授,2007 年获得普利策诗歌奖,是美国桂冠诗人(2012—2014),密西西比州桂冠诗人(2012—2016)。

Faulkner's Joe Christmas was born in winter, like Jesus, given his name for the day he was left at the orphanage, his race unknown in Mississippi.

My father was reading *War and Peace* when he gave me my name.
I was born near Easter, 1966, in Mississippi.

When I turned 33 my father said, It's your Jesus year—you're the same age he was when he died. It was spring, the hills green in Mississippi.

I know more than Joe Christmas did. Natasha is a Russian name—
though I'm not; it means Christmas child, even in Mississippi.

Questions for Discussion

1. Comment on the topic reflected in the poem "We Wear the Mask".
2. Please illustrate the implied meaning in the poem "If We Must Die".
3. How can we Chinese students fully understand the meaning of African American poetry?
4. What are the distinctive features revealed in African American poetry selected here?

African American Drama
非裔美国戏剧简介

  与非裔美国诗歌相比,非裔美国戏剧的发展相对滞后,直到 1823 年才有布朗的剧作《沙塔威国王的戏剧》在美国上演。时隔一个世纪之后,理查逊的剧作《拾荒老妪的财产》于 1923 年在百老汇上演,轰动一时,是第一部在百老汇上演的非裔美国戏剧。其间,关于美国黑人的戏剧主要是滑稽剧——大多由白人化妆成黑人表演,对黑人进行类型化的刻板再现,主要对内战前的美国南方的种植园生活进行浪漫化处理,且大言不惭地声称,奴隶制是对黑人最好的保护等,引起许多著名黑人作家、社会活动家如道格拉斯、德莱尼等人的强烈谴责。20 世纪上半叶,虽然有杜波伊斯、休斯等著名非裔美国作家的剧作问世,重视社会抗议主题,但是真正产生巨大社会影响的剧本到 20 世纪 50 年代才重新出现。

  年轻的非裔美国剧作家汉丝贝利创作的《阳光下的干葡萄》,获得纽约剧评人奖,不仅再现了当时白人文化对黑人的歧视,也因聚焦 20 世纪 50 年代美国的"融合"主题,以及对非洲文化的憧憬式礼赞引人关注,成为第一部非裔美国女性创作的、非裔美国艺术家导演的、在百老汇上演的非喜剧性剧作。60 年代和 70 年代,虽然有多部剧作上演,但是真正产生较大社会反响的当推巴拉卡的《荷兰人》(1964)和戈尔登的《无处成名》(1970),后者因真诚审视黑人个体与群体的身份追寻,获得普利策奖,这是第一部获此殊荣的非裔美国戏剧。

  进入 80 年代,非裔美国戏剧更加蓬勃发展,富勒的《士兵的报酬》(1981)及威尔逊的《栅栏》(1987)双双获得普利策奖,威尔逊更是以反映(非裔)美国社会与文化的系列剧为评论界瞩目。有论者指出,80 年代和 90 年代是威尔逊独领风骚的时代,除了《栅栏》之外,《钢琴课》也获得 1990 年普利策奖,他的其他剧作,如《马雷尼大妈的黑臀》(1982)、《两列奔驰的火车》(1992)、《七把吉他》(1996)等也都非常成功。年轻剧作家帕克斯可以说是 21 世纪初非裔美国戏剧界的翘楚,其《输家/赢家》获得 2002 年普利策奖;当下最红的剧作家当属诺塔奇,其《劳役》获得 2017 年普利策奖,显示出非裔美国戏剧界后继有人,兴旺发达。

1. A Raisin in the Sun

虽然过早被癌症夺去生命,但是洛林·汉丝贝利(Lorraine Hansberry)(1930—1965)短暂的一生精彩纷呈,令人瞩目;虽然只有两部剧作问世,但是她依然被尊奉为美国最重要的黑人剧作家之一。她在剧作中打破了肤色界限,抗议美国黑人的不幸遭遇,尝试利用舞台唤醒白人与黑人观众的社会意识与政治意识,成为当时反对美国种族隔离,为民权奋争的代表人物。因此,她不仅是著名剧作家,也是积极的社会活动家与女性主义者。

1930 年 5 月 19 日,汉丝贝利出生于芝加哥的黑人中产阶级家庭。1938 年,他们家在芝加哥白人中产阶级社区购买了一处房子,但是饱受种族歧视与隔离之苦。她的父亲勇敢挑战当时盛行的吉姆·克劳种族隔离法令,并在伊利诺伊州最高法院打赢了这场反对种族隔离的官司,父亲的勇气和对公平正义的执着追求对汉丝贝利产生了非常大的影响,这也明显地体现在她的成名作《阳光下的干葡萄》(1959)中。

汉丝贝利中学阶段就喜欢文学与历史,深受杜波伊斯、罗宾逊、休斯与埃林顿等人的影响。她特别欣赏休斯的诗歌,认同他对黑人复杂生活的反映,及其对美国黑人美梦难寻的描绘,《阳光下的干葡萄》就源自休斯的一句诗歌。在威斯康星大学读书期间,她学习英语、艺术与舞台设计。1950 年,她在纽约市工作,为罗宾逊的激进黑人刊物《自由》撰稿,扩展了自己对当时国内及国际问题的理解。1952 年,她出任该刊的副主编,1953 年离职,全身心地投入戏剧创作,1959 年,她出版《阳光下的干葡萄》,获得当年纽约戏剧书评人奖,成为第一位获此殊荣的黑人剧作家。该剧上演了 500 多场,不仅反映了黑人与白人的矛盾与冲突,也真实、形象地刻画了黑人家庭成员之间的矛盾。虽然本剧中的杨格一家身陷芝加哥南岸,但是他们有克服自身缺陷及美国主流文化藩篱的勇气与行动。

1965 年,汉丝贝利因癌症去世,她的遗作由前夫整理出版。直至今日,她依然被视为当代杰出的非裔美国剧作家之一,对后来的巴拉卡、布林斯、威尔逊等剧作家产生较大影响,引领其他非裔美国剧作家与演艺人员继续前行。

本剧围绕住在芝加哥南岸黑人区的杨格一家应该如何使用老杨格留下的一万美金遗产展开。笃信宗教的母亲莉娜认为,应该以此购买一处好房子,为自己的孙子提供一个稳定、健康的成长环境,另外,用于改善小女碧妮莎的教育;而儿子小杨格则认为,自己现在是一家之主,这笔钱应该归自己支配,用来投资酒店,由此改善全家的生活。从大的方面来说,本剧旨在探讨什么对家庭最重要,以及家庭成员怎样实现美国梦这样的大问题。

美国社会对美国梦的宣传与强调往往忽略很多前提,不同族裔、不同阶层乃至不同性别的人们,他们能否实现"美国梦"也因此各有差异。强调通过个人奋斗,改善自己的物质生活,实现自己人生梦想的美国梦对不同族裔、不同阶级甚至不同性别的人来说有着较大的差异,这本是不争的事实。本剧以一个黑人家庭为例,通过黑人社区不同代际之间的矛盾,揭示非裔美国人对"平等"的渴望及不同理解。

更为重要的是,作为二战以后世界上最富庶的国度,美国不同社会成员之间的"富庶"程度各不相同。因为反差巨大，饱受种族隔离与种族歧视之苦的黑人成员更加渴望能够实现平等、富足、自由的美国梦，由此引发的矛盾冲突更为醒目。而 20 世纪 50 年代末上演的《阳光下的干葡萄》对这些问题的关注与思考，直接预示了 60 和 70 年代美国社会对自由、平等、公正等权力的追寻，及其在非裔美国文学如诗歌、戏剧等文类中的体现。

此外，男性气概也是本剧的重要着力点。父亲老杨格已经去世，母亲莉娜对儿子小杨格是否具有男性气概，能否承担起家庭重担非常怀疑，作为儿子，他需要证明自己的男性气概。一方面，小杨格抱怨白人不把他当男人看待，另外他也指责女性拉他的后腿，使他不能像个真正的男人。难能可贵的是，在本剧临近结束时，面对白人社区代表试图以高价收买自己，收买母亲莉娜的梦想时，小杨格断然拒绝，极好地体现了自己作为"一家之主"的男性的担当。

本剧对三位女性人物的探讨进一步丰富了黑人女性人物画廊。作为母亲的莉娜体现了老一辈传统女性的"主内"身份，儿媳鲁斯属于过渡性人物，对自己能否进行堕胎犹豫不已（这对笃信宗教的母亲莉娜来说根本不能考虑），而小女儿碧妮莎则代表新一代黑人女性，崇尚独立，对结婚、由男人照顾没有兴趣，而是渴望成为医生（过去，这通常是男性从事的职业）。她坚信，无论是母亲信奉的上帝，还是她哥哥小杨格或嫂子鲁斯或任何人，都无法为自己选择未来的生活道路，她必须自己进行选择，体现了新一代黑人女性的自强与自立精神。

The action of the play is set in Chicago's Southside, sometime between World War II and the present.

A RAISIN IN THE SUN was first presented by Philip Rose and David J. Cogan at the Ethel Barrymore Theatre, New York City, March 11, 1959, with the following cast:
(In order of appearance)
RUTH YOUNGER: Daughter-in-law;
TRAVIS YOUNGER: Grandson;
WALTER LEE YOUNGER: Son;
BENEATHA YOUNGER: Daughter;
LENA YOUNGER: MAMA;
JOSEPH ASAGAI: Student.

Act I

Scene One: Friday morning.
Scene Two: The following morning.

Act II

Scene One: Later, the same day.
Scene Two: Friday night, a few weeks later.
Scene Three: Moving day, one week later.

Act III

An hour late.

ACT I
SCENE ONE

The YOUNGER living room would be a comfortable and well-ordered room if it were not for a number of indestructible contradictions to this state of being. Its furnishings are typical and undistinguished and their primary feature now is that they have clearly had to accommodate the living of too many people for too many years—and they are tired. Still，we can see that at some time, a time probably no longer remembered by the family（except perhaps for MAMA）, the furnishings of this room were actually selected with care and love and even hope—and brought to this apartment and arranged with taste and pride.

That was a long time ago. Now the once loved pattern of the couch upholstery has to fight to show itself from under acres of crocheted doilies and couch covers which have themselves finally come to be more important than the upholstery. And here a table or a chair has been moved to disguise the worn places in the carpet; but the carpet has fought back by showing its weariness, with depressing uniformity, elsewhere on its surface.

Weariness has，in fact，won in this room. Everything has been polished, washed, sat on，used, scrubbed too often. All pretenses but living itself have long since vanished from the very atmosphere of this room.

Moreover, a section of this room, for it is not really a room unto itself, though the landlord's lease would make it seem so, slopes backward to provide a small kitchen area, where the family prepares the meals that are eaten in the living room proper, which must also serve as dining room. The single window that has been provided for these "two" rooms is located in this kitchen area. The sole natural light the family may enjoy in the course of a day is only that which fights its way through this little window.

At left，a door leads to a bedroom which is shared by MAMA and her daughter，BENEATHA. At right，opposite，is a second room（which in the beginning of the life of this apartment was probably a breakfast room）which serves as a bedroom for WALTER and his wife，RUTH.

Time：Sometime between World War II and the present. ①

Place：Chicago's Southside. ②

At Rise：It is morning dark in the living room，TRAVIS is asleep on the make-down bed at center. An alarm clock sounds from within the bedroom at right，and presently RUTH enters from that room and closes the door behind her. She crosses sleepily toward the window. As she passes her sleeping son she reaches down and shakes him a little. At the window she raises the shade and a dusky Southside morning light comes in feebly. She fills a pot with water and puts it on to boil. She calls to the boy，between yawns，in a slightly muffled voice.

---

① 二战后，美国成为世界上最富裕的国家,但是很多黑人依然生活在经济上贫困、政治上不平等的状态下。1954 年美国最高法院判定 1896 年美国高院通过的"隔离但是平等"的"吉姆·克劳"种族隔离法案违宪。20 世纪 50 年代中期开始,美国黑人争取平等权利的民权运动蓬勃展开。

② 芝加哥南岸为黑人集聚区,很多著名黑人政治家如 20 世纪 80 年代参加总统竞选的杰克逊,2008 年获得美国总统大选的奥巴马都从芝加哥南岸开始自己的政治生涯。

RUTH is about thirty. We can see that she was a pretty girl, even exceptionally so, but now it is apparent that life has been little that she expected, and disappointment has already begun to hang in her face. In a few years, before thirty-five even, she will be known among her people as a "settled woman."

She crosses to her son and gives him a good, final, rousing shake.

RUTH: Come on now, boy, it's seven thirty! (Her son sits up at last, in a stupor of sleepiness) I say hurry up, Travis! You ain't the only person in the world got to use a bathroom! (The child, a sturdy, handsome little boy of ten or eleven, drags himself out of the bed and almost blindly takes his towels and "today's clothes" from drawers and a closet and goes out to the bathroom, which is in an outside hall and which is shared by another family or families on the same floor, RUTH crosses to the bedroom door at right and opens it and calls in to her husband) Walter Lee! ... It's after seven thirty! Lemme see you do some waking up in there now! (She waits) You better get up from there, man! It's after seven thirty I tell you. (She waits again) All right, you just go ahead and lay there and next thing you know Travis be finished and Mr. Johnson'll be in there and you'll be fussing and cussing round here like a madman! And be late too! (She waits, at the end of patience) Walter Lee—it's time for you to GET UP!

(She waits another second and then starts to go into the bedroom, but is apparently satisfied that her husband has begun to get up. She stops, pulls the door to, and returns to the kitchen area. She wipes her face with a moist cloth and runs her fingers through her sleep-disheveled hair in a vain effort and ties an apron around her housecoat. The bedroom door at right opens and her husband stands in the doorway in his pajamas, which are rumpled and mismated. He is a lean, intense young man in his middle thirties, inclined to quick nervous movements and erratic speech habits—and always in his voice there is a quality of indictment)

WALTER: Is he out yet?

RUTH: What you mean out? He ain't hardly got in there good yet.

WALTER: (Wandering in, still more oriented to sleep than to a new day) Well, what was you doing all that yelling for if I can't even get in there yet? (Stopping and thinking) Check coming today?

RUTH: They said Saturday and this is just Friday and I hopes to God you ain't going to get up here first thing this morning and start talking to me 'bout no money—'cause I 'bout don't want to hear it.

WALTER: Something the matter with you this morning?

RUTH: No—I'm just sleepy as the devil. What kind of eggs you want?

WALTER: Not scrambled, (RUTH starts to scramble eggs) Paper come? (RUTH points impatiently to the rolled up Tribune on the table, and he gets it and spreads it out and vaguely reads the front page) Set off another bomb yesterday.

RUTH: (Maximum indifference) Did they?

WALTER: (Looking up) What's the matter with you?

RUTH: Ain't nothing the matter with me. And don't keep asking me that this morning.

WALTER: Ain't nobody bothering you. (Reading the news of the day absently again) Say Colonel McCormick is sick.

RUTH: (Affecting tea-party interest) Is he now? Poor thing.

WALTER: (Sighing and looking at his watch) Oh, me. (He waits) Now what is that boy doing in that bathroom all this time? He just going to have to start getting up earlier. I can't be being late to work on account of him fooling around in there.

RUTH: (Turning on him)Oh, no he ain't going to be getting up no earlier no such thing! It ain't his fault that he can't get to bed no earlier nights 'cause he got a bunch of crazy good-for-nothing clowns sitting up running their mouths in what is supposed to be his bedroom after ten o'clock at night ...

WALTER: That's what you mad about, ain't it? The things I want to talk about with my friends just couldn't be important in your mind, could they?

(He rises and finds a cigarette in her handbag on the table and crosses to the little window and looks out, smoking and deeply enjoying this first one)

RUTH: (Almost matter of factly, a complaint too automatic to deserve emphasis) Why you always got to smoke before you eat in the morning?

WALTER: (At the window) Just look at 'em down there ... Running and racing to work ... (He turns and faces his wife and watches her a moment at the stove, and then, suddenly) You look young this morning, baby.

RUTH: (Indifferently) Yeah?

WALTER: Just for a second—stirring them eggs. Just for a second it was—you looked real young again. (He reaches for her; she crosses away. Then, drily) It's gone now—you look like yourself again!

RUTH: Man, if you don't shut up and leave me alone.

WALTER: (Looking out to the street again) First thing a man ought to learn in life is not to make love to no colored woman first thing in the morning. You all some eeeevil people at eight o'clock in the morning. (TRAVIS appears in the hall doorway, almost fully dressed and quite wide awake now, his towels and pajamas across his shoulders. He opens the door and signals for his father to make the bathroom in a hurry)

TRAVIS: (Watching the bathroom) Daddy, come on! (WALTER gets his bathroom utensils and flies out to the bathroom)

RUTH: Sit down and have your breakfast, Travis.

TRAVIS: Mama, this is Friday. (Gleefully) Check coming tomorrow, huh?

RUTH: You get your mind off money and eat your breakfast.

TRAVIS: (Eating) This is the morning we supposed to bring the fifty cents to school.

RUTH: Well, I ain't got no fifty cents this morning.

TRAVIS: Teacher say we have to.

RUTH: I don't care what teacher say. I ain't got it. Eat your breakfast, Travis.

TRAVIS: I am eating.

RUTH: Hush up now and just eat! (The boy gives her an exasperated look for her lack of understanding, and eats grudgingly)

TRAVIS: You think Grandmama would have it?

RUTH: No! And I want you to stop asking your grandmother for money, you hear me?

TRAVIS: (Outraged) Gaaaleee! I don't ask her, she just gimme it sometimes!

RUTH: Travis Willard Younger—I got too much on me this morning to be—

TRAVIS: Maybe Daddy—

RUTH: Travis! (The boy hushes abruptly. They are both quiet and tense for several seconds)

TRAVIS: (Presently) Could I maybe go carry some groceries in front of the supermarket for a little while after school then?

RUTH: Just hush, I said. (Travis jabs his spoon into his cereal bowl viciously, and rests his head in anger upon his fists) If you through eating, you can get over there and make up your bed. (The boy obeys stiffly and crosses the room, almost mechanically, to the bed and more or less folds the bedding into a heap, then angrily gets his books and cap)

TRAVIS: (Sulking and standing apart from her unnaturally) I'm gone.

RUTH: (Looking up from the stove to inspect him automatically) Come here. (He crosses to her and she studies his head) If you don't take this comb and fix this here head, you better! (TRAVIS puts down his books with a great sigh of oppression, and crosses to the mirror. His mother mutters under her breath about his "slubbornness") 'Bout to march out of here with that head looking just like chickens slept in it! I just don't know where you get your slubborn ways ... And get your jacket, too. Looks chilly out this morning.

TRAVIS: (With conspicuously brushed hair and jacket) I'm gone.

RUTH: Get carfare and milk money—(Waving one finger)—and not a single penny for no caps, you hear me?

TRAVIS: (With sullen politeness) Yes'm. (He turns in outrage to leave. His mother watches after him as in his frustration he approaches the door almost comically. When she speaks to him, her voice has become a very gentle tease)

RUTH: (Mocking; as she thinks he would say it) Oh, Mama makes me so mad sometimes, I don't know what to do! (She waits and continues to his back as he stands stock-still in front of the door) I wouldn't kiss that woman good-bye for nothing in this world this morning! (The boy finally turns around and rolls his eyes at her, knowing the mood has changed and he is vindicated; he does not, however, move toward her yet) Not for nothing in this world! (She finally laughs aloud at him and holds out her arms to him and we see that it is a way between them, very old and practiced. He crosses to her and allows her to embrace him warmly but keeps his face fixed with masculine rigidity. She holds him back from her presently and looks at him and runs her fingers over the features of his face. With utter gentleness—) Now—whose little old angry man are you?

TRAVIS: (The masculinity and gruffness start to fade at last) Aw gaalee—Mama ...

RUTH: (Mimicking) Aw gaaaaalleeeee, Mama! (She pushes him, with rough playfulness and finality, toward the door) Get on out of here or you going to be late.

TRAVIS: (In the face of love, new aggressiveness) Mama, could I please go carry groceries?

RUTH: Honey, it's starting to get so cold evenings.

WALTER: (Coming in from the bathroom and drawing a make-believe gun from a make-believe holster and shooting at his son) What is it he wants to do?

RUTH: Go carry groceries after school at the supermarket.

WALTER: Well, let him go ...

TRAVIS: (Quickly, to the ally) I have to—she won't gimme the fifty cents ...

WALTER: (To his wife only) Why not?

RUTH: (Simply, and with flavor) 'Cause we don't have it.

WALTER: (To RUTH only) What you tell the boy things like that for? (Reaching down into his pants with a rather important gesture) Here, son—(He hands the boy the coin, but his eyes are directed to his wife's, TRAVIS takes the money happily)

TRAVIS: Thanks, Daddy. (He starts out. RUTH watches both of them with murder in her eyes. WALTER stands and stares back at her with defiance, and suddenly reaches into his pocket again on an afterthought)

WALTER: (Without even looking at his son, still staring hard at his wife) In fact, here's another fifty cents ... Buy yourself some fruit today—or take a taxicab to school or something!

TRAVIS: Whoopee—(He leaps up and clasps his father around the middle with his legs, and they face each other in mutual appreciation; slowly WALTER LEE peeks around the boy to catch the violent rays from his wife's eyes and draws his head back as if shot)

WALTER: You better get down now—and get to school, man.

TRAVIS: (At the door) O. K. Good-bye. (He exits)

WALTER : (After him, pointing with pride) That's my boy. (She looks at him in disgust and turns back to her work) You know what I was thinking 'bout in the bathroom this morning?

RUTH: No.

WALTER: How come you always try to be so pleasant!

RUTH: What is there to be pleasant 'bout!

WALTER: You want to know what I was thinking 'bout in the bathroom or not!

RUTH: I know what you thinking 'bout.

WALTER: (Ignoring her)'Bout what me and Willy Harris was talking about last night.

RUTH: (Immediately—a refrain) Willy Harris is a good-for-nothing loudmouth.

WALTER: Anybody who talks to me has got to be a good-for-nothing loudmouth, ain't he? And what you know about who is just a good-for-nothing loudmouth? Charlie Atkins was just a "good-for-nothing loudmouth" too, wasn't he! When he wanted me to go in the dry-cleaning business with him. And now—he's grossing a hundred thousand a year. A hundred thousand dollars a year! You still call him a loudmouth!

RUTH: (Bitterly) Oh, Walter Lee ... (She folds her head on her arms over the table)

WALTER: (Rising and coming to her and standing over her) You tired, ain't you? Tired of everything. Me, the boy, the way we live—this beat-up hole—everything. Ain't you?

(She doesn't look up, doesn't answer) So tired—moaning and groaning all the time, but you wouldn't do nothing to help, would you? You couldn't be on my side that long for nothing, could you?

RUTH: Walter, please leave me alone.

WALTER: A man needs for a woman to back him up ...

RUTH: Walter—

WALTER: Mama would listen to you. You know she listen to you more than she do me and Bennie. She think more of you. All you have to do is just sit down with her when you drinking your coffee one morning and talking 'bout things like you do and—(He sits down beside her and demonstrates graphically what he thinks her methods and tone should be)—you just sip your coffee, see, and say easy like that you been thinking 'bout that deal Walter Lee is so interested in, 'bout the store and all, and sip some more coffee, like what you saying ain't really that important to you—And the next thing you know, she be listening good and asking you questions and when I come home—I can tell her the details. This ain't no fly-by-night proposition, baby. I mean we figured it out, me and Willy and Bobo.

RUTH: (With a frown) Bobo?

WALTER: Yeah. You see, this little liquor store we got in mind cost seventy-five thousand and we figured the initial investment on the place be 'bout thirty thousand, see. That be ten thousand each. Course, there's a couple of hundred you got to pay so's you don't spend your life just waiting for them clowns to let your license get approved—

RUTH: You mean graft?

WALTER: (Frowning impatiently) Don't call it that. See there, that just goes to show you what women understand about the world. Baby, don't nothing happen for you in this world 'less you pay somebody off!

RUTH: Walter, leave me alone! (She raises her head and stares at him vigorously—then says, more quietly) Eat your eggs, they gonna be cold.

WALTER: (Straightening up from her and looking off) That's it. There you are. Man say to his woman: I got me a dream. His woman say: Eat your eggs. (Sadly, but gaining in power) Man say: I got to take hold of this here world, baby! And a woman will say: Eat your eggs and go to work. (Passionately now) Man say: I got to change my life, I'm choking to death, baby! And his woman say—(In utter anguish as he brings his fists down on his thighs)—Your eggs is getting cold!

RUTH: (Softly) Walter, that ain't none of our money.

WALTER: (Not listening at all or even looking at her) This morning, I was lookin' in the mirror and thinking about it ... I'm thirty-five years old; I been married eleven years and I got a boy who sleeps in the living room—(Very, very quietly)—and all I got to give him is stories about how rich white people live ...

RUTH: Eat your eggs, Walter.

WALTER: (Slams the table and jumps up)—DAMN MY EGGS—DAMN ALL THE EGGS THAT EVER WAS!

RUTH: Then go to work.

WALTER: (Looking up at her) See—I'm trying to talk to you 'bout myself—(Shaking his head with the repetition)—and all you can say is eat them eggs and go to work.

RUTH: (Wearily) Honey, you never say nothing new. I listen to you every day, every night and every morning, and you never say nothing new. (Shrugging) So you would rather be Mr. Arnold than be his chauffeur. So—I would rather be living in Buckingham Palace.

WALTER: That is just what is wrong with the colored woman in this world ... Don't understand about building their men up and making 'em feel like they somebody. Like they can do something.

RUTH: (Drily, but to hurt) There are colored men who do things.

WALTER: No thanks to the colored woman.

RUTH: Well, being a colored woman, I guess I can't help myself none. (She rises and gets the ironing board and sets it up and attacks a huge pile of rough-dried clothes, sprinkling them in preparation for the ironing and then rolling them into tight fat balls)

WALTER: (Mumbling) We one group of men tied to a race of women with small minds!

(His sister BENEATHA enters. She is about twenty, as slim and intense as her brother. She is not as pretty as her sister-in-law, but her lean, almost intellectual face has a handsomeness of its own. She wears a bright-red flannel nightie, and her thick hair stands wildly about her head. Her speech is a mixture of many things; it is different from the rest of the family's insofar as education has permeated her sense of English—and perhaps the Midwest rather than the South has finally—at last—won out in her inflection; but not altogether, because over all of it is a soft slurring and transformed use of vowels which is the decided influence of the Southside. She passes through the room without looking at either RUTH or WALTER and goes to the outside door and looks, a little blindly, out to the bathroom. She sees that it has been lost to the Johnsons. She closes the door with a sleepy vengeance and crosses to the table and sits down a little defeated)

BENEATHA: I am going to start timing those people.

WALTER: You should get up earlier.

BENEATHA: (Her face in her hands. She is still fighting the urge to go back to bed) Really—would you suggest dawn? Where's the paper?

WALTER: (Pushing the paper across the table to her as he studies her almost clinically, as though he has never seen her before) You a horrible-looking chick at this hour.

BENEATHA: (Drily) Good morning, everybody.

WALTER: (Senselessly) How is school coming?

BENEATHA: (In the same spirit) Lovely. Lovely. And you know, biology is the greatest. (Looking up at him) I dissected something that looked just like you yesterday.

WALTER: I just wondered if you've made up your mind and everything.

BENEATHA: (Gaining in sharpness and impatience) And what did I answer yesterday

— 20 —

morning—and the day before that?

RUTH: (From the ironing board, like someone disinterested and old) Don't be so nasty, Bennie.

BENEATHA: (Still to her brother) And the day before that and the day before that!

WALTER: (Defensively) I'm interested in you. Something wrong with that? Ain't many girls who decide—

WALTER: and BENEATHA (In unison)—"to be a doctor." (Silence)

WALTER: Have we figured out yet just exactly how much medical school is going to cost?

RUTH: Walter Lee, why don't you leave that girl alone and get out of here to work?

BENEATHA: (Exits to the bathroom and bangs on the door) Come on out of there, please! (She comes back into the room)

WALTER: (Looking at his sister intently) You know the check is coming tomorrow.

BENEATHA: (Turning on him with a sharpness all her own) That money belongs to Mama, Walter, and it's for her to decide how she wants to use it. I don't care if she wants to buy a house or a rocket ship or just nail it up somewhere and look at it. It's hers. Not ours—*hers*.

WALTER: (Bitterly) Now ain't that fine! You just got your mother's interest at heart, ain't you, girl? You such a nice girl—but if Mama got that money she can always take a few thousand and help you through school too—can't she?

BENEATHA: I have never asked anyone around here to do anything for me!

WALTER: No! And the line between asking and just accepting when the time comes is big and wide—ain't it!

BENEATHA: (With fury) What do you want from me, Brother—that I quit school or just drop dead, which!

WALTER: I don't want nothing but for you to stop acting holy 'round here. Me and Ruth done made some sacrifices for you—why can't you do something for the family?

RUTH: Walter, don't be dragging me in it.

WALTER: You are in it—Don't you get up and go work in somebody's kitchen for the last three years to help put clothes on her back?

RUTH: Oh, Walter—that's not fair ...

WALTER: It ain't that nobody expects you to get on your knees and say thank you, Brother; thank you, Ruth; thank you, Mama—and thank you, Travis, for wearing the same pair of shoes for two semesters—

BENEATHA: (Dropping to her knees) Well—I do—all right? —thank everybody! And forgive me for ever wanting to be anything at all! (Pursuing him on her knees across the floor) FORGIVE ME, FORGIVE ME, FORGIVE ME!

RUTH: Please stop it! Your mama'll hear you.

WALTER: Who the hell told you you had to be a doctor? If you so crazy 'bout messing 'round with sick people—then go be a nurse like other women—or just get married and be quiet ...

BENEATHA: Well—you finally got it said ... It took you three years but you finally got it said. Walter, give up; leave me alone—it's Mama's money.

WALTER: He was my father, too!

BENEATHA: So what? He was mine, too—and Travis' grandfather—but the insurance money belongs to Mama. Picking on me is not going to make her give it to you to invest in any liquor stores—(Underbreath, dropping into a chair)—and I for one say, God bless Mama for that!

WALTER: (To RUTH) See—did you hear? Did you hear!

RUTH: Honey, please go to work.

WALTER: Nobody in this house is ever going to understand me.

BENEATHA: Because you're a nut.

WALTER: Who's a nut?

BENEATHA: You—you are a nut. Thee is mad, boy.

WALTER: (Looking at his wife and his sister from the door, very sadly) The world's most backward race of people, and that's a fact.

BENEATHA: (Turning slowly in her chair) And then there are all those prophets who would lead us out of the wilderness—(WALTER slams out of the house)—into the swamps!

RUTH: Bennie, why you always gotta be pickin' on your brother? Can't you be a little sweeter sometimes? (Door opens, WALTER walks in. He fumbles with his cap, starts to speak, clears throat, looks everywhere but at RUTH. Finally:)

WALTER: (To RUTH) I need some money for carfare.

RUTH: (Looks at him, then warms; teasing, but tenderly) Fifty cents? (She goes to her bag and gets money) Here—take a taxi! (WALTER exits, MAMA enters. She is a woman in her early sixties, full-bodied and strong. She is one of those women of a certain grace and beauty who wear it so unobtrusively that it takes a while to notice. Her dark-brown face is surrounded by the total whiteness of her hair, and, being a woman who has adjusted to many things in life and overcome many more, her face is full of strength. She has, we can see, wit and faith of a kind that keep her eyes lit and full of interest and expectancy. She is, in a word, a beautiful woman. Her bearing is perhaps most like the noble bearing of the women of the Hereros of Southwest Africa—rather as if she imagines that as she walks she still bears a basket or a vessel upon her head. Her speech, on the other hand, is as careless as her carriage is precise—she is inclined to slur everything—but her voice is perhaps not so much quiet as simply soft)

MAMA: Who that 'round here slamming doors at this hour? (She crosses through the room, goes to the window, opens it, and brings in a feeble little plant growing doggedly in a small pot on the windowsill. She feels the dirt and puts it back out)

RUTH: That was Walter Lee. He and Bennie was at it again.

MAMA: My children and they tempers. Lord, if this little old plant don't get more sun than it's been getting it ain't never going to see spring again. (She turns from the window) What's the matter with you this morning, Ruth? You looks right peaked. You aiming to iron all them things? Leave some for me. I'll get to 'em this afternoon. Bennie honey, it's too drafty for you to be sitting 'round half dressed. Where's your robe?

BENEATHA: In the cleaners.

MAMA: Well, go get mine and put it on.

BENEATHA: I'm not cold, Mama, honest.

MAMA: I know—but you so thin ...

BENEATHA: (Irritably) Mama, I'm not cold.

MAMA: (Seeing the make-down bed as TRAVIS has left it) Lord have mercy, look at that poor bed. Bless his heart—he tries, don't he? (She moves to the bed TRAVIS has sloppily made up)

RUTH: No—he don't half try at all 'cause he knows you going to come along behind him and fix everything. That's just how come he don't know how to do nothing right now—you done spoiled that boy so.

MAMA: (Folding bedding) Well—he's a little boy. Ain't supposed to know 'bout housekeeping. My baby, that's what he is. What you fix for his breakfast this morning?

RUTH: (Angrily) I feed my son, Lena!

MAMA: I ain't meddling—(Underbreath; busy-bodyish) I just noticed all last week he had cold cereal, and when it starts getting this chilly in the fall a child ought to have some hot grits or something when he goes out in the cold—

RUTH: (Furious) I gave him hot oats—is that all right!

MAMA: I ain't meddling. (Pause) Put a lot of nice butter on it? (RUTH shoots her an angry look and does not reply) He likes lots of butter.

RUTH: (Exasperated) Lena—

MAMA: (To BENEATHA. MAMA is inclined to wander conversationally sometimes) What was you and your brother fussing 'bout this morning?

BENEATHA: It's not important, Mama. (She gets up and goes to look out at the bathroom, which is apparently free, and she picks up her towels and rushes out)

MAMA: What was they fighting about?

RUTH: Now you know as well as I do.

MAMA: (Shaking her head) Brother still worrying hisself sick about that money?

RUTH: You know he is.

MAMA: You had breakfast?

RUTH: Some coffee.

MAMA: Girl, you better start eating and looking after yourself better. You almost thin as Travis.

RUTH: Lena—

MAMA: Un-hunh

RUTH: What are you going to do with it?

MAMA: Now don't you start, child. It's too early in the morning to be talking about money. It ain't Christian.

RUTH: It's just that he got his heart set on that store—

MAMA: You mean that liquor store that Willy Harris want him to invest in?

RUTH: Yes—

MAMA: We ain't no business people, Ruth. We just plain working folks.

RUTH: Ain't nobody business people till they go into business. Walter Lee say colored people ain't never going to start getting ahead till they start gambling on some different kinds of things in the world—investments and things.

MAMA: What done got into you, girl? Walter Lee done finally sold you on investing.

RUTH: No. Mama, something is happening between Walter and me. I don't know what it is—but he needs something—something I can't give him anymore. He needs this chance, Lena.

MAMA: (Frowning deeply) But liquor, honey—

RUTH: Well—like Walter say—I spec people going to always be drinking themselves some liquor.

MAMA: Well—whether they drinks it or not ain't none of my business. But whether I go into business selling it to 'em is, and I don't want that on my ledger this late in life. (Stopping suddenly and studying her daughter-in-law) Ruth Younger, what's the matter with you today? You look like you could fall over right there.

RUTH: I'm tired.

MAMA: Then you better stay home from work today.

RUTH: I can't stay home. She'd be calling up the agency and screaming at them, "My girl didn't come in today—send me somebody! My girl didn't come in!" Oh, she just have a fit …

MAMA: Well, let her have it. I'll just call her up and say you got the flu—

RUTH: (Laughing) Why the flu?

MAMA: 'Cause it sounds respectable to 'em. Something white people get, too. They know 'bout the flu. Otherwise they think you been cut up or something when you tell 'em you sick.

RUTH: I got to go in. We need the money.

MAMA: Somebody would of thought my children done all but starved to death the way they talk about money here late. Child, we got a great big old check coming tomorrow.

RUTH: (Sincerely, but also self-righteously) Now that's your money. It ain't got nothing to do with me. We all feel like that—Walter and Bennie and me—even Travis.

MAMA: (Thoughtfully, and suddenly very far away) Ten thousand dollars—

RUTH: Sure is wonderful.

MAMA: Ten thousand dollars.

RUTH: You know what you should do, Miss Lena? You should take yourself a trip somewhere. To Europe or South America or someplace—

MAMA: (Throwing up her hands at the thought) Oh, child!

RUTH: I'm serious. Just pack up and leave! Go on away and enjoy yourself some. Forget about the family and have yourself a ball for once in your life—

MAMA: (Drily) You sound like I'm just about ready to die. Who'd go with me? What I look like wandering 'round Europe by myself?

RUTH: Shoot—these here rich white women do it all the time. They don't think nothing of packing up they suitcases and piling on one of them big steamships and—swoosh! —they gone, child.

MAMA: Something always told me I wasn't no rich white woman.

RUTH: Well—what are you going to do with it then?

MAMA: I ain't rightly decided. (Thinking. She speaks now with emphasis) Some of it got to be put away for Beneatha and her schoolin'—and ain't nothing going to touch that part of it. Nothing. (She waits several seconds, trying to make up her mind about something, and looks at RUTH a little tentatively before going on) Been thinking that we maybe could meet the notes on a little old two-story somewhere, with a yard where Travis could play in the summertime, if we use part of the insurance for a down payment and everybody kind of pitch in. I could maybe take on a little day work again, few days a week—

RUTH: (Studying her mother-in-law furtively and concentrating on her ironing, anxious to encourage without seeming to) Well, Lord knows, we've put enough rent into this here rat trap to pay for four houses by now ...

MAMA: (Looking up at the words "rat trap" and then looking around and leaning back and sighing—in a suddenly reflective mood—) "Rat trap"—yes, that's all it is. (Smiling) I remember just as well the day me and Big Walter moved in here. Hadn't been married but two weeks and wasn't planning on living here no more than a year. (She shakes her head at the dissolved dream) We was going to set away, little by little, don't you know, and buy a little place out in Morgan Park. We had even picked out the house. (Chuckling a little) Looks right dumpy today. But Lord, child, you should know all the dreams I had 'bout buying that house and fixing it up and making me a little garden in the back—(She waits and stops smiling) And didn't none of it happen. (Dropping her hands in a futile gesture)

RUTH: (Keeps her head down, ironing) Yes, life can be a barrel of disappointments, sometimes.

MAMA: Honey, Big Walter would come in here some nights back then and slump down on that couch there and just look at the rug, and look at me and look at the rug and then back at me—and I'd know he was down then ... really down. (After a second very long and thoughtful pause; she is seeing back to times that only she can see) And then, Lord, when I lost that baby—little Claude—I almost thought I was going to lose Big Walter too. Oh, that man grieved hisself! He was one man to love his children.

RUTH: Ain't nothin' can tear at you like losin' your baby.

MAMA: I guess that's how come that man finally worked hisself to death like he done. Like he was fighting his own war with this here world that took his baby from him.

RUTH: He sure was a fine man, all right. I always liked Mr. Younger.

MAMA: Crazy 'bout his children! God knows there was plenty wrong with Walter Younger—hard-headed, mean, kind of wild with women—plenty wrong with him. But he sure loved his children. Always wanted them to have something—be something. That's where Brother gets all these notions, I reckon. Big Walter used to say, he'd get right wet in the eyes sometimes, lean his head back with the water standing in his eyes and say, "Seem like God didn't see fit to give the black man nothing but dreams—but He did give us children to make them dreams seem worth while." (She smiles) He could talk like that, don't you know.

RUTH: Yes, he sure could. He was a good man, Mr. Younger.

MAMA: Yes, a fine man—just couldn't all. (BENEATHA comes in, brushing her hair and looking up to the ceiling, where the sound of a vacuum cleaner has started up)

BENEATHA: What could be so dirty on that woman's rugs that she has to vacuum them every single day?

RUTH: I wish certain young women 'round here who I could name would take inspiration about certain rugs in a certain apartment I could also mention.

BENEATHA: (Shrugging) How much cleaning can a house need, for Christ's sakes.

MAMA: (Not liking the Lord's name used thus) Bennie!

RUTH: Just listen to her—just listen!

BENEATHA: Oh, God!

MAMA: If you use the Lord's name just one more time—

BENEATHA: (A bit of a whine) Oh, Mama—

RUTH: Fresh—just fresh as salt, this girl!

BENEATHA: (Drily) Well—if the salt never catch up with his dreams, that's loses its savor—

MAMA: Now that will do. I just ain't going to have you 'round here reciting the scriptures in vain—you hear me?

BENEATHA: How did I manage to get on everybody's wrong side by just walking into a room?

RUTH: If you weren't so fresh—

BENEATHA: Ruth, I'm twenty years old.

MAMA: What time you be home from school today?

BENEATHA: Kind of late. (With enthusiasm) Madeline is going to start my guitar lessons today. (MAMA and RUTH look up with the same expression)

MAMA: Your what kind of lessons?

BENEATHA: Guitar.

RUTH: Oh, Father!

MAMA: How come you done taken it in your mind to learn to play the guitar?

BENEATHA: I just want to, that's all.

MAMA: (Smiling) Lord, child, don't you know what to do with yourself? How long it going to be before you get tired of this now—like you got tired of that little playacting group you joined last year? (Looking at RUTH) And what was it the year before that?

RUTH: The horseback-riding club for which she bought that fifty-five-dollar riding habit that's been hanging in the closet ever since!

MAMA: (To BENEATHA) Why you got to flit so from one thing to another, baby?

BENEATHA: (Sharply) I just want to learn to play the guitar. Is there anything wrong with that?

MAMA: Ain't nobody trying to stop you. I just wonders sometimes why you has to flit so from one thing to another all the time. You ain't never done nothing with all that camera equipment you brought home—

BENEATHA: I don't flit! I—I experiment with different forms of expression—

RUTH: Like riding a horse?

BENEATHA: —People have to express themselves one way or another.

MAMA: What is it you want to express?

BENEATHA: (Angrily) Me! (MAMA and RUTH look at each other and burst into raucous laughter) Don't worry—I don't expect you to understand.

MAMA: (To change the subject) Who you going out with tomorrow night?

BENEATHA: (With displeasure) George Murchison again.

MAMA: (Pleased) Oh—you getting a little sweet on him?

RUTH: You ask me, this child ain't sweet on nobody but herself—(Underbreath) Express herself!

(They laugh)

BENEATHA: Oh—I like George all right, Mama. I mean I like him enough to go out with him and stuff, but—

RUTH: (For devilment) What does and stuff mean?

BENEATHA: Mind your own business.

MAMA: Stop picking at her now, Ruth. (She chuckles—then a suspicious sudden look at her daughter as she turns in her chair for emphasis) What DOES it mean?

BENEATHA: (Wearily) Oh, I just mean I couldn't ever really be serious about George. He's—he's so shallow.

RUTH: Shallow—what do you mean he's shallow? He's rich!

MAMA: Hush, Ruth.

BENEATHA: I know he's rich. He knows he's rich, too.

RUTH: Well—what other qualities a man got to have to satisfy you, little girl?

BENEATHA: You wouldn't even begin to understand. Anybody who married Walter could not possibly understand.

MAMA: (Outraged) What kind of way is that to talk about your brother?

BENEATHA: Brother is a flip—let's face it.

MAMA: (To RUTH, helplessly) What's a flip?

RUTH: (Glad to add kindling) She's saying he's crazy.

BENEATHA: Not crazy. Brother isn't really crazy yet—he—he's an elaborate neurotic.

MAMA: Hush your mouth!

BENEATHA: As for George. Well. George looks good—he's got a beautiful car and he takes me to nice places and, as my sister-in-law says, he is probably the richest boy I will ever get to know and I even like him sometimes—but if the Youngers are sitting around waiting to see if their little Bennie is going to tie up the family with the Murchisons, they are wasting their time.

RUTH: You mean you wouldn't marry George Murchison if he asked you someday? That pretty, rich thing? Honey, I knew you was odd—

BENEATHA: No I would not marry him if all I felt for him was what I feel now. Besides,

George's family wouldn't really like it.

MAMA: Why not?

BENEATHA: Oh, Mama—The Murchisons are honest-to-God-real-foe-rich colored people, and the only people in the world who are more snobbish than rich white people are rich colored people. I thought everybody knew that. I've met Mrs. Murchison. She's a scene!

MAMA: You must not dislike people 'cause they well off, honey.

BENEATHA: Why not? It makes just as much sense as disliking people 'cause they are poor, and lots of people do that.

RUTH: (A wisdom-of-the-ages manner. To MAMA) Well, she'll get over some of this—

BENEATHA: Get over it? What are you talking about, Ruth? Listen, I'm going to be a doctor. I'm not worried about who I'm going to marry yet—if I ever get married.

MAMA and RUTH: If!

MAMA: Now, Bennie—

BENEATHA: Oh, I probably will ... but first I'm going to be a doctor, and George, for one, still thinks that's pretty funny. I couldn't be bothered with that. I am going to be a doctor and everybody around here better understand that!

MAMA: (Kindly) 'Course you going to be a doctor, honey, God willing.

BENEATHA: (Drily) God hasn't got a thing to do with it.

MAMA: Beneatha—that just wasn't necessary.

BENEATHA: Well—neither is God. I get sick of hearing about God.

MAMA: Beneatha!

BENEATHA: I mean it! I'm just tired of hearing about God all the time. What has He got to do with anything? Does he pay tuition?

MAMA: You 'bout to get your fresh little jaw slapped!

RUTH: That's just what she needs, all right!

BENEATHA: Why? Why can't I say what I want to around here, like everybody else?

MAMA: It don't sound nice for a young girl to say things like that—you wasn't brought up that way. Me and your father went to trouble to get you and Brother to church every Sunday.

BENEATHA: Mama, you don't understand. It's all a matter of ideas, and God is just one idea I don't accept. It's not important. I am not going out and be immoral or commit crimes because I don't believe in God. I don't even think about it. It's just that I get tired of Him getting credit for all the things the human race achieves through its own stubborn effort. There simply is no blasted God—there is only man and it is he who makes miracles! (MAMA absorbs this speech, studies her daughter and rises slowly and crosses to BENEATHA and slaps her powerfully across the face. After, there is only silence and the daughter drops her eyes from her mother's face, and MAMA is very tall before her)

MAMA: Now—you say after me, in my mother's house there is still God. (There is a long pause and BENEATHA stares at the floor wordlessly. MAMA repeats the phrase with precision and cool emotion) In my mother's house there is still God.

BENEATHA: In my mother's house there is still God. (A long pause)

MAMA: (Walking away from BENEATHA, too disturbed for triumphant posture.

Stopping and turning back to her daughter) There are some ideas we ain't going to have in this house. Not long as I am at the head of this family.

BENEATHA: Yes, ma'am. (MAMA walks out of the room)

RUTH: (Almost gently, with profound understanding) You think you a woman, Bennie— but you still a little girl. What you did was childish—so you got treated like a child.

BENEATHA: I see. (Quietly) I also see that everybody thinks it's all right for Mama to be a tyrant. But all the tyranny in the world will never put a God in the heavens! (She picks up her books and goes out. Pause)

RUTH: (Goes to MAMA's door) She said she was sorry.

MAMA: (Coming out, going to her plant) They frightens me, Ruth. My children.

RUTH: You got good children, Lena. They just a little off sometimes—but they're good.

MAMA: No—there's something come down between me and them that don't let us understand each other and I don't know what it is. One done almost lost his mind thinking 'bout money all the time and the other done commence to talk about things I can't seem to understand in no form or fashion. What is it that's changing, Ruth.

RUTH: (Soothingly, older than her years) Now ... you taking it all too seriously. You just got strong-willed children and it takes a strong woman like you to keep 'em in hand.

MAMA: (Looking at her plant and sprinkling a little water on it) They spirited all right, my children. Got to admit they got spirit—Bennie and Walter. Like this little old plant that ain't never had enough sunshine or nothing—and look at it ... (She has her back to RUTH, who has had to stop ironing and lean against something and put the back of her hand to her forehead)

RUTH: (Trying to keep MAMA from noticing) You ... sure ... loves that little old thing, don't you? ...

MAMA: Well, I always wanted me a garden like I used to see sometimes at the back of the houses down home. This plant is close as I ever got to having one. (She looks out of the window as she replaces the plant) Lord, ain't nothing as dreary as the view from this window on a dreary day, is there? Why ain't you singing this morning, Ruth? Sing that "No Ways Tired." That song always lifts me up so—(She turns at last to see that RUTH has slipped quietly to the floor, in a state of semiconsciousness) Ruth! Ruth honey—what's the matter with you ... Ruth!

Curtain

Questions for discussion

1. What's the big conflict in the play?
2. Walter Younger wants to be a responsible man and creates a better future for his family, and why is his dream deferred?
3. Are there any racial or gender discriminations represented in Act I?

2. Dutchman

当代著名非裔美国诗人阿米利·巴拉卡(Amiri Baraka)(1934—2014)出生于纽瓦克黑人中产阶级家庭,先后在拉特格斯大学与霍华德大学就读,1954 年获得英语学士学位,毕业后曾在美国空军服役,曾因向共产主义刊物投稿诗作被开除军籍。他非常多产,除了诗歌创作之外,还发表了许多论文、短篇小说、音乐批评等,是与杜波伊斯、赖特、鲍德温等齐名的 20 世纪美国重要作家与文化批评家。

巴拉卡早年住在纽约著名的格林威治村,是当时垮掉派艺术家中最具才华的黑人,他与白人犹太女性海蒂结婚,有两个孩子。1960 年,他受邀访问古巴后,文艺思想与创作理念出现戏剧性的变化,他不再相信欧裔美国社会与文化,出版《布鲁斯人民:白人美国的黑人音乐》(1963),创作了《奴隶》(1964)和《洗手间》(1964)等戏剧作品,但是真正奠定他剧作家地位,为他赢得广泛赞誉的是他 1963 年在外百老汇上演的《荷兰人》。剧中黑人男性柯雷与白人女子卢拉之间的关系,隐喻了当时美国社会与文化环境中白人对黑人的毁灭性伤害。著名非裔美国文学批评家特纳(Darwin T. Turner)认为,这两位人物之间的关系表明,美国黑人如果在智识方面对白人形成威胁,就可能遭受柯雷这样的灭顶之灾;此剧同时也表明,如果美国黑人不直面白人的压迫,那么他的梦想、追求只会破灭。

在美国民权运动如火如荼的 20 世纪 60 年代,特别是马尔科姆·艾克斯被暗杀之后,巴拉卡更加强调非裔美国文艺服务于黑人民族的功能,甚至不无极端地把文艺的宣传功能提升到极致,创作出类似于"我们的诗歌应该能够杀戮//能够暗杀//诗歌能够射杀//诗歌是投枪"这样的诗句。1968 年,他与志同道合者尼尔共同编辑了富有典型时代特征的美国黑人革命文学选集《黑人的怒火》。

离开纽约回到新泽西后,巴拉卡创立民族主义的泛非组织"非洲人民议会",建立"精神之家",加入"美国黑人政治学会"等机构,其剧作《警察》、《要么武装自己要么伤害自己》直面美国警察在城市黑人社区的残暴行径。为了表明自己的种族与文化立场,他与白人妻子海蒂离婚,与非裔美国女性塞维尔·罗宾逊结婚,把自己的名字由原来的琼斯改为巴拉卡(Imamu Amiri Baraka),全身心地投入到黑人解放与黑人民族主义的斗争中去。1968—1975 年间,巴拉卡成为当时最具影响的年轻激进分子。

后来因为对黑人穆斯林及黑人民族主义意识形态感到失望,巴拉卡转而拥抱马克思-列宁主义,他对美国种族问题的思考更加成熟,艺术创作方面也更为沉稳,获得了多种荣誉,如古根海姆奖、福克纳笔会奖、洛克菲勒戏剧奖、休斯奖等,并成为新泽西州的桂冠诗人。巴拉卡的文艺创作与批评极好地反映了 20 世纪 60 年代和 70 年代黑人民权运动及黑人权力运动时期非裔美国文学中的激进与偏颇,值得我们认真反思与分析。

1964 年,《荷兰人》在外百老汇上演,1967 年被拍成电影,成为巴拉卡最受人关注的剧作,曾经获得奥比奖。有趣的是,本剧的背景设在纽约地铁上,舞台上重点呈现的是黑人男性柯雷与白人女性卢拉,并没有出现什么"荷兰人"。有论者指出,本剧的标题让人想起《飞翔的荷兰人》中受到诅咒、重复自己旅程的幽灵船,巴拉卡仿佛以之暗示,非裔美国人,就像这艘传说中的船,不仅在重复非洲黑人穿越大西洋中间航道的生死经历,而且在重现美国黑人生活在奴隶制中的悲惨命运,因此极具象征意义。本剧中黑人男主人公柯雷遭遇白人女性卢拉诱惑,在地铁车厢被卢拉刺杀身亡,预示着后续登台的黑人可能会遭遇同样的诱惑与死亡命运,反映了黑人男性青年的悲惨宿命。

以黑人男性柯雷与白人女性卢拉为呈现对象的《荷兰人》不仅再现了类型化的黑人男女,也通过对发生在美国南方特定历史时期、针对黑人男性的私刑出现在北方城市纽约地铁上的情景再现。使观众清楚地看到具有"自由主义"打扮,吃着苹果的卢拉如何被柯雷"原始"的男性魅力打动,主动与其调情,却在临近演出结束时,轻巧地把一柄小刀插进柯雷的心脏,若无其事地等待下一个牺牲品的全过程。

巴拉卡通过此剧表明,在 60 年代民权运动如火如荼的美国,黑人在继续寻找自己文化身份的过程中,更加清醒地认识到白人"自由主义"文化的"欺骗性",那些貌似"左翼",有时"甜言蜜语"的白人可能掩盖了自己种族主义者的真面目,他们虽然在言辞上同情黑人族群遭受的不公正待遇,但是几乎始终保有居高临下的主宰身份,不仅威胁着黑人的安全,而且腐蚀着黑人的心灵及其族群的文化。

令人欣慰的是,黑人男主人公柯雷虽然像许多悲剧英雄一样,难以摆脱死亡的命运,但是在生命的最后瞬间,他意识到自己必须主宰自己的命运,不能受白人文化的摆布,必须跳出美国历史的束缚,才能摆脱奴役,获得自由。巴拉卡的《荷兰人》极好地再现了美国转型时期——由 20 世纪 50 年代的融合主义转向 60 年代的分离主义——的历史画卷。

Characters

Clay,twenty-year-old Negro

Lula,thirty-year-old white woman

Riders of coach,white and black

Young negro

Conductor

In the flying underbelly of the city. Steaming hot, and summer on top, outside. Underground. The subway heaped in modern myth.

Opening scene is a man sitting in a subway seat, holding a magazine but looking vacantly just above its wilting pages. Occasionally he looks blankly toward the window on his right. Dim lights and darkness whistling by against the glass. (Or paste the lights, as admitted props, right on the subway windows. Have them move, even dim and flicker. But give the sense of speed. Also stations, whether the train is stopped or the glitter and activity of these stations merely flashes by the windows.)

The man is sitting alone. That is, only his seat is visible, though the rest of the car is outfitted as a complete subway car. But only his seat is shown. There might be, for a time, as the play begins, a loud scream of the actual train. And it can recur throughout the play, or continue on a lower key once the dialogue starts.

The train slows after a time, pulling to a brief stop at one of the stations. The man looks idly up, until he sees a woman's face staring at him through the window; when it realizes that the man has noticed the face, it begins very premeditatedly to smile. The man smiles too, for a moment, without a trace of self-consciousness. Almost an instinctive though undesirable response. Then a kind of awkwardness or embarrassment sets in, and the man makes to look away, is further embarrassed, so he brings back his eyes to where the face was, but by now the train is moving again, and the face would seem to be left behind by the way the man turns his head to look back through the other windows at the slowly fading platform. He smiles then; more comfortably confident, hoping perhaps that his memory of this brief encounter will be pleasant. And then he is idle again.

Scene 1

Train roars. Lights flash outside the windows.

Lula *enters from the rear of the car in bright, skimpy summer clothes and sandals. She carries a net bag full of paper books, fruit, and other anonymous articles. She is wearing sunglasses, which she pushes up on her forehead from time to time. Lula is a tall, slender, beautiful woman with long red hair hanging straight down her back, wearing only loud lipstick in somebody's good taste. She is eating an apple, very daintily. Coming down the car toward* Clay. *She stops beside* Clay's *seat and hangs languidly from the strap, still managing to eat the apple. It is apparent that she is going to sit in the seat next to* Clay, *and that she is only waiting for him to notice her before she sits.*

Clay *sits as before, looking just beyond his magazine, now and again pulling the magazine slowly back and forth in front of his face in a hopeless effort to fan himself. Then he sees the woman hanging there beside him and he looks up into her face, smiling quizzically.*

Lula: Hello.

Clay: Uh, hi're you?

Lula: I'm going to sit down. ...O. K.?

Clay: Sure.

Lula: [*Swings down onto the seat, pushing her legs straight out as if she is very weary*] Oooof! Too much weight.

Clay: Ha, doesn't look like much to me. [*Leaning back against the window, a little surprised and maybe stiff*]

Lula: It's so anyway. [*And she moves her toes in the sandals, then pulls her right leg up on the left knee, better to inspect the bottoms of the sandals and the back of her heel. She appears for a second not to notice that* Clay *is sitting next to her or that she has spoken to him just a second before.* Clay *looks at the magazine, then out the black window. As he does this, she turns very quickly toward him*] Weren't you staring at me through the window?

Clay: [*Wheeling around and very much stiffened*] What?

Lula: Weren't you staring at me through the window? At the last stop?

Clay: Staring at you? What do you mean?

Lula: Don't you know what staring means?

Clay: I saw you through the window ... if that's what it means. I don't know if I was staring. Seems to me you were staring through the window at me.

Lula: I was. But only after I'd turned around and saw you staring through that window down in the vicinity of my ass and legs.

Clay: Really?

Lula: Really. I guess you were just taking those idle potshots. Nothing else to do. Run your mind over people's flesh.

Clay: Oh boy. Wow, now I admit I was looking in your direction. But the rest of that weight is yours. ①

Lula: I suppose.

Clay: Staring through train windows is weird business. Much weirder than staring very sedately at abstract asses.

Lula: That's why I came looking through the window ... so you'd have more than that to go on. I even smiled at you.

Clay: That's right.

Lula: I even got into this train, going some other way than mine. Walked down the aisle ... searching you out.

Clay: Really? That's pretty funny.

Lula: That's pretty funny. ... God, you're dull.

Clay: Well, I'm sorry, lady, but I really wasn't prepared for party talk.

Lula: No, you're not. What are you prepared for? [*Wrapping the apple core in a Kleenex and dropping it on the floor*]

Clay: [*Takes her conversation as pure sex talk. He turns to confront her squarely with this idea*] I'm prepared for anything. How about you?

Lula: [*Laughing loudly and cutting it off abruptly*] What do you think you're doing?

Clay: What?

Lula: You think I want to pick you up, get you to take me somewhere and screw me, huh?

Clay: Is that the way I look?

Lula: You look like you been trying to grow a beard. That's exactly what you look like. You look like you live in New Jersey with your parents and are trying to grow a beard. That's what. You look like you've been reading Chinese poetry and drinking lukewarm sugarless tea. [*Laughs, uncrossing and recrossing her legs*] You look like death eating a soda cracker.

Clay: [*Cocking his head from one side to the other, embarrassed and trying to make some comeback, but also intrigued by what the woman is saying ... even the sharp city coarseness of her voice, which is still a kind of gentle sidewalk throb*] Really? I look like all that?

Lula: Not all of it. [*She feints a seriousness to cover an actual somber tone*] I lie a lot. [*Smiling*] It helps me control the world.

---

① 本剧这种"颠倒黑白"的处理方式颠覆了传统(非裔)美国文学中白人男性骚扰/侵害黑人女性的性别关系,而居主宰地位的"种族"关系依然继续在此发挥作用。但是,黑人男性柯雷直接点出白人女性"欲加之罪何患无辞"的潜台词,既预示着美国黑人名义上的进步,也表明依然处于受压迫状态的黑人的无奈。

Clay: [*Relieved and laughing louder than the humor*] Yeah, I bet.

Lula: But it's true, most of it, right? Jersey? Your bumpy neck?

Clay: How'd you know all that? Huh? Really, I mean about Jersey ... and even the beard. I met you before? You know Warren Enright?

Lula: You tried to make it with your sister when you were ten. [*Clay leans back hard against the back of the seat, his eyes opening now, still trying to look amused*] But I succeeded a few weeks ago. [*She starts to laugh again*]

Clay: What're you talking about? Warren tell you that? You're a friend of Georgia's?

Lula: I told you I lie. I don't know your sister. I don't know Warren Enright.

Clay: You mean you're just picking these things out of the air?

Lula: Is Warren Enright a tall skinny black black boy with a phony English accent?

Clay: I figured you knew him.

Lula: But I don't. I just figured you would know somebody like that. [*Laughs*]

Clay: Yeah, yeah.

Lula: You're probably on your way to his house now.

Clay: That's right.

Lula: [*Putting her hand on Clay's closest knee, drawing it from the knee up to the thigh's hinge, then removing it, watching his face very closely, and continuing to laugh, perhaps more gently than before*] Dull, dull, dull. I bet you think I'm exciting.

Clay: You're O. K.

Lula: Am I exciting you now?

Clay: Right. That's not what's supposed to happen?

Lula: How do I know? [*She returns her hand, without moving it, then takes it away and plunges it in her bag to draw out an apple*] You want this?

Clay: Sure.

Lula: [*She gets one out of the bag for herself*] Eating apples together is always the first step. Or walking up uninhabited Seventh Avenue in the twenties on weekends. [*Bites and giggles, glancing at Clay and speaking in loose singsong*] Can get you involved ... boy! Get us involved. Um-huh. [*Mock seriousness*] Would you like to get involved with me, Mister Man?

Clay: [*Trying to be as flippant as Lula, whacking happily at the apple*] Sure. Why not? A beautiful woman like you. Huh, I'd be a fool not to.

Lula: And I bet you're sure you know what you're talking about. [*Taking him a little roughly by the wrist, so he cannot eat the apple, then shaking the wrist*] I bet you're sure of almost everything anybody ever asked you about ... right? [*Shakes his wrist harder*] Right?

Clay: Yeah, right. ... Wow, you're pretty strong, you know? Whatta you, a lady wrestler or something?

Lula: What's wrong with lady wrestlers? And don't answer because you never knew any. Huh. [*Cynically*] That's for sure. They don't have any lady wrestlers in that part of Jersey. That's for sure.

Clay: Hey, you still haven't told me how you know so much about me.

Lula: I told you I didn't know anything about *you* ... you're a well-known type.

Clay: Really?

Lula: Or at least I know the type very well. And your skinny English friend too.

Clay: Anonymously?

Lula: [*Settles back in seat, single-mindedly finishing her apple and humming snatches of rhythm and blues song*] What?

Clay: Without knowing us specifically?

Lula: Oh boy. [*Looking quickly at* Clay] What a face. You know, you could be a handsome man.

Clay: I can't argue with you.

Lula: [*Vague, off-center response*] What?

Clay: [*Raising his voice, thinking the train noise has drowned part of his sentence*] I can't argue with you.

Lula: My hair is turning gray. A gray hair for each year and type I've come through.

Clay: Why do you want to sound so old?

Lula: But it's always gentle when it starts. [*Attention drifting*] Hugged against tenements, day or night.

Clay: What?

Lula: [*Refocusing*] Hey, why don't you take me to that party you're going to?

Clay: You must be a friend of Warren's to know about the party.

Lula: Wouldn't you like to take me to the party? [*Imitates clinging vine*] Oh, come on, ask me to your party.

Clay: Of course I'll ask you to come with me to the party. And I'll bet you're a friend of Warren's.

Lula: Why not be a friend of Warren's? Why not? [*Taking his arm*] Have you asked me yet?

Clay: How can I ask you when I don't know your name?

Lula: Are you talking to my name?

Clay: What is it, a secret?

Lula: I'm Lena the Hyena.

Clay: The famous woman poet?

Lula: Poetess! The same!

Clay: Well, you know so much about me ... what's my name?

Lula: Morris the Hyena.

Clay: The famous woman poet?

Lula: The same. [*Laughing and going into her bag*] You want another apple?

Clay: Can't make it, lady. I only have to keep one doctor away a day.

Lula: I bet your name is ... something like ... uh, Gerald or Walter. Huh?

Clay: God, no.

Lula: Lloyd, Norman? One of those hopeless colored names creeping out of New Jersey. Leonard? Gag. ...

Clay: Like Warren?

Lula: Definitely. Just exactly like Warren. Or Everett.

Clay: Gag. ...

Lula: Well, for sure, it's not Willie.

Clay: It's Clay.

Lula: Clay? Really? Clay what?

Clay: Take your pick. Jackson, Johnson, or Williams.

Lula: Oh, really? Good for you. But it's got to be Williams. You're too pretentious to be a Jackson or Johnson.

Clay: That's right.

Lula: But Clay's O. K.

Clay: So's Lena.

Lula: It's Lula.

Clay: Oh?

Lula: Lula the Hyena.

Clay: Very good.

Lula: [*Starts laughing again*] Now you say to me, "Lula, Lula, why don't you go to this party with me tonight?" It's your turn, and let those be your lines.

Clay: Lula, why don't you go to this party with me tonight, Huh?

Lula: Say my name twice before you ask, and no huh's.

Clay: Lula, Lula, why don't you go to this party with me tonight?

Lula: I'd like to go, Clay, but how can you ask me to go when you barely know me?

Clay: That is strange, isn't it?

Lula: What kind of reaction is that? You're supposed to say, "Aw, come on, we'll get to know each other better at the party."

Clay: That's pretty corny.

Lula: What are you into anyway? [*Looking at him half sullenly but still amused*] What thing are you playing at, Mister? Mister Clay Williams? [*Grabs his thigh, up near the crotch*] What are *you* thinking about?

Clay: Watch it now, you're gonna excite me for real.

Lula: [*Taking her hand away and throwing her apple core through the window*] I bet. [*She slumps in the seat and is heavily silent*]

Clay: I thought you knew everything about me? What happened? [Lula *looks at him, then looks slowly away, then over where the other aisle would be. Noise of the train. She reaches in her bag and pulls out one of the paper books. She puts it on her leg and thumbs the pages listlessly. Clay cocks his head to see the title of the book. Noise of the train. Lula flips pages and her eyes drift. Both remain silent*] Are you going to the party with me, Lula?

Lula: [*Bored and not even looking*] I don't even know you.

Clay: You said you know my type.

Lula: [*Strangely irritated*] Don't get smart with me, Buster. I know you like the palm of my hand.

Clay: The one you eat the apples with?

Lula: Yeh. And the one I open doors late Saturday evening with. That's my door. Up at the top of the stairs. Five flights. Above a lot of Italians and lying Americans. And scrape carrots with. Also ... [*Looks at him*] the same hand I unbutton my dress with, or let my skirt fall down. Same hand. Lover.

Clay: Are you angry about anything? Did I say something wrong?

Lula: Everything you say is wrong. [*Mock smile*] That's what makes you so attractive. Ha. In that funnybook jacket with all the buttons. [*More animate, taking hold of his jacket*] What've you got that jacket and tie on in all this heat for? And why're you wearing a jacket and tie like that? Did your people ever burn witches or start revolutions over the price of tea? Boy, those narrow-shoulder clothes come from a tradition you ought to feel oppressed by. A three-button suit. What right do you have to be wearing a threebutton suit and striped tie? Your grandfather was a slave, he didn't go to Harvard.

Clay: My grandfather was a night watchman.

Lula: And you went to a colored college where everybody thought they were Averell Harriman.

Clay: All except me.

Lula: And who did you think you were? Who do you think you are now?

Clay: [*Laughs as if to make light of the whole trend of the conversation*] Well, in college I thought I was Baudelaire. But I've slowed down since.

Lula: I bet you never once thought you were a black nigger. [*Mock serious, then she howls with laughter.* Clay *is stunned but after initial reaction, he quickly tries to appreciate the humor.* Lula *almost shrieks*] A black Baudelaire.

Clay: That's right.

Lula: Boy, are you corny. I take back what I said before. Everything you say is not wrong. It's perfect. You should be on television.

Clay: You act like you're on television already.

Lula: That's because I'm an actress.

Clay: I thought so.

Lula: Well, you're wrong. I'm no actress. I told you I always lie. I'm nothing, honey, and don't you ever forget it. [*Lighter*] Although my mother was a Communist. The only person in my family ever to amount to anything.

Clay: My mother was a Republican.

Lula: And your father voted for the man rather than the party.

Clay: Right!

Lula: Yea for him. Yea, yea for him.

Clay: Yea!

Lula: And yea for America where he is free to vote for the mediocrity of his choice! Yea!

Clay: Yea!

Lula: And yea for both your parents who even though they differ about so crucial a matter as the body politic still forged a union of love and sacrifice that was destined to flower at the birth of the noble Clay ... what's your middle name?

Clay: Clay.

Lula: A union of love and sacrifice that was destined to flower at the birth of the noble Clay Clay Williams. Yea! And most of all yea yea for you, Clay Clay. The Black Baudelaire! Yes! [*And with knifelike cynicism*] My Christ. My Christ.

Clay: Thank you, ma'am.

Lula: May the people accept you as a ghost of the future. And love you, that you might not kill them when you can.

Clay: What?

Lula: You're a murderer, Clay, and you know it. [*Her voice darkening with significance*] You know goddamn well what I mean.

Clay: I do?

Lula: So we'll pretend the air is light and full of perfume.

Clay: [*Sniffing at her blouse*] It is.

Lula: And we'll pretend the people cannot see you. That is, the citizens. And that you are free of your own history. And I am free of my history. We'll pretend that we are both anonymous beauties smashing along through the city's entrails. [*She yells as loud as she can*] GROOVE!

Scene 2

Scene is the same as before, though now there are other seats visible in the car. And throughout the scene other people get on the subway. There are maybe one or two seated in the car as the scene opens, though neither Clay *nor* Lula *notices them.* Clay's *tie is open.* Lula *is hugging his arm.*

Clay: The party!

Lula: I know it'll be something good. You can come in with me, looking casual and significant. I'll be strange, haughty, and silent, and walk with long slow strides.

Clay: Right.

Lula: When you get drunk, pat me once, very lovingly on the flanks, and I'll look at you cryptically, licking my lips.

Clay: It sounds like something we can do.

Lula: You'll go around talking to young men about your mind, and to old men about your plans. If you meet a very close friend who is also with someone like me, we can stand together, sipping our drinks and exchanging codes of lust. The atmosphere will be slithering in love and half-love and very open moral decision.

Clay: Great. Great.

Lula: And everyone will pretend they don't know your name, and then ... [*She pauses heavily*] later, when they have to, they'll claim a friendship that denies your sterling character.

Clay: [*Kissing her neck and fingers*] And then what?

Lula: Then? Well, then we'll go down the street, late night, eating apples and winding very deliberately toward my house.

Clay: Deliberately?

Lula: I mean, we'll look in all the shop windows, and make fun of the queers. Maybe we'll meet a Jewish Buddhist and flatten his conceits over some very pretentious coffee.

Clay: In honor of whose God?

Lula: Mine.

Clay: Who is ... ?

Lula: Me ... and you?

Clay: A corporate Godhead.

Lula: Exactly. Exactly. [Notices one of the other people entering]

Clay: Go on with the chronicle. Then what happens to us?

Lula: [A mild depression, but she still makes her description triumphant and increasingly direct] To my house, of course.

Clay: Of course.

Lula: And up the narrow steps of the tenement.

Clay: You live in a tenement?

Lula: Wouldn't live anywhere else. Reminds me specifically of my novel form of insanity.

Clay: Up the tenement stairs.

Lula: And with my apple-eating hand I push open the door and lead you, my tender big-eyed prey, into my ... God, what can I call it ... into my hovel.

Clay: Then what happens?

Lula: After the dancing and games, after the long drinks and long walks, the real fun begins.

Clay: Ah, the real fun. [Embarrassed, in spite of himself] Which is ... ?

Lula: [Laughs at him] Real fun in the dark house. Hah! Real fun in the dark house, high up above the street and the ignorant cowboys. I lead you in, holding your wet hand gently in my hand ...

Clay: Which is not wet?

Lula: Which is dry as ashes.

Clay: And cold?

Lula: Don't think you'll get out of your responsibility that way. It's not cold at all. You Fascist! Into my dark living room. Where we'll sit and talk endlessly, endlessly.

Clay: About what?

Lula: About what? About your manhood, what do you think? What do you think we've been talking about all this time?

Clay: Well, I didn't know it was that. That's for sure. Every other thing in the world but that. [Notices another person entering, looks quickly, almost involuntarily up and down the car, seeing the other people in the car] Hey, I didn't even notice when those people got on.

Lula: Yeah, I know.

Clay: Man, this subway is slow.

Lula: Yeah, I know.

Clay: Well, go on. We were talking about my manhood.

Lula: We still are. All the time.

Clay: We were in your living room.

Lula: My dark living room. Talking endlessly.

Clay: About my manhood.

Lula: I'll make you a map of it. Just as soon as we get to my house.

Clay: Well, that's great.

Lula: One of the things we do while we talk. And screw.

Clay: [*Trying to make his smile broader and less shaky*] We finally got there.

Lula: And you'll call my rooms black as a grave. You'll say, "This place is like Juliet's tomb."

Clay: [*Laughs*] I might.

Lula: I know. You've probably said it before.

Clay: And is that all? The whole grand tour?

Lula: Not all. You'll say to me very close to my face, many, many times, you'll say, even whisper, that you love me.

Clay: Maybe I will.

Lula: And you'll be lying.

Clay: I wouldn't lie about something like that.

Lula: Hah. It's the only kind of thing you will lie about. Especially if you think it'll keep me alive.

Clay: Keep you alive? I don't understand.

Lula: [*Bursting out laughing, but too shrilly*] Don't understand? Well, don't look at me. It's the path I take, that's all. Where both feet take me when I set them down. One in front of the other.

Clay: Morbid. Morbid. You sure you're not an actress? All that self-aggrandizement.

Lula: Well, I told you I wasn't an actress ... but I also told you I lie all the time. Draw your own conclusions.

Clay: Morbid. Morbid. You sure you're not an actress? All scribed? There's no more?

Lula: I've told you all I know. Or almost all.

Clay: There's no funny parts?

Lula: I thought it was all funny.

Clay: But you mean peculiar, not ha-ha.

Lula: You don't know what I mean.

Clay: Well, tell me the almost part then. You said almost all. What else? I want the whole story.

Lula: [*Searching aimlessly through her bag. She begins to talk breathlessly, with a light and silly tone*] All stories are whole stories. All of 'em. Our whole story ... nothing but change. How could things go on like that forever? Huh? [*Slaps him on the shoulder, begins finding things in her bag, taking them out and throwing them over her shoulder into the aisle*] Except I do go on as I do. Apples and long walks with deathless intelligent lovers. But you mix it up. Look out the window, all the time. Turning pages. Change change change. Till, shit, I don't know you. Wouldn't, for that matter. You're too serious. I bet you're even too serious to be psychoanalyzed. Like all those Jewish poets from Yonkers, who leave their mothers looking for other mothers, or others' mothers, on whose baggy tits they lay their fumbling heads. Their poems are always funny, and all about sex.

Clay: They sound great. Like movies.

Lula: But you change. [*Blankly*] And things work on you till you hate them. [*More people come into the train. They come closer to the couple, some of them not sitting, but swinging drearily on the straps, staring at the two with uncertain interest*]

Clay: Wow. All these people, so suddenly. They must all come from the same place.

Lula: Right. That they do.

Clay: Oh? You know about them too?

Lula: Oh yeah. About them more than I know about you. Do they frighten you?

Clay: Frighten me? Why should they frighten me?

Lula: 'Cause you're an escaped nigger.

Clay: Yeah?

Lula: 'Cause you crawled through the wire and made tracks to my side.

Clay: Wire?

Lula: Don't they have wire around plantations?

Clay: You must be Jewish. All you can think about is wire. Plantations didn't have any wire. Plantations were big open whitewashed places like heaven, and everybody on 'em was grooved to be there. Just strummin' and hummin' all day.

Lula: Yes, yes.

Clay: And that's how the blues was born.

Lula: Yes, yes. And that's how the blues was born. [*Begins to make up a song that becomes quickly hysterical. As she sings she rises from her seat, still throwing things out of her bag into the aisle, beginning a rhythmical shudder and twistlike wiggle, which she continues up and down the aisle, bumping into many of the standing people and tripping over the feet of those sitting. Each time she runs into a person she lets out a very vicious piece of profanity, wiggling and stepping all the time*] And that's how the blues was born. Yes. Yes. Son of a bitch, get out of the way. Yes. Quack. Yes. Yes. And that's how the blues was born. Ten little niggers sitting on a limb, but none of them ever looked like him. [*Points to* Clay, *returns toward the seat, with her hands extended for him to rise and dance with her*] And that's how blues was born. Yes. Come on, Clay. Let's do the nasty. Rub bellies. Rub bellies.

Clay: [*Waves his hands to refuse. He is embarrassed, but determined to get a kick out of the proceedings*] Hey, what was in those apples? Mirror, mirror on the wall, who's the fairest one of all? Snow White, baby, and don't you forget it.

Lula: [*Grabbing for his hands, which he draws away*] Come on, Clay. Let's rub bellies on the train. The nasty. The nasty. Do the gritty grind, like your ol' rag-head mammy. Grind till you lose your mind. Shake it, shake it, shake it, shake it! OOOOweeee! Come on, Clay. Let's do the choo-choo train shuffle, the navel scratcher.

Clay: Hey, you coming on like the lady who smoked up her grass skirt.

Lula: [*Becoming annoyed that he will not dance, and becoming more animated as if to embarrass him still further*] Come on, Clay … let's do the thing. Uhh! Uhh! Clay! Clay! You middle-class black bastard. Forget your social-working mother for a few seconds and let's knock stomachs. Clay, you liver-lipped white man. You would-be Christian. You ain't no nigger, you're just a dirty white man. Get up, Clay. Dance with me, Clay.

Clay: Lula! Sit down, now. Be cool.

Lula: [*Mocking him, in wild dance*] Be cool. Be cool. That's all you know … shaking that wildroot cream-oil on your knotty head, jackets buttoning up to your chin, so full of white man's words. Christ. God. Get up and scream at these people. Like scream meaningless shit in these hopeless faces. [*She screams at people in train, still dancing*] Red trains cough Jewish underwear for keeps! Expanding smells of silence. Gravy snot whistling like sea birds. Clay. Clay, you got to break out. Don't sit there dying the way they want you to die. Get up.

Clay: Oh, sit the fuck down. [*He moves to restrain her*] Sit down, goddamn it.

Lula: [*Twisting out of his reach*] Screw yourself, Uncle Tom. Thomas Woolly-head. [*Begins to dance a kind of jig, mocking* Clay *with loud forced humor*] There is Uncle Tom … I mean, Uncle Thomas Woolly-Head. With old white matted mane. He hobbles on his wooden cane. Old Tom. Old Tom. Let the white man hump his ol' mama, and he jes' shuffle off in the woods and hide his gentle gray head. Ol' Thomas Woolly-Head. [*Some of the other riders are laughing now. A drunk gets up and joins* Lula *in her dance, singing, as best he can, her "song."* Clay *gets up out of his seat and visibly scans the faces of the other riders*]

Clay: Lula! Lula! [*She is dancing and turning, still shouting as loud as she can. The drunk too is shouting, and waving his hands wildly*] Lula … you dumb bitch. Why don't you stop it? [*He rushes half stumbling from his seat, and grabs one of her flailing arms*]

Lula: Let me go! You black son of a bitch. [*She struggles against him*] Let me go! Help! [Clay *is dragging her towards her seat, and the drunk seeks to interfere. He grabs* Clay *around the shoulders and begins wrestling with him.* Clay *clubs the drunk to the floor without releasing* Lula, *who is still screaming.* Clay *finally gets her to the seat and throws her into it*]

Clay: Now you shut the hell up. [*Grabbing her shoulders*] Just shut up. You don't know what you're talking about. You don't know anything. So just keep your stupid mouth closed.

Lula: You're afraid of white people. And your father was. Uncle Tom Big Lip!

Clay: [*Slaps her as hard as he can, across the mouth.* Lula's *head bangs against the back of the seat. When she raises it again,* Clay *slaps her again*] Now shut up and let me talk. [*He turns toward the other riders, some of whom are sitting on the edge of their seats. The drunk is on one knee, rubbing his head, and singing softly the same song. He shuts up too when he sees* Clay *watching him. The others go back to newspapers or stare out the windows*] Shit, you don't have any sense, Lula, nor feelings either. I could murder you now. Such a tiny ugly throat. I could squeeze it flat, and watch you turn blue, on a humble. For dull kicks. And all these weak-faced ofays squatting around here, staring over their papers at me. Murder them too. Even if they expected it. That man there … [*Points to well-dressed man*] I could rip that *Times* right out of his hand, as skinny and middle-classed as I am, I could rip that paper out of his hand and just as easily rip out his throat. It takes no great effort. For what? To kill you soft idiots? You don't understand anything but luxury.

Lula: You fool!

Clay: [*Pushing her against the seat*] I'm not telling you again, Tallulah Bankhead! Luxury. In your face and your fingers. You telling me what I ought to do. [*Sudden scream frightening the whole coach*] Well, don't! Don't you tell me anything! If I'm a middleclass fake white man … let me be. And let me be in the way I want. [*Through his teeth*] I'll rip your lousy breasts off! Let me be who I feel like being. Uncle Tom. ①Thomas. Whoever. It's none of your business. You don't know anything except what's there for you to see. An act. Lies. Device. Not the pure heart, the pumping black heart. You don't ever know that. And I sit here, in this buttoned-up suit, to keep myself from cutting all your throats. I mean wantonly. You great liberated whore! You fuck some black man, and right away you're an expert on black people. What a lotta shit that is. The only thing you know is that you come if he bangs you hard enough. And that's all. The belly rub? You wanted to do the belly rub? Shit, you don't even know how. You don't know how. That ol' dipty-dip shit you do, rolling your ass like an elephant. That's not my kind of belly rub. Belly rub is not Queens. Belly rub is dark places, with big hats and overcoats held up with one arm. Belly rub hates you. Old bald-headed four-eyed ofays popping their fingers … and don't know yet what they're doing. They say, "I love Bessie Smith." And don't even understand that Bessie Smith is saying, "Kiss my ass, kiss my black unruly ass." Before love, suffering, desire, anything you can explain, she's saying, and very plainly, "Kiss my black ass." And if you don't know that, it's you that's doing the kissing. Charlie Parker? Charlie Parker. All the hip white boys scream for Bird. And Bird saying, "Up your ass, feebleminded ofay! Up your ass." And they sit there talking about the tortured genius of Charlie Parker. Bird would've played not a note of music if he just walked up to East Sixty-seventh Street and killed the first ten white people he saw. Not a note! And I'm the great would-be poet. Yes. That's right! Poet. Some kind of bastard literature … all it needs is a simple knife thrust. Just let me bleed you, you loud whore, and one poem vanished. A whole people of neurotics, struggling to keep from being sane. And the only thing that would cure the neurosis would be your murder. Simple as that. I mean if I murdered you, then other white people would begin to understand me. You understand? No. I guess not. If Bessie Smith had killed some white people she wouldn't have needed that music. She could have talked very straight and plain about the world. No metaphors. No grunts. No

---

① 汤姆叔叔是斯托夫人的小说《汤姆叔叔的小屋》中善良、温顺、虔敬上帝、忠诚于奴隶主人的黑人男性,是不敢直接反抗奴隶主/白人的懦弱形象的代表。

wiggles in the dark of her soul. Just straight two and two are four. Money. Power. Luxury. Like that. All of them. Crazy niggers turning their backs on sanity. When all it needs is that simple act. Murder. Just murder! Would make us all sane. [*Suddenly weary*] Ahhh. Shit. But who needs it? I'd rather be a fool. Insane. Safe with my words, and no deaths, and clean, hard thoughts, urging me to new conquests. My people's madness. Hah! That's a laugh. My people. They don't need me to claim them. They got legs and arms of their own. Personal insanities. Mirrors. They don't need all those words. They don't need any defense. But listen, though, one more thing. And you tell this to your father, who's probably the kind of man who needs to know at once. So he can plan ahead. Tell him not to preach so much rationalism and cold logic to these niggers. Let them alone. Let them sing curses at you in code and see your filth as simple lack of style. Don't make the mistake, through some irresponsible surge of Christian charity, of talking too much about the advantages of Western rationalism, or the great intellectual legacy of the white man, or maybe they'll begin to listen. And then, maybe one day, you'll find they actually do understand exactly what you are talking about, all these fantasy people. All these blues people. And on that day, as sure as shit, when you really believe you can "accept" them into your fold, as half-white trusties late of the subject peoples. With no more blues, except the very old ones, and not a watermelon in sight, the great missionary heart will have triumphed, and all of those ex-coons will be stand-up Western men, with eyes for clean hard useful lives, sober, pious and sane, and they'll murder you. They'll murder you, and have very rational explanations. Very much like your own. They'll cut your throats, and drag you out to the edge of your cities so the flesh can fall away from your bones, in sanitary isolation.

Lula: [*Her voice takes on a different, more businesslike quality*] I've heard enough.

Clay: [*Reaching for his books*] I bet you have. I guess I better collect my stuff and get off this train. Looks like we won't be acting out that little pageant you outlined before.

Lula: No. We won't. You're right about that, at least. [*She turns to look quickly around the rest of the car*] All right! [*The others respond*]

Clay: [*Bending across the girl to retrieve his belongings*] Sorry, baby, I don't think we could make it. [*As he is bending over her, the girl brings up a small knife and plunges it into* Clay's *chest. Twice. He slumps across her knees, his mouth working stupidly*]

Lula: Sorry is right. [*Turning to the others in the car who have already gotten up from their seats*] Sorry is the rightest thing you've said. Get this man off me! Hurry, now! [*The others come and drag* Clay's *body down the aisle*] Open the door and throw his body out. [*They throw him off*] And all of you get off at the next stop. [Lula *busies herself straightening her things. Getting everything in order. She takes out a notebook and makes a quick scribbling note. Drops it in her bag. The train apparently stops and all the others get off, leaving her alone in the coach. Very soon a young Negro of about twenty comes into the coach, with a couple of books under his arm. He sits a few seats in back of* Lula. *When he is seated she turns and gives him a long slow look. He looks up from his book and drops the book on his lap. Then an old Negro conductor comes into the car, doing a sort of restrained soft shoe, and half mumbling the words of some song. He looks at the young man, briefly, with a quick greeting*]

Conductor: Hey, brother!①

Young man: Hey. [*The conductor continues down the aisle with his little dance and the mumbled song. Lula turns to stare at him and follows his movements down the aisle. The conductor tips his hat when he reaches her seat, and continues out the car*]

Curtain

1964

Questions for Discussion

1. Lula claims to know the type of Clay or the "colored man", what does this suggest?

2. How to understand Lula's "I lie a lot. It helps me to control the world"?

3. Clay is stabbed to death in the play, do you think it is an accident? What does this incident suggest?

---

① 如此结尾有故伎重演的味道,可参看当代电影《逃出绝命镇》。

3. Fences

奥古斯特·威尔逊(August Wilson)(1945—2005)是 20 世纪 80 年代美国剧坛崛起的一位极负盛名的黑人剧作家。纽约时报著名戏剧评论家弗兰克·里奇把威尔逊的脱颖而出称为美国戏剧界的一个重要发现;更有其他一些剧评家认为他是继尤金·奥尼尔、田纳西·威廉斯和阿瑟·米勒之后美国诞生的又一位伟大戏剧家。遗憾的是,他英年早逝。2005 年 10 月,美国百老汇的弗吉尼亚剧院更名为奥古斯特·威尔逊剧院,以纪念这位伟大的戏剧家。威尔逊由此成为首位获此殊荣的非裔美国作家。

威尔逊倾注了毕生精力创作"20 世纪黑人体验史"系列剧,大致以每十年为一阶段,选取其中代表性的事件为剧本题材,以编年史的方式全方位地记录美国黑人过去百年的生命历程,有力地激发了他们重新审视历史的信念。他是一位多产作家,代表性作品有《马雷尼大妈的黑臀》(1984)、《栅栏》(1985)、《乔·特纳来了又走了》(1986)、《钢琴课》(1987)等。这些作品让威尔逊收获了巨大成功,先后荣获普利策戏剧奖、纽约剧评奖、托尼奖等各种著名戏剧奖项。其中,凭借《栅栏》和《钢琴课》,威尔逊获得 1987 年和 1990 年普利策戏剧奖。五年内两度荣获普利策奖,这在美国文学史上是极为罕见的。他后期的作品还有《两列奔驰的火车》(1990)、《七把吉他》(1995)、《郝德利王二世》(1999)等。从整体来看,一个贯穿威尔逊系列剧作始终的主题是,美国黑人需要重新追溯历史,重新认识自己,认清自己既是一个美国人,又是一个黑人的事实。

作品简介与赏析

《栅栏》(*Fences*, 1985)被很多评论家誉为奥古斯特·威尔逊最具代表性的作品。该剧以上演 525 场、单年赢利 1 100 万美元的佳绩创造了百老汇非音乐剧种的纪录,并且把美国戏剧界最权威、最具影响力的三大奖项全部收入囊中:普利策戏剧奖、托尼奖和纽约剧评人奖。

该剧描述的是 20 世纪 60 年代一个美国黑人家庭中发生的故事,深刻反映了美国社会中的种族问题对黑人生活造成的巨大影响。主人公特洛伊·马克森是一个饱尝生活艰辛、心灵受过摧残的黑人。他已经 53 岁,坐过牢,当过运动员,现在干着垃圾清扫的工作。他曾经是位优秀的棒球运动员,但由于肤色的原因,未能进入任何著名球队。在种族歧视严重的美国社会,他着实际遇不佳。扭曲的生活导致了他复杂又矛盾的性格。他尽力照顾因二战期间受伤而造成智力障碍的可怜哥哥,但又私自挪用哥哥的抚恤金;他设法帮助自己在橄榄球方面有天分的儿子科里,却阻止他获取一份颁发给橄榄球星的大学奖学金;他爱自己的妻子,但却和别的女人生孩子。剧中的其他人物也在痛苦挣扎中求生存。儿子想成为橄榄球明星的梦想被父亲扼杀在摇篮里。他试图对抗、超越父亲,却潜移默化地继承了父亲身上的一些特质。善良的妻子罗斯最终答应收养丈夫和别的女人生的孩子,但却离开了丈夫。兄弟之间、父子之间、夫妻之间,思想上无法沟通,矛盾复杂交织,整个家庭处于濒临破裂的边缘。

《栅栏》这个剧名意味深长。男主人公特洛伊在自家后院里用结实的硬木修筑起一堵栅栏,希望用它来防止外界的侵袭,保护自己和自己的家庭。栅栏给这个黑人家庭带来了些许安全感。然而与此同时,他也筑起了一道无形的围墙,把自己和亲人围了进去,让家庭成员与外界彻底隔绝，孤立无援。栅栏更是横在了他们灵魂深处，让他们倍感窒息。

    威尔逊出生于美国贫穷动荡的黑人聚居区匹兹堡。他的母亲是黑人，在穷人区的两间屋子里艰难带大了包括威尔逊在内的六个孩子。由于种族主义的根深蒂固，威尔逊很早就辍学。独特的成长经历使他对美国黑人生活有着极为深刻的体会和认识。在《栅栏》的创作中，他用细腻的笔锋生动而真实地还原了种族歧视下美国黑人的苦难生活。他曾经说过自己创作的目的就是为了把美国黑人的传统形象有血有肉地展现在人们面前。与空泛的说教不同的是，他力求从社会学和文学的双重角度剖析美国黑人的悲惨处境，启发人们关注美国黑人的社会地位，并最终引导美国黑人开启找寻自我身份之路。

    威尔逊对当代美国戏剧的巨大贡献，不仅仅体现在他宏大的历史主题上，更体现在他通过独具匠心的戏剧艺术对美国黑人自我身份所进行的深刻探索上。他大胆继承前辈们的创作手法和技巧，对其进行创造性的发展，最终形成自己独特的写作风格。他坚持基于纯黑人的文化传统进行写作。布鲁斯音乐、讲故事模式和隐喻性语言等黑人文化传统形式在作品中的巧妙融合构成了作家最鲜明的戏剧创作特色，也成为作家成熟卓越的戏剧艺术技巧的最完美诠释。通过独特的戏剧表现手法，威尔逊成功地为美国黑人同胞寻找到一条通向自我身份之路。

    选篇出自剧本《栅栏》的第一幕第一场。

Characters

Troy Maxson

Jim Bono：Troy's *friend*

Rose：   Troy's *wife*

Lyons：   Troy's *oldest son by previous marriage*

Gabriel： Troy's *brother*

Cory：   Troy *and* Rose's *son*

Raynell： Troy's *daughter*

Setting

    The setting is the yard which fronts the only entrance to the Maxson household, an ancient two-story brick house set back off a small alley in a big-city neighborhood. The entrance to the house is gained by two or three steps leading to a wooden porch badly in need of paint.

    A relatively recent addition to the house and running its full width, the porch lacks congruence. It is a sturdy porch with a flat roof. One or two chairs of dubious value sit at one end where the kitchen window opens onto the porch. An old-fashioned icebox stands silent guard at the opposite end.

    The yard is a small dirt yard, partially fenced, except for the last scene, with a wooden sawhorse, a pile of lumber, and other fence-building equipment set off to the side. Opposite is a tree from which hangs a ball made of rags. A baseball bat leans against the tree. Two oil drums serve as garbage receptacles and sit near the house at right to complete the setting.

The Play

Near the turn of the century, the destitute of Europe sprang on the city with tenacious claws and an honest and solid dream. The city devoured them. They swelled its belly until it burst into a thousand furnaces and sewing machines, a thousand butcher shops and bakers' ovens, a thousand churches and hospitals and funeral parlors and money-lenders. The city grew. It nourished itself and offered each man a partnership limited only by his talent, his guile, and his willingness and capacity for hard work. For the immigrants of Europe, a dream dared and won true.

The descendants of African slaves were offered no such welcome or participation. They came from places called the Carolinas and the Virginias, Georgia, Alabama, Mississippi, and Tennessee. They came strong, eager, searching. The city rejected them and they fled and settled along the riverbanks and under bridges in shallow, ramshackle houses made of sticks and tar-paper. They collected rags and wood. They sold the use of their muscles and their bodies. They cleaned houses and washed clothes, they shined shoes, and in quiet desperation and vengeful pride, they stole, and lived in pursuit of their own dream. That they could breathe free, finally, and stand to meet life with the force of dignity and whatever eloquence the heart could call upon.

By 1957, the hard-won victories of the European immigrants had solidified the industrial might of America. War had been confronted and won with new energies that used loyalty and patriotism as its fuel. Life was rich, full, and flourishing. The Milwaukee Braves won the World Series, and the hot winds of change that would make the sixties a turbulent, racing, dangerous, and provocative decade had not yet begun to blow full.

Act One

Scene One

It is 1957. Troy *and* Bono *enter the yard, engaged in conversation.* Troy *is fifty-three years old, a large man with thick, heavy hands; it is this largeness that he strives to fill out and make an accommodation with. Together with his blackness, his largeness informs his sensibilities and the choices he has made in his life.*

Of the two men, Bono *is obviously the follower. His commitment to their friendship of thirty-odd years is rooted in his admiration of* Troy's *honesty, capacity for hard work, and his strength, which* Bono *seeks to emulate.*

It is Friday night, payday, and the one night of the week the two men engage in a ritual of talk and drink. Troy *is usually the most talkative and at times he can be crude and almost vulgar, though he is capable of rising to profound heights of expression. The men carry lunch buckets and wear or carry burlap aprons and are dressed in clothes suitable to their jobs as garbage collectors.*

Bono: Troy, you ought to stop that lying!
Troy: I ain't lying! The nigger had a watermelon this big. [*He indicates with his hands.*] Talking about ... "What watermelon, Mr. Rand?" I liked to fell out! "What watermelon,

Mr. Rand?"... And it sitting there big as life.

Bono: What did Mr. Rand say?

Troy: Ain't said nothing. Figure if the nigger too dumb to know he carrying a watermelon, he wasn't gonna get much sense out of him. Trying to hide that great big old watermelon under his coat. Afraid to let the white man see him carry it home.

Bono: I'm like you ... I ain't got no time for them kind of people.

Troy: Now what he look like getting mad cause he see the man from the union talking to Mr. Rand?

Bono: He come to me talking about ... "Maxson gonna get us fired." I told him to get away from me with that. He walked away from me calling you a troublemaker. What Mr. Rand say?

Troy: Ain't said nothing. He told me to go down the Commissioner's office next Friday. They called me down there to see them.

Bono: Well, as long as you got your complaint filed, they can't fire you. That's what one of them white fellows tell me.

Troy: I ain't worried about them firing me. They gonna fire me cause I asked a question? That's all I did. I went to Mr. Rand and asked him, "Why? Why you got the white mens driving and the colored lifting?" Told him, "what's the matter, don't I count? You think only white fellows got sense enough to drive a truck. That ain't no paper job! Hell, anybody can drive a truck. How come you got all whites driving and the colored lifting? He told me "take it to the union." Well, hell, that's what I done! Now they wanna come up with this pack of lies.

Bono: I told Brownie if the man come and ask him any questions ... just tell the truth! It ain't nothing but something they done trumped up on you cause you filed a complaint on them.

Troy: Brownie don't understand nothing. All I want them to do is change the job description. Give everybody a chance to drive the truck. Brownie can't see that. He ain't got that much sense.

Bono: How you figure he be making out with that gal be up at Taylors' all the time ... that Alberta gal?

Troy: Same as you and me. Getting just as much as we is. Which is to say nothing.

Bono: It is, huh? I figure you doing a little better than me ... and I ain't saying what I'm doing.

Troy: Aw, nigger, look here ... I know you. If you had got anywhere near that gal, twenty minutes later you be looking to tell somebody. And the first one you gonna tell ... that you gonna want to brag to ... is gonna be me.

Bono: I ain't saying that. I see where you be eyeing her.

Troy: I eye all the women. I don't miss nothing. Don't never let nobody tell you Troy Maxson don't eye the women.

Bono: You been doing more than eyeing her. You done bought her a drink or two.

Troy: Hell yeah, I bought her a drink! What that mean? I bought you one, too. What that mean cause I buy her a drink? I'm just being polite.

Bono: It's alright to buy her one drink. That's what you call being polite. But when you wanna be buying two or three ... that's what you call eyeing her.

Troy: Look here, as long as you known me ... you ever known me to chase after women?

Bono: Hell yeah! Long as I done known you. You forgetting I knew you when.

Troy: Naw, I'm talking about since I been married to Rose?

Bono: Oh, not since you been married to Rose. Now, that's the truth, there. I can say that.

Troy: Alright then! Case closed.

Bono: I see you be walking up around Alberta's house. You supposed to be at Taylors' and you be walking up around there.

Troy: What you watching where I'm walking for? I ain't watching after you.

Bono: I seen you walking around there more than once.

Troy: Hell, you liable to see me walking anywhere! That don't mean nothing cause you see me walking around there.

Bono: Where she come from anyway? She just kinda showed up one day.

Troy: Tallahassee. You can look at her and tell she one of them Florida gals. They got some big healthy women down there. Grow them right up out the ground. Got a little bit of Indian in her. Most of them niggers down in Florida got some Indian in them.

Bono: I don't know about that Indian part. But she damn sure big and healthy. Woman wear some big stockings. Got them great big old legs and hips as wide as the Mississippi River.

Troy: Legs don't mean nothing. You don't do nothing but push them out of the way. But them hips cushion the ride!

Bono: Troy, you ain't got no sense.

Troy: It's the truth! Like you riding on Goodyears!

[Rose *enters from the house. She is ten years younger than* Troy, *her devotion to him stems from her recognition of the possibilities of her life without him: a succession of abusive men and their babies, a life of partying and running the streets, the Church, or aloneness with its attendant pain and frustration. She recognizes* Troy's *spirit as a fine and illuminating one and she either ignores or forgives his faults, only some of which she recognizes. Though she doesn't drink, her presence is an integral part of the Friday night rituals. She alternates between the porch and the kitchen, where supper preparations are under way.*]

Rose: What you all out here getting into?

Troy: What you worried about what we getting into for? This is men talk, woman.

Rose: What I care what you all talking about? Bono, you gonna stay for supper?

Bono: No, I thank you, Rose. But Lucille say she cooking up a pot of pigfeet.

Troy: Pigfeet! Hell, I'm going home with you! Might even stay the night if you got some pigfeet. You got something in there to top them pigfeet, Rose?

Rose: I'm cooking up some chicken. I got some chicken and collard greens.

Troy: Well, go on back in the house and let me and Bono finish what we was talking about. This is men talk. I got some talk for you later. You know what kind of talk I mean. You go on and powder it up.

Rose: Troy Maxson, don't you start that now!

Troy: [*Puts his arm around her.*] Aw, woman ... come here. Look here, Bono ... when I met this woman ... I got out that place, say, "Hitch up my pony, saddle up my mare ... there's a woman out there for me somewhere. I looked here. Looked there. Saw Rose and latched on to her." I latched on to her and told her—I'm gonna tell you the truth—I told her, "Baby, I don't wanna marry, I just wanna be your man." Rose told me ... tell him what you told me, Rose.

Rose: I told him if he wasn't the marrying kind, then move out the way so the marrying kind could find me.

Troy: That's what she told me. "Nigger, you in my way. You blocking the view! Move out the way so I can find me a husband." I thought it over two or three days. Come back—

Rose: Ain't no two or three days nothing. You was back the same night.

Troy: Come back, told her ... "Okay, baby ... but I'm gonna buy me a banty rooster and put him out there in the backyard ... and when he see a stranger come, he'll flap his wings and crow ..." Look here, Bono, I could watch the front door by myself ... it was that back door I was worried about.

Rose: Troy, you ought not talk like that. Troy ain't doing nothing but telling a lie.

Troy: Only thing is ... when we first got married ... forget the rooster ... we ain't had no yard!

Bono: I hear you tell it. Me and Lucille was staying down there on Logan Street. Had two rooms with the outhouse in the back. I ain't mind the outhouse none. But when that goddamn wind blow through there in the winter ... that's what I'm talking about! To this day I wonder why in the hell I ever stayed down there for six long years. But see, I didn't know I could do no better. I thought only white folks had inside toilets and things.

Rose: There's a lot of people don't know they can do no better than they doing now. That's just something you got to learn. A lot of folks still shop at Bella's.

Troy: Ain't nothing wrong with shopping at Bella's. She got fresh food.

Rose: I ain't said nothing about if she got fresh food. I'm talking about what she charge. She charge ten cents more than the A & P.

Troy: The A & P ain't never done nothing for me. I spends my money where I'm treated right. I go down to Bella, say, "I need a loaf of bread, I'll pay you Friday." She give it to me. What sense that make when I got money to go and spend it somewhere else and ignore the person who done right by me? That ain't in the Bible.

Rose: We ain't talking about what's in the Bible. What sense it make to shop there when she overcharge?

Troy: You shop where you want to. I'll do my shopping where the people been good to me.

Rose：Well，I don't think it's right for her to overcharge. That's all I was saying.

Bono：Look here ... I got to get on. Lucille going be raising all kind of hell.

Troy：Where you going，nigger? We ain't finished this pint. Come here，finish this pint.

Bono：Well，hell，I am ... if you ever turn the bottle loose.

Troy：[*Hands him the bottle.*] The only thing I say about the A & P is I'm glad Cory got that job down there. Help him take care of his school clothes and things. Gabe done moved out and things getting tight around here. He got that job. ... He can start to look out for himself.

Rose：Cory done went and got recruited by a college football team.

Troy：I told that boy about that football stuff. The white man ain't gonna let him get nowhere with that football. I told him when he first come to me with it. Now you come telling me he done went and got more tied up in it. He ought to go and get recruited in how to fix cars or something where he can make a living.

Rose：He ain't talking about making no living playing football. It's just something the boys in school do. They gonna send a recruiter by to talk to you. He'll tell you he ain't talking about making no living playing football. It's a honor to be recruited.

Troy：It ain't gonna get him nowhere. Bono'll tell you that.

Bono：If he be like you in the sports ... he's gonna be alright. Ain't but two men ever played baseball as good as you. That's Babe Ruth[①] and Josh Gibson[②]. Them's the only two men ever hit more home runs than you.

Troy：What it ever get me? Ain't got a pot to piss in or a window to throw it out of.

Rose：Times have changed since you was playing baseball，Troy. That was before the war. Times have changed a lot since then.

Troy：How in hell they done changed?

Rose：They got lots of colored boys playing ball now. Baseball and football.

Bono：You right about that，Rose. Times have changed，Troy. You just come along too early.

Troy：There ought not never have been no time called too early! Now you take that fellow ... what's that fellow they had playing right field for the Yankees back then? You know who I'm talking about，Bono. Used to play right field for the Yankees.

Rose：Selkirk[③]?

Troy：Selkirk! That's it! Man batting. 269，understand? .269. What kind of sense that make? I was hitting .432 with thirty-seven home runs! Man batting .269 and playing right field for the Yankees! I saw Josh Gibson's daughter yesterday. She walking around with raggedy shoes on her feet. Now I bet you Selkirk's daughter ain't walking around with

---

① George Herman "Babe" Ruth, Jr. (1895—1948)：美国职业棒球运动员，美国棒球史上最有名的球员，有"棒球之神"的美称。作为 20 世纪 20 年代和 30 年代美国职业棒球史上的扬基强打者，他曾经连续三次打破大联盟全垒打纪录，1936 年入选棒球名人堂(Baseball Hall of Fame)。

② Josh Gibson (1911—1947)：美国职业棒球运动员，1972 年入选棒球名人堂。

③ George Alexander Selkirk (1908—1987)：美国职业棒球运动员，绰号 Twinkletoes，该名称来自他特殊的跑垒姿势，生涯九年皆效力于纽约扬基队，是贝比·鲁斯(Babe Ruth)的接班人。

raggedy shoes on her feet! I bet you that!

Rose：They got a lot of colored baseball players now. Jackie Robinson^① was the first. Folks had to wait for Jackie Robinson.

Troy：I done seen a hundred niggers play baseball better than Jackie Robinson. Hell，I know some teams Jackie Robinson couldn't even make! What you talking about Jackie Robinson. Jackie Robinson wasn't nobody. I'm talking about if you could play ball then they ought to have let you play. Don't care what color you were. Come telling me I come along too early. If you could play ... then they ought to have let you play. [Troy *takes a long drink from the bottle*.]

Rose：You gonna drink yourself to death. You don't need to be drinking like that.

Troy：Death ain't nothing. I done seen him. Done wrassled with him. You can't tell me nothing about death. Death ain't nothing but a fastball on the outside corner. And you know what I'll do to that! Lookee here，Bono ... am I lying? You get one of them fastballs, about waist high，over the outside corner of the plate where you can get the meat of the bat on it ... and good god! You can kiss it goodbye. Now，am I lying?

Bono：Naw，you telling the truth there. I seen you do it.

Troy：If I'm lying ... that 450 feet worth of lying! [*Pause*.] That's all death is to me. A fastball on the outside corner.

Rose：I don't know why you want to get on talking about death.

Troy：Ain't nothing wrong with talking about death. That's part of life. Everybody gonna die. You gonna die，I'm gonna die. Bono's gonna die. Hell，we all gonna die.

Rose：But you ain't got to talk about it. I don't like to talk about it.

Troy：You the one brought it up. Me and Bono was talking about baseball ... you tell me I'm gonna drink myself to death. Ain't that right，Bono? You know I don't drink this but one night out of the week. That's Friday night. I'm gonna drink just enough to where I can handle it. Then I cuts it loose. I leave it alone. So don't you worry about me drinking myself to death. 'Cause I ain't worried about Death. I done seen him. I done wrestled with him.

Look here，Bono ... I looked up one day and Death was marching straight at me. Like Soldiers on Parade! The Army of Death was marching straight at me. The middle of July，1941. It got real cold just like it be winter. It seem like Death himself reached out and touched me on the shoulder. He touch me just like I touch you. I got cold as ice and Death standing there grinning at me.

Rose：Troy，why don't you hush that talk.

Troy：I say ... What you want，Mr. Death? You be wanting me? You done brought your army to be getting me? I looked him dead in the eye. I wasn't fearing nothing. I was ready to tangle. Just like I'm ready to tangle now. The Bible say be ever vigilant. That's why I don't get but so drunk. I got to keep watch.

---

① Jackie Robinson（1919—1972）：美国职业棒球运动员，美国职业棒球大联盟（Major League Baseball）史上第一位非裔美国人球员，1962 年入选棒球名人堂。

Rose: Troy was right down there in Mercy Hospital. You remember he had pneumonia? Laying there with a fever talking plumb out of his head.

Troy: Death standing there staring at me ... carrying that sickle in his hand. Finally he say, "You want bound over for another year?" See, just like that ... "You want bound over for another year?" I told him, "Bound over hell! Let's settle this now!"

It seem like he kinda fell back when I said that, and all the cold went out of me. I reached down and grabbed that sickle and threw it just as far as I could throw it ... and me and him commenced to wrestling.

We wrestled for three days and three nights. I can't say where I found the strength from. Every time it seemed like he was gonna get the best of me, I'd reach way down deep inside myself and find the strength to do him one better.

Rose: Every time Troy tell that story he find different ways to tell it. Different things to make up about it.

Troy: I ain't making up nothing. I'm telling you the facts of what happened. I wrestled with Death for three days and three nights and I'm standing here to tell you about it. [Pause.] Alright. At the end of the third night we done weakened each other to where we can't hardly move. Death stood up, throwed on his robe ... had him a white robe with a hood on it. He throwed on that robe and went off to look for his sickle. Say, "I'll be back." Just like that. "I'll be back." I told him, say, "Yeah, but ... you gonna have to find me!" I wasn't no fool. I wasn't going looking for him. Death ain't nothing to play with. And I know he's gonna get me. I know I got to join his army ... his camp followers. But as long as I keep my strength and see him coming ... as long as I keep up my vigilance ... he's gonna have to fight to get me. I ain't going easy.

Bono: Well, look here, since you got to keep up your vigilance ... let me have the bottle.

Troy: Aw hell, I shouldn't have told you that part. I should have left out that part.

Rose: Troy be talking that stuff and half the time don't even know what he be talking about.

Troy: Bono know me better than that.

Bono: That's right. I know you. I know you got some Uncle Remus in your blood. You got more stories than the devil got sinners.

Troy: Aw hell, I done seen him too! Done talked with the devil.

Rose: Troy, don't nobody wanna be hearing all that stuff.

[Lyons *enters the yard from the street. Thirty-four years old*, Troy's *son by a previous marriage, he sports a neatly trimmed goatee, sport coat, white shirt, tieless and buttoned at the collar. Though he fancies himself a musician, he is more caught up in the rituals and "idea" of being a musician than in the actual practice of the music. He has come to borrow money from* Troy, *and while he knows he will be successful, he is uncertain as to what extent his lifestyle will be held up to scrutiny and ridicule.*]

Lyons: Hey, Pop.

Troy: What you come "Hey, Popping" me for?

Lyons: How you doing, Rose? [*He kisses her.*] Mr. Bono. How you doing?

Bono: Hey, Lyons ... how you been?

Troy: He must have been doing alright. I ain't seen him around here last week.

Rose: Troy, leave your boy alone. He come by to see you and you wanna start all that nonsense.

Troy: I ain't bothering Lyons. [Offers him the bottle.] Here ... get you a drink. We got an understanding. I know why he come by to see me and he know I know.

Lyons: Come on, Pop ... I just stopped by to say hi ... see how you was doing.

Troy: You ain't stopped by yesterday.

Rose: You gonna stay for supper, Lyons? I got some chicken cooking in the oven.

Lyons: No, Rose ... thanks. I was just in the neighborhood and thought I'd stop by for a minute.

Troy: You was in the neighborhood alright, nigger. You telling the truth there. You was in the neighborhood cause it's my payday.

Lyons: Well, hell, since you mentioned it ... let me have ten dollars.

Troy: I'll be damned! I'll die and go to hell and play blackjack with the devil before I give you ten dollars.

Bono: That's what I wanna know about ... that devil you done seen.

Lyons: What ... Pop done seen the devil? You too much, Pops.

Troy: Yeah, I done seen him. Talked to him too!

Rose: You ain't seen no devil. I done told you that man ain't had nothing to do with the devil. Anything you can't understand, you want to call it the devil.

Troy: Look here, Bono ... I went down to see Hertzberger about some furniture. Got three rooms for two-ninety-eight. That what it say on the radio. "Three rooms ... two-ninety-eight." Even made up a little song about it. Go down there ... man tell me I can't get no credit. I'm working every day and can't get no credit. What to do? I got an empty house with some raggedy furniture in it. Cory ain't got no bed. He's sleeping on a pile of rags on the floor. Working every day and can't get no credit. Come back here—Rose'll tell you— madder than hell. Sit down ... try to figure what I'm gonna do. Come a knock on the door. Ain't been living here but three days. Who know I'm here? Open the door ... devil standing there bigger than life. White fellow ... got on good clothes and everything. Standing there with a clipboard in his hand. I ain't had to say nothing. First words come out of his mouth was ... "I understand you need some furniture and can't get no credit." I liked to fell over. He say "I'll give you all the credit you want, but you got to pay the interest on it." I told him, "Give me three rooms worth and charge whatever you want." Next day a truck pulled up here and two men unloaded them three rooms. Man what drove the truck give me a book. Say send ten dollars, first of every month to the address in the book and everything will be alright. Say if I miss a payment the devil was coming back and it'll be hell to pay. That was fifteen years ago. To this day ... the first of the month I send my ten dollars, Rose'll tell you.

Rose: Troy lying.

Troy: I ain't never seen that man since. Now you tell me who else that could have been but the devil? I ain't sold my soul or nothing like that, you understand. Naw, I wouldn't have truck with the devil about nothing like that. I got my furniture and pays my ten dollars the first of the month just like clockwork.

Bono: How long you say you been paying this ten dollars a month?

Troy: Fifteen years!

Bono: Hell, ain't you finished paying for it yet? How much the man done charged you.

Troy: Aw hell, I done paid for it. I done paid for it ten times over! The fact is I'm scared to stop paying it.

Rose: Troy lying. We got that furniture from Mr. Glickman. He ain't paying no ten dollars a month to nobody.

Troy: Aw hell, woman. Bono know I ain't that big a fool.

Lyons: I was just getting ready to say ... I know where there's a bridge for sale.

Troy: Look here, I'll tell you this ... it don't matter to me if he was the devil. It don't matter if the devil give credit. Somebody has got to give it.

Rose: It ought to matter. You going around talking about having truck with the devil ... God's the one you gonna have to answer to. He's the one gonna be at the Judgment.

Lyons: Yeah, well, look here, Pop ... let me have that ten dollars. I'll give it back to you. Bonnie got a job working at the hospital.

Troy: What I tell you, Bono? The only time I see this nigger is when he wants something. That's the only time I see him.

Lyons: Come on, Pop, Mr. Bono don't want to hear all that. Let me have the ten dollars. I told you Bonnie working.

Troy: What that mean to me? "Bonnie working." I don't care if she working. Go ask her for the ten dollars if she working. Talking about "Bonnie working." Why ain't you working?

Lyons: Aw, Pop, you know I can't find no decent job. Where am I gonna get a job at? You know I can't get no job.

Troy: I told you I know some people down there. I can get you on the rubbish if you want to work. I told you that the last time you came by here asking me for something.

Lyons: Naw, Pop ... thanks. That ain't for me. I don't wanna be carrying nobody's rubbish. I don't wanna be punching nobody's time clock.

Troy: What's the matter, you too good to carry people's rubbish? Where you think that ten dollars you talking about come from? I'm just supposed to haul people's rubbish and give my money to you cause you too lazy to work. You too lazy to work and wanna know why you ain't got what I got.

Rose: What hospital Bonnie working at? Mercy?

Lyons: She's down at Passavant working in the laundry.

Troy: I ain't got nothing as it is. I give you that ten dollars and I got to eat beans the rest of the week. Naw ... you ain't getting no ten dollars here.

Lyons: You ain't got to be eating no beans. I don't know why you wanna say that.

Troy: I ain't got no extra money. Gabe done moved over to Miss Pearl's paying her the rent and things done got tight around here. I can't afford to be giving you every payday.

Lyons: I ain't asked you to give me nothing. I asked you to loan me ten dollars. I know you got ten dollars.

Troy: Yeah, I got it. You know why I got it? Cause I don't throw my money away out there in the streets. You living the fast life ... wanna be a musician ... running around in them clubs and things ... then, you learn to take care of yourself. You ain't gonna find me going and asking nobody for nothing. I done spent too many years without.

Lyons: You and me is two different people, Pop.

Troy: I done learned my mistake and learned to do what's right by it. You still trying to get something for nothing. Life don't owe you nothing. You owe it to yourself. Ask Bono. He'll tell you I'm right.

Lyons: You got your way of dealing with the world ... I got mine. The only thing that matters to me is the music.

Troy: Yeah, I can see that! It don't matter how you gonna eat ... where your next dollar is coming from. You telling the truth there.

Lyons: I know I got to eat. But I got to live too. I need something that gonna help me to get out of the bed in the morning. Make me feel like I belong in the world. I don't bother nobody. I just stay with my music cause that's the only way I can find to live in the world. Otherwise there ain't no telling what I might do. Now I don't come criticizing you and how you live. I just come by to ask you for ten dollars. I don't wanna hear all that about how I live.

Troy: Boy, your mama did a hell of a job raising you.

Lyons: You can't change me, Pop. I'm thirty-four years old. If you wanted to change me, you should have been there when I was growing up. I come by to see you ... ask for ten dollars and you want to talk about how I was raised. You don't know nothing about how I was raised.

Rose: Let the boy have ten dollars, Troy.

Troy: [To Lyons.] What the hell you looking at me for? I ain't got no ten dollars. You know what I do with my money. [To Rose.] Give him ten dollars if you want him to have it.

Rose: I will. Just as soon as you turn it loose.

Troy: [Handing Rose the money.] There it is. Seventy-six dollars and forty-two cents. You see this, Bono? Now, I ain't gonna get but six of that back.

Rose: You ought to stop telling that lie. Here, Lyons. [She hands him the money.]

Lyons: Thanks, Rose. Look ... I got to run ... I'll see you later.

Troy: Wait a minute. You gonna say, "thanks, Rose" and ain't gonna look to see where she got that ten dollars from? See how they do me, Bono?

Lyons: I know she got it from you, Pop. Thanks. I'll give it back to you.

Troy: There he go telling another lie. Time I see that ten dollars ... he'll be owing me thirty more.

Lyons: See you, Mr. Bono.

Bono: Take care, Lyons!

Lyons: Thanks, Pop. I'll see you again. [Lyons *exits the yard*.]

Troy: I don't know why he don't go and get him a decent job and take care of that woman he got.

Bono: He'll be alright, Troy. The boy is still young.

Troy: The *boy* is thirty-four years old.

Rose: Let's not get off into all that.

Bono: Look here ... I got to be going. I got to be getting on. Lucille gonna be waiting.

Troy: [*Puts his arm around* Rose.] See this woman, Bono? I love this woman. I love this woman so much it hurts. I love her so much ... I done run out of ways of loving her. So I got to go back to basics. Don't you come by my house Monday morning talking about time to go to work ... 'cause I'm still gonna be stroking!

Rose: Troy! Stop it now!

Bono: I ain't paying him no mind, Rose. That ain't nothing but gin-talk. Go on, Troy. I'll see you Monday.

Troy: Don't you come by my house, nigger! I done told you what I'm gonna be doing. [*The lights go down to black*.]

Questions for Discussion

1. As the play's namesake, "fences" is the center metaphor of the play. Please talk about the function and significance of it.

2. Troy Maxson is the protagonist of the play. What is revealed through Troy's characterization in Act One, Scene One?

3. Identify and discuss the conflicts introduced in Act One, Scene One. Predict the outcomes of these conflicts.

African American Fiction
非裔美国小说简介

  非裔美国小说主要指由非裔美国人创作的虚构作品,具有比较悠久的历史,无论在奴隶制时期,吉姆·克劳种族隔离时期,还是在民权运动时期,非裔美国小说都主要关注美国社会普遍存在的白人对黑人的歧视以及制度化的不平等。由于欧洲著名思想家康德、休谟等人以能否进行文艺创作作为衡量、判断一个民族优劣的标志,因此,早期非裔美国小说家的创作带有明显的"回应"与"证明"的特点:尝试以自己的创作,证明美国黑人具有和白人一样的人性,因此,黑人民族主义与社会抗议仿佛成为非裔美国小说家的必然选择,与之相适应,现实主义的创作原则仿佛成为许多美国黑人作家的自觉选择。后来,揭露美国社会的种族歧视与压迫,以及寻找自我身份、种族身份、文化身份等成为许多小说家关注的重要主题。

  如果说 20 世纪之前的非裔美国小说主要聚焦奴隶制的残暴与非人性,以及对黑人女性的性剥削,那么 20 世纪以来的非裔美国小说在现实主义的旗帜下发展壮大,不仅在创作主题方面突破了原来的种族对抗意识形态,如以赖特的《土生子》为代表的社会抗议小说,而且在创作风格方面由原来比较单一的现实主义,转向复杂多样的创作实践,汲取现代主义及后现代主义的创作风格,如里德、莫里森、埃弗雷特的文本实践等。

  进入 21 世纪,虽然美国社会有诸多关于"后种族"的讨论,但是深层次的种族歧视依然几乎无处不在,黑人遭受的不公正对待或"另眼相待"依然普遍存在,也继续对黑人族群产生较大的影响。新世纪非裔美国小说创作如何能够在"淡化""种族"或"族裔"因素的同时,真实、客观地反映非裔美国人民的生存状态,依然是对非裔美国艺术家,特别是对非裔美国小说家的严峻考验,而当代非裔美国小说家丰富的创作实践与艺术成就仿佛已经证明,他们能够做到。

1. Their Eyes Were Watching God

作家简介

佐拉·尼尔·赫斯顿(Zora Neale Hurston)(1891—1960)是哈莱姆文艺复兴时期的重要代表人物,杰出的美国黑人女作家和人类学家,被誉为"南方的天才"。

赫斯顿出生于美国南方,在没有种族歧视的黑人小城伊顿维尔度过自己的童年时光。1904年,她的家庭在她母亲去世后解体,她无忧无虑的童年生活也随之结束;离开伊顿维尔后,她才开始意识到种族歧视的存在。1918—1924年就读于霍华德大学期间,她结识了许多黑人作家,开始进行文学创作。1925年,她来到当时黑人文学的中心、哈莱姆黑人文艺复兴的发祥地纽约,成为哈莱姆文艺复兴运动中的活跃分子,与兰斯顿·休斯等共同创办了文学杂志《火》;1926年秋,她进入巴纳德学院,在著名人类学家博厄斯教授的指导下学习人类学,1928年毕业后进入哥伦比亚大学攻读硕士学位,在梅森夫人的资助下,回到南方从事黑人民间故事和传说的收集、整理工作。

1934年,赫斯顿出版自己第一部小说《约拿的葫芦藤》,反映了20世纪30年代美国黑人的感受;1935年,她出版《骡子与人》,这是第一部由美国黑人收集、整理出版的美国黑人民间故事集。1937年,在加勒比地区进行人种史研究时,她创作了被誉为美国黑人文学史上里程碑式的经典之作《他们眼望上苍》,这部作品塑造了一位个性鲜明的黑人女性人物珍妮·斯塔克斯,表现了美国黑人女性意识的觉醒。

1938年,赫斯顿出版旅游札记《告诉我的马》,描写自己在海地的见闻和当地的民俗与风土人情;此外,她发表小说《摩西,山的主宰》(1939),仿照《圣经》中的《出埃及记》塑造了黑人摩西的形象。40年代,她发表自传《道路上的尘迹》(1942)、小说《苏旺尼的六翼天使》(1948),以及多篇涉及种族问题的文章,如"白人出版商不想出版的东西""漂泊的黑人"和"我最难以启齿的吉姆·克劳经历"等。

赫斯顿共创作4部长篇小说、2本黑人民间故事集、1部自传、50多篇短篇故事。虽然她的文学创作成绩斐然,但是多部作品生前绝版,70年代才被重新发现,其代表作《他们眼望上苍》更是成为现代(非裔)美国文学经典。赫斯顿对自己的黑人身份非常自豪,毕生致力于收集、整理和保护黑人民族的传统文化遗产,其作品深刻揭示了当时黑人社区内部存在的自我鄙视,以及这种内化的种族主义思想对黑人灵魂的腐蚀,力图唤醒黑人对自己身份的肯定和热爱。当代著名黑人女作家艾丽斯·沃克认为,赫斯顿不遗余力地去捕捉乡间黑人语言表达之美。别的作家看到的只是黑人不能完美地掌握英语,而她看到的却是诗一般的语言。赫斯顿着力表现的是黑人文化语境下的黑人经验,她的作品从未停止为受到压迫的黑人说话,为美国黑人创造和谐、平等的生存环境是她一生的追求。

作品简介与赏析

长篇小说《他们眼望上苍》描写了反抗传统习俗的束缚、争取自己做人权利的珍妮的一生,是赫斯顿的代表作,被公认为是美国黑人文学史上的经典之作。通过描写女主人公珍妮的三次婚姻,以及她在三次婚姻中的不断成长,赫斯顿让黑人妇女独领风骚,使被遮蔽的女性自信与自强重新成为社会的关注点,塑造出一个寻找自我、表现自我、肯定自我的黑人女性,是黑人文学中第一部充分展示黑人女性意识觉醒的作品,在黑人女性形象塑造方面具有里程碑式的意义,开启黑人女性主义文学先河。

1940 年,赖特的《土生子》轰动美国文坛,抗议小说仿佛代表了美国黑人文学的发展趋势,赖特批评《他们眼望上苍》"没有主题,没有启示性,没有思想"。在赖特作品风靡于世的年代,赫斯顿的作品因缺乏种族抗议和种族斗争而遭受冷落,直到女权运动高涨的 70 年代,她作品的价值才重新为人们所重视。艾丽斯·沃克认为赫斯顿是"一个伟大的作家。一个有勇气、有令人难以置信的幽默感的作家,所写的每一行里都有诗",并说,"对我来说,再也没有比这本小说(《他们眼望上苍》)更为重要的书了"。《诺顿非裔美国文学选集》将这部作品列为"哈莱姆文艺复兴时期最伟大的作品之一"。

小说以珍妮自述的方式开始。在第一、二章中,珍妮在丈夫甜点死后回到伊顿维尔的家中,伴随她的是邻居的不解与指责;在珍妮向好友讲述自己一生追求、实现生命意义的过程中,小说展示了姐妹情谊的美好情景。

珍妮女性意识觉醒的每一个阶段,都展示出她对生活的热爱。在珍妮的三次婚姻中,她对自己丈夫的看法都和梨树相关:第一任丈夫洛根·基利克斯"玷污了梨树的纯洁",第二任丈夫也"并不代表太阳升起和梨树的开花授粉";只有第三任丈夫才是"蜜蜂找到了梨花——盛开的梨花"。另一个与女人关系密切的重要意象是骡子。在父权制中,女人就像骡子一样,处于受压迫的他者地位。在小说开始,祖母就告诉她"黑人女性的命运和骡子是相同的",这不但说明黑人女性要承担沉重的劳动,而且说明她们的地位极其低下,这也体现在珍妮的婚姻生活中。经历过三次婚姻后,珍妮从一个单纯的小女孩成长为独立成熟的女性,她用自己的行动感染着身边的人,让她们觉醒,为寻找更加和谐、平等的社会地位而努力。

Chapter 1

Ships at a distance have every man's wish on board. For some they come in with the tide. For others they sail forever on the horizon, never out of sight, never landing until the Watcher turns his eyes away in resignation, his dreams mocked to death by Time. That is the life of men.

Now, women forget all those things they don't want to remember, and remember everything they don't want to forget. The dream is the truth. Then they act and do things accordingly.

So the beginning of this was a woman and she had come back from burying the dead. Not the dead of sick and ailing with friends at the pillow and the feet. She had come back from the sodden and the bloated; the sudden dead, their eyes flung wide open in judgment.

The people all saw her come because it was sundown. The sun was gone, but he had left his footprints in the sky. It was the time for sitting on porches beside the road. It was the time to hear things and talk. These sitters had been tongueless, earless, eyeless conveniences all day long. Mules and other brutes had occupied their skins. But now, the sun and the bossman were gone, so the skins felt powerful and human. They became lords of sounds and lesser things. They passed nations through their mouths. They sat in judgment.

Seeing the woman as she was made them remember the envy they had stored up from other times. So they chewed up the back parts of their minds and swallowed with relish. They made burning statements with questions, and killing tools out of laughs. It was mass cruelty. A mood come alive. Words walking without masters; walking altogether like harmony in a song.

"What she doin' coming back here in dem overhalls? Can't she find no dress to put on? —Where's dat blue satin dress she left here in? —Where all dat money her husband took and died and left her? —What dat ole forty year ole 'oman doin' wid her hair swingin' down her back lak some young gal? —Where she left dat young lad of a boy she went off here wid? —Thought she was going to marry? —Where he left her? —What he done wid all her money? —Betcha he off wid some gal so young she ain't even got no hairs—why she don't stay in her class?

When she got to where they were she turned her face on the bander log and spoke. They scrambled a noisy "good evenin'" and left their mouths setting open and their ears full of hope. Her speech was pleasant enough, but she kept walking straight on to her gate. The porch couldn't talk for looking.

The men noticed her firm buttocks like she had grapefruits in her hip pockets; the great rope of black hair swinging to her waist and unraveling in the wind like a plume; then her pugnacious breasts trying to bore holes in her shirt. They, the men, were saving with the mind what they lost with the eye. The women took the faded shirt and muddy overalls and laid them away for remembrance. It was a weapon against her strength and if it turned out of no significance, still it was a hope that she might fall to their level some day.

But nobody moved, nobody spoke, nobody even thought to swallow spit until after her gate slammed behind her.

Pearl Stone opened her mouth and laughed real hard because she didn't know what else to do. She fell all over Mrs. Sumpkins while she laughed. Mrs. Sumpkins snorted violently and sucked her teeth.

"Humph! Y'all let her worry yuh. You ain't like me. Ah ain't got her to study 'bout. If she ain't got manners enough to stop and let folks know how she been makin' out, let her g'wan!"

"She ain't even worth talkin' after," Lulu Moss drawled through her nose. "She sits high, but she looks low. Dat's what Ah say 'bout dese ole women runnin' after young boys."

Pheoby Watson hitched her rocking chair forward before she spoke. "Well, nobody don't know if it's anything to tell or not. Me, Ah'm her best friend, and Ah don't know."

"Maybe us don't know into things lak you do, but we all know how she went 'way from here and us sho seen her come back. 'Tain't no use in your tryin' to cloak no ole woman lak Janie Starks, Pheoby, friend or no friend."

"At dat she ain't so ole as some of y'all dat's talking.

"She's way past forty to my knowledge, Pheoby."

"No more'n forty at de outside."

"She's 'way too old for a boy like Tea Cake."

"Tea Cake ain't been no boy for some time. He's round thirty his ownself."

"Don't keer what it was, she could stop and say a few words with us. She act like we done done something to her," Pearl Stone complained. "She de one been doin' wrong."

"You mean, you mad 'cause she didn't stop and tell us all her business. Anyhow, what you ever know her to do so bad as y'all make out? The worst thing Ah ever knowed her to do was taking a few years offa her age and dat ain't never harmed nobody. Y'all makes me tired. De way you talkin' you'd think de folks in dis town didn't do nothin' in de bed 'cept praise de Lawd. You have to 'scuse me, 'cause Ah'm bound to go take her some supper." Pheoby stood up sharply.

"Don't mind us," Lulu smiled, "just go right ahead, us can mind yo' house for you till you git back. Mah supper is done. You bettah go see how she feel. You kin let de rest of us know."

"Lawd," Pearl agreed, "Ah done scorched-up dat lil meat and bread too long to talk about. Ah kin stay 'way from home long as Ah please. Mah husband ain't fussy."

"Oh, er, Pheoby, if youse ready to go, Ah could walk over dere wid you," Mrs. Sumpkins volunteered. "It's sort of duskin' down dark. De booger man might ketch yuh."

"Naw, Ah thank yuh. Nothin' couldn't ketch me dese few steps Ah'm goin'. Anyhow mah husband tell me say no first class booger would have me. If she got anything to tell yuh, you'll hear it."

Pheoby hurried on off with a covered bowl in her hands. She left the porch pelting her back with unasked questions. They hoped the answers were cruel and strange. When she arrived at the place, Pheoby Watson didn't go in by the front gate and down the palm walk to the front door. She walked around the fence corner and went in the intimate gate with her heaping plate of mulatto rice. Janie must be round that side.

She found her sitting on the steps of the back porch with the lamps all filled and the chimneys cleaned.

"Hello, Janie, how you comin'?" "Aw, pretty good, Ah'm tryin' to soak some uh de tiredness and de dirt outa mah feet." She laughed a little. "Ah see you is. Gal, you sho looks good. You looks like youse yo' own daughter." They both laughed. "Even wid dem overhalls on, you shows yo' womanhood."

"G'wan! G'wan! You must think Ah brought yuh somethin'. When Ah ain't brought home a thing but mahself." "Dat's a gracious plenty. Yo' friends wouldn't want nothin' better."

"Ah takes dat flattery offa you, Pheoby, 'cause Ah know it's from de heart." Janie extended her hand. "Good Lawd, Pheoby! ain't you never goin' tuh gimme dat lil rations you brought me? Ah ain't had a thing on mah stomach today exceptin' mah hand." They both laughed easily. "Give it here and have a seat."

"Ah knowed you'd be hongry. No time to be huntin' stove wood after dark. Mah mulatto rice ain't so good dis time. Not enough bacon grease, but Ah reckon it'll kill hongry."

"Ah'll tell you in a minute," Janie said, lifting the cover. "Gal, it's too good! you switches a mean fanny round in a kitchen."

"Aw, dat ain't much to eat, Janie. But Ah'm liable to have something sho nuff good tomorrow, 'cause you done come."

Janie ate heartily and said nothing. The varicolored cloud dust that the sun had stirred up in the sky was settling by slow degrees.

"Here, Pheoby, take yo' ole plate. Ah ain't got a bit of use for a empty dish. Dat grub sho come in handy.

Pheoby laughed at her friend's rough joke. "Youse just as crazy as you ever was."

"Hand me dat wash-rag on dat chair by you, honey. Lemme scrub mah feet." She took the cloth and rubbed vigorously. Laughter came to her from the big road.

"Well, Ah see Mouth-Almighty is still sittin' in de same place. And Ah reckon they got me up in they mouth now."

"Yes indeed. You know if you pass some people and don't speak tuh suit 'em dey got tuh go way back in yo' life and see whut you ever done.

They know mo' 'bout yuh than you do yo' self. An envious heart makes a treacherous ear. They done 'heard' 'bout you just what they hope done happened."

"If God don't think no mo' 'bout 'em then Ah do, they's a lost ball in de high grass.

"Ah hears what they say 'cause they just will collect round mah porch 'cause it's on de big road. Mah husband git so sick of 'em sometime he makes 'em all git for home."

"Sam is right too. They just wearin' out yo' sittin' chairs."

"Yeah, Sam say most of 'em goes to church so they'll be sure to rise in Judgment[①]. Dat's de day dat every secret is s'posed to be made known. They wants to be there and hear it all."

"Sam is too crazy! You can't stop laughin' when youse round him."

"Uuh hunh. He says he aims to be there hisself so he can find out who stole his corn-cob pipe."

"Pheoby, dat Sam of your'n just won't quit! Crazy thing!"

"Most of dese zigaboos is so het up over yo' business till they liable to hurry theyself to Judgment to find out about you if they don't soon know. You better make haste and tell 'em 'bout you and Tea Cake gittin' married, and if he taken all yo' money and went off wid some young gal, and where at he is now and where at is all yo' clothes dat you got to come back here in overhalls."

"Ah don't mean to bother wid tellin' 'em nothin', Pheoby. 'Tain't worth de trouble. You can tell 'em what Ah say if you wants to. Dat's just de same as me 'cause mah tongue is in mah friend's mouf."

"If you so desire Ah'll tell 'em what you tell me to tell 'em."

"To start off wid, people like dem wastes up too much time puttin' they mouf on things they don't know nothin' about. Now they got to look into me loving Tea Cake and see whether it was done right or not! They don't know if life is a mess of corn-meal dumplings, and if love is a bed-quilt!"

"So long as they get a name to gnaw on they don't care whose it is, and what about, 'specially if they can make it sound like evil."

"If they wants to see and know, why they don't come kiss and be kissed? Ah could then sit down and tell 'em things. Ah been a delegate to de big 'ssociation of life. Yessuh! De Grand Lodge, de big convention of livin' is just where Ah been dis year and a half y'all ain't seen me."

They sat there in the fresh young darkness close together. Pheoby eager to feel and do through Janie, but hating to show her zest for fear it might be thought mere curiosity. Janie full of that oldest human longing—self-revelation. Pheoby held her tongue for a long time, but she couldn't help moving her feet. So Janie spoke.

"They don't need to worry about me and my overhalls long as Ah still got nine hundred dollars in de bank. Tea Cake got me into wearing 'em—following behind him. Tea Cake ain't wasted up no money of mine, and he ain't left me for no young gal, neither. He give me every consolation in de world. He'd tell 'em so too, if he was here. If he wasn't gone."

Pheoby dilated all over with eagerness, "Tea Cake gone?"

"Yeah, Pheoby, Tea Cake is gone. And dat's de only reason you see me back here— cause Ah ain't got nothing to make me happy no more where Ah was at. Down in the Everglades there, down on the muck."

"It's hard for me to understand what you mean, de way you tell it. And then again Ah'm hard of understandin' at times."

"Naw, 'tain't nothin' lak you might think. So 'tain't no use in me telling you somethin' unless Ah give you de understandin' to go 'long wid it. Unless you see de fur, a mink skin ain't no different from a coon hide. Looka heah, Pheoby, is Sam waitin' on you for his supper?"

"It's all ready and waitin'. If he ain't got sense enough to eat it, dat's his hard luck."

"Well then, we can set right where we is and talk. Ah got the house all opened up to let dis breeze get a little catchin'."

"Pheoby, we been kissin'-friends for twenty years, so Ah depend on you for a good thought. And Ah'm talking to you from dat standpoint."

Time makes everything old so the "Pheoby, we been kissin'-friends for twenty years, so Ah depend on you for a good thought. And Ah'm talking to you from dat standpoint."

Time makes everything old so the kissing, young darkness became a monstropolous old thing while Janie talked.

Chapter 2

Janie saw her life like a great tree in leaf with the things suffered, things enjoyed, things done and undone. Dawn and doom was in the branches. "Ah know exactly what Ah got to tell yuh, but it's hard to know where to start at.

"Ah ain't never seen mah papa. And Ah didn't know 'im if Ah did. Mah mama neither. She was gone from round dere long before Ah wuz big enough tuh know. Mah grandma raised me. Mah grandma and de white folks she worked wid. She had a house out in de back-yard and dat's where Ah wuz born. They was quality white folks up dere in West Florida. Named Washburn. She had four gran'chillun on de place and all of us played together and dat's how come Ah never called mah Grandma nothin' but Nanny, 'cause dat's what everybody on de place called her. Nanny used to ketch us in our devilment and lick every youngun on de place and Mis' Washburn did de same. Ah reckon dey never hit us ah lick amiss 'cause dem three boys and us two girls wuz pretty aggravatin', Ah speck.

"Ah was wid dem white chillun so much till Ah didn't know Ah wuzn't white till Ah was round six years old. Wouldn't have found it out then, but a man come long takin' pictures and without askin' anybody, Shelby, dat was de oldest boy, he told him to take us. Round a week later de man brought de picture for Mis' Washburn to see and pay him which she did, then give us all a good lickin'.

"So when we looked at de picture and everybody got pointed out there wasn't nobody left except a real dark little girl with long hair standing by Eleanor. Dat's where Ah wuz s'posed to be, but Ah couldn't recognize dat dark chile as me. So Ah ast, 'where is me? Ah don't see me.'

"Everybody laughed, even Mr. Washburn. Miss Nellie, de Mama of de chillun who come back home after her husband dead, she pointed to de dark one and said, 'Dat's you, Alphabet, don't you know yo' ownself?'

"Dey all useter call me Alphabet 'cause so many people had done named me different names. Ah looked at de picture a long time and seen it was mah dress and mah hair so Ah said:

"'Aw, aw! Ah'm colored!'

"Den dey all laughed real hard. But before Ah seen de picture Ah thought Ah wuz just like de rest.

"Us lived dere havin' fun till de chillum at school got to teasin' me 'bout livin' in de white folks' back-yard. Dere wuz uh knotty head gal name Mayrella dat useter git mad every time she look at me. Mis' Washburn useter dress me up in all de clothes her gran'chillun didn't need no mo' which still wuz better'n whut de rest uh de colored chillun had. And then she useter put hair ribbon on mah head fuh me tuh wear. Dat useter rile Mayrella uh lot. So she would pick at me all de time and put some others up tuh do de same. They'd push me 'way from de ring plays and make out they couldn't play wid nobody dat lived on premises. Den they'd tell me not to be takin' on over mah looks 'cause they mama told 'em 'bout de hound dawgs huntin' mah papa all night long. 'Bout Mr. Washburn and de sheriff puttin' de bloodhounds on de trail tuh ketch mah papa for whut he done tuh mah mama. Dey didn't tell about how he wuz seen tryin' tuh git in touch wid mah mama later on so he could marry her. Naw, dey didn't talk dat part of it atall. Dey made it sound real bad so as tuh crumple mah feathers. None of 'em didn't even remember whut his name wuz, but dey all knowed de bloodhound part by heart. Nanny didn't love tuh see me wid mah head hung down, so she figgered it would be mo' better fuh me if us had uh house. She got de land and everything and then Mis' Washburn helped out uh whole heap wid things."

Pheoby's hungry listening helped Janie to tell her story. So she went on thinking back to her young years and explaining them to her friend in soft, easy phrases while all around the house, the night time put on flesh and blackness.

She thought awhile and decided that her conscious life had commenced at Nanny's gate. On a late afternoon Nanny had called her to come inside the house because she had spied Janie letting Johnny Taylor kiss her over the gatepost.

It was a spring afternoon in West Florida. Janie had spent most of the day under a blossoming pear tree in the back-yard. She had been spending every minute that she could steal from her chores under that tree for the last three days. That was to say, ever since the first tiny bloom had opened. It had called her to come and gaze on a mystery. From barren brown stems to glistening leaf-buds; from the leaf-buds to snowy virginity of bloom. It stirred her tremendously. How? Why? It was like a flute song forgotten in another existence and remembered again. What? How? Why? This singing she heard that had nothing to do with her ears. The rose of the world was breathing out smell. It followed her through all her waking moments and caressed her in her sleep. It connected itself with other vaguely felt matters that had struck her outside observation and buried themselves in her flesh. Now they emerged and quested about her consciousness.

She was stretched on her back beneath the pear tree soaking in the alto chant of the visiting bees, the gold of the sun and the panting breath of the breeze when the inaudible voice of it all came to her. She saw a dust-bearing bee sink into the sanctum of a bloom; the thousand sister-calyxes arch to meet the love embrace and the ecstatic shiver of the tree from root to tiniest branch creaming in every blossom and frothing with delight. So this was a marriage! She had been summoned to behold a revelation. Then Janie felt a pain remorseless sweet that left her limp and languid.

After a while she got up from where she was and went over the little garden field entire. She was seeking confirmation of the voice and vision, and everywhere she found and acknowledged answers. A personal answer for all other creations except herself. She felt an answer seeking her, but where? When? How? She found herself at the kitchen door and stumbled inside. In the air of the room were flies tumbling and singing, marrying and giving in marriage. When she reached the narrow hallway she was reminded that her grandmother was home with a sick headache. She was lying across the bed asleep so Janie tipped on out of the front door. Oh to be a pear tree—any tree in bloom! With kissing bees singing of the beginning of the world! She was sixteen. She had glossy leaves and bursting buds and she wanted to struggle with life but it seemed to elude her. Where were the singing bees for her? Nothing on the place nor in her grandma's house answered her. She searched as much of the world as she could from the top of the front steps and then went on down to the front gate and leaned over to gaze up and down the road. Looking, waiting, breathing short with impatience. Waiting for the world to be made.

Through pollinated air she saw a glorious being coming up the road. In her former blindness she had known him as shiftless Johnny Taylor, tall and lean. That was before the golden dust of pollen had beglamored his rags and her eyes.

In the last stages of Nanny's sleep, she dreamed of voices. Voices far-off but persistent, and gradually coming nearer. Janie's voice. Janie talking in whispery snatches with a male voice she couldn't quite place. That brought her wide awake. She bolted upright and peered out of the window and saw Johnny Taylor lacerating her Janie with a kiss.

"Janie!"

The old woman's voice was so lacking in command and reproof, so full of crumbling dissolution,—that Janie half believed that Nanny had not seen her. So she extended herself outside of her dream and went inside of the house. That was the end of her childhood.

Nanny's head and face looked like the standing roots of some old tree that had been torn away by storm. Foundation of ancient power that no longer mattered. The cooling palma christi leaves that Janie had bound about her grandma's head with a white rag had wilted down and become part and parcel of the woman. Her eyes didn't bore and pierce. They diffused and melted Janie, the room and the world into one comprehension.

"Janie, youse uh 'oman, now, so—" "Naw, Nanny, naw Ah ain't no real 'oman yet."

The thought was too new and heavy for Janie. She fought it away.

Nanny closed her eyes and nodded a slow, weary affirmation many times before she gave it voice.

"Yeah, Janie, youse got yo' womanhood on yuh. So Ah mout ez well tell yuh whut Ah been savin' up for uh spell. Ah wants to see you married right away.

"Me, married? Naw, Nanny, no ma'am! Whut Ah know 'bout uh husband?"

"Whut Ah seen just now is plenty for me, honey, Ah don't want no trashy nigger, no breath-and-britches, lak Johnny Taylor usin' yo' body to wipe his foots on."

Nanny's words made Janie's kiss across the gatepost seem like a manure pile after a rain.

"Look at me, Janie. Don't set dere wid yo' head hung down. Look at yo' ole grandma!" Her voice began snagging on the prongs of her feelings. "Ah don't want to be talkin' to you lak dis. Fact is Ah done been on mah knees to mah Maker many's de time askin' please—for Him not to make de burden too heavy for me to bear."

"Nanny, Ah just—Ah didn't mean nothin' bad."

"Dat's what makes me skeered. You don't mean no harm. You don't even know where harm is at. Ah'm ole now. Ah can't be always guidin' yo' feet from harm and danger. Ah wants to see you married right away.

"Who Ah'm goin' tuh marry off-hand lak dat? Ah don't know nobody."

"De Lawd will provide. He know Ah done bore de burden in de heat uh de day. Somebody done spoke to me 'bout you long time ago. Ah ain't said nothin' 'cause dat wasn't de way Ah placed you. Ah wanted yuh to school out and pick from a higher bush and a sweeter berry. But dat ain't yo' idea, Ah see."

"Nanny, who—who dat been askin' you for me?"

"Brother Logan Killicks. He's a good man, too."

"Naw, Nanny, no ma'am! Is dat whut he been hangin' round here for? He look like some ole skullhead in de grave yard.

The older woman sat bolt upright and put her feet to the floor, and thrust back the leaves from her face.

"So you don't want to marry off decent like, do yuh? You just wants to hug and kiss and feel around with first one man and then another, huh? You wants to make me suck de same sorrow yo' mama did, eh? Mah ole head ain't gray enough. Mah back ain't bowed enough to suit yuh!"

The vision of Logan Killicks was desecrating the pear tree, but Janie didn't know how to tell Nanny that. She merely hunched over and pouted at the floor.

"Janie."

"Yes, ma'am."

"You answer me when Ah speak. Don't you set dere poutin' wid me after all Ah done went through for you!"

She slapped the girl's face violently, and forced her head back so that their eyes met in struggle. With her hand uplifted for the second blow she saw the huge tear that welled up from Janie's heart and stood in each eye. She saw the terrible agony and the lips tightened down to hold back the cry and desisted. Instead she brushed back the heavy hair from Janie's face and stood there suffering and loving and weeping internally for both of them.

"Come to yo' Grandma, honey. Set in her lap lak yo' use tuh. Yo' Nanny wouldn't harm a hair uh yo' head. She don't want nobody else to do it neither if she kin help it. Honey, de white man is de ruler of everything as fur as Ah been able tuh find out. Maybe it's some place way off in de ocean where de black man is in power, but we don't know nothin' but what we see. So de white man throw down de load and tell de nigger man tuh pick it up. He pick it up because he have to, but he don't tote it. He hand it to his womenfolks. De nigger woman is de mule uh de world so fur as Ah can see. Ah been prayin' fuh it tuh be different wid you. Lawd, Lawd, Lawd!"

For a long time she sat rocking with the girl held tightly to her sunken breast. Janie's long legs dangled over one arm of the chair and the long braids of her hair swung low on the other side. Nanny half sung, half sobbed a running chant-prayer over the head of the weeping girl.

"Lawd have mercy! It was a long time on de way but Ah reckon it had to come. Oh Jesus! Do, Jesus! Ah done de best Ah could."

Finally, they both grew calm.

"Janie, how long you been 'lowin' Johnny Taylor to kiss you?"

"Only dis one time, Nanny. Ah don't love him at all. Whut made me do it is—oh, Ah don't know."

"Thank yuh, Massa Jesus."

"Ah ain't gointuh do it no mo', Nanny. Please don't make me marry Mr. Killicks."

"'Tain't Logan Killicks Ah wants you to have, baby, it's protection. Ah ain't gittin' ole, honey. Ah'm done ole. One mornin' soon, now, de angel wid de sword is gointuh stop by here. De day and de hour is hid from me, but it won't be long. Ah ast de Lawd when you was uh infant in mah arms to let me stay here till you got grown. He done spared me to see de day. Mah daily prayer now is tuh let dese golden moments rolls on a few days longer till Ah see you safe in life." "Lemme wait, Nanny, please, jus' a lil bit mo'."

"Don't think Ah don't feel wid you, Janie, 'cause Ah do. Ah couldn't love yuh no more if Ah had uh felt yo' birth pains mahself. Fact uh de matter, Ah loves yuh a whole heap more'n Ah do yo' mama, de one Ah did birth. But you got to take in consideration you ain't no everyday chile like most of 'em. You ain't got no papa, you might jus' as well say no mama, for de good she do yuh. You ain't got nobody but me. And mah head is ole and tilted towards de grave. Neither can you stand alone by yo'self. De thought uh you bein' kicked around from pillar tuh post is uh hurtin' thing. Every tear you drop squeezes a cup uh blood outa mah heart. Ah got tuh try and do for you befo' mah head is cold."

A sobbing sigh burst out of Janie. The old woman answered her with little soothing pats of the hand.

"You know, honey, us colored folks is branches without roots and that makes things come round in queer ways. You in particular. Ah was born back due in slavery so it wasn't for me to fulfill my dreams of whut a woman oughta be and to do. Dat's one of de hold-backs of slavery. But nothing can't stop you from wishin'. You can't beat nobody down so low till you can rob 'em of they will. Ah didn't want to be used for a work-ox and a brood-sow and Ah didn't want mah daughter used dat way neither. It sho wasn't mah will for things to happen lak they did. Ah even hated de way you was born. But, all de same Ah said thank God, Ah got another chance. Ah wanted to preach a great sermon about colored women sittin' on high, but they wasn't no pulpit for me. Freedom found me wid a baby daughter in mah arms, ① so Ah said Ah'd take a broom and a cook-pot and throw up a highway through de wilderness for her. She would expound what Ah felt. But somehow she got lost offa de highway and next thing Ah knowed here you was in de world. So whilst Ah was tendin' you of nights Ah said Ah'd save de text for you. Ah been waitin' a long time, Janie, but nothin' Ah been through ain't too much if you just take a stand on high ground lak Ah dreamed."

Old Nanny sat there rocking Janie like an infant and thinking back and back. Mind-pictures brought feelings, and feelings dragged out dramas from the hollows of her heart.

"Dat mornin' on de big plantation close to Savannah, a rider come in a gallop tellin' 'bout Sherman takin' Atlanta. Marse Robert's son had done been kilt at Chickamauga. So he grabbed his gun and straddled his best horse and went off wid de rest of de gray-headed men and young boys to drive de Yankees back into Tennessee.

"They was all cheerin' and cryin' and shoutin' for de men dat was ridin' off. Ah couldn't see nothin' cause yo' mama wasn't but a week old, and Ah was flat uh mah back. But pretty soon he let on he forgot somethin' and run into mah cabin and made me let down mah hair for de last time. He sorta wropped his hand in it, pulled mah big toe, lak he always done, and was gone after de rest lak lightnin'. Ah heard 'em give one last whoop for him. Then de big house and de quarters got sober and silent.

---

① 美国内战(1861—1865)结束以后,黑人奴隶制被废除,黑人得以解放,获得自由。

"It was de cool of de evenin' when Mistis come walkin' in mah door. She throwed de door wide open and stood dere lookin' at me outa her eyes and her face. Look lak she been livin' through uh hundred years in January without one day of spring. She come stood over me in de bed.

"'Nanny, Ah come to see that baby uh yourn.

"Ah tried not to feel de breeze off her face, but it got so cold in dere dat Ah was freezin' to death under the kivvers. So Ah couldn't move right away lak Ah aimed to. But Ah knowed Ah had to make haste and do it.

"'You better git dat kivver offa dat youngun and dat quick!' she clashed at me. 'Look lak you don't know who is Mistis on dis plantation, Madam. But Ah aims to show you.'

"By dat time I had done managed tuh unkivver mah baby enough for her to see de head and face.

"'Nigger, whut's yo' baby doin' wid gray eyes and yaller hair?' She begin tuh slap mah jaws ever which a'way. Ah never felt the fust ones' cause Ah wuz too busy gittin' de kivver back over mah chile. But dem last lick burnt me lak fire. Ah had too many feelin's tuh tell which one tuh follow so Ah didn't cry and Ah didn't do nothin' else. But then she kept on astin me how come mah baby look white. She asted me dat maybe twenty-five or thirty times, lak she got tuh sayin' dat and couldn't help herself. So Ah told her, 'Ah don't know nothin' but what Ah'm told tuh do,' 'cause Ah ain't nothin' but uh nigger and uh slave.'

"Instead of pacifyin' her lak Ah thought, look lak she got madder. But Ah reckon she was tired and wore out 'cause she didn't hit me no more. She went to de foot of de bed and wiped her hands on her handksher. 'Ah wouldn't dirty mah hands on yuh. But first thing in de mornin' de overseer will take you to de whippin' post and tie you down on yo' knees and cut de hide offa yo' yaller back. One hundred lashes wid a raw-hide on yo' bare back. Ah'll have you whipped till de blood run down to yo' heels! Ah mean to count de licks mahself. And if it kills you Ah'll stand de loss. Anyhow, as soon as dat brat is a month old Ah'm going to sell it offa dis place.'

"She flounced on off and let her wintertime wid me. Ah knowed mah body wasn't healed, but Ah couldn't consider dat. In de black dark Ah wrapped mah baby de best Ah knowed how and made it to de swamp by de river. Ah knowed de place was full uh moccasins and other bitin' snakes, but Ah was more skeered uh whut was behind me. Ah hide in dere day and night and suckled de baby every time she start to cry, for fear somebody might hear her and Ah'd git found. Ah ain't sayin' uh friend or two didn't feel mah care. And den de Good Lawd seen to it dat Ah wasn't taken. Ah don't see how come mah milk didn't kill mah chile, wid me so skeered and worried all de time. De noise uh de owls skeered me; de limbs of dem cypress trees took to crawlin' and movin' round after dark, and two three times Ah heered panthers prowlin' round. But nothin' never hurt me 'cause de Lawd knowed how it was.

"Den, one night Ah heard de big guns boomin' lak thunder. It kept up all night long. And de next mornin' Ah could see uh big ship at a distance and a great stirrin' round. So

Ah wrapped Leafy up in moss and fixed her good in a tree and picked mah way on down to de landin'. The men was all in blue①, and Ah heard people say Sherman was comin' to meet de boats in Savannah, and all of us slaves was free. So Ah run got mah baby and got in quotation wid people and found a place Ah could stay.

"But it was a long time after dat befo' de Big Surrender at Richmond②. Den de big bell ring in Atlanta and all de men in gray uniforms③ had to go to Moultrie, and bury their swords in de ground to show they was never to fight about slavery no mo'. So den we knowed we was free.

"Ah wouldn't marry nobody, though Ah could have uh heap uh times, cause Ah didn't want nobody mistreating mah baby. So Ah got with some good white people and come down here in West Florida to work and make de sun shine on both sides of de street for Leafy.

"Mah Madam help me wid her just lak she been doin' wid you. Ah put her in school when it got so it was a school to put her in. Ah was 'spectin' to make a school teacher outa her.

"But one day she didn't come home at de usual time and Ah waited and waited, but she never come all dat night. Ah took a lantern and went round askin' everybody but nobody ain't seen her. De next mornin' she come crawlin' in on her hands and knees. A sight to see. Dat school teacher had done hid her in de woods all night long, and he had done raped mah baby and run on off just before day.

"She was only seventeen, and somethin' lak dat to happen! Lawd a'mussy! Look lak Ah kin see it all over again. It was a long time before she was well, and by dat time we knowed you was on de way. And after you was born she took to drinkin' likker and stayin' out nights. Couldn't git her to stay here and nowhere else. Lawd knows where she is right now. She ain't dead, 'cause Ah'd know it by mah feelings, but sometimes Ah wish she was at rest.

"And, Janie, maybe it wasn't much, but Ah done de best Ah kin by you. Ah raked and scraped and bought dis lil piece uh land so you wouldn't have to stay in de white folks' yard and tuck yo' head befo' other chillun at school. Dat was all right when you was little. But when you got big enough to understand things, Ah wanted you to look upon yo'self. Ah don't want yo' feathers always crumpled by folks throwin' up things in yo' face. And Ah can't die easy thinkin' maybe de menfolks white or black is makin' a spit cup outa you: Have some sympathy fuh me. Put me down easy, Janie, Ah'm a cracked plate."

Questions for Discussion

1. What kind of black feminist ideas does Zora Neale Hurston express in *Their Eyes Were Watching God*?
2. How can we interpret the writing strategies used in *Their Eyes Were Watching God* from the perspective of postcolonialism?
3. What's the big conflict represented in the novel, and how can we understand the misunderstanding among black folks?

---

① 在美国内战中,穿着蓝色军服的士兵属于北方联邦的军队。
② 在美国内战中,南方军队战败,在里士满投降。
③ 在美国内战中,穿着灰色军服的士兵属于南方联邦的军队。

2. Invisible Man

作者简介

　　拉尔夫·艾里森(1914—1994)是20世纪最重要的美国作家之一,一生只出版了一部小说《看不见的人》,但创作了大量评论性文章和短篇故事。艾里森于1914年出生于俄克拉荷马城的一个贫寒之家,父亲在1916年的一场事故中去世,母亲独自承担了养育孩子的重任。小学时他首次接触到音乐教育,对音乐的热爱伴随了他的一生,音乐影响了他的小说和批评创作。1933年,他高中毕业前往阿拉巴马州的塔斯克基学院学习作曲。虽然受到古典音乐的训练,但他深爱爵士乐和摇摆乐,并将这两种风格揉入自己的作曲中,这使得他与学院上下的保守风气格格不入。此时他的兴趣部分地转向文学,接触到艾略特的现代主义诗歌,其现代主义风格对艾里森后来创作《看不见的人》影响很大。1936年,他离开塔斯克基学院,北上纽约哈莱姆,结识了兰斯顿·休斯和理查德·赖特,进入哈莱姆文人团体,也由此接触到设立在哈莱姆的美国共产党总部。在为联邦作家项目工作期间,艾里森收集了大量非裔美国民间故事和奴隶叙事,头脑中渐渐形成了很多之后在创作《看不见的人》时的想法和意象。二战中他在美国商船上服役,同时出版了几篇最知名的短篇故事,包括"宾戈游戏之王"和"飞回家"等。1952年《看不见的人》出版后,艾里森立刻着手开始创作第二部小说,但1967年的一场大火毁掉了他的手稿,虽然艾里森后来一直试图重写这部小说,但直至1994年患癌去世也未能完成。在他去世后,这部小说最终以《六月庆典》(1999)为题出版。艾里森一生创作了数量惊人的短篇故事、书评和评论。他有关文学、艺术、文化、民主和爵士乐的文章至今仍是对美国社会最明晰最具鉴赏力的评述。此类文章主要收集在《影子与行动》(*Shadow and Act*, 1964)、《去高地》(*Going to the Territory*, 1986)以及他去世后由别人编辑整理出版的《艾里森文选》(1994)中,他对20世纪美国黑人文学第二次浪潮的兴起做出了巨大贡献。

作品简介与赏析

　　小说的无名主人公曾是生活在美国南方的一个好孩子,从懂事起就一直努力按照学校教育所灌输的一整套价值观念塑造自己,直到大学期间无意间让一名白人校董看到了校长布莱索希望掩盖的黑人的真实生活后,他受到惩罚,被学校除名。北上纽约寻找工作时,他一再受挫,最后终于在一家油漆厂找到了工作,却被其他工人视为工贼。油漆厂发生爆炸,他身受重伤,厂医院却将他当实验品,致使他一度失去意识。流浪哈莱姆时,他在街头为一对黑人老夫妇仗义执言,其演讲口才颇为左翼组织"兄弟会"首领杰克兄弟赏识,允其加入,但只是被当作拉选票的工具。最后,主人公为兄弟会所不容,又遭到黑人民族主义极端分子拉斯的追杀,只能遁入地下,栖居在纽约一所公寓的地下室,与社会断绝往来。小说揭示了美国社会的悖论:这个国家依照先辈的理想建国,然而现实表明它早已背叛了这些理想。

　　《看不见的人》于1952年由兰登书屋出版,获得广泛好评。第二年获得国家图书奖,艾里森成为第一位获此殊荣的非裔美国作家。1965年,《图书周刊》经过问卷调查,将《看不见的人》推选为1945年以来美国最出色的一部作品。在一片赞誉声中也不乏批评的声音。有人责难艾里森没有从"抗议小说"的立场出发进行创作。对此,艾里森回应道:"我要求把我的小说作为艺术来评价;如果失败,那是美学上的失败,而不是因为我是否进行过意识形态的斗争。"事实上,这部作品经受了时间的考验,被誉为美国最伟大的小说之一,跻身于经典美国文学的殿堂。

　　小说结构由序曲、正文和尾声三部分组成,以第一人称叙述人"沦为看不见的人后藏身于地下"开头,中间回忆他曾经的地上生活,结尾则叙述他重新回到地下,组成了一个环形结构。在时间的处理上,叙事由现在的状态,追溯以往,之后又回到现在,从而将叙述者的过去、现在和将来连成一个有机整体。就类型而言,它属于成长小说,记录了叙述人认识社会和自我的成长经历。与主人公的成长经历相对应的是小说采用了流浪汉小说的模式。小说中事件发生地频繁转换:从偏僻乡间到高等学府,从南方到北方,从工厂到医院,从客栈到社区。小说追随着主人公的脚步,从童年走入成年,从天真走入觉醒。与此同时,社会的方方面面和各色人等透过他的眼睛,呈现在读者面前。

　　下文选自小说的序曲和第一章。主人公兼叙事人"我"用倒叙的手法讲述了自己为何藏身地下,成为一个看不见的人。而小说以一句"我是一个看不见的人"开启全书的灵魂——序曲,奠定了全书的主题、形式和基调。序曲中"我"以社会反叛者的姿态描述了自己的地下生活,揭开美国文化的疮疤:"我的洞温暖如春,光线充足。确实是光线充足。恐怕走遍整个纽约也找不到像我这个洞这样明亮的地方,即使百老汇也不例外。帝国大厦晚上灯火通明,连摄影师也觉得光线理想,但也比不上我的洞。那是骗人的。这两个地方看来明亮,其实是我们整个文明最为黑暗的场所——请原谅,我该说我们整个文化最为黑暗的地方"……主人公自述自己20年来过着行尸走肉的生活,"直到发现自己是个看不见的人,才意识到自己是个活人。"

　　第一章中的主人公追述了自己中学毕业前夕的一件往事。作为优秀学生代表,"我"被邀请在本镇白人头面人物的集会上发表自己的毕业演说。"我"赶到集会地,却发现自己必须参加一场以娱乐白人为目的的格斗。格斗者由黑人青少年组成,为争取奖金开展一场你死我活的格斗,同时受尽白人戏耍侮辱。格斗结束,"我"遍体鳞伤,仍然努力完成自己的演讲。作为奖励,"我"得到一只高级公文包,里面是一张州立黑人学院的奖学金证书。当晚"我"梦见自己打开公文包,发现里面无数信封套着的一封短信,上面写着:"敬启者,务必让这个小黑鬼不停地跑下去。"这句话无情地揭示了美国社会种族关系的本质。

Prologue

I am an invisible man. No, I am not a spook like those who haunted Edgar Allan Poe; nor am I one of your Hollywood-movie ectoplasms. I am a man of substance, of flesh and bone, fiber and liquids—and I might even be said to possess a mind. I am invisible, understand, simply because people refuse to see me. Like the bodiless heads you see sometimes in circus sideshows, it is as though I have been surrounded by mirrors of hard, distorting glass. When they approach me they see only my surroundings, themselves, or figments of their imagination—indeed, everything and anything except me.

Nor is my invisibility exactly a matter of a biochemical accident to my epidermis. That invisibility to which I refer occurs because of a peculiar disposition of the eyes of those with whom I come in contact. A matter of the construction of their *inner* eyes, those eyes with which they look through their physical eyes upon reality. I am not complaining, nor am I protesting either. It is sometimes advantageous to be unseen, although it is most often rather wearing on the nerves. Then too, you're constantly being bumped against by those of poor vision. Or again, you often doubt if you really exist. You wonder whether you aren't simply a phantom in other people's minds. Say, a figure in a nightmare which the sleeper tries with all his strength to destroy. It's when you feel like this that, out of resentment, you begin to bump people back. And, let me confess, you feel that way most of the time. You ache with the need to convince yourself that you do exist in the real world, that you're a part of all the sound and anguish, and you strike out with your fists, you curse and you swear to make them recognize you. And, alas, it's seldom successful.

One night I accidentally bumped into a man, and perhaps because of the near darkness he saw me and called me an insulting name. I sprang at him, seized his coat lapels and demanded that he apologize. He was a tall blond man, and as my face came close to his he looked insolently out of his blue eyes and cursed me, his breath hot in my face as he struggled. I pulled his chin down sharp upon the crown of my head, butting him as I had seen the West Indians do, and I felt his flesh tear and the blood gush out, and I yelled, "Apologize! Apologize!" But he continued to curse and struggle, and I butted him again and again until he went down heavily, on his knees, profusely bleeding. I kicked him repeatedly, in a frenzy because he still uttered insults though his lips were frothy with blood. Oh yes, I kicked him! And in my outrage I got out my knife and prepared to slit his throat, right there beneath the lamplight in the deserted street, holding him in the collar with one hand, and opening the knife with my teeth—when it occurred to me that the man had not *seen* me, actually; that he, as far as he knew, was in the midst of a walking nightmare! And I stopped the blade, slicing the air as I pushed him away, letting him fall back to the street. I stared at him hard as the lights of a car stabbed through the darkness. He lay there, moaning on the asphalt; a man almost killed by a phantom. It unnerved me. I was both disgusted and ashamed. I was like a drunken man myself, wavering about on weakened legs. Then I was amused: Something in this man's thick head had sprung out and beaten him within an inch of his life①. I began to laugh at this crazy discovery. Would he have awakened at the point of death? Would Death himself have freed him for wakeful living? But I didn't linger. I ran away into the dark, laughing so hard I feared I might rupture myself. The next day I saw his picture in the *Daily News*, beneath a caption stating that he had been "mugged." Poor fool, poor blind fool, I thought with sincere compassion, mugged by an invisible man!

Most of the time (although I do not choose as I once did to deny the violence of my days by ignoring it) I am not so overtly violent. I remember that I am invisible and walk softly so as not to awaken the sleeping ones. Sometimes it is best not to awaken them; there are few things in the world as dangerous as sleepwalkers. I learned in time though that it is possible to carry on a fight against them without their realizing it. For instance, I have been carrying on a fight with Monopolated Light & Power② for some time now. I use their service and pay them nothing at all, and they don't know it. Oh, they suspect that power is being drained off, but they don't know where. All they know is that according to the master meter back there in their power station a hell of a lot of free current is

---

① within an inch of his life: 使他几乎丧命。
② Monopolated Light & Power: 独营电灯电力公司。

disappearing somewhere into the jungle of Harlem. The joke, of course, is that I don't live in Harlem but in a border area. Several years ago (before I discovered the advantages of being invisible) I went through the routine process of buying service and paying their outrageous rates. But no more. I gave up all that, along with my apartment, and my old way of life: That way based upon the fallacious assumption that I, like other men, was visible. Now, aware of my invisibility, I live rent-free in a building rented strictly to whites, in a section of the basement that was shut off and forgotten during the nineteenth century, which I discovered when I was trying to escape in the night from Ras the Destroyer[①]. But that's getting too far ahead of the story, almost to the end, although the end is in the beginning and lies far ahead.

The point now is that I found a home—or a hole in the ground, as you will. Now don't jump to the conclusion that because I call my home a "hole" it is damp and cold like a grave; there are cold holes and warm holes. Mine is a warm hole. And remember, a bear retires to his hole for the winter and lives until spring; then he comes strolling out like the Easter chick breaking from its shell. I say all this to assure you that it is incorrect to assume that, because I'm invisible and live in a hole, I am dead. I am neither dead nor in a state of suspended animation. Call me Jack-the-Bear[②], for I am in a state of hibernation.

My hole is warm and full of light. Yes, *full* of light. I doubt if there is a brighter spot in all New York than this hole of mine, and I do not exclude Broadway. Or the Empire State Building on a photographer's dream night. But that is taking advantage of you. Those two spots are among the darkest of our whole civilization—pardon me, our whole *culture* (an important distinction, I've heard)—which might sound like a hoax, or a contradiction, but that (by contradiction, I mean) is how the world moves: Not like an arrow, but a boomerang. (Beware of those who speak of the *spiral* of history; they are preparing a boomerang. Keep a steel helmet handy.) I know; I have been boomeranged across my head so much that I now can see the darkness of lightness. And I love light. Perhaps you'll think it strange that an invisible man should need light, desire light, love light. But maybe it is exactly because I *am* invisible. Light confirms my reality, gives birth to my form. A beautiful girl once told me of a recurring nightmare in which she lay in the center of a large dark room and felt her face expand until it filled the whole room, becoming a formless mass while her eyes ran in bilious jelly up the chimney. And so it is with me. Without light I am not only invisible, but formless as well; and to be unaware of one's form is to live a death. I myself, after existing some twenty years, did not become alive until I discovered my invisibility.

That is why I fight my battle with Monopolated Light & Power. The deeper reason, I mean: It allows me to feel my vital aliveness. I also fight them for taking so much of my money before I learned to protect myself. In my hole in the basement there are exactly 1, 369 lights. I've wired the entire ceiling, every inch of it. And not with fluorescent bulbs,

---

① Ras the Destroyer:煞星拉斯,小说中的黑人极端主义分子。

② Jack-the-Bear:爵士音乐家艾灵顿(Duke Ellington)(1899—1974)和他的乐队在 1940 年的一个唱片标题。

but with the older, more-expensive-to-operate kind, the filament type. An act of sabotage, you know. I've already begun to wire the wall. A junk man I know, a man of vision, has supplied me with wire and sockets. Nothing, storm or flood, must get in the way of our need for light and ever more and brighter light. The truth is the light and light is the truth. When I finish all four walls, then I'll start on the floor. Just how that will go, I don't know. Yet when you have lived invisible as long as I have you develop a certain ingenuity. I'll solve the problem. And maybe I'll invent a gadget to place my coffee pot on the fire while I lie in bed, and even invent a gadget to warm my bed—like the fellow I saw in one of the picture magazines who made himself a gadget to warm his shoes! Though invisible, I am in the great American tradition of tinkers. That makes me kin to Ford, Edison and Franklin. 4 Call me, since I have a theory and a concept, a "thinker-tinker." Yes, I'll warm my shoes; they need it, they're usually full of holes. I'll do that and more.

Now I have one radio-phonograph; I plan to have five. There is a certain acoustical deadness in my hole, and when I have music I want to *feel* its vibration, not only with my ear but with my whole body. I'd like to hear five recordings of Louis Armstrong[①] playing and singing "What Did I Do to Be so Black and Blue"—all at the same time. Sometimes now I listen to Louis while I have my favorite dessert of vanilla ice cream and sloe gin. I pour the red liquid over the white mound, watching it glisten and the vapor rising as Louis bends that military instrument into a beam of lyrical sound. Perhaps I like Louis Armstrong because he's made poetry out of being invisible. I think it must be because he's unaware that he *is* invisible. And my own grasp of invisibility aids me to understand his music. Once when I asked for a cigarette, some jokers gave me a reefer, which I lighted when I got home and sat listening to my phonograph. It was a strange evening. Invisibility, let me explain, gives one a slightly different sense of time, you're never quite on the beat. Sometimes you're ahead and sometimes behind. Instead of the swift and imperceptible flowing of time, you are aware of its nodes, those points where time stands still or from which it leaps ahead. And you slip into the breaks and look around. That's what you hear vaguely in Louis' music.

Once I saw a prizefighter boxing a yokel. The fighter was swift and amazingly scientific. His body was one violent flow of rapid rhythmic action. He hit the yokel a hundred times while the yokel held up his arms in stunned surprise. But suddenly the yokel, rolling about in the gale of boxing gloves, struck one blow and knocked science, speed and footwork as cold as a well-digger's posterior. The smart money hit the canvas. The long shot got the nod. The yokel had simply stepped inside of his opponent's sense of time. So under the spell of the reefer I discovered a new analytical way of listening to music. The unheard sounds came through, and each melodic line existed of itself, stood out clearly from all the rest, said its piece, and waited patiently for the other voices to speak. That night I found myself hearing not only in time, but in space as well. I not only

---

① Louis Armstrong:路易斯·阿姆斯特朗(1900—1971),美国著名爵士音乐家。

entered the music but descended, like Dante①, into its depths. And *beneath the swiftness of the hot tempo there was a slower tempo and a cave and I entered it and looked around and heard an old woman singing a spiritual as full of Weltschmerz as flamenco②, and beneath that lay a still lower level on which I saw a beautiful girl the color of ivory pleading in a voice like my mother's as she stood before a group of slaveowners who bid for her naked body, and below that I found a lower level and a more rapid tempo and I heard someone shout:*

"Brothers and sisters, my text this morning is the 'Blackness of Blackness.'"

And a congregation of voices answered: "That blackness is most black, brother, most black ... "

"In the beginning ... "

"At the very start," they cried.

" .. there was blackness ... "

"Preach it ... "

"... and the sun ... "

"The sun, Lawd ... "

"... was bloody red ... "

"Red ... "

"Now black is ... " the preacher shouted.

"Bloody ... "

"I said black is ... "

"Preach it, brother ... "

"... an' black ain't ... "

"Red, Lawd, red: He said it's red!"

"Amen, brother ... "

"Black will git you ... "

"Yes, it will ... "

"Yes, it will ... "

"... an' black won't ... "

"Now, it won't!"

"It do ... "

"It do, Lawd ... "

"... an' it don't."

"Halleluiah ... "

"... It'll put you, glory, glory, Oh my Lawd, in the whale's belly."

"Preach it, dear brother ... "

"... .an' make you tempt ... "

"Good God a-mighty!"

"Old Aunt Nelly!"

---

① Dante:但丁,意大利诗人,文艺复兴运动的先驱人物,代表作是史诗《神曲》。
② flamenco:弗拉门科舞曲,一种西班牙舞。

"Black will make you ..."

"Black ..."

"... or black will un-make you ..."

"Ain't it the truth, Lawd?"

And at that point a voice of trombone timbre screamed at me, "Git out of here, you fool! Is you ready to commit treason?"

And I tore myself away, hearing the old singer of spirituals moaning, "Go curse your God, boy, and die."

I stopped and questioned her, asked her what was wrong.

"I dearly loved my master, son," she said.

"You should have hated him," I said.

"He gave me several sons," she said, "and because I loved my sons I learned to love their father though I hated him too."

"I too have become acquainted with ambivalence," I said. "That's why I'm here."

"What's that?"

"Nothing, a word that doesn't explain it. Why do you moan?"

"I moan this way 'cause he's dead," she said.

"Then tell me, who is that laughing upstairs?"

"Them's my sons. They glad."

"Yes, I can understand that too," I said.

"I laughs too, but I moans too. He promised to set us free but he never could bring hisself to do it. Still I loved him ..."

"Loved him? You mean ...?"

"Oh yes, but I loved something else even more."

"What more?"

"Freedom."

"Freedom," I said. "Maybe freedom lies in hating."

"Naw, son, it's in loving. I loved him and give him the poison and he withered away like a frost-bit apple. Them boys would a tore him to pieces with they homemade knives."

"A mistake was made somewhere," I said, "I'm confused." And I wished to say other things, but the laughter upstairs became too loud and moan-like for me and I tried to break out of it, but I couldn't. Just as I was leaving I felt an urgent desire to ask her what freedom was and went back. She sat with her head in her hands, moaning softly; her leather-brown face was filled with sadness.

"Old woman, what is this freedom you love so well?" I asked around a corner of my mind.

She looked surprised, then thoughtful, then baffled. "I done forgot, son. It's all mixed up. First I think it's one thing, then I think it's another. It gits my head to spinning. I guess now it ain't nothing but knowing how to say what I got up in my head. But it's a hard job, son. Too much is done happen to me in too short a time. Hit's like I have a fever. Ever' time I starts to walk my head gits to swirling and I falls down. Or if it ain't that, it's the boys; they gits to laughing and wants to kill up the white folks. They's bitter, that's what they is ... "

"But what about freedom?"

"Leave me 'lone, boy; my head aches!"

I left her, feeling dizzy myself. I didn't get far.

Suddenly one of the sons, a big fellow six feet tall, appeared out of nowhere and struck me with his fist.

"What's the matter, man?" I cried.

"You made Ma cry!"

"But how?" I said, dodging a blow.

"Askin' her them questions, that's how. Git outa here and stay, and next time you got questions like that, ask yourself!"

He held me in a grip like cold stone, his fingers fastening upon my windpipe until I thought I would suffocate before he finally allowed me to go. I stumbled about dazed, the music beating hysterically in my ears. It was dark. My head cleared and I wandered down a dark narrow passage, thinking I heard his footsteps hurrying behind me. I was sore, and into my being had come a profound craving for tranquillity, for peace and quiet, a state I felt I could never achieve. For one thing, the trumpet was blaring and the rhythm was too hectic. A tom-tom beating like heart-thuds began drowning out the trumpet, filling my ears. I longed for water and I heard it rushing through the cold mains my fingers touched as I felt my way, but I couldn't stop to search because of the footsteps behind me.

"Hey, Ras," I called. "Is it you, Destroyer? Rinehart?"

No answer, only the rhythmic footsteps behind me. Once I tried crossing the road, but a speeding machine struck me, scraping the skin from my leg as it roared past.

Then somehow I came out of it, ascending hastily from this underworld of sound to hear Louis Armstrong innocently asking,

> What did I do
> To be so black
> And blue?

At first I was afraid; this familiar music had demanded action, the kind of which I was incapable, and yet had I lingered there beneath the surface I might have attempted to act. Nevertheless, I know now that few really listen to this music. I sat on the chair's edge in a soaking sweat, as though each of my 1, 369 bulbs had every one become a klieg light in an individual setting for a third degree with Ras and Rinehart in charge. It was exhausting—as though I had held my breath continuously for an hour under the terrifying serenity that comes from days of intense hunger. And yet, it was a strangely satisfying experience for an invisible man to hear the silence of sound. I had discovered unrecognized compulsions of my being—even though I could not answer "yes" to their promptings. I haven't smoked a reefer since, however; not because they're illegal, but because to *see* around corners is enough (that is not unusual when you are invisible). But to hear around them is too much; it inhibits action. And despite Brother Jack① and all that sad, lost period of the Brotherhood, I believe in nothing if not in action.

Please, a definition: A hibernation is a covert preparation for a more overt action.

Besides, the drug destroys one's sense of time completely. If that happened, I might forget to dodge some bright morning and some cluck would run me down with an orange and yellow street car, or a bilious bus! Or I might forget to leave my hole when the moment for action presents itself.

Meanwhile I enjoy my life with the compliments of Monopolated Light & Power. Since you never recognize me even when in closest contact with me, and since, no doubt, you'll hardly believe that I exist, it won't matter if you know that I tapped a power line leading into the building and ran it into my hole in the ground. Before that I lived in the darkness into which I was chased, but now I see. I've illuminated the blackness of my invisibility— and vice versa. And so I play the invisible music of my isolation. The last statement doesn't seem just right, does it? But it is; you hear this music simply because music is heard and seldom seen, except by musicians. Could this compulsion to put invisibility down in black and white be thus an urge to make music of invisibility? But I am an orator, a rabble-rouser—Am? I *was*, and perhaps shall be again. Who knows? All sickness is not unto death, neither is invisibility.

I can hear you say, "What a horrible, irresponsible bastard!" And you're right. I leap to agree with you. I am one of the most irresponsible beings that ever lived. Irresponsibility is part of my invisibility; any way you face it, it is a denial. But to whom can I be responsible, and why should I be, when you refuse to see me? And wait until I reveal how truly irresponsible I am. Responsibility rests upon recognition, and recognition is a form of agreement. Take the man whom I almost killed: Who was responsible for that near murder—I? I don't think so, and I refuse it. I won't buy it. You can't give it to me. *He* bumped *me*, *he* insulted *me*. Shouldn't he, for his own personal safety, have recognized my hysteria, my "danger potential"? He, let us say, was lost in a dream world. But didn't *he* control that dream world—which, alas, is only too real! —and didn't *he* rule me out of it? And if he had yelled for a policeman, wouldn't *I* have been taken for the offending one? Yes, yes, yes! Let me agree with you, I was the irresponsible one; for I should have used my knife to protect the higher interests of society. Some day that kind of foolishness will cause us tragic trouble. All dreamers and sleepwalkers must pay the price, and even the invisible victim is responsible for the fate of all. But I shirked that responsibility; I became too snarled in the incompatible notions that buzzed within my brain. I was a coward ...

But what did *I* do to be so blue? Bear with me.

Chapter 1

It goes a long way back, some twenty years. All my life I had been looking for

---

① Brother Jack:兄弟会头目杰克兄弟,书中人物。

— 81 —

something, and everywhere I turned someone tried to tell me what it was. I accepted their answers too, though they were often in contradiction and even self-contradictory. I was naïve. I was looking for myself and asking everyone except myself questions which I, and only I, could answer. It took me a long time and much painful boomeranging of my expectations to achieve a realization everyone else appears to have been born with: That I am nobody but myself. But first I had to discover that I am an invisible man!

And yet I am no freak of nature, nor of history. I was in the cards, other things having been equal (or unequal) eighty-five years ago. I am not ashamed of my grandparents for having been slaves. I am only ashamed of myself for having at one time been ashamed. About eighty-five years ago they were told that they were free, united with others of our country in everything pertaining to the common good, and, in everything social, separate like the fingers of the hand. And they believed it. They exulted in it. They stayed in their place, worked hard, and brought up my father to do the same. But my grandfather is the one. He was an odd old guy, my grandfather, and I am told I take after him. It was he who caused the trouble. On his deathbed he called my father to him and said, "Son, after I'm gone I want you to keep up the good fight. I never told you, but our life is a war and I have been a traitor all my born days, a spy in the enemy's country ever since I give up my gun back in the Reconstruction①. Live with your head in the lion's mouth. I want you to overcome 'em with yeses, undermine 'em with grins, agree 'em to death and destruction, let 'em swoller you till they vomit or bust wide open." They thought the old man had gone out of his mind. He had been the meekest of men. The younger children were rushed from the room, the shades drawn and the flame of the lamp turned so low that it sputtered on the wick like the old man's breathing. "Learn it to the younguns," he whispered fiercely; then he died.

But my folks were more alarmed over his last words than over his dying. It was as though he had not died at all, his words caused so much anxiety. I was warned emphatically to forget what he had said and, indeed, this is the first time it has been mentioned outside the family circle. It had a tremendous effect upon me, however. I could never be sure of what he meant. Grandfather had been a quiet old man who never made any trouble, yet on his deathbed he had called himself a traitor and a spy, and he had spoken of his meekness as a dangerous activity. It became a constant puzzle which lay unanswered in the back of my mind. And whenever things went well for me I remembered my grandfather and felt guilty and uncomfortable. It was as though I was carrying out his advice in spite of myself. And to make it worse, everyone loved me for it. I was praised by the most lily-white men of the town. I was considered an example of desirable conduct— just as my grandfather had been. And what puzzled me was that the old man had defined it as *treachery*. When I was praised for my conduct I felt a guilt that in some way I was doing something that was really against the wishes of the white folks, that if they had understood they would have desired me to act just the opposite, that I should have been sulky and

---

① Reconstruction:美国南方重建时期(1865—1877)。

mean, and that that really would have been what they wanted, even though they were fooled and thought they wanted me to act as I did. It made me afraid that some day they would look upon me as a traitor and I would be lost. Still I was more afraid to act any other way because they didn't like that at all. The old man's words were like a curse. On my graduation day I delivered an oration in which I showed that humility was the secret, indeed, the very essence of progress. (Not that I believed this—how could I, remembering my grandfather? —I only believed that it worked.) It was a great success. Everyone praised me and I was invited to give the speech at a gathering of the town's leading white citizens. It was a triumph for our whole community.

It was in the main ballroom of the leading hotel. When I got there I discovered that it was onthe occasion of a smoker, and I was told that since I was to be there anyway I might as well take part in the battle royal to be fought by some of my schoolmates as part of the entertainment. The battle royal came first.

All of the town's big shots were there in their tuxedoes, wolfing down the buffet foods, drinking beer and whiskey and smoking black cigars. It was a large room with a high ceiling. Chairs were arranged in neat rows around three sides of a portable boxing ring. The fourth side was clear, revealing a gleaming space of polished floor. I had some misgivings over the battle royal, by the way. Not from a distaste for fighting, but because I didn't care too much for the other fellows who were to take part. They were tough guys who seemed to have no grandfather's curse worrying their minds. No one could mistake their toughness. And besides, I suspected that fighting a battle royal might detract from the dignity of my speech. In those pre-invisible days I visualized myself as a potential Booker T. Washington①. But the other fellows didn't care too much for me either, and there were nine of them. I felt superior to them in my way, and I didn't like the manner in which we were all crowded together into the servants' elevator. Nor did they like my being there. In fact, as the warmly lighted floors flashed past the elevator we had words over the fact that I, by taking part in the fight, had knocked one of their friends out of a night's work.

We were led out of the elevator through a rococo16 hall into an anteroom and told to get into our fighting togs. Each of us was issued a pair of boxing gloves and ushered out into the big mirrored hall, which we entered looking cautiously about us and whispering, lest we might accidentally be heard above the noise of the room. It was foggy with cigar smoke. And already the whiskey was taking effect. I was shocked to see some of the most important men of the town quite tipsy. They were all there—bankers, lawyers, judges, doctors, fire chiefs, teachers, merchants. Even one of the more fashionable pastors. Something we could not see was going on up front. A clarinet was vibrating sensuously and the men were standing up and moving eagerly forward. We were a small tight group, clustered together, our bare upper bodies touching and shining with anticipatory sweat; while up front the big shots were becoming increasingly excited over something we still could not see. Suddenly I heard the school superintendent, who had told me to come, yell,

---

① Booker T. Washington：布克·华盛顿，黑奴出生的美国教育家，强调美国黑人的经济平等胜过社会平等。

"Bring up the shines①, gentlemen! Bring up the little shines!"

We were rushed up to the front of the ballroom, where it smelled even more strongly of tobacco and whiskey. Then we were pushed into place. I almost wet my pants. A sea of faces, some hostile, some amused, ringed around us, and in the center, facing us, stood a magnificent blonde—stark naked. There was dead silence. I felt a blast of cold air chill me. I tried to back away, but they were behind me and around me. Some of the boys stood with lowered heads, trembling. I felt a wave of irrational guilt and fear. My teeth chattered, my skin turned to goose flesh, my knees knocked. Yet I was strongly attracted and looked in spite of myself. Had the price of looking been blindness, I would have looked. The hair was yellow like that of a circus kewpie doll, the face heavily powdered and rouged, as though to form an abstract mask, the eyes hollow and smeared a cool blue, the color of a baboon's butt. I felt a desire to spit upon her as my eyes brushed slowly over her body. Her breasts were firm and round as the domes of East Indian temples, and I stood so close as to see the fine skin texture and beads of pearly perspiration glistening like dew around the pink and erected buds of her nipples. I wanted at one and the sametime to run from the room, to sink through the floor, or go to her and cover her from my eyes and the eyes of the others with my body; to feel the soft thighs, to caress her and destroy her, to love her and murder her, to hide from her, and yet to stroke where below the small American flag tattooed upon her belly her thighs formed a capital V. I had a notion that of all in the room she saw only me with her impersonal eyes.

And then she began to dance, a slow sensuous movement; the smoke of a hundred cigars clinging to her like the thinnest of veils. She seemed like a fair bird-girl girdled in veils calling to me from the angry surface of some gray and threatening sea. I was transported. Then I became aware of the clarinet playing and the big shots yelling at us. Some threatened us if we looked and others if we did not. On my right I saw one boy faint. And now a man grabbed a silver pitcher from a table and stepped close as he dashed ice water upon him and stood him up and forced two of us to support him as his head hung and moans issued from his thick bluish lips. Another boy began to plead to go home. He was the largest of the group, wearing dark red fighting trunks much too small to conceal the erection which projected from him as though in answer to the insinuating low-registered moaning of the clarinet. He tried to hide himself with his boxing gloves.

And all the while the blonde continued dancing, smiling faintly at the big shots who watched her with fascination, and faintly smiling at our fear. I noticed a certain merchant who followed her hungrily, his lips loose and drooling. He was a large man who wore diamond studs in a shirtfront which swelled with the ample paunch underneath, and each time the blonde swayed her undulating hips he ran his hand through the thin hair of his bald head and, with his arms upheld, his posture clumsy like that of an intoxicated panda, wound his belly in a slow and obscene grind. This creature was completely hypnotized. The music had quickened. As the dancer flung herself about with a detached expression on her

---

① shines: (贬)黑家伙。

face, the men began reaching out to touch her. I could see their beefy fingers sink into the soft flesh. Some of the others tried to stop them and she began to move around the floor in graceful circles, as they gave chase, slipping and sliding over the polished floor. It was mad. Chairs went crashing, drinks were spilt, as they ran laughing and howling after her. They caught her just as she reached a door, raised her from the floor, and tossed her as college boys are tossed at a hazing, and above her red, fixed-smiling lips I saw the terror and disgust in her eyes, almost like my own terror and that which I saw in some of the other boys. As I watched, they tossed her twice and her soft breasts seemed to flatten against the air and her legs flung wildly as she spun. Some of the more sober ones helped her to escape. And I started off the floor, heading for the anteroom with the rest of the boys.

Some were still crying and in hysteria. But as we tried to leave we were stopped and ordered to get into the ring. There was nothing to do but what we were told. All ten of us climbed under the ropes and allowed ourselves to be blindfolded with broad bands of white cloth. One of the men seemed to feel a bit sympathetic and tried to cheer us up as we stood with our backs against the ropes. Some of us tried to grin. "See that boy over there?" one of the men said. "I want you to run across at the bell and give it to him right in the belly. If you don't get him, I'm going to get you. I don't like his looks." Each of us was told the same. The blindfolds were put on. Yet even then I had been going over my speech. In my mind each word was as bright as flame. I felt the cloth pressed into place, and frowned so that it would be loosened when I relaxed.

But now I felt a sudden fit of blind terror. I was unused to darkness. It was as though I had suddenly found myself in a dark room filled with poisonous cottonmouths. I could hear the bleary voices yelling insistently for the battle royal to begin.

"Get going in there!"

"Let me at that big nigger!"

I strained to pick up the school superintendent's voice, as though to squeeze some security out of that slightly more familiar sound.

"Let me at those black sonsabitches!" someone yelled.

"No, Jackson, no!" another voice yelled. "Here, somebody, help me hold Jack."

"I want to get at that ginger-colored nigger. Tear him limb from limb," the first voice yelled.

I stood against the ropes trembling. For in those days I was what they called gingercolored, and he sounded as though he might crunch me between his teeth like a crisp ginger cookie.

Quite a struggle was going on. Chairs were being kicked about and I could hear voices grunting as with a terrific effort. I wanted to see, to see more desperately than ever before. But the blindfold was tight as a thick skin-puckering scab and when I raised my gloved hands to push the layers of white aside a voice yelled, "Oh, no you don't, black bastard! Leave that alone!"

"Ring the bell before Jackson kills him a coon①!" someone boomed in the sudden

---

① coon：黑鬼。

silence. And I heard the bell clang and the sound of the feet scuffing forward.

A glove smacked against my head. I pivoted, striking out stiffly as someone went past, and felt the jar ripple along the length of my arm to my shoulder. Then it seemed as though all nine of the boys had turned upon me at once. Blows pounded me from all sides while I struck out as best I could. So many blows landed upon me that I wondered if I were not the only blindfolded fighter in the ring, or if the man called Jackson hadn't succeeded in getting me after all.

Blindfolded, I could no longer control my motions. I had no dignity. I stumbled about like a baby or a drunken man. The smoke had become thicker and with each new blow it seemed to sear and further restrict my lungs. My saliva became like hot bitter glue. A glove connected with my head, filling my mouth with warm blood. It was everywhere. I could not tell if the moisture I felt upon my body was sweat or blood. A blow landed hard against the nape of my neck. I felt myself going over, my head hitting the floor. Streaks of blue light filled the black world behind the blindfold. I lay prone, pretending that I was knocked out, but felt myself seized by hands and yanked to my feet. "Get going, black boy! Mix it up!" My arms were like lead, my head smarting from blows. I managed to feel my way to the ropes and held on, trying to catch my breath. A glove landed in my mid-section and I went over again, feeling as though the smoke had become a knife jabbed into my guts. Pushed this way and that by the legs milling around me, I finally pulled erect and discovered that I could see the black, sweat-washed forms weaving in the smoky-blue atmosphere like drunken dancers weaving to the rapid drum-like thuds of blows.

Everyone fought hysterically. It was complete anarchy. Everybody fought everybody else. No group fought together for long. Two, three, four, fought one, then turned to fight each other, were themselves attacked. Blows landed below the belt and in the kidney, with the gloves open as well as closed, and with my eye partly opened now there was not so much terror. I moved carefully, avoiding blows, although not too many to attract attention, fighting from group to group. The boys groped about like blind, cautious crabs crouching to protect their mid-sections, their heads pulled in short against their shoulders, their arms stretched nervously before them, with their fists testing the smoke-filled air like the knobbed feelers of hypersensitive snails. In one corner I glimpsed a boy violently punching the air and heard him scream in pain as he smashed his hand against a ring post. For a second I saw him bent over holding his hand, then going down as a blow caught his unprotected head. I played one group against the other, slipping in and throwing a punch then stepping out of range while pushing the others into the melee to take the blows blindly aimed at me. The smoke was agonizing and there were no rounds, no bells at three-minute intervals to relieve our exhaustion. The room spun round me, a swirl of lights, smoke, sweating bodies surrounded by tense white faces. I bled from both nose and mouth, the blood spattering upon my chest.

The men kept yelling, "Slug him, black boy! Knock his gets out!"

"Uppercut him! Kill him! Kill that big boy!"

Taking a fake fall, I saw a boy going down heavily beside me as though we were felled by a single blow, saw a sneaker-clad foot shoot into his groin as the two who had knocked him down stumbled upon him. I rolled out of range, feeling a twinge of nausea.

The harder we fought the more threatening the men became. And yet, I had begun to worry about my speech again. How would it go? Would they recognize my ability? What would they give me?

I was fighting automatically when suddenly I noticed that one after another of the boys was leaving the ring. I was surprised, filled with panic, as though I had been left alone with an unknown danger. Then I understood. The boys had arranged it among themselves. It was the custom for the two men left in the ring to slug it out for the winner's prize. I discovered this too late. When the bell sounded two men in tuxedoes leaped into the ring and removed the blindfold. I found myself facing Tatlock, the biggest of the gang. I felt sick at my stomach. Hardly had the bell stopped ringing in my ears than it clanged again and I saw him moving swiftly toward me. Thinking of nothing else to do I hit him smash on the nose. He kept coming, bringing the rank sharp violence of stale sweat. His face was a black blank of a face, only his eyes alive—with hate of me and aglow with a feverish terror from what had happened to us all. I became anxious. I wanted to deliver my speech and he came at me as though he meant to beat it out of me. I smashed him again and again, taking his blows as they came. Then on a sudden impulse I struck him lightly and as we clinched, I whispered, "Fake like I knocked you out, you can have the prize."

"I'll break your behind," he whispered hoarsely.

"For *them*?"

"For *me*, sonofabitch!"

They were yelling for us to break it up and Tatlock spun me half around with a blow, and as a joggled camera sweeps in a reeling scene, I saw the howling red faces crouching tense beneath the cloud of blue-gray smoke. For a moment the world wavered, unraveled, flowed, then my head cleared and Tatlock bounced before me. That fluttering shadow before my eyes was his jabbing left hand. Then falling forward, my head against his damp shoulder, I whispered,

"I'll make it five dollars more."

"Go to hell!"

But his muscles relaxed a trifle beneath my pressure and I breathed, "Seven?"

"Give it to your ma," he said, ripping me beneath the heart.

And while I still held him I butted him and moved away. I felt myself bombarded with punches. I fought back with hopeless desperation. I wanted to deliver my speech more than anything else in the world, because I felt that only these men could judge truly my ability, and now this stupid clown was ruining my chances. I began fighting carefully now, moving in to punch him and out again with my greater speed. A lucky blow to his chin and I had him going too—until I heard a loud voice yell, "I got my money on the big boy."

Hearing this, I almost dropped my guard. I was confused: Should I try to win against the voice out there? Would not this go against my speech, and was not this a moment for humility, for nonresistance? A blow to my head as I danced about sent my right eye popping like a jack-in-the-box and settled my dilemma. The room went red as I fell. It was a dream fall, my body languid and fastidious as to where to land, until the floor became impatient and smashed up to meet me. A moment later I came to. An hypnotic voice said FIVE emphatically. And I lay there, hazily watching a dark red spot of my own blood shaping itself into a butterfly, glistening and soaking into the soiled gray world of the canvas.

When the voice drawled TEN I was lifted up and dragged to a chair. I sat dazed. My eye pained and swelled with each throb of my pounding heart and I wondered if now I would be allowed to speak. I was wringing wet, my mouth still bleeding. We were grouped along the wall now. The other boys ignored me as they congratulated Tatlock and speculated as to how much they would be paid. One boy whimpered over his smashed hand. Looking up front, I saw attendants in white jackets rolling the portable ring away and placing a small square rug in the vacant space surrounded by chairs. Perhaps, I thought, I will stand on the rug to deliver my speech.

Then the M. C. ① called to us, "Come on up here boys and get your money."

We ran forward to where the men laughed and talked in their chairs, waiting. Everyone seemed friendly now.

"There it is on the rug," the man said. I saw the rug covered with coins of all dimensions and a few crumpled bills. But what excited me, scattered here and there, were the gold pieces.

"Boys, it's all yours," the man said. "You get all you grab."

"That's right, Sambo②," a blond man said, winking at me confidentially.

I trembled with excitement, forgetting my pain. I would get the gold and the bills, I thought. I would use both hands. I would throw my body against the boys nearest me to block them from the gold.

"Get down around the rug now," the man commanded, "and don't anyone touch it until I give the signal."

"This ought to be good," I heard.

As told, we got around the square rug on our knees. Slowly the man raised his freckled hand as we followed it upward with our eyes.

I heard, "These niggers look like they're about to pray!"

Then, "Ready," the man said. "Go!"

I lunged for a yellow coin lying on the blue design of the carpet, touching it and sending a surprised shriek to join those rising around me. I tried frantically to remove my hand but could not let go. A hot, violent force tore through my body, shaking me like a wet rat. The rug was electrified. The hair bristled up on my head as I shook myself free. My muscles jumped, my nerves jangled, writhed. But I saw that this was not stopping the other boys. Laughing in fear and embarrassment, some were holding back and scooping up the coins knocked off by the painful contortions of the others. The men roared above us as

---

① M. C.: master of ceremonies, 司仪。
② Sambo:(贬)傻宝,黑鬼。

we struggled.

"Pick it up, goddamnit, pick it up!" someone called like a bass-voiced parrot. "Go on, get it!"

I crawled rapidly around the floor, picking up the coins, trying to avoid the coppers and to get greenbacks and the gold. Ignoring the shock by laughing, as I brushed the coins off quickly, I discovered that I could contain the electricity—a contradiction, but it works. Then the men began to push us onto the rug. Laughing embarrassedly, we struggled out of their hands and kept after the coins. We were all wet and slippery and hard to hold. Suddenly I saw a boy lifted into the air, glistening with sweat like a circus seal, and dropped, his wet back landing flush upon the charged rug, heard him yell and saw him literally dance upon his back, his elbows beating a frenzied tattoo upon the floor, his muscles twitching like the flesh of a horse stung by many flies. When he finally rolled off, his face was gray and no one stopped him when he ran from the floor amid booming laughter.

"Get the money," the M. C. called. "That's good hard American cash!"

And we snatched and grabbed, snatched and grabbed. I was careful not to come too close to the rug now, and when I felt the hot whiskey breath descend upon me like a cloud of foul air I reached out and grabbed the leg of a chair. It was occupied and I held on desperately.

"Leggo, nigger! Leggo!"

The huge face wavered down to mine as he tried to push me free. But my body was slippery and he was too drunk. It was Mr. Colcord, who owned a chain of movie houses and "entertainment palaces." Each time he grabbed me I slipped out of his hands. It became a real struggle. I feared the rug more than I did the drunk, so I held on, surprising myself for a moment by trying to topple *him* upon the rug. It was such an enormous idea that I found myself actually carrying it out. I tried not to be obvious, yet when I grabbed his leg, trying to tumble him out of the chair, he raised up roaring with laughter, and, looking at me with soberness dead in the eye, kicked me viciously in the chest. The chair leg flew out of my hand and I felt myself going and rolled. It was as though I had rolled through a bed of hot coals. It seemed a whole century would pass before I would roll free, a century in which I was seared through the deepest levels of my body to the fearful breath within me and the breath seared and heated to the point of explosion. It'll all be over in a flash, I thought as I rolled clear. It'll all be over in a flash.

But not yet, the men on the other side were waiting, red faces swollen as though from apoplexy as they bent forward in their chairs. Seeing their fingers coming toward me I rolled away as a fumbled football rolls off the receiver's fingertips, back into the coals. That time I luckily sent the rug sliding out of place and heard the coins ringing against the floor and the boys scuffling to pick them up and the M. C. calling, "All right, boys, that's all. Go get dressed and get your money."

I was limp as a dish rag. My back felt as though it had been beaten with wires.

When we had dressed the M. C. came in and gave us each five dollars, except Tatlock, who got ten for being last in the ring. Then he told us to leave. I was not to get a chance to deliver my speech, I thought. I was going out into the dim alley in despair when I was stopped and told to go back. I returned to the ballroom, where the men were pushing back their chairs and gathering in groups to talk.

The M. C. knocked on a table for quiet. "Gentlemen," he said, "we almost forgot an important part of the program. A most serious part, gentlemen. This boy was brought here to deliver a speech which he made at his graduation yesterday ... "

"Bravo!"

"I'm told that he is the smartest boy we've got out there in Greenwood. I'm told that he knows more big words than a pocket-sized dictionary."

Much applause and laughter.

"So now, gentlemen, I want you to give him your attention."

There was still laughter as I faced them, my mouth dry, my eye throbbing. I began slowly, but evidently my throat was tense, because they began shouting, "Louder! Louder!"

"We of the younger generation extol the wisdom of that great leader and educator[①]," I shouted, "who first spoke these flaming words of wisdom: 'A ship lost at sea for many days suddenly sighted a friendly vessel. From the mast of the unfortunate vessel was seen a signal: "Water, water; we die of thirst!" The answer from the friendly vessel came back: "Cast down your bucket where you are." The captain of the distressed vessel, at last heeding the injunction, cast down his bucket, and it came up full of fresh sparkling water from the mouth of the Amazon River. ' And like him I say, and in his words, 'To those of my race who depend upon bettering their condition in a foreign land, or who underestimate the importance of cultivating friendly relations with the southern white man, who is his next-door neighbor, I would say: "Cast down your bucket where you are"—cast it down in making friends in every manly way of the people of all races by whom we are surrounded ... '"

I spoke automatically and with such fervor that I did not realize that the men were still talking and laughing until my dry mouth, filling up with blood from the cut, almost strangled me. I coughed, wanting to stop and go to one of the tall brass, sand-filled spittoons to relieve myself, but a few of the men, especially the superintendent, were listening and I was afraid. So I gulped it down, blood, saliva and all, and continued. (What powers of endurance I had during those days! What enthusiasm! What a belief in the rightness of things!) I spoke even louder in spite of the pain. But still they talked and still they laughed, as though deaf with cotton in dirty ears. So I spoke with greater emotional emphasis. I closed my ears and swallowed blood until I was nauseated. The speech seemed a hundred times as long as before, but I could not leave out a single word. All had to be said, each memorized nuance considered, rendered. Nor was that all. Whenever I uttered a word of three or more syllables a group of voices would yell for me to repeat it. I used the phrase "social responsibility" and they yelled:

---

① that great leader and educator: 指布克·华盛顿。

"What's that word you say, boy?"

"Social responsibility," I said.

"What?"

"Social ..."

"Louder."

"... responsibility."

"More!"

"Respon—"

"Repeat!"

"—sibility."

The room filled with the uproar of laughter until, no doubt distracted by having to gulp down my blood, I made a mistake and yelled a phrase I had often seen denounced in newspaper editorials, heard debated in private.

"Social ..."

"What?" they yelled.

"... equality—"

The laughter hung smokelike in the sudden stillness. I opened my eyes, puzzled. Sounds of displeasure filled the room. The M. C. rushed forward. They shouted hostile phrases at me. But I did not understand.

A small dry mustached man in the front row blared out, "Say that slowly, son!"

"What, sir?"

"What you just said!"

"Social responsibility, sir," I said.

"You weren't being smart, were you, boy?" he said, not unkindly.

"No, sir!"

"You sure that about 'equality' was a mistake?"

"Oh, yes, sir," I said. "I was swallowing blood."

"Well, you had better speak more slowly so we can understand. We mean to do right by you, but you've got to know your place at all times. All right, now, go on with your speech."

I was afraid. I wanted to leave but I wanted also to speak and I was afraid they'd snatch me down.

"Thank you, sir," I said, beginning where I had left off, and having them ignore me as before.

Yet when I finished there was a thunderous applause. I was surprised to see the superintendent come forth with a package wrapped in white tissue paper, and, gesturing for quiet, address the men.

"Gentlemen, you see that I did not overpraise this boy. He makes a good speech and some day he'll lead his people in the proper paths. And I don't have to tell you that that is important in these days and times. This is a good, smart boy, and so to encourage him in the right direction, in the name of the Board of Education I wish to present him a prize in the form of this ..."

He paused, removing the tissue paper and revealing a gleaming calfskin brief case.

"...in the form of this first-class article from Shad Whitmore's shop."

"Boy," he said, addressing me, "take this prize and keep it well. Consider it a badge of office. Prize it. Keep developing as you are and some day it will be filled with important papers that will help shape the destiny of your people."

I was so moved that I could hardly express my thanks. A rope of bloody saliva forming a shape like an undiscovered continent drooled upon the leather and I wiped it quickly away. I felt an importance that I had never dreamed.

"Open it and see what's inside," I was told.

My fingers a-tremble, I complied, smelling the fresh leather and finding an official-looking document inside. It was a scholarship to the state college for Negroes. My eyes filled with tears and I ran awkwardly off the floor.

I was overjoyed; I did not even mind when I discovered that the gold pieces I had scrambled for were brass pocket tokens advertising a certain make of automobile.

When I reached home everyone was excited. Next day the neighbors came to congratulate me. I even felt safe from grandfather, whose deathbed curse usually spoiled my triumphs. I stood beneath his photograph with my brief case in hand and smiled triumphantly into his stolid black peasant's face. It was a face that fascinated me. The eyes seemed to follow everywhere I went.

That night I dreamed I was at a circus with him and that he refused to laugh at the clowns no matter what they did. Then later he told me to open my brief case and read what was inside and I did, finding an official envelope stamped with the state seal; and inside the envelope I found another and another, endlessly, and I thought I would fall of weariness. "Them's years," he said. "Now open that one." And I did and in it I found an engraved document containing a short message in letters of gold. "Read it," my grandfather said. "Out loud!"

"To Whom It May Concern," I intoned. "Keep This Nigger-Boy Running."

I awoke with the old man's laughter ringing in my ears.

(It was a dream I was to remember and dream again for many years after. But at that time I had no insight into its meaning. First I had to attend college.)

Questions for Discussion

1. The novel is entitled "*Invisible Man*" and the invisible man is the narrator and protagonist of the story. Is his invisibility literal or figurative? What does it mean for a black to be invisible in a white world?

2. How does the narrator/protagonist feel upon hearing his grandfather's words at deathbed? What causes the feeling?

3. How do you relate the invisible man as a model black citizen in the South to the ideas advocated by Booker T. Washington, who is mentioned many times in this novel?

3. The Color Purple

作者简介

艾丽斯·沃克(1944—　)是当代美国黑人文学最有影响力的人物之一,黑人女性主义的倡导人,提出"妇女主义"以区别于白人女性主义。她出生于佐治亚州一个贫苦佃农家庭,8岁时,一只眼睛被打瞎。高中毕业后去了亚特兰大的斯佩尔曼学院读书,后转到纽约的萨拉·劳伦斯学院。大学三年级时她去非洲访问,非洲后来成为她小说的一个背景。1965年大学毕业后,她前往密西西比州工作,积极投身民权运动,这段经历为她的小说《梅丽蒂恩》提供了素材。1970年,她重新发现了哈莱姆文艺复兴时期的黑人女作家赫斯顿,后者对沃克产生了重大影响。

沃克的创作包括长篇小说、诗歌、短篇故事以及文学批评。主要有长篇小说《格兰奇·科普兰的第三次生命》(1970)、《梅丽蒂恩》(1976)、《紫色》(1982)、《我熟悉的一切之神庙》(1989)、《拥有欢乐的秘密》(1992)、《我父亲的微笑之光》(1989)、《魔鬼是我的敌人》(2008),诗集《一度》(1968)、《笃信地球之善》(2003),短篇小说集《爱情与麻烦:黑人妇女的故事》(1973)、《伤心前行》(2000),及批评文集《寻找我们母亲的花园》(1983)等。

作品简介与赏析

沃克的代表作《紫色》为她赢得美国国家图书奖和普利策小说奖,刻画了20世纪初挣扎在社会最底层的美国黑人妇女的生活原貌和心路历程。全书采用书信体,以朴素的文字、真挚的情感和生动的黑人土语记录了黑人妇女们当下的生活。全书由主人公西丽及其妹妹的书信组成。西丽14岁时被继父强暴,生下两个孩子都被他送人,孤苦无依的西丽只能给上帝写信倾诉痛苦。嫁给某某先生后,常遭丈夫打骂;妹妹耐蒂为躲避继父纠缠前来投靠,却因拒绝某某先生的示爱被后者赶走。耐蒂后来去非洲当传教士,她给西丽的来信却被某某先生藏了起来。知道了实情的西丽非常愤怒,在某某先生的情人萨格的帮助下,离家前往孟菲斯做裁缝谋生,获得了经济上的独立。某某先生后来也逐渐意识到自己的错误而真心忏悔,两人言归于好。小说结尾,耐蒂带着西丽的孩子从非洲回来,一家人最终团聚。

沃克把《紫色》称为一部历史小说,但它不同于通常意义上的"正史",而是民间的历史,聚焦黑人家庭,尤其是黑人妇女当下生活的历史。这样的历史叙事与人们意识之中的传统历史有着很大出入。小说呈现了南方黑人妇女那段无人提及的历史,揭示了黑人内部的性别压迫和两性冲突,如继父和丈夫某某先生对西丽的凌辱和欺压,儿媳索菲亚的女性抗争意识以及由此引发的与丈夫之间的矛盾。在刻画黑人妇女追求自我解放和尊严的同时,沃克也准确抓住了黑人男性的复杂心理:他们既是受害者,同时又是施害者,他们将种族歧视带给自己的创伤和无力感转移、发泄到妻儿身上。

从底层黑人妇女的视角出发来记录历史是该小说的一大特色。此外,作家对文类的选择和语言的运用也独具匠心。

首先,沃克对书信体小说的挪用深化了黑人女性主体复归这一主题。在《紫色》中,书信既是贯穿全文的内容,也构成了小说的叙事框架。值得注意的是,西丽的大部分信件都是写给上帝这个不存在的读者的,在受述人缺席的情况下,原本作为叙述核心的叙述内容让位于叙述行为本身,后者对于叙述人本人的意义得以凸显。写信上升为小说最为重要的情节,正是写信这一行为,使得西丽从失语状态中挣脱出来,让她在自己日益变得自信强大的声音中找回自我。书信见证了西丽的成长,让她从逆来顺受的无知少女转变为自立坚强的新女性,这个历程使黑人女性书写本身成为小说的主题。

其次,西丽用黑人土语写信,而受过教育的妹妹则用标准英语写信。相比之下,后者的语言显然不如前者那样生动传神,因为西丽富于本土特色的表达抓住了黑人民间语言的精髓,得以和思想、话语紧密联系起来。换句话说,基于共同现实和心理意识的黑人语言负载着黑人文化及其价值观,以一种差异性的重复,改写了白人的标准英语及其内含的价值观,在与主流话语形成对抗的同时消解后者。

此外,沃克提出的"妇女主义"概念是其作品解读的重要索引。赫斯顿的小说,特别是《他们眼望上苍》,以浓厚的南方黑人文化和黑人女性特有的语言、形象和象征,深深地影响着沃克。无论从主题还是形式上来看,沃克的作品都是对这位"精神向导"的文学先辈的致敬。如今,《紫色》已成为"黑人妇女小说的一种格式"。可以说,沃克的"妇女主义"模式,正是将赫斯顿的作品作为黑人女性写作的范本,建构出来的现代黑人妇女文学的经典模式。沃克致力于塑造那些经历了女性意识和族群意识的双重觉醒,自立自强、互相关爱的黑人妇女形象,致力于建构一个黑人民族两性和谐的理想社会。换句话说,妇女主义体现了女性主义的多元性,它既从种族的视角去审视女性主义研究,又从性属的视角去审视黑人研究,以差异性的表述——汇合了种族、性属、阶级的多声话语——拓展了二者,是黑人妇女独特的文化经历在美学上的表述。

《紫色》发表后好评如潮,1985年被改编成电影,2005年又被改编成音乐剧,进一步扩大了作者的影响力。

下面的选文出自《紫色》的三封信。第一封信叙述了西丽的儿媳——性格勇猛刚烈的索菲亚——的不幸遭遇。因为对市长太太顶嘴,又用拳头回敬了市长的耳光,索菲亚被一群警察殴打致残后关进了监狱。第二封信记录了索菲亚在狱中遭受的非人待遇,以及她虽然表面顺从,却日夜想着杀人的疯狂的心理状态。第三封信和前两封信在时间上相隔近12年,讲述索菲亚被亲朋好友设法弄出监狱后在市长家度过十来年奴隶般的帮佣生活,终于得以回家与亲人相聚,却变得畏畏缩缩,失去了以往的斗志。席上西丽宣布自己的计划——要离开某某先生,追随萨格前往孟菲斯开创新生活。此举引起轩然大波,遭到某某先生的极力反对,却得到家中妇女们的一致赞同。西丽等女性的勇气和姐妹情谊极大地鼓舞了索菲亚,她的抗争精神开始复苏。三封信都出自西丽,用黑人口语体创作,与标准英语在拼写和语法上都有着较大差异。

Dear God,

Harpo① mope. Wipe the counter, light a cigarette, look outdoors, walk up and down. Little Squeak② run long all up under him trying to git his tension. Baby this, she say, Baby that. Harpo look through her head, blow smoke.

Squeak come over to the corner where me and Mr. _____③ at. She got two bright gold teef in the side of her mouth, generally grin all the time. Now she cry. Miss Celie, she say, What the matter with Harpo?

---

① Harpo:哈波,西丽丈夫某某先生的长子。
② Squeak:哈波的情人。
③ Mr. _____:某某先生,西丽的丈夫。

Sofia① in jail, I say.

In jail? She look like I say Sofia on the moon.

What she in jail for? she ast.

Sassing the mayor's wife, I say.

Squeak pull up a chair. Look down my throat.

What your real name? I ast her. She say, Mary Agnes.

Make Harpo call you by your real name, I say. Then maybe he see you even when he trouble.

She look at me puzzle. I let it go. I tell her what one of Sofia sister tell me and Mr. _____.

Sofia and the prizefighter② and all the children got in the prizefighter car and went to town. Clam out on the street looking like somebody. Just then the mayor and his wife come by.

All these children, say the mayor's wife, digging in her pocketbook. Cute as little buttons though, she say. She stop, put her hand on one of the children head. Say, and such strong white teef.

Sofia and the prizefighter don't say nothing. Wait for her to pass. Mayor wait too, stand back and tap his foot, watch her with a little smile. Now Millie, he say. Always going on over colored. ③ Miss Millie finger the children some more, finally look at Sofia and the prizefighter. She look at the prizefighter car. She eye Sofia wristwatch. She say to Sofia, All your children so clean, she say, would you like to work for me, be my maid?

Sofia say, Hell no.

She say, What you say?

Sofia say, Hell no.

Mayor look at Sofia, push his wife out the way. Stick out his chest. Girl, what you say to Miss Millie?

Sofia say, I say, Hell no.

He slap her.

I stop telling it right there.

Squeak on the edge of her seat. She wait. Look down my throat some more.

No need to say no more, Mr. _____ say. You know what happen if somebody slap Sofia.

Squeak go white as a sheet. Naw, she say.

Naw nothing, I say. Sofia knock the man down.

The polices come, start slinging the children off the mayor, bang they heads together. Sofia really start to fight. They drag her to the ground.

This far as I can go with it, look like. My eyes git full of water and my throat close.

---

① Sofia：索菲亚，哈波的妻子。

② the prizefighter：拳击手，索菲亚的情人。

③ Always going on over colored：你老要打量这些黑人。

Poor Squeak all scrunch down in her chair, trembling.

They beat Sofia, Mr. _____ say.

Squeak fly up like she sprung, run over hind the counter to Harpo, put her arms round him. They hang together a long time, cry.

What the prizefighter do in all this? I ast Sofia sister, Odessa. ①

He want to jump in, she say. Sofia say No, take the children home.

Polices have they guns on him anyway. One move, he dead. Six of them, you know.

Mr. _____ go plead with the sheriff to let us see Sofia. Bub② be in so much trouble, look so much like the sheriff, he and Mr. _____ almost on family terms. Just long as Mr. _____ know he colored.

Sheriff say, She a crazy woman, your boy's wife. You know that?

Mr. _____ say, Yassur, us do know it. Been trying to tell Harpo she crazy for twelve years. Since way before they marry. Sofia come from crazy peoples, Mr. _____ say, it not all her fault. And then again, the sheriff know how womens is, anyhow.

Sheriff think bout the women he know, say, Yep, you right there.

Mr. _____ say, Wegon tell her she crazy too, if us ever do git in to see her.

Sheriff say, Well make sure you do. And tell her she lucky she alive.

When I see Sofia I don't know why she still alive. They crack her skull, they crack her ribs. They tear her nose loose on one side. They blind her in one eye. She swole from head to foot. Her tongue the size of my arm, it stick out tween her teef like a piece of rubber. She can't talk. And she just about the color of a eggplant.

Scare me so bad I near bout drop my grip. But I don't. I put it on the floor of the cell, take out comb and brush, nightgown, witch hazel and alcohol and I start to work on her. The colored tendant bring me water to wash her with, and I start at her two little slits for eyes.

Dear God,

They put Sofia to work in the prison laundry. All day long from five to eight she washing clothes. Dirty convict uniforms, nasty sheets and blankets piled way over her head. Us see her twice a month for half a hour. Her face yellow and sickly, her fingers look like fatty sausage.

Everything nasty here, she say, even the air. Food bad enough to kill you with it. Roaches here, mice, flies, lice and even a snake or two. If you say anything they strip you, make you sleep on a cement floor without a light.

How you manage? us ast.

Every time they ast me to do something, Miss Celie, I act like I'm you. I jump right up and do just what they say.

She look wild when she say that, and her bad eye wander round the room.

---

① Odessa：奥德莎，索菲亚的姐姐。
② Bub：鲍勃，某某先生的次子。

Mr. _____ suck in his breath. Harpo groan. Miss Shug① cuss. She come from Memphis special to see Sofia.

I can't fix my mouth to say how I feel.

I'm a good prisoner, she say. Best convict they ever see. They can't believe I'm the one sass the mayor's wife, knock the mayor down. She laugh. It sound like something from a song. The part where everybody done gone home but you.

Twelve years a long time to be good though, she say.

Maybe you git out on good behavior, say Harpo.

Good behavior ain't good enough for them, say Sofia. Nothing less than sliding on your belly with your tongue on they boots can even git they attention. I dream of murder, she say, I dream of murder sleep or wake.

Us don't say nothing.

How the children? she ast.

They all fine, say Harpo. Tween Odessa and Squeak, they git by.

Say thank you to Squeak, she say. Tell Odessa I think about her.

Dear Nettie②,

When I told Shug I'm writing to you instead of to God, she laugh. Nettie don't know these people, she say. Considering who I been writing to, this strike me funny.

It was Sofia you saw working as the mayor's maid. The woman you saw carrying the white woman's packages that day in town. Sofia Mr. _____'s son Harpo's wife. Polices lock her up for sassing the mayor's wife and hitting the mayor back. First she was in prison working in the laundry and dying fast. Then us got her move to the mayor's house. She had to sleep in a little room up under the house, but it was better than prison. Flies, maybe, but no rats.

Anyhow, they kept her eleven and a half years, give her six months off for good behavior so she could come home early to her family. Her bigger children married and gone, and her littlest children mad at her, don't know who she is. Think she act funny, look old and dote on that little white gal she raise.

Yesterday us all had dinner at Odessa's house. Odessa Sofia's sister. She raise the kids. Her and her husband Jack. Harpo's woman Squeak, and Harpo himself.

Sofia sit down at the big table like there's no room for her. Children reach cross her like she not there. Harpo and Squeak act like a old married couple. Children call Odessa mama. Call Squeak little mama. Call Sofia "Miss." The only one seem to pay her any tention at all is Harpo and Squeak's little girl, Suzie Q. She sit cross from Sofia and squinch up her eyes at her.

As soon as dinner over, Shug push back her chair and light a cigarette. Now is come the time to tell yall, she say.

---

① Shug：萨格，布鲁斯歌手，某某先生的情人，后成为西丽的好友和情人，并帮助她觉醒和成长。
② Nettie：耐蒂，西丽的妹妹。

Tell us what? Harpo ast.

Us leaving, she say.

Yeah? say Harpo, looking round for the coffee. And then looking over at Grady.

Us leaving, Shug say again. Mr. _____ look struck, like he always look when Shug say she going anywhere. He reach down and rub his stomach, look off side her head like nothing been said.

Grady say, Such good peoples, that's the truth. The salt of the earth. ① But—time to move on.

Squeak not saying nothing. She got her chin glued to her plate. I'm not saying nothing either. I'm waiting for the feathers to fly. ②

Celie is coming with us, say Shug.

Mr. _____ 's head swivel back straight. Say what? he ast.

Celie is coming to Memphis with me.

Over my dead body, Mr. _____ say.

You satisfied that what you want, Shug say, cool as clabber. ③

Mr. _____ start up from his seat, look at Shug, plop back down again. He look over at me. I thought you was finally happy, he say. What wrong now?

You a lowdown dog is what's wrong, I say. It's time to leave you and enter into the Creation. And your dead body just the welcome mat I need.

Say what? he ast. Shock.

All round the table folkses mouths be dropping open.

You took my sister Nettie away from me, I say. And she was the only person love me in the world.

Mr. _____ start to sputter. ButButButButBut. Sound like some kind of motor.

But Nettie and my children coming home soon, I say. And when she do, all us together gon whup your ass.

Nettie and your children! say Mr. ____. You talking crazy.

I got children, I say. Being brought up in Africa. Good schools, lots of fresh air and exercise. Turning out a heap better than the fools you didn't even try to raise.

Hold on, say Harpo.

Oh, hold on hell, I say. If you hadn't tried to rule over Sofia the white folks never would have caught her.

Sofia so surprise to hear me speak up she ain't chewed for ten minutes.

That's a lie, say Harpo.

A little truth in it, say Sofia.

Everybody look at her like they surprise she there. It like a voice speaking from the grave.

---

① The salt of the earth：都是些高尚的人。

② I'm waiting for the feathers to fly：我等着吵架呢。

③ Shug say, cool as clabber：萨格很冷静地说。

You was all rotten children, I say. You made my life a hell on earth. And your daddy here ain't dead horse's shit.

Mr. _____ reach over to slap me. I jab my case knife in his hand.

You bitch, he say. What will people say, you running off to Memphis like you don't have a house to look after?

Shug say, Albert. Try to think like you got some sense. Why any woman give a shit what people think is a mystery to me.

Well, say Grady, trying to bring light. A woman can't git a man if peoples talk.

Shug look at me and us giggle. Then us laugh sure nuff. Then Squeak start to laugh. Then Sofia. All us laugh and laugh.

Shug say, Ain't they something? Us say um hum, and slap the table, wipe the water from our eyes.

Harpo look at Squeak. Shut up Squeak, he say. It bad luck for women to laugh at men.

She say, Okay. She sit up straight, suck in her breath, try to press her face together.

He look at Sofia. She look at him and laugh in his face. I already had my bad luck, she say. I had enough to keep me laughing the rest of my life.

Harpo look at her like he did the night she knock Mary Agnes down. A little spark fly cross the table. ①

I got six children by this crazy woman, he mutter.

Five, she say.

He so outdone he can't even say, Say what?

He look over at the youngest child. She sullen, mean, mischeevous and too stubborn to live in this world. But he love her best of all. Her name Henrietta.

Henrietta, he say.

She say, Yesssss ... like they say it on the radio.

Everything she say confuse him. Nothing, he say. Then he say, Gogit me a cool glass of water.

She don't move.

Please, he say.

She go git the water, put it by his plate, give him a peck on the cheek. Say, Poor Daddy. Sit back down.

You not gitting a penny of my money, Mr. _____ say to me. Not one thin dime.

Did I ever ast you for money? I say. I never ast you for nothing. Not even for your sorry hand in marriage.

Shug break in right there. Wait, she say. Hold it. Somebody else going with us too. No use in Celie being the only one taking the weight.

Everybody sort of cut they eyes at Sofia. She the one they can't quite find a place for. She the stranger.

---

① A little spark fly cross the table：桌上空气紧张得快冒火星了。

It ain't me, she say, and her look say, Fuck you for entertaining the thought. She reach for a biscuit and sort of root her behind deeper into her seat. One look at this big stout graying, wildeyed woman and you know not even to ast. Nothing.

But just to clear this up neat and quick, she say, I'm home. Period.

Her sister Odessa come and put her arms round her. Jack① move up close.

Course you is, Jack say.

Mama crying? ast one of Sofia children.

Miss Sofia too, another one say.

But Sofia cry quick, like she do most things.

Who going? she ast.

Nobody say nothing. It so quiet you can hear the embers dying back in the stove. Sound like they falling in on each other.

Finally, Squeak look at everybody from under her bangs. Me, she say. I'm going North.

You going What? say Harpo. He so surprise. He begin to sputter, sputter, just like his daddy. Sound like I don't know what.

I want to sing, say Squeak.

Sing! say Harpo.

Yeah, say Squeak. Sing. I ain't sung in public since Jolentha was born. Her name Jolentha. They call her Suzie Q.

You ain't had to sing in public since Jolentha was born. Everything you need I done provided for.

I need to sing, say Squeak.

Listen Squeak, say Harpo. You can't go to Memphis. That's all there is to it.

Mary Agnes, say Squeak.

Squeak, Mary Agnes, what difference do it make?

It make a lot, say Squeak. When I was Mary Agnes I could sing in public.

Just then a little knock come on the door.

Odessa and Jack look at each other. Come in, say Jack.

A skinny little white woman stick most of herself through the door.

Oh, you all are eating dinner, she say. Excuse me.

That's all right, say Odessa. Us just finishing up. But there's plenty left. Why don't you sit down and join us. Or I could fix you something to eat on the porch.

Oh lord, say Shug.

It Eleanor Jane②, the white girl Sofia used to work for.

She look round till she spot Sofia, then she seem to let her breath out. No thank you, Odessa, she say. I ain't hungry. I just come to see Sofia.

Sofia, she say. Can I see you on the porch for a minute.

---

① Jack：奥德莎的丈夫，索菲亚的姐夫。
② Eleanor Jane：埃莉诺·简，市长的女儿，索菲亚带大的白人女孩。

All right, Miss Eleanor, she say. Sofia push back from the table and they go out on the porch. A few minutes later us hear Miss Eleanor sniffling. Then she really boo-hoo.

What the matter with her? Mr. _____ ast.

Henrietta say, Prob-limbszzzz ... like somebody on the radio.

Odessa shrug. She always underfoot, she say.

A lot of drinking in that family, say Jack. Plus, they can't keep that boy of theirs in college. He get drunk, aggravate his sister, chase women, hunt niggers, and that ain't all.

That enough, say Shug. Poor Sofia.

Pretty soon Sofia come back in and sit down.

What the matter? ast Odessa.

A lot of mess back at the house, say Sofia.

You got to go back up there? Odessa ast.

Yeah, say Sofia. In a few minutes. But I'll try to be back before the children go to bed.

Henrietta ast to be excuse, say she got a stomach ache.

Squeak and Harpo's little girl come over, look up at Sofia, say, You gotta go Misofia?

Sofia say, Yeah, pull her up on her lap. Sofia on parole, she say. Got to act nice.

Suzie Q lay her head on Sofia chest. Poor Sofia, she say, just like she heard Shug. Poor Sofia.

Mary Agnes, darling, say Harpo, look how Suzie Q take to Sofia.

Yeah, say Squeak, children know good when they see it. She and Sofia smile at one nother.

Go on sing, say Sofia, I'll look after this one till you come back.

You will? say Squeak.

Yeah, say Sofia.

And look after Harpo, too, say Squeak. Please ma'am.

Amen

Questions for Discussion

1. In the first letter, what does the incident which leads up to Sofia's ending up in jail tell us about U. S. racial relations in the story? And how does the incident reveal Sofia's personality?

2. How do you understand Sofia's statement in the second letter that she's the best convict yet at the same time dreaming of murder sleep or wake?

3. At the beginning of the third letter, Sofia's experience as a prisoner and as a maid for the mayor's family turns her into a different person. Yet with the conflict between men and women in Mr. _____'s household unfolding, her old defiant self returns. What do you think effects the change?

4. Why does Squeak, in the third letter, emphasize her real name Mary Agnes? What does a name mean to a black woman, given the glaring sexism within the black community in the story?

4. Beloved

作者简介

托妮·莫里森(1931—2019)是当代美国黑人文坛最耀眼的明星,获得包括普利策奖和诺贝尔文学奖在内的诸多奖项。她在黑人传统文学的基础上不断探索,形成了自己的创作特色,是继赖特、埃里森之后美国黑人文学史上的又一座高峰。

莫里森出生于美国中西部俄亥俄州洛雷恩镇的一个黑人家庭。父母对黑人音乐和民间故事的热爱让莫里森从小就深受黑人文化的熏陶。1949 年,她考入霍华德大学,主修英语,副修古典文学。本科毕业后前往康奈尔大学深造,获文学硕士学位,硕士论文是关于福克纳和伍尔夫的小说。1958 年,她与牙买加建筑师哈罗德·莫里森结婚。1964 年离婚后,她独自抚养两个儿子。从 1965 年到 1984 年,莫里森担任兰登书屋出版公司的教科书编辑和小说类图书编辑。在此期间编辑了《黑人之书》(*The Black Book*,1974)——一部汇集了记载美国黑人历史的照片和文本的大作。从 1984 到 1989 年,她在纽约州立大学任教,1989 年后在普林斯顿大学任教,笔耕不辍,至今已经出版 11 部长篇小说,包括《最蓝的眼睛》(1970)、《秀拉》(1973)、《所罗门之歌》(1977)、《柏油娃》(1981),反映美国黑人百年历史的三部曲《宠儿》(1987)、《爵士乐》(1992)、《乐园》(1998);进入 21 世纪以来陆续发表《爱》(2003)、《恩惠》(2008)、《家园》(2012),和《愿上帝保佑你,孩子》(2015)。除长篇小说之外,她还创作了戏剧、短篇故事、儿童书籍以及批评文集《在黑暗中嬉戏——白人性与文学想象》(1992)、《他者之源》(2017)和《自尊之源》(2019)。

作品简介与赏析

《宠儿》是莫里森最知名的小说,出版后一年即获得普利策奖,作者也因这部小说获得诺贝尔文学奖。2006 年,《纽约时报书评》组织 100 名作家和编辑评选 25 年来美国最佳小说,《宠儿》高居榜首。小说主人公塞丝以真实的美国历史人物——逃亡黑奴玛格丽特·加纳为原型。1855 年,从肯塔基州的种植园"甜蜜之家"出逃到俄亥俄州的女黑奴塞丝面对前来抓捕的白人,为避免自己的孩子重蹈奴隶的悲惨命运,她亲手杀死不到两岁的女儿,出狱后让人在其墓碑上刻上"宠儿"二字。18 年后,一个自称名叫宠儿的年轻女子走进了塞丝的生活,从此一切都改变了……故事的开头是 1873 年,处于重建时期的美国南方依然盛行着蓄奴制时代的种族暴行。塞丝和女儿丹芙独自住在辛辛那提城郊,基本不与人往来。之前同在"甜蜜之家"为奴的保罗·D 来到她家,引发了她对过去的痛苦回忆。与此同时,18 年前被母亲杀死的女儿宠儿的鬼魂重返人间,前来向塞丝索爱。在设计赶走保罗·D 后,宠儿无限度地向塞丝提出各种要求,让后者变成母爱的奴隶。最后,丹芙带着一群黑人邻居前来驱鬼,宠儿终于消失,塞丝也从过去的阴影中走了出来。

《宠儿》着力刻画了蓄奴制对已获自由的美国黑人的身心伤害,体现了作家在小说创作中惯常表现的政治敏锐性。20 世纪的最后 25 年,一种新的文类——新奴隶叙事在美国黑人文坛悄然兴起。以埃里克斯·哈利的《根》为标志,一大批新奴隶叙事体小说次第登场。为了辨明后民权运动时代自由的含义,这批作品重新开启了对奴隶制的探讨,其中最受赞誉的便是《宠儿》。《宠儿》以深刻的批判意识和高度的人文关怀,改写了被主流历史观所忽视与边缘化的黑人历史,还原了他们的生存状态,讲述美国南方重建时期,已成为自由人的黑奴重建自我身份的故事。小说对外部世界着墨不多,重点追踪人物的内心发展轨迹,通过倒叙的方式,由几个主要人物的叙事声音将情节依次推进。透过主要叙事人也是主人公塞丝的意识和回忆,大部分的故事情节得以浮现。

小说的叙事技巧堪称完美。首先,它打破了传统的时间顺序和线形叙事,将过去的点点滴滴穿插到现在的时间层面上,不仅使得故事的进展十分缓慢,而且混淆了过去与现在的时间界限,使二者浑然一体。这种表现手法淋漓尽致地展现了人物不愿却不得不面对过去的痛苦而混乱的心境。其次,小说基于声音和听觉的叙事特点十分明显。在小说起始的寥寥数页里,第三人称叙事人的叙事声音就已不露痕迹地迅速将书中几个主要人物推上前台。如果说叙事声音在编织情节的过程中将不同的身份赋予人物,那么人物形象的逐渐丰满乃至呼之欲出,则应归功于书中出现的其他种种声音:人物的对话、内心独白、歌谣、布道、多声部的合唱等,它们构成一部波澜壮阔的交响乐,成为黑人重建自我、缔结家庭纽带关系、从群体中汲取力量的重要手段。再次,则是作者对黑人口语体的大量运用。她在小说中成功地吸取和发扬了黑人文化传统独特的魅力,把从黑奴时代起就开始流传的民间口头文学的传统运用到自己的创作中。作品多处采用口吻亲切、如同唠家常一般的口语体,字里行间透露出听者和说者双方的默契,同时在书中零星散落条条线索,留下了一处处空白,需要读者用自己的想象力和经验来填补。这使文本具有了强大的召唤力,在文本与读者之间形成一种动态交流。读者不再是被动地接受文本,而是必须主动参与到小说情节的建构和想象中。

虽然属于基于事实的新奴隶叙事体,作家却将现实与超现实相结合,赋予小说魔幻现实主义的色彩。比如,小说第一章就以"凶宅闹鬼"的情节牢牢抓住读者,把哥特式小说元素放在这部取材于真人真事的故事中,其颠覆意味跃然纸上。西方理性主义传统把鬼视为被排斥、被压制、被放逐的对象,而宠儿这个冤鬼却能肉身还魂,回到人间索取那过早丢失的母爱。与宠儿的鬼魂相比,真正可怕的其实是蓄奴制,尽管已在法律层面被废除,但它的余响依然如鬼魅般如影随形,是黑人心中不可触及的伤痕。这种情节安排也反映了莫里森与黑人本土文化的契合。她的小说富含神话寓言、民俗仪式、民间传说、民间信仰、黑人音乐等黑人传统文化的因素,也带有明显的非洲传统宗教观和生死观的印记。相信、接受、容忍鬼魂的存在,甚至与之交流的情形,在书中随处可见。在一次访谈中,莫里森明确表示她相信鬼魂的存在。对这一主题的渲染其实反衬出她所倡导的黑人民族传统对现代文明既定秩序的有力反驳。

莫里森还善于通过塑造身份神秘、性格模糊的人物形象来构建开放性的小说文本。宠儿究竟是人是鬼?这是个至今依然争议不休的问题。实际上,小说的开放性表明,莫里森在小说中交叉运用了偏重双重意识的非裔美国人的视角,和重视多样性、多声部和过程的后现代视角,结合了西方传统文学的精髓和黑人口头文学的特质,体现了艺术性和思想性的完美融合,成为20世纪后半叶唯有《看不见的人》能与之比肩的最具影响力的美国黑人小说。

下文选自《宠儿》第一章。凶宅闹鬼与故人来访的重合开启了女主人公的意识流动,记忆深处的过往点滴泛起,作者以高超的叙事技巧将过去与现在、现实与幻象巧妙地编织在一起,吸引着读者去探寻故事的真相。

One

124 WAS SPITEFUL. Full of a baby's venom. The women in the house knew it and so did the children. For years each put up with the spite in his own way, but by 1873 Sethe and her daughter Denver were its only victims. The grandmother, Baby Suggs, was dead,

and the sons, Howard and Buglar, had run away by the time they were thirteen years old—
as soon as merely looking in a mirror shattered it (that was the signal for Buglar); as soon
as two tiny hand prints appeared in the cake (that was it for Howard). Neither boy waited
to see more; another kettleful of chickpeas smoking in a heap on the floor; soda crackers
crumbled and strewn in a line next to the door sill. Nor did they wait for one of the relief
periods: the weeks, months even, when nothing was disturbed. No. Each one fled at
once—the moment the house committed what was for him the one insult not to be borne or
witnessed a second time. Within two months, in the dead of winter, leaving their
grandmother, Baby Suggs; Sethe, their mother; and their little sister, Denver, all by
themselves in the gray and white house on Bluestone Road. It didn't have a number then,
because Cincinnati didn't stretch that far. In fact, Ohio had been calling itself a state only
seventy years when first one brother and then the next stuffed quilt packing into his hat,
snatched up his shoes, and crept away from the lively spite the house felt for them.

Baby Suggs didn't even raise her head. From her sickbed she heard them go but that
wasn't the reason she lay still. It was a wonder to her that her grandsons had taken so long
to realize that every house wasn't like the one on Bluestone Road. Suspended between the
nastiness of life and the meanness of the dead, she couldn't get interested in leaving life or
living it, let alone the fright of two creeping-off boys. Her past had been like her
present—intolerable—and since she knew death was anything but forgetfulness, she used
the little energy left her for pondering color.

"Bring a little lavender in, if you got any. Pink, if you don't."

And Sethe would oblige her with anything from fabric to her own tongue. Winter in
Ohio was especially rough if you had an appetite for color. Sky provided the only drama,
and counting on a Cincinnati horizon for life's principal joy was reckless indeed. So Sethe
and the girl Denver did what they could, and what the house permitted, for her. Together
they waged a perfunctory battle against the outrageous behavior of that place; against
turned-over slop jars, smacks on the behind, and gusts of sour air. For they understood the
source of the outrage as well as they knew the source of light.

Baby Suggs died shortly after the brothers left, with no interest whatsoever in their
leave-taking or hers, and right afterward Sethe and Denver decided to end the persecution
by calling forth the ghost that tried them so. Perhaps a conversation, they thought, an
exchange of views or something would help. So they held hands and said, "Come on.
Come on. You may as well just come on."

The sideboard took a step forward but nothing else did.

"Grandma Baby must be stopping it," said Denver. She was ten and still mad at Baby
Suggs for dying.

Sethe opened her eyes. "I doubt that," she said.

"Then why don't it come?"

"You forgetting how little it is," said her mother. "She wasn't even two years old
when she died. Too little to understand. Too little to talk much even."

"Maybe she don't want to understand," said Denver.

"Maybe. But if she'd only come, I could make it clear to her." Sethe released her daughter's hand and together they pushed the sideboard back against the wall. Outside a driver whipped his horse into the gallop local people felt necessary when they passed 124.

"For a baby she throws a powerful spell," said Denver.

"No more powerful than the way I loved her," Sethe answered and there it was again. The welcoming cool of unchiseled headstones; the one she selected to lean against on tiptoe, her knees wide open as any grave. Pink as a fingernail it was, and sprinkled with glittering chips. Ten minutes, he said. You got ten minutes I'll do it for free.

Ten minutes for seven letters. With another ten could she have gotten "Dearly" too? She had not thought to ask him and it bothered her still that it might have been possible— that for twenty minutes, a half hour, say, she could have had the whole thing, every word she heard the preacher say at the funeral (and all there was to say, surely) engraved on her baby's headstone: Dearly Beloved. But what she got, settled for, was the one word that mattered. She thought it would be enough, rutting① among the headstones with the engraver, his young son looking on, the anger in his face so old; the appetite in it quite new. That should certainly be enough. Enough to answer one more preacher, one more abolitionist and a town full of disgust.

Counting on the stillness of her own soul, she had forgotten the other one: the soul of her baby girl. Who would have thought that a little old baby could harbor so much rage? Rutting among the stones under the eyes of the engraver's son was not enough. Not only did she have to live out her years in a house palsied by the baby's fury at having its throat cut, but those ten minutes she spent pressed up against dawn-colored stone studded with star chips, her knees wide open as the grave, were longer than life, more alive, more pulsating than the baby blood that soaked her fingers like oil.

"We could move," she suggested once to her mother-in-law.

"What'd be the point?" asked Baby Suggs. "Not a house in the country ain't packed to its rafters with some dead Negro's grief. We lucky this ghost is a baby. My husband's spirit was to come back in here? or yours? Don't talk to me. You lucky. You got three left. Three pulling at your skirts and just one raising hell from the other side. Be thankful, why don't you? I had eight. Every one of them gone away from me. Four taken, four chased, and all, I expect, worrying somebody's house into evil." Baby Suggs rubbed her eyebrows. "My first-born. All I can remember of her is how she loved the burned bottom of bread. Can you beat that? Eight children and that's all I remember."

"That's all you let yourself remember," Sethe had told her, but she was down to one herself—one alive, that is—the boys chased off by the dead one, and her memory of Buglar was fading fast. Howard at least had a head shape nobody could forget. As for the rest, she worked hard to remember as close to nothing as was safe. Unfortunately her brain was devious. She might be hurrying across a field, running practically, to get to the pump quickly and rinse the chamomile sap from her legs. Nothing else would be in her

---

① rutting: 苟合。

mind. The picture of the men coming to nurse her was as lifeless as the nerves in her back where the skin buckled like a washboard. Nor was there the faintest scent of ink or the cherry gum and oak bark from which it was made. Nothing. Just the breeze cooling her face as she rushed toward water. And then sopping the chamomile away with pump water and rags, her mind fixed on getting every last bit of sap off—on her carelessness in taking a shortcut across the field just to save a half mile, and not noticing how high the weeds had grown until the itching was all the way to her knees. Then something. The plash of water, the sight of her shoes and stockings awry on the path where she had flung them; or Here Boy lapping in the puddle near her feet, and suddenly there was Sweet Home[①] rolling, rolling, rolling out before her eyes, and although there was not a leaf on that farm that did not make her want to scream, it rolled itself out before her in shameless beauty. It never looked as terrible as it was and it made her wonder if hell was a pretty place too. Fire and brimstone all right, but hidden in lacy groves. Boys hanging from the most beautiful sycamores in the world. It shamed her—remembering the wonderful soughing trees rather than the boys. Try as she might to make it otherwise, the sycamores beat out the children every time and she could not forgive her memory for that.

When the last of the chamomile was gone, she went around to the front of the house, collecting her shoes and stockings on the way. As if to punish her further for her terrible memory, sitting on the porch not forty feet away was Paul D, the last of the Sweet Home men. And although she she said, "Is that you?"

"What's left." He stood up and smiled. "How you been, girl, besides barefoot?"

When she laughed it came out loose and young. "Messed up my legs back yonder. Chamomile."

He made a face as though tasting a teaspoon of something bitter. "I don't want to even hear 'bout it. Always did hate that stuff."

Sethe balled up her stockings and jammed them into her pocket. "Come on in."

"Porch is fine, Sethe. Cool out here." He sat back down and looked at the meadow on the other side of the road, knowing the eagerness he felt would be in his eyes.

"Eighteen years," she said softly.

"Eighteen," he repeated. "And I swear I been walking every one of em. Mind if I join you?" He nodded toward her feet and began unlacing his shoes.

"You want to soak them? Let me get you a basin of water." She moved closer to him to enter the house.

"No, uh uh. Can't baby feet. A whole lot more tramping they got to do yet."

"You can't leave right away, Paul D. You got to stay awhile."

"Well, long enough to see Baby Suggs, anyway. Where is she?"

"Dead."

"Aw no. When?"

"Eight years now. Almost nine."

---

① Sweet Home: "甜蜜之家",塞丝出逃之前所在的种植园的名字。

"Was it hard? I hope she didn't die hard."

Sethe shook her head. "Soft as cream. Being alive was the hard part. Sorry you missed her though. Is that what you came by for?"

"That's some of what I came for. The rest is you. But if all the truth be known, I go anywhere these days. Anywhere they let me sit down."

"You looking good."

"Devil's confusion. He lets me look good long as I feel bad." He looked at her and the word "bad" took on another meaning.

Sethe smiled. This is the way they were—had been. All of the Sweet Home men, before and after Halle, treated her to a mild brotherly flirtation, so subtle you had to scratch for it.

Except for a heap more hair and some waiting in his eyes, he looked the way he had in Kentucky. Peachstone skin; straight-backed. For a man with an immobile face it was amazing how ready it was to smile, or blaze or be sorry with you. As though all you had to do was get his attention and right away he produced the feeling you were feeling. With less than a blink, his face seemed to change—underneath it lay the activity.

"I wouldn't have to ask about him, would I? You'd tell me if there was anything to tell, wouldn't you?" Sethe looked down at her feet and saw again the sycamores.

"I'd tell you. Sure I'd tell you. I don't know any more now than I did then." Except for the churn, he thought, and you don't need to know that. "You must think he's still alive."

"No. I think he's dead. It's not being sure that keeps him alive."

"What did Baby Suggs think?"

"Same, but to listen to her, all her children is dead. Claimed she felt each one go the very day and hour."

"When she say Halle went?"

"Eighteen fifty-five. The day my baby was born."

"You had that baby, did you? Never thought you'd make it."

He chuckled. "Running off pregnant."

"Had to. Couldn't be no waiting." She lowered her head and thought, as he did, how unlikely it was that she had made it. And if it hadn't been for that girl looking for velvet, she never would have.

"All by yourself too." He was proud of her and annoyed by her. Proud she had done it; annoyed that she had not needed Halle or him in the doing.

"Almost by myself. Not all by myself. A whitegirl helped me."

"Then she helped herself too, God bless her."

"You could stay the night, Paul D."

"You don't sound too steady in the offer."

Sethe glanced beyond his shoulder toward the closed door. "Oh it's truly meant. I just hope you'll pardon my house. Come on in. Talk to Denver while I cook you something."

Paul D tied his shoes together, hung them over his shoulder and followed her through the door straight into a pool of red and undulating light that locked him where he stood.

"You got company?" he whispered, frowning.

"Off and on," said Sethe.

"Good God." He backed out the door onto the porch. "What kind of evil you got in here?"

"It's not evil, just sad. Come on. Just step through."

He looked at her then, closely. Closer than he had when she first rounded the house on wet and shining legs, holding her shoes and stockings up in one hand, her skirts in the other. Halle's girl—the one with iron eyes and backbone to match. He had never seen her hair in Kentucky. And though her face was eighteen years older than when last he saw her, it was softer now. Because of the hair. A face too still for comfort; irises the same color as her skin, which, in that still face, used to make him think of a mask with mercifully punched out eyes. Halle's woman. Pregnant every year including the year she sat by the fire telling him she was going to run. Her three children she had already packed into a wagonload of others in a caravan of Negroes crossing the river. They were to be left with Halle's mother near Cincinnati. Even in that tiny shack, leaning so close to the fire you could smell the heat in her dress, her eyes did not pick up a flicker of light. They were like two wells into which he had trouble gazing. Even punched out they needed to be covered, lidded, marked with some sign to warn folks of what that emptiness held. So he looked instead at the fire while she told him, because her husband was not there for the telling. Mr. Garner was dead and his wife had a lump in her neck the size of a sweet potato and unable to speak to anyone. She leaned as close to the fire as her pregnant belly allowed and told him, Paul D, the last of the Sweet Home men.

There had been six of them who belonged to the farm, Sethe the only female. Mrs. Garner, crying like a baby, had sold his brother to pay off the debts that surfaced the minute she was widowed. Then schoolteacher arrived to put things in order. But what he did broke three more Sweet Home men and punched the glittering iron out of Sethe's eyes, leaving two open wells that did not reflect firelight.

Now the iron was back but the face, softened by hair, made him trust her enough to step inside her door smack into a pool of pulsing red light.

She was right. It was sad. Walking through it, a wave of grief soaked him so thoroughly he wanted to cry. It seemed a long way to the normal light surrounding the table, but he made it—dry-eyed and lucky.

"You said she died soft. Soft as cream," he reminded her.

"That's not Baby Suggs," she said.

"Who then?"

"My daughter. The one I sent ahead with the boys."

"She didn't live?"

"No. The one I was carrying when I run away is all I got left. Boys gone too. Both of em walked off just before Baby Suggs died."

Paul D looked at the spot where the grief had soaked him. The red was gone but a kind of weeping clung to the air where it had been.

Probably best, he thought. If a Negro got legs he ought to use them. Sit down too long, somebody will figure out a way to tie them up. Still ... if her boys were gone ...

"No man? You here by yourself?"

"Me and Denver," she said.

"That all right by you?"

"That's all right by me."

She saw his skepticism and went on. "I cook at a restaurant in town. And I sew a little on the sly.

Paul D smiled then, remembering the bedding dress. Sethe was thirteen when she came to Sweet Home and already iron-eyed. She was a timely present for Mrs. Garner who had lost Baby Suggs to her husband's high principles. The five Sweet Home men looked at the new girl and decided to let her be. They were young and so sick with the absence of women they had taken to calves. Yet they let the iron-eyed girl be, so she could choose in spite of the fact that each one would have beaten the others to mush to have her. It took her a year to choose—a long, tough year of thrashing on pallets eaten up with dreams of her. A year of yearning, when rape seemed the solitary gift of life. The restraint they had exercised possible only because they were Sweet Home men—the ones Mr. Garner bragged about while other farmers shook their heads in warning at the phrase.

"Y'all got boys," he told them. "Young boys, old boys, picky boys, stroppin boys. Now at Sweet Home, my niggers is men every one of em. Bought em thataway, raised em thataway. Men every one."

"Beg to differ, Garner. Ain't no nigger men."

"Not if you scared, they ain't." Garner's smile was wide. "But if you a man yourself, you'll want your niggers to be men too."

"I wouldn't have no nigger men round my wife."

It was the reaction Garner loved and waited for. "Neither would I," he said. "Neither would I," and there was always a pause before the neighbor, or stranger, or peddler, or brother-in-law or whoever it was got the meaning. Then a fierce argument, sometimes a fight, and Garner came home bruised and pleased, having demonstrated one more time what a real Kentuckian was: one tough enough and smart enough to make and call his own niggers men.

And so they were: Paul D Garner, Paul F Garner, Paul A Garner, Halle Suggs and Sixo, the wild man. All in their twenties, minus women, fucking cows, dreaming of rape, thrashing on pallets, rubbing their thighs and waiting for the new girl—the one who took Baby Suggs' place after Halle bought her with five years of Sundays. Maybe that was why she chose him. A twenty-year-old man so in love with his mother he gave up five years of Sabbaths just to see her sit down for a change was a serious recommendation.

She waited a year. And the Sweet Home men abused cows while they waited with her. She chose Halle and for their first bedding she sewed herself a dress on the sly.

"Won't you stay on awhile? Can't nobody catch up on eighteen years in a day."

Out of the dimness of the room in which they sat, a white staircase climbed toward the blue-and-white wallpaper of the second floor. Paul D could see just the beginning of the paper; discreet flecks of yellow sprinkled among a blizzard of snowdrops all backed by blue. The luminous white of the railing and steps kept him glancing toward it. Every sense he had told him the air above the stairwell was charmed and very thin. But the girl who walked down out of that air was round and brown with the face of an alert doll.

Paul D looked at the girl and then at Sethe who smiled saying, "Here she is my Denver. This is Paul D, honey, from Sweet Home."

"Good morning, Mr. D."

"Garner, baby. Paul D Garner."

"Yes sir."

"Glad to get a look at you. Last time I saw your mama, you were pushing out the front of her dress."

"Still is," Sethe smiled, "provided she can get in it."

Denver stood on the bottom step and was suddenly hot and shy. It had been a long time since anybody (good-willed whitewoman, preacher, speaker or newspaperman) sat at their table, their sympathetic voices called liar by the revulsion in their eyes. For twelve years, long before Grandma Baby died, there had been no visitors of any sort and certainly no friends. No colored people. Certainly no hazelnut man with too long hair and no notebook, no charcoal, no oranges, no questions. Someone her mother wanted to talk to and would even consider talking to while barefoot. Looking, in fact acting, like a girl instead of the quiet, queenly woman Denver had known all her life. The one who never looked away, who when a man got stomped to death by a mare right in front of Sawyer's restaurant did not look away; and when a sow began eating her own litter did not look away then either. And when the baby's spirit picked up Here Boy and slammed him into the wall hard enough to break two of his legs and dislocate his eye, so hard he went into convulsions and chewed up his tongue, still her mother had not looked away. She had taken a hammer, knocked the dog unconscious, wiped away the blood and saliva, pushed his eye back in his head and set his leg bones. He recovered, mute and off-balance, more because of his untrustworthy eye than his bent legs, and winter, summer, drizzle or dry, nothing could persuade him to enter the house again.

Now here was this woman with the presence of mind to repair a dog gone savage with pain rocking her crossed ankles and looking away from her own daughter's body. As though the size of it was more than vision could bear. And neither she nor he had on shoes. Hot, shy, now Denver was lonely. All that leaving: first her brothers, then her grandmother—serious losses since there were no children willing to circle her in a game or hang by their knees from her porch railing. None of that had mattered as long as her mother did not look away as she was doing now, making Denver long, downright long, for a sign of spite from the baby ghost.

"She's a fine-looking young lady," said Paul D. "Fine-looking. Got her daddy's sweet face."

"You know my father?"

"Knew him. Knew him well."

"Did he, Ma'am?" Denver fought an urge to realign her affection.

"Of course he knew your daddy. I told you, he's from Sweet Home."

Denver sat down on the bottom step. There was nowhere else gracefully to go. They were a twosome, saying "Your daddy" and "Sweet Home" in a way that made it clear both belonged to them and not to her. That her own father's absence was not hers. Once the absence had belonged to Grandma Baby—a son, deeply mourned because he was the one who had bought her out of there. Then it was her mother's absent husband. Now it was this hazelnut stranger's absent friend. Only those who knew him ("knew him well") could claim his absence for themselves. Just as only those who lived in Sweet Home could remember it, whisper it and glance sideways at one another while they did. Again she wished for the baby ghost—its anger thrilling her now where it used to wear her out. Wear her out.

"We have a ghost in here," she said, and it worked. They were not a twosome anymore. Her mother left off swinging her feet and being girlish. Memory of Sweet Home dropped away from the eyes of the man she was being girlish for. He looked quickly up the lightning-white stairs behind her.

"So I hear," he said. "But sad, your mama said. Not evil."

"No sir," said Denver, "not evil. But not sad either."

"What then?"

"Rebuked. Lonely and rebuked."

"Is that right?" Paul D turned to Sethe.

"I don't know about lonely," said Denver's mother. "Mad, maybe, but I don't see how it could be lonely spending every minute with us like it does."

"Must be something you got it wants."

Sethe shrugged. "It's just a baby."

"My sister," said Denver. "She died in this house."

Paul D scratched the hair under his jaw. "Reminds me of that headless bride back behind Sweet Home. Remember that, Sethe? Used to roam them woods regular."

"How could I forget? Worrisome ... "

"How come everybody run off from Sweet Home can't stop talking about it? Look like if it was so sweet you would have stayed."

"Girl, who you talking to?"

Paul D laughed. "True, true. She's right, Sethe. It wasn't sweet and it sure wasn't home." He shook his head.

"But it's where we were," said Sethe. "All together. Comes back whether we want it to or not." She shivered a little. A light ripple of skin on her arm, which she caressed back into sleep. "Denver," she said, "start up that stove. Can't have a friend stop by and don't feed him."

"Don't go to any trouble on my account," Paul D said.

"Bread ain't trouble. The rest I brought back from where I work. Least I can do, cooking from dawn to noon, is bring dinner home. You got any objections to pike?"

"If he don't object to me I don't object to him."

At it again, thought Denver. Her back to them, she jostled the kindlin and almost lost the fire. "Why don't you spend the night, Mr. Garner? You and Ma'am can talk about Sweet Home all night long."

Sethe took two swift steps to the stove, but before she could yank Denver's collar, the girl leaned forward and began to cry.

"What is the matter with you? I never knew you to behave this way."

"Leave her be," said Paul D. "I'm a stranger to her."

"That's just it. She got no cause to act up with a stranger. Oh baby, what is it? Did something happen?"

But Denver was shaking now and sobbing so she could not speak. The tears she had not shed for nine years wetting her far too womanly breasts.

"I can't no more. I can't no more."

"Can't what? What can't you?"

"I can't live here. I don't know where to go or what to do, but I can't live here. Nobody speaks to us. Nobody comes by. Boys don't like me. Girls don't either."

"Honey, honey."

"What's she talking 'bout nobody speaks to you?" asked Paul D.

"It's the house. People don't—"

"It's not! It's not the house. It's us! And it's you!"

"Denver!"

"Leave off, Sethe. It's hard for a young girl living in a haunted house. That can't be easy."

"It's easier than some other things."

"Think, Sethe. I'm a grown man with nothing new left to see or do and I'm telling you it ain't easy. Maybe you all ought to move. Who owns this house?"

Over Denver's shoulder Sethe shot Paul D a look of snow. "What you care?"

"They won't let you leave?"

"No."

"Sethe."

"No moving. No leaving. It's all right the way it is."

"You going to tell me it's all right with this child half out of her mind?"

Something in the house braced, and in the listening quiet that followed Sethe spoke.

"I got a tree on my back and a haint in my house, and nothing in between but the daughter I am holding in my arms. No more running—from nothing. I will never run from another thing on this earth. I took one journey and I paid for the ticket, but let me tell you something, Paul D Garner: it cost too much! Do you hear me? It cost too much. Now sit down and eat with us or leave us be."

Paul D fished in his vest for a little pouch of tobacco—concentrating on its contents and the knot of its string while Sethe led Denver into the keeping room that opened off the large room he was sitting in. He had no smoking papers, so he fiddled with the pouch and listened through the open door to Sethe quieting her daughter. When she came back she avoided his look and went straight to a small table next to the stove. Her back was to him and he could see all the hair he wanted without the distraction of her face.

"What tree on your back?"

"Huh." Sethe put a bowl on the table and reached under it for flour.

"What tree on your back? Is something growing on your back? I don't see nothing growing on your back."

"It's there all the same."

"Who told you that?"

"Whitegirl. That's what she called it. I've never seen it and never will. But that's what she said it looked like. A chokecherry tree. Trunk, branches, and even leaves. Tiny little chokecherry leaves. But that was eighteen years ago. Could have cherries too now for all I know."

Sethe took a little spit from the tip of her tongue with her forefinger. Quickly, lightly she touched the stove. Then she trailed her fingers through the flour, parting, separating small hills and ridges of it, looking for mites. Finding none, she poured soda and salt into the crease of her folded hand and tossed both into the flour. Then she reached into a can and scooped half a handful of lard. Deftly she squeezed the flour through it, then with her left hand sprinkling water, she formed the dough.

"I had milk," she said. "I was pregnant with Denver but I had milk for my baby girl. I hadn't stopped nursing her when I sent her on ahead with Howard and Buglar."

Now she rolled the dough out with a wooden pin. "Anybody could smell me long before he saw me. And when he saw me he'd see the drops of it on the front of my dress. Nothing I could do about that. All I knew was I had to get my milk to my baby girl. Nobody was going to nurse her like me. Nobody was going to get it to her fast enough, or take it away when she had enough and didn't know it. Nobody knew that she couldn't pass her air if you held her up on your shoulder, only if she was lying on my knees. Nobody knew that but me and nobody had her milk but me. I told that to the women in the wagon. Told them to put sugar water in cloth to suck from so when I got there in a few days she wouldn't have forgot me. The milk would be there and I would be there with it."

"Men don't know nothing much," said Paul D, tucking his pouch back into his vest pocket, "but they do know a suckling can't be away from its mother for long."

"Then they know what it's like to send your children off when your breasts are full."

"We was talking 'bout a tree, Sethe."

"After I left you, those boys came in there and took my milk. That's what they came in there for. Held me down and took it. I told Mrs. Garner on em. She had that lump and couldn't speak but her eyes rolled out tears. Them boys found out I told on em. Schoolteacher made one open up my back, and when it closed it made a tree. It grows there still."

"They used cowhide on you?"

"And they took my milk."

"They beat you and you was pregnant?"

"And they took my milk!"

The fat white circles of dough lined the pan in rows. Once more Sethe touched a wet forefinger to the stove. She opened the oven door and slid the pan of biscuits in. As she raised up from the heat she felt Paul D behind her and his hands under her breasts. She straightened up and knew, but could not feel, that his cheek was pressing into the branches of her chokecherry tree.

Not even trying, he had become the kind of man who could walk into a house and make the women cry. Because with him, in his presence, they could. There was something blessed in his manner. Women saw him and wanted to weep—to tell him that their chest hurt and their knees did too. Strong women and wise saw him and told him things they only told each other: that way past the Change of Life, desire in them had suddenly become enormous, greedy, more savage than when they were fifteen, and that it embarrassed them and made them sad; that secretly they longed to die—to be quit of it— that sleep was more precious to them than any waking day. Young girls sidled up to him to confess or describe how well-dressed the visitations were that had followed them straight from their dreams. Therefore, although he did not understand why this was so, he was not surprised when Denver dripped tears into the stovefire. Nor, fifteen minutes later, after telling him about her stolen milk, her mother wept as well. Behind her, bending down, his body an arc of kindness, he held her breasts in the palms of his hands. He rubbed his cheek on her back and learned that way her sorrow, the roots of it; its wide trunk and intricate branches. Raising his fingers to the hooks of her dress, he knew without seeing them or hearing any sigh that the tears were coming fast. And when the top of her dress was around her hips and he saw the sculpture her back had become, like the decorative work of an ironsmith too passionate for display, he could think but not say, "Aw, Lord, girl." And he would tolerate no peace until he had touched every ridge and leaf of it with his mouth, none of which Sethe could feel because her back skin had been dead for years. What she knew was that the responsibility for her breasts, at last, was in somebody else's hands.

Would there be a little space, she wondered, a little time, some way to hold off eventfulness, to push busyness into the corners of the room and just stand there a minute or two, naked from shoulder blade to waist, relieved of the weight of her breasts, smelling the stolen milk again and the pleasure of baking bread? Maybe this one time she could stop dead still in the middle of a cooking meal—not even leave the stove—and feel the hurt her back ought to. Trust things and remember things because the last of the Sweet Home men was there to catch her if she sank?

The stove didn't shudder as it adjusted to its heat. Denver wasn't stirring in the next room. The pulse of red light hadn't come back and Paul D had not trembled since 1856 and then for eighty-three days in a row. Locked up and chained down, his hands shook so bad he couldn't smoke or even scratch properly. Now he was trembling again but in the legs this time. It took him a while to realize that his legs were not shaking because of worry, but because the floorboards were and the grinding, shoving floor was only part of it. The house itself was pitching. Sethe slid to the floor and struggled to get back into her dress. While down on all fours, as though she were holding her house down on the ground, Denver burst from the keeping room, terror in her eyes, a vague smile on her lips.

"God damn it! Hush up!" Paul D was shouting, falling, reaching for anchor. "Leave the place alone! Get the hell out!" A table rushed toward him and he grabbed its leg. Somehow he managed to stand at an angle and, holding the table by two legs, he bashed it about, wrecking everything, screaming back at the screaming house. "You want to fight, come on! God damn it! She got enough without you. She got enough!"

The quaking slowed to an occasional lurch, but Paul D did not stop whipping the table around until everything was rock quiet. Sweating and breathing hard, he leaned against the wall in the space the sideboard left. Sethe was still crouched next to the stove, clutching her salvaged shoes to her chest. The three of them, Sethe, Denver, and Paul D, breathed to the same beat, like one tired person. Another breathing was just as tired.

It was gone. Denver wandered through the silence to the stove. She ashed over the fire and pulled the pan of biscuits from the oven. The jelly cupboard was on its back, its contents lying in a heap in the corner of the bottom shelf. She took out a jar, and, looking around for a plate, found half of one by the door. These things she carried out to the porch steps, where she sat down.

Questions for Discussion

1. Mr. Garner calls his slaves "men" while other farmers call them "boys". Though treated with kindness, do you think there's a real difference between Mr. Garner's slaves and other blacks under slavery? Why?
2. What does the "chokecherry tree" on Sethe's back refer to? What is it symbolic of?
3. Sethe lives in a house numbered 124. What does the address imply?
4. In Chapter 1, the story is told from the perspective of Sethe in the form of stream of consciousness. Despite her efforts to repress her past, it surfaces time and again against her will. What does the juxtaposition of past with present serve to do?

5. Erasure

作者简介

当代非裔美国作家帕西瓦尔·埃弗雷特（Percival Everett）（1956—　）出生于乔治亚州的戈登，在南卡罗来纳的哥伦比亚长大；他 1977 年毕业于迈阿密大学，获得学士学位，1982 年毕业于布朗大学，获得硕士学位。他做过多种工作，如爵士乐师、农场工人等；1985 年以来，他在美国多所大学教授创意写作等课程，目前任南加州大学杰出教授。

在创作方面，埃弗雷特是个多面手，喜欢实验性写作，欣赏对话、互文与解构策略，不仅出版小说、诗歌，还创作绘画，已经获得多项荣誉，逐步迈入当代非裔美国经典作家的行列，以《抹除》为代表的多部作品进入美国中学、大学的必读书目，影响越来越大。

从处女作《萨德》（1983）开始，他就十分关注生活中的荒诞，以及如何从荒诞的生活中活出意义这一主题，之后有多部相同主题的作品问世；1990 年起，《他的黑皮肤》（1990）开始改写古希腊神话，并以《上帝的国度》（1994）进军美国"西部"文化，破解美国西部"神话"及其种族意涵。21 世纪以来，他更加关注美国社会与文化中无处不在的种族歧视及其对黑人的心理伤害，代表作《抹除》（2001）极尽讽刺调侃之能事，重新呈现人们习以为常且高度固化的黑人家庭、普通黑人民众（特别是黑人女性）、黑人知识分子、黑人文化工业等，不仅意在颠覆美国黑人经典《土生子》中黑白对立的种族关系，更以夸张的手法嘲弄美国文化工业的驯服机制。

作为杰出的后现代派作家，埃弗雷特注重主题的拓展及文体与技法方面的创新，之后陆续发表《我非西德尼·波迪尔》（2009）、《假设》（2011）、《非裔美国人民的历史》（2004）、《如此悲伤》（2017）等，不仅延续了前期作品中对"身份追寻""异化的影响"以及暴力与喜剧的"奇怪"混合等主题，而且予以深化，突出上述主题在美国特定历史时期的再现。他不仅与非裔美国文学传统作家与作品形成主题鲜明的对话，而且为美国文学中十分强调的追寻自由、公正，凸显个人主义与个体尊严等主题添加非裔美国视角，极大地丰富了美国文学主题与表现形式。

作品简介与赏析

《抹除》的主人公埃里森在大学做助理教授，喜欢实验性创作，对自己的作品不够畅销，读者不太多等问题，本来有足够的心理预期，但是当他看到别人用类型化的黑人、用社会广为接受的偏见为基础创作出来的黑人隔都小说成为畅销书，成为人们了解、认识黑人个体、家庭、社区，乃至于黑人文化的"经典"之作，而自己最近完成的小说又多次被退稿时，他再也按捺不住，决定以调侃的方式，聚焦当代黑人内城生活，以现实主义的方式，再现当代美国"内城""真实的"黑人（特别是黑人男性）的生活。

埃里森化名"斯塔格·雷"创作了名为《我的帕雯洛基》的新作——后来直接改名为《操》，以非裔美国经典作家赖特的《土生子》为故事原型，以当代美国黑人女作家萨菲尔的小说《进取》（1997）为调侃对象，塑造了为富有的黑人老板开车，扶黑人老板女儿回房间的黑人青年詹金斯这一形象——他不识字，整天怨天尤人，力比多四溢而且极度暴力。他没有像《土生子》中的黑人主人公别格一样，杀死自己白人老板的女儿玛丽，而是利用自己黑人老板女儿的醉酒，直接与其发生性关系；此外，他与多名黑人女性有染，与四位不同女性生下四个孩子。更为搞笑的是，面对抓捕，他的第一反应不是羞愧，而是，"瞧，我上电视了。"

更为重要的是,这部以破碎英语写成的调侃之作《我的帕枭洛基》(《操》)居然获得类似美国国家图书奖评委会的高度肯定,专家们几乎一致认为,这部不可多得的现实主义杰作,精彩地再现了"真实的"当代黑人生活,好莱坞愿意预付高价,获得这部作品的电影改编权。特别反讽的是,这本戏仿之作的作者埃里森本人就是当时评委会成员之一,而且始终坚持认为,这部作品非常垃圾,全都是类型化的偏见,没有任何真实性可言,是胡编乱造的典型。他想让其他评委认识到,这部作品极具攻击性,"写得很糟",非常"种族主义",但是评委会的其他专家对他的这些论述全都不以为然,认为他应该为自己的黑人族人获得此项殊荣感到由衷的高兴,这时候泼冷水,纯粹是妒忌心作祟。

我们可以想象,作为勤勉的实验小说家,此时的埃里森恐怕是悲喜交集。喜的是,自己的严肃之作之前因"不够真实",或者说"不够黑"而屡遭退稿,无人问津,现在成功突然不期而至;悲的是,自己视为荒诞,予以调侃的"虚假的"东西居然被视为"真实",成为黑人族群生活的代表,他该如何面对文学,如何思考想象与真实。埃弗雷特以这种文本戏仿的方式进行种族想象,揭示美国文化工业的偏狭与荒诞及其对非裔美国族裔及其文化的扭曲。

Chapter 1

My journal is a private affair, but as I cannot know the time of my coming death, and since I am not disposed, however unfortunately, to the serious consideration of self-termination, I am afraid that others will see these pages. Since however I will be dead, it should not much matter to me who sees what or when. My name is Thelonious Ellison. And I am a writer of fiction. This admission pains me only at the thought of my story being found and read, as I have always been severely put off by any story which had as its main character a writer. So, I will claim to be something else, if not instead, then in addition, and that shall be a son, a brother, a fisher-man, an art lover, a woodworker. If for no other reason, I choose this last, callous-building occupation because of the shame it caused my mother, who for years called my pickup truck a station wagon. I am Thelonious Ellison. Call me Monk.

I have dark brown skin, curly hair, a broad nose, some of my ancestors were slaves and I have been detained by pasty white policemen in New Hampshire, Arizona and Georgia and so the society in which I live tells me I am black; that is my race. Though I am fairly athletic, I am no good at basketball. I listen to Mahler, Aretha Franklin, Charlie Parker and Ry Cooder on vinyl records and compact discs. I graduated summa cum laude from Harvard, hating every minute of it. I am good at math. I cannot dance. I did not grow up in any inner city or the rural south. My family owned a bungalow near Annapolis. My grandfather was a doctor. My father was a doctor. My brother and sister were doctors. [1]

While in college I was a member of the Black Panther Party, defunct as it was, mainly because I felt I had to prove I was *black* enough. Some people in the society in which I

---

① 完全不同于人们视为当然的黑人家庭及黑人男性形象。

live, described as being black, tell me I am not *black* enough.① Some people whom the society calls white tell me that same thing. I have heard this mainly about my novels, from editors who have rejected me and reviewers whom I have apparently confused and, on a couple of occasions, on a basketball court when upon missing a shot I muttered *Egads*. From a reviewer:

> The novel is finely crafted, with fully developed characters, rich language and subtle play with the plot, but one is lost to understand what this reworking of Aeschylus's The Persians has to do with the African American experience.

One night at a party in New York, one of the tedious affairs where people who write mingle with people who want to write and with people who can help either group begin or continue to write, a tall, thin, rather ugly book agent told me that I could sell many books if I'd forget about writing retellings of Euripides and parodies of French poststructuralists and settle down to write the true, gritty real stories of black life. I told him that I was living a *black* life, far blacker than he could ever know, that I had lived one, that I would be living one. He left me to chat with an on-the-rise performance artist/novelist who had recently posed for seventeen straight hours in front of the governor's mansion as a lawn jockey. He familiarly flipped one of her braided extensions and tossed a thumb back in my direction.

The hard, *gritty* truth of the matter is that I hardly ever think about race. Those times when I did think about it a lot I did so because of my guilt for not thinking about it. I don't believe in race. I believe there are people who will shoot me or hang me or cheat me and try to stop me because they do believe in race, because of my brown skin, curly hair, wide nose and slave ancestors. But that's just the way it is.

Saws cut wood. They either rip with the grain or cut across it. A ripsaw will slice smoothly along the grain, but chew up the wood if it goes against the grain. It is all in the geometry of the teeth, the shape, size and set of them, how they lean away from the blade. Crosscut teeth are typically smaller than rip teeth. The large teeth of ripsaws shave material away quickly and there are deep gaps between them which allow shavings to fall away, keeping the saw from binding. Crosscut teeth make a wider path, are raked back and beveled to points. The points allow the crosscut saw to score and cleave the grain cleanly.

I arrived in Washington to give a paper, for which I had only moderate affection, at a conference, a meeting of the *Nouveau Roman* Society. I decided to attend out of no great affinity for the organization or its members or its mission, but because my mother and sister still lived in D. C. and it had been three years since my last visit.

My mother had wanted to meet me at the airport, but I refused to give her my flight

① not black enough: 所谓“不够黑”即并非人们熟知的传统的黑人形象。

information. For that matter, I also did not tell her at which hotel I'd be staying. My sister did not offer to pick me up. Lisa probably didn't hate me, her younger brother, but it became fairly clear rather early in our lives, and still, that she had little use for me. I was too flighty for her, lived in a swirl of abstracts, removed from the *real world*. While she had struggled through medical school, I had somehow, apparently, breezed through college "without cracking a book." A falsehood, but a belief to which she held fast. While she was risking her life daily by crossing picket lines to offer poor women health care which included abortions if they wanted, I was fishing, sawing wood, or writing dense, obscure novels or teaching a bunch of green California intellects about Russian formalism. But if she was cool to me, she was frozen to my brother, the high rolling plastic surgeon in Scottsdale, Arizona. Bill had a wife and two kids, but we all knew he was gay. Lisa didn't dislike Bill because of his sexuality, but because he practiced medicine for no reason other than the accumulation of great wealth.

I fancied occasionally that my brother and sister were proud of me, for my books, even if they found them unreadable, boring, mere curiosities. As my brother pointed out once while my parents were extolling my greatness to some friends, "You could rub your shit on a shingle and they'd act like that." I knew this before he'd said it, but still it was rather deflating. He then added, "Not that they don't have a right to be proud." What went unsaid, but clearly implied, was that they had a right but not a reason to be proud of me. I must have cared some then, because I was angered by his words. By now however, I appreciated Bill and what he had said, though I hadn't seen him in four years.

The conference was at the Mayflower Hotel, but as I disliked meetings and had little interest in the participants of such affairs, I took a room at a little B & B off Dupont Circle called the Tabbard Inn. The most attractive feature of the place to me was the absence of a phone in the room. I checked in, unpacked and showered. I then called my sister at her clinic from the phone in the lobby.

"So, you're here," Lisa said.

I didn't point out to her how much better *So, you made it* might have sounded, but said, "Yep."

"Have you called Mother yet?"

"No. I figured she'd be taking her afternoon siesta about now."

Lisa grunted what sounded like an agreement. "So, shall I pick you up and we can swing by and get the old lady for dinner?"

"Okay. I'm at the Tabbard Inn."

"I know it. Be there in an hour." She hung up before I could say *Goodbye* or *I'll be ready* or *Don't bother, just go to hell*. But I wouldn't have said that to Lisa. I admired her far too much and in many ways I wished I were more like her. She'd dedicated her life to helping people, but it was never clear to me that she liked them all that much. That idea of service, she got from my father, who, however wealthy his practice made him, never collected fees from half his patients.

My father's funeral had been a simple, yet huge, somewhat organic event in

Northwest Washington. The street outside the Episcopal church my parents never attended was filled with people, nearly all of them teary-eyed and claiming to have been delivered into this world by the great Dr. Ellison, this in spite of most of them being clearly too young to have been born while he was still practicing. I as yet have been unable to come to an understanding or create some meaning for the spectacle.

Lisa arrived exactly one hour later. We hugged stiffly, as was our wont, and walked to the street. I got into her luxury coupe, sank into the leather and said, "Nice car."

"What's that supposed to mean?" she asked.

"Comfortable car," I said. "Plush, well appointed, not shitty, nicer than my car. What do you think it means?"

She turned the key. "I hope you are ready."

I looked at her, watched as she slipped the automatic transmission into drive.

"Mother's a little weird these days," she said.

"She sounds okay on the phone," I said, knowing full well it was a stupid thing to say, but still my bit in all this was to allow segue from minor complaint to reports of coming doom.

"You think you'd be able to tell anything during those five minute check-ins you call conversation's?"

I had in fact called them just that, but I would no longer.

"She forgets things, forgets that you've told her things just minutes later."

"She an old woman."

"That's exactly what I'm telling you." Lisa slammed the heel of her palm against the horn, then lowered her windows. She yelled at the driver in front of us who had stopped in a manner to her disliking, "Eat shit and die, you colon polyp!"

"You should be careful," I said. "That guy could be a nut or something."

"Fuck him," she said. "Four months ago Mother paid all her bills twice. All of them. Guess who writes the checks now." she turned her head to look at me, awaiting a response.

"You do."

"Damn right, I do. You're out in California and Pretty Boy Floyd is butchering people in Fartsdale and I'm the only one here."

"What about Lorraine?"

"Lorraine is still around. Where else is she going to be? She's still stealing little things here and there. Do you think she complained when she got paid twice? I'm being run ragged."

"I'm sorry, Lisa. It really isn't a fair setup." I didn't know what to say short of offering to move back to D.C. and in with my mother.

"She can't even remember that I'm divorced. She can recall every nauseating detail about Barry, but she can't remember that he ran off with his secretary. You'll see. First thing out of her mouth will be, 'Are you and Barry pregnant yet?' Christ."

"Is there anything you want me to take care of in the house?" I asked.

"Yeah, right. You come home, fix a radiator and she'll remember that for six years. 'Monksie fixed that squeaky door. Why can't you fix anything? You'd think with all that education you could fix something.' Don't touch anything in that house." Lisa didn't reach for a pack of cigarettes, don't make motions like she was reaching for one or lighting one, but that's exactly what she was doing. In her mind, she was holding a Bic lighter to a Marlboro and blowing out a cloud of smoke. She looked at me again. "So, how are you doing, little brother?"

"Okay, I guess."

"What are you doing in town?"

"I'm giving a paper at the *Nouveau Roman* Society meeting." Her silence seemed to request elaboration. "I'm working on a novel, I guess you'd call it a novel, which treats this critical text by Roland Barthes, *S/Z* exactly as it treats its so-called subject text which is Balzac's *Sarrasine*."

Lisa grunted something friendly enough sounding. "You know, I just can't read that stuff you write."

"Sorry."

"It's my fault, I'm sure."

"How is your practice?"

Lisa shook her head, "I hate this country. These anti-abortionist creeps are out front every day, with their signs and their big potato heads. They're scary. I suppose you heard about that mess in Maryland."

I had in fact read about the sniper who shot the nurse through the clinic window; I nodded.

Lisa was tapping the steering wheel rapid fire with her index fingers. As always, my sister and her problems seemed so much larger than me and mine. And I could offer her nothing in the way of solutions, advice or even commiseration. Even in her car, in spite of her small size and soft features, she towered over me.

"You know why I like you, Monk," she said after a long break. "I like you because you're smart. You understand stuff I could never get and you don't even think about it. I mean, you're just one of those people." There was a note of resentment in her compliment. "I mean, Bill is a jerk, probably a good butcher, but a butcher nonetheless. He doesn't care about anything but being a good butcher and making butcher money. But you, you don't have to think about this crap, but you do." She put out her imaginary cigarette. "I just wish you'd write something I could read."

"I'll see what I can do."

My mother had just awakened from her nap when we arrived at her house on Underwood, but as always she was dressed as if to go out. She wore blush in the old way, showing clearly on her light cheeks, but her age let her pull it off. She seemed shorter than ever and she hugged me somewhat less stiffly than my sister had and said, "My little

Monksie is home."

I lifted her briefly from the floor, she always liked that, and kissed her cheek. I observed the expectant expression on my sister's face as the old woman turned to her.

"So, Lisa, are you and Barry pregnant yet?"

"Barry is," Lisa said. She then spoke into our mother's puzzled face. "Barry and I are divorced, Mother. The idiot ran off with another woman."

"I'm so sorry, dear." She patted Lisa's arm. "That's just life, honey. Don't worry. You'll get through it. As your father used to say, 'One way or another.'"

"Thank you, Mother."

"We're taking you out to dinner, madam," I said. "What do you think of that?"

"I think it's lovely, just lovely. Let me freshen up and grab my bag."

Lisa and I wandered around the living room while she was gone. I went to the mantel and looked at the photographs that had remained the same for fifteen years, my father posed gallantly in his uniform from the war in Korea, my mother looking more like Dorothy Dandridge than my mother, and the children, looking sweeter and cleaner than we ever were. I looked down into the fireplace. "Hey, Lisa, there are ashes in the fireplace."

"What?"

"Look. Ashes." I pointed.

The fireplace in the house had never been used. Our mother was so afraid of fire that she'd insisted on electric stoves and electric baseboard heat throughout the house. Mother came back with her bag and her face powdered.

"How did these ashes get here?" Lisa asked, sidling up to the subject in her way.

"When you burn things, you make ashes," Mother said. "You should know that, with your education."

"What was burned?"

"I promised your father I'd burn some of his papers when he died. Well, he died."

"Father died seven years ago," Lisa said.

"I know that, dear. I just finally got around to it. You know how I hate fire." Her point was a reasonable one.

"What kind of papers?" Lisa asked.

"That's none of your business," Mother said. "Why do you think your father asked me to burn them? Now, let's go to dinner."

At the door, Mother fumbled with her key in the lock, complained that the mechanism had become sticky lately. I offered to help. "Here," I said. "If you turn the key this way and then back, it turns easily."

"Monksie fixed my lock," she said.

Lisa groaned and stepped down ahead of us to her car.

Mother spoke softly to me, "I think there's a problem with Lisa and Barry."

"Yes, Mother."

"Are you married yet?" she asked. I held her arm as she walked down the porch steps.

"Not yet."

"You'd better get started. You don't want to be fifty with little kids. They'll run your tail into the ground."

My father had been considerably older than my mother. In June, when school ended, we would drive to the house in Highland Beach, Maryland, and open it for the summer. We'd open all the windows, sweep, clear cobwebs and chase away stray cats. Then for the rest of the summer we would all remain at the beach and Father would join us on weekends. But I remember how the first cleaning always wore him out and when it came time to take a break before dinner and play softball or croquet, he would resign to a seat on the porch and watch. He would cheer Mother on when she took the bat, giving her pointers, then sitting back as if worn out by thinking about it. He had more energy in the mornings and for some reason he and I took early strolls together. We walked to the beach, out onto the pier, then back, past the Douglass house and over to the tidal creek where we'd sit and watch the crabs scurrying with the tide. Sometimes we'd take a bucket and a net and he'd coach me while I snagged a couple dozen crabs for lunch.

Once he fell to his butt in the sand and said, "Thelonious, you're a good boy."

I looked back at him from the ankle-deep water.

"You're not like your brother and sister. Of course, they're not like each other either. But they're more alike than they're willing to admit. Anyway, you're different."

"Is that good, Father?" I asked.

"Yes," he said, as if figuring out the answer right then. He pointed to the water. "There's a nice fat one. Come at him from farther away."

I followed his instructions and scooped up the crab.

"Good boy. You have a special mind. The way you see things. If I had the patience to figure out what you were saying sometimes, I know you'd make me a smarter man."

I don't know what he was telling me, but I understood the flattering tone and appreciated it.

"And you're so relaxed. Hang on to that trait, son. That might serve you better than anything else in life."

"Yes, Father."

"It will also prove handy for upsetting your siblings." Then he leaned back and proceeded to have a heart attack.

I ran to him. He grabbed my arm and said, "Now, stay relaxed and go get help."

That turned out to be the first of four heart attacks he would suffer just out and shooting himself one unseasonably warm February evening while Mother was off meeting with her bridge club. His suicide apparently came as no surprise to my mother, as she called each of us, in order of age, and said the same thing, "You must come home for your father's funeral."

Dinner was typical, nothing more or less. My mother said things that made my sister roll her eyes while she smoked an entire pack of imaginary cigarettes. Mother told me about telling all her bridge buddies about my books, asking as she always did if there wasn't a better word for *fuck* than *fuck*. Then my sister dropped me at my hotel and perfunctorily committed herself to lunch with me the next day.

I was scheduled to present my paper at nine the next morning, so my intention was to get to bed early and maybe sleep through it. However, when I entered my room I found a note that had been slipped under the door that told me to return a call to Linda Mallory at the Mayflower. I went to the lobby for the telephone.

"I was hoping you would come to the conference." Linda said. "The secretary in your department told me where you'd be staying."

"How are you, Linda?"

"I've been better. You know, Lars and I broke up."

"I didn't know you were together. I suppose asking who Lars is at this juncture is pointless."

"Are you tired? I mean, it's early yet and we are still on California clock, right?"

"Is that Bay area talk? *California clock?*" I looked at my watch. 8:20. "My paper's at nine in the morning."

"But it's only eight o'clock," she said. "That's five for us. You can't expect me to believe you're going to bed at five. I can be over in fifteen."

"No, I'll come there," I said, fearing that if I declined completely, she would show up anyway. "I'll meet you in the bar."

"There's one of those little bars in my room."

"In the bar at eight-forty-five." I hung up.

Linda Mallory and I had slept together three times, two of those times we had sex. Twice in Berkeley when I was doing some readings and once in Los Angeles when she was down doing the same. She was a tall, knock-kneed, rather shapeless-however-thin woman with a weak chin and a sharp wit, a sharp wit when men and sex weren't involved at any rate. She zeroed in on male attention like a Rottweiler on a porkchop and it became all she could see. In fact, before her ears perked to male attention she could be called attractive, dark eyes and thick hair, lean and with an easy smile. She liked to fuck, she said, but I believed she liked saying it more than doing it. She could be pushy. And she was completely without literary talent, which was both irritating and, in a weird way, refreshing. Linda had published one volume of predictably strange and stereotypically *innovative* short fictions (as she liked to call them). She'd fallen into a circle of *innovative* writers who had survived the sixties by publishing each others' stories in their periodicals and each others' books collectively, thus amassing publications, so achieving tenure at their various universities, and establishing a semblance of credibility in the so-called real world. Sadly, these people made up a good portion of the membership of the *Nouveau Roman* Society. They all hated me. For a couple of reasons: One was that I had published and had moderate success with a realistic novel some years earlier, and two, I made no secret, in print or radio interviews, what I thought of their work. Finally, however, I was hated because the French, whom they so adored, seemed to hold my work in high regard. To me, a mere strange footnote to my obscure and very quiet literary career. To them, a slap in the face perhaps.

Linda was already in the bar when I arrived. She wrapped me up in a hug and I remembered how much like a bicycle she had felt in bed.

"So," she said, in that way people use the word to introduce beating around the bush. "We had to come three thousand miles to see each other when we live in the same state."

"Funny how things work out."

We sat and I ordered a scotch. Linda asked for another Gibson. She played with the onion in her glass, stabbing it with the red plastic sword.

"Are you on the program?" I asked. I hadn't seen her name, but then I hadn't looked.

"I'm on a panel with Davis Gimbel, Willis Lloyd and Lewis Rosenthal."

"What's the panel?" I asked.

"'The Place of Burroughs in American Fiction.'"

I groaned. "Sounds pleasant enough."

"I saw the tide of your paper. I don't get it." She ate the onion off her sword just as our drinks arrived. "What's it about?"

"You'll hear it. I'm sick of the damn thing. It's not going to make me any friends, I'll tell you that." I looked around the bar and saw no familiar faces. "I can just feel the creepiness here."

"Why did you come then?" she complained.

"Because this way my trip is paid for." I swallowed some scotch and was sorry I hadn't requested a water back. "I'd rather admit to that than say I came here because I care about the proceedings of the NRS."

"You have a point." Linda ate her second onion. "Would you like to go up to my room?"

"Smooth," I said. "What if we don't have sex and say we did?" After an awkward spell, I said, "So, how's Berkeley?"

"It's fine. I'm up for tenure this year."

"How does it look?" I asked, knowing full well it couldn't look good for her.

"Your family's here," she said.

"My mother and sister." I finished my scotch and became painfully aware that I had nothing to say to Linda. I didn't know enough about her personal life to ask questions and I didn't want to bring up her recent breakup, so I stared into my glass.

The waitress came over and asked if I wanted another drink. I said no and gave her enough for the two Gibsons and my scotch. Linda watched my hands.

"I'd better get some rest," I said. "I'll see you tomorrow."

"Probably."

Questions for Discussion

1. Why was "I" described as not black enough by both black and white people?

2. "I" don't believe in race, and those who do believe in race will "shoot me or hang me or cheat me and try to stop me" because of "my" brown skin, curly hair, wide nose and slave ancestors, please comment on it.

3. Monk introduces his family members briefly, do you find any differences between his family and those of others?

6. The Known World

作家简介

　　与 20 世纪很多著名非裔美国作家非常类似的是,爱德华·琼斯(1951—　　)也出身贫寒,不识字的母亲是家中的经济支柱。但是幸运的是,他接受了高等教育,1979 年在马萨诸塞耶稣会学校圣十字学院获得英语专业学士学位,1981 年在弗吉尼亚大学获得艺术硕士学位;其后 20 年间,他白天为一家金融杂志工作,晚上进行小说创作,经过多年的不懈努力,终于开始收获成功的果实,成为知名作家。

　　酷爱读书的琼斯特别喜欢沃特斯的《他的眼睛望着麻雀》和赖特的《土生子》,觉得书中的人物非常熟悉,好像在对自己说话,而且他对黑人也能创作如此美好的东西感到非常震惊;读完埃里森的小说《看不见的人》之后,他看到作者的照片,再次坚定黑人也能创作美好作品的信念。此外,对他的创作产生影响的黑人作家还有小说家佩里、邓巴和布鲁克斯,以及美国白人作家福克纳、俄国作家契诃夫,但是对他的短篇小说创作产生无可替代影响的是英国作家乔伊斯的《都柏林人》。

　　他的第一部短篇小说集《迷失在都市》(1992)收录 14 篇短篇小说,获得海明威笔会奖,并进入美国国家图书奖的决赛名单,对一个文坛"新手"来说,这份荣誉非常难得。书中收录的这些故事都以 20 世纪 60 年代和 70 年代华盛顿特区穷苦社区为背景,主要讲述人们在这个冷酷、残忍的世界中的挣扎以及精神方面的坚守与收获。琼斯非常高妙地捕捉到了这个"迷失都市"的脉搏,描绘人们如何面对灾祸不断的世界,以及如何维系家庭与社区的脆弱联系。

　　2003 年,他的第一部长篇小说《已知世界》获得普利策文学奖。批评家认为,这部作品非常与众不同、迷人、有力,可与福克纳、莫里森及马尔克斯的作品相媲美。琼斯在访谈中指出,自己想通过这部作品,揭示使人们挺过艰难岁月的精神力量,他认为是家庭的力量让奴隶们得以挺住。更为重要的是,他认为,人们一直面临这样的难题:家庭的分崩离析及其难以承受的后果,家庭意味着人们具有超越自身的爱,是人们得以幸存的关键。

　　琼斯对待写作非常认真,惜墨如金,对当下非裔美国文学的商业化写作不以为然,他明确表示,自己不会写"无知""绝望"与"脆弱"或者写人们去夜店、去做蠢事。他想创作出能够表达人们坚韧、顽强的东西,如爱、荣誉、智识,以及非裔美国人民作为一个民族的强大力量。他的杰作《已知世界》很好地体现了这一理念。

作品简介与赏析

　　《已知世界》是琼斯的第一部长篇小说,故事背景设在 1855 年弗吉尼亚州的曼彻斯特县,围绕前黑人奴隶亨利·汤森德展开,讲述他赢得自由后,获得 50 英亩土地,摇身一变,成为拥有 33 位奴隶的黑人奴隶主的故事。

　　熟悉美国南方奴隶制的读者,他们脑海中经常会萦绕着三类人:一是残暴的白人奴隶主,二是受苦受难的黑人奴隶,三是被奴隶主欺凌、侮辱的女黑奴。而 21 世纪初出版的《已知世界》完全颠覆了人们对奴隶制的普遍认知。这部作品描绘了获得自由的黑人成为奴隶主的故事,而且他这个黑人奴隶主所做的事情与人们熟悉的白人奴隶主并没有本质上的区别;另外一位肤色白皙,获得自由的前奴隶法纳·尔斯泰,也成为与亨利类似的黑人女奴隶主,与一位男奴保持着性关系。人们不禁会问:琼斯此举是否旨在讨好白人社会,减少他们良心上的内疚,还是想借此探讨奴隶制的体制性罪恶——重要的不是作为个体的奴隶主(无论他们是白人还是黑人)有多么邪恶,而是奴隶制所具有的体制性的邪恶,使善良之辈也可能成为暴虐之徒。

虽然本书的重要主题之一是奴隶制,但作者并非只关注肤色,而是非常重视权力的作用,特别是权力的腐蚀作用及其矛盾之处。虽然大部分奴隶制的牺牲品都是黑人,但琼斯也在作品中融入一些小的涉及白人奴隶的故事;尽管黑人奴隶主亨利是书中的重要角色,但是在人物刻画方面,作者对白人警长约翰·斯基潘顿更加关注,把他描绘成当时权力结构中性格最复杂的人物。这位警长非常体面,不愿意拥有奴隶,当有人送给他一个黑人小女孩作为结婚礼物时,他把她当成自己的女儿一样抚养,体现出他人性中非常美好的方面;但是作为警长,职责使然,他也不得不做一些无情杀害自由奴隶的事情。他牢房墙上挂着的名为"已知世界"的旧地图,可以很好地代表他的状况。这幅过时的地图,就像他当差的这个县的社会舆论,既偏颇又片面,只能为他了解这个真实的世界提供非常有限的知识。与之相对应的是艾莉丝·奈特的挂毯,涵盖过去、现在与未来,而非局限于某时某刻,预示着整部作品的基调。

这部广受赞誉的小说没有满足于提供一个善恶分明的故事,而是坚持追问:个体的脆弱与坚强如何体现,奴隶制体制性的罪恶如何得以维系等,为新世纪的美国读者反思历史,勇敢面对历史的复杂性提供了新的思路。

Chapter 1
Liaison. The Warmth of Family. Stormy Weather.

The evening his master died he worked again well after he ended the day for the other adults, his own wife among them, and sent them back with hunger and tiredness to their cabins. The young ones, his son among them, had been sent out of the fields an hour or so before the adults, to prepare the late supper and, if there was time enough, to play in the few minutes of sun that were left. When he, Moses, finally freed himself of the ancient and brittle harness that connected him to the oldest mule his master owned, all that was left of the sun was a five-inch-long memory of red orange laid out in still waves across the horizon between two mountains on the left and one on the right. He had been in the fields for all of fourteen hours. He paused before leaving the fields as the evening quiet wrapped itself about him. The mule quivered, wanting home and rest. Moses closed his eyes and bent down and took a pinch of the soil and ate it with no more thought than if it were a spot of cornbread. He worked the dirt around in his mouth and swallowed, leaning his head back and opening his eyes in time to see the strip of sun fade to dark blue and then to nothing. He was the only man in the realm, slave or free, who ate dirt, but while the bondage women, particularly the pregnant ones, ate it for some incomprehensible need, for that something that ash cakes and apples and fatback did not give their bodies, he ate it not only to discover the strengths and weaknesses of the field, but because the eating of it tied him to the only thing in his small world that meant almost as much as his own life.

This was July, and July dirt tasted even more like sweetened metal than the dirt of June or May. Something in the growing crops unleashed a metallic life that only began to dissipate in mid-August, and by harvest time that life would be gone altogether, replaced by a sour moldiness he associated with the coming of fall and winter, the end of a relationship he had begun with the first taste of dirt back in March, before the first hard spring rain. Now, with the sun gone and no moon and the darkness having taken a nice hold of him, he walked to the end of the row, holding the mule by the tail. In the clearing he dropped the tail and moved around the mule toward the barn.

The mule followed him, and after he had prepared the animal for the night and came out, Moses smelled the coming of rain. He breathed deeply, feeling it surge through him. Believing he was alone, he smiled. He knelt down to be closer to the earth and breathed deeply some more. Finally, when the effect began to dwindle, he stood and turned away, for the third time that week, from the path that led to the narrow lane of the quarters with its people and his own cabin, his woman and his boy. His wife knew enough now not to wait for him to come and eat with them. On a night with the moon he could see some of the smoke rising from the world that was the lane—home and food and rest and what passed in many cabins for the life of family. He turned his head slightly to the right and made out what he thought was the sound of playing children, but when he turned his head back, he could hear far more clearly the last bird of the day as it evening-chirped in the small forest far off to the left.

He went straight ahead, to the farthest edge of the cornfields to a patch of woods that had yielded nothing of value since the day his master bought it from a white man who had gone broke and returned to Ireland. "I did well over there," that man lied to his people back in Ireland, his dying wife standing hunched over beside him, "but I longed for all of you and for the wealth of my homeland." The patch of woods of no more than three acres did yield some soft, blue grass that no animal would touch and many trees that no one could identify. Just before Moses stepped into the woods, the rain began, and as he walked on the rain became heavier. Well into the forest the rain came in torrents through the trees and the mighty summer leaves, and after a bit Moses stopped and held out his hands and collected water that he washed over his face. Then he undressed down to his nakedness and lay down. To keep the rain out of his nose, he rolled up his shirt and placed it under his head so that it tilted just enough for the rain to flow down about his face. When he was an old man and rheumatism chained up his body, he would look back and blame the chains on evenings such as these, and on nights when he lost himself completely and fell asleep and didn't come to until morning, covered with dew. The ground was almost soaked. The leaves seemed to soften the hard rain as it fell and it hit his body and face with no more power than the gentle tapping of fingers. He opened his mouth; it was rare for him and the rain to meet up like this. His eyes had remained open, and after taking in all that he could without turning his head, he took up his thing and did it. When he was done, after a few strokes, he closed his eyes, turned on his side and dozed. After a half hour or so the rain stopped abruptly and plunged everything into silence, and that silence woke him. He came to his feet with the usual reluctance. All about his body was mud and leaves and debris for the rain had sent a wind through the woods. He wiped himself with his pants and remembered that the last time he had been there in the rain, the rain had lasted long enough to wash him clean. He had been seized then by an even greater happiness and had laughed and twirled himself around and around in what someone watching him might have called a dance. He did not know it, but Alice, a woman people said had lost her mind, was watching him now, only the first time in her six months of wandering about in the night that she had come upon him. Had he known she was there, he would not have thought she had sense enough to know what was going on, given how hard, the story went, the mule had kicked her on the plantation in a faraway county whose name only she remembered. In her saner moments, which were very rare since the day Moses's master bought her, Alice could describe everything about the Sunday the mule kicked her in the head and sent all common sense flying out of her. No one questioned her because her story was so vivid, so sad—another slave without freedom and now she had a mind so addled she wandered in the night like a cow without a bell. No one knew enough about the place she had come from to know that her former master was terrified of mules and would not have them on his place, had even banished pictures and books about mules from his little world.

Moses walked out of the forest and into still more darkness toward the quarters, needing no moon to light his way. He was thirty-five years old and for every moment of those years he had been someone's slave, a white man's slave and then another white man's slave and now, for nearly ten years, the overseer slave for a black master.

Caldonia Townsend, his master's wife, had for the last six days and nights only been catnapping, as her husband made his hard way toward death. The white people's doctor had come the morning of the first day, as a favor to Caldonia's mother, who believed in the magic of white people, but that doctor had only pronounced that Moses's master, Henry Townsend, was going through a bad spell and would recover soon. The ailments of white people and black people were different, and a man who specialized in one was not expected to know much about the other, and that was something he believed Caldonia should know without him telling her. If her husband was dying, the doctor didn't know anything about it. And he left in the heat of the day, having pocketed 75 cents from Caldonia, 60 cents for looking at Henry and 15 cents for the wear and tear on himself and his buggy and his one-eyed horse.

Henry Townsend—a black man of thirty-one years with thirty-three slaves and more than fifty acres of land that sat him high above many others, white and black and Indian, in Manchester County, Virginia—sat up in bed for most of his dying days, eating a watery porridge and looking out his window at land his wife, Caldonia, kept telling him he would walk and ride over again. But she was young and naively vigorous and had known but one death in her life, that of her father, who had been secretly poisoned by his own wife. On the fourth day on his way to death, Henry found sitting up difficult and lay down. He spent that night trying to reassure his wife. "Nothin hurts," he said more than once that day, a day in July 1855. "Nothin hurts."

"Would you tell me if it did?" Caldonia said. It was near about three in the morning, two hours or so after she had dismissed for the evening Loretta, her personal maid, the one who had come with her marriage to Henry.

"I ain't took on the habit of not tellin you the truth," Henry said that fourth evening. "I can't start now." He had received some education when he was twenty and twenty-one, educated just enough to appreciate a wife like Caldonia, a colored woman born free and who had been educated all her days. Finding a wife had been near the end of a list of things he planned to do with his life. "Why don't you go on to bed, darlin?" Henry said. "I can feel sleep comin on and you shouldn't wait for it to get here." He was in what the slaves who worked in the house called the "sick and gettin well room," where he had taken himself that first sick day to give Caldonia some peace at night. "I'm fine right here," she said. The night had gotten cooler and he was in fresh nightclothes, having sweated through the ones they had put him in at about nine o'clock. "Should I read to you?" Caldonia asked, covered in a lace shawl Henry had seen in Richmond. He had paid a white boy to go into the white man's shop to purchase it for him, because the shop would have no black customers. "A bit of Milton? Or the Bible?" She was curled up in a large horsehair chair that had been pulled up to his bed. On each side of the bed were small tables just large enough for a book and a candelabrum that held three candles as thick as a woman's wrist. The candelabrum on the right side was dark, and the one on the left had only one burning candle. There was no fire in the hearth.

"I been so weary of Milton," Henry said. "And the Bible suits me better in the day, when there's sun and I can see what all God gave me." Two days before he had told his parents to go home, that he was doing better, and he had indeed felt some improvement, but on the next day, after his folks were back at their place, Henry took a turn back to bad. He and his father had not been close for more than ten years, but his father was a man strong enough to put aside disappointment in his son when he knew his flesh and blood was sick. In fact, the only time his father had come to see Henry on the plantation was when the son had been doing poorly. Some seven times in the course of ten years or so. When Henry's mother visited alone, whether he was ill or well, she stayed in the house, two rooms down from her son and Caldonia. The day Henry sent them home, his parents had come upstairs and kissed his smiling face good-bye, his mother on the lips and his father on the forehead, the way it had been done since Henry was a boy. His parents as a couple had never slept in the home he and Moses the slave had built, choosing to stay in whatever cabin was available down in the quarters. And they would do it that way when they came to bury their only child.

"Shall I sing?" Caldonia said, and reached over and touched his hand resting at the side of the bed. "Shall I sing till the birds wake up?" She had been educated by a freed black woman who herself had been educated in Washington, D.C., and Richmond. That woman, Fern Elston, had returned to her own plantation after visiting the Townsends three days ago to continue making part of her living in Manchester County teaching the freed black children whose parents could afford her. Caldonia said, "You think you've heard all my songs, Henry Townsend, but you haven't. You really haven't." Fern Elston had married a man who was supposed to be a farmer, but he lived to gamble, and as Fern told herself in those moments when she was able to put love aside and see her husband for what he was, he seemed to be driving them the long way around to the poorhouse. Fern and her husband had twelve slaves to their names. In 1855 in Manchester County, Virginia, there were thirty-four free black families, with a mother and father and one child or more, and eight of those free families owned slaves, and all eight knew one another's business. When the War between the States came, the number of slave-owning blacks in Manchester would be down to five, and one of those included an extremely morose man who, according to the U.S. census of 1860, legally owned his own wife and five children and three grandchildren. The census of 1860 said there were 2,670 slaves in Manchester County, but the census taker, a U.S. marshal who feared God, had argued with his wife the day he sent his report to Washington, D.C., and all his arithmetic was wrong because he had failed to carry a one.

Henry said, "No. Best save the singin for some other time, darlin." What he wanted was to love her, to get up from the sickbed and walk under his own power and take his wife to the bed they had been happy in all their married days. When he died, late the evening of the seventh day, Fern Elston would be with Caldonia in his death room. "I always thought you did right in marrying him," Fern would say, in the first stages of grief for Henry, a former student. After the War between the States, Fern would tell a pamphlet writer, a white immigrant from Canada, that Henry had been the brightest of her students, someone she would have taught for free. Loretta, Caldonia's maid, would be there as well when Henry died, but she would be silent. She merely closed her master's eyes after a time and covered his face with a quilt, a Christmas present from three slave women who had made it in fourteen days.

Moses the overseer walked the lane of the quarters down to his cabin, the one nearest the house where his master and mistress lived. Next to Moses's cabin, Elias sat on a damp tree stump before his own cabin, whittling a piece of pinewood that would be the body of a doll he was making for his daughter. It was the first thing he had ever given her. He had a lamp hanging from a nail beside his door but the light had been failing and he was as close to working blind as a body could get. But his daughter and his two sons, one only thirteen months old, were heaven and earth to him and somehow the knife cut into the pinewood in just the right way and began what would be the doll's right eye.

Moses, a few feet before passing Elias, said, "You gotta meet that mule in the mornin."

"I know," Elias said. Moses had not stopped walking. "I ain't hurtin a soul here."

Elias said. "Just fixin on some wood." Now Moses stopped and said, "I ain't carin if you fixin God's throne. I said you gotta meet that mule in the mornin. That mule sleepin right now, so maybe you should follow after him." Elias said nothing and he did not move. Moses said, "I ain't but two minutes off you, fella, and you seem to wanna keep forgettin that." Moses had found Elias a great bother in the mind from the day Henry Townsend drove up with Elias from the slave market, a one-day affair held out in the open twice a year at the eastern edge of the town of Manchester, in the spring and in the fall after harvest. The very day Elias was bought by Henry some white people had talked about building a permanent structure for the slave market—that was the year it rained every spring day the market was held, and many white people caught colds as a result. One woman died of pneumonia. But God was generous with his blessings the following fall and each day was perfect for buying and selling slaves, and not a soul said anything about constructing a permanent place, so fine was the roof God himself had provided for the market.

Now Moses said to Elias, "If you ain't waitin for me here when the sun come up, not even Massa Henry will save you." Moses continued on to his cabin. Moses was the first slave Henry Townsend had bought: $325 and a bill of sale from William Robbins, a white man. It took Moses more than two weeks to come to understand that someone wasn't fiddling with him and that indeed a black man, two shades darker than himself, owned him and any shadow he made. Sleeping in a cabin beside Henry in the first weeks after the sale, Moses had thought that it was already a strange world that made him a slave to a white man, but God had indeed set it twirling and twisting every which way when he put black people to owning their own kind. Was God even up there attending to business anymore?

With one foot Elias swept the shavings from his other foot and started whittling again. The right leg of the doll was giving him trouble: He wanted the figure to be running but he had not been able to get the knee to bend just right. Someone seeing it might think it was just a doll standing still, and he didn't want that. He was afraid that if the knee did not bend soon he would have to start again with a new piece of wood. Finding a good piece would be hard. But then the right leg of his own wife, Celeste, did not bend the way it should either, so maybe in the long run it might not matter with the doll. Celeste had been limping from the first step she took into the world.

Moses went into his cabin and met the darkness and a dead hearth. Outside, the light of Elias's lamp leaned this way and that and then it dimmed even more. Elias had never believed in a sane God and so had never questioned a world where colored people could be the owners of slaves, and if at that moment, in the near dark, he had sprouted wings, he would not have questioned that either. He would simply have gone on making the doll. Inside Elias's cabin his crippled wife and three children slept and the hearth had enough embers to last the night, which promised to be cold again. Elias left the doll's right leg alone and returned to the head, which he already thought was as perfect as anything he had seen made by a man. He had gotten better since carving the first comb for Celeste. He wanted to attach corn silk to the doll's head but the kind of dark silk he wanted would not be ready until early fall. Immature silk would have to do.

Moses was not hungry and so did not complain to his wife or the boy about the darkness. He lay down on the straw pallet beside his wife, Priscilla. Their son was on the other side of her, snoring. Priscilla watched her husband as he slowly drifted into sleep, and once he was asleep, she took hold of his hand and put it to her face and smelled all of the outside world that he had brought in with him and then she tried to find sleep herself.

That last day, the day Henry Townsend died, Fern Elston returned early in a buggy driven by a sixty-five-year-old slave her husband had inherited from his father.

Fern and Caldonia spent a few hours in the parlor, drinking a milk-and-honey brew Caldonia's mother was fond of making. Upstairs during that time, Zeddie, the cook, and then Loretta, Caldonia's maid, sat with Henry. About seven in the evening, Caldonia told Fern she had best go on to bed, but Fern had not been sleeping well and she told Caldonia they might as well sit together with Henry. Fern had been a teacher not only to Caldonia but to her twin brother as well. There were not that many free educated women in Manchester County to pass her time with and so Fern had made a friend of a woman who, as a girl, had found too much to giggle about in the words of William Shakespeare.

The two women went up about eight and Caldonia told Loretta she would call her if she needed her and Loretta nodded and went out and down to her small room at the end of the hall. The three, Fern and Henry and Caldonia, started in talking about the Virginia heat and the way it wore away a body. Henry had seen North Carolina once and thought Virginia's heat could not compare. That last evening was fairly cold again. Henry had not had to change the night-clothes he had put on at six. About nine he fell asleep and woke not long after. His wife and Fern were discussing a Thomas Gray poem. He thought he knew the one they were talking about but as he formed some words to join the conversation, death stepped into the room and came to him: Henry walked up the steps and into the tiniest of houses, knowing with each step that he did not own it, that he was only renting. He was ever so disappointed; he heard footsteps behind him and death told him it was Caldonia, coming to register her own disappointment. Whoever was renting the house to him had promised a thousand rooms, but as he traveled through the house he found less than four rooms, and all the rooms were identical and his head touched their ceilings. "This will not do," Henry kept saying to himself, and he turned to share that thought with his wife, to say, "Wife, wife, look what they done done," and God told him right then, "Not a wife, Henry, but a widow."

It was several minutes before Caldonia and Fern knew Henry was no more and they went on talking about a widowed white woman with two slaves to her name on a farm in some distant part of Virginia, in a place near Montross where her nearest white neighbors were miles and miles away. The news of the young woman, Elizabeth Marson, was more than one year old but it was only now reaching the people of Manchester County, so the women in the room with dead Henry spoke as if it had all happened to Elizabeth just that morning. After the white woman's husband died, her slaves, Mirtha and Destiny, had taken over and kept the woman prisoner for months, working her ragged with only a few hours rest each day until her hair turned white and her pores sweated blood. Caldonia said she understood that Mirtha and Destiny had been sold to try to compensate Elizabeth, to settle her away from that farm with its memories, but Fern said she understood that the slave women had been killed by the law. When Elizabeth was finally rescued, she did not remember that she was supposed to be the owner, and it was a long time before she could be taught that again. Caldonia, noticing her husband's stillness, went to him. She gave a cry as she shook him. Loretta came in silently and took a hand mirror from atop the dresser. It seemed to Caldonia as she watched Loretta place the mirror under Henry's nose that he had only stepped away and that if she called loudly enough to him, put her mouth quite close to his ear, and called loud enough for any slave in the quarters to hear, he might turn back and be her husband again. She took Henry's hand in both of hers and put it to her cheek. It was warm, she noticed, thinking there might yet be enough life in it for him to reconsider. Caldonia was twenty-eight years old and she was childless.

Alice, the woman without a mind who had watched Moses be with himself in the woods, had been Henry and Caldonia's property for some six months the night he died. From the first week, Alice had started going about the land in the night, singing and talking to herself and doing things that sometimes made the hair on the backs of the slave patrollers' necks stand up. She spit at and slapped their horses for saying untrue things about her to her neighbors, especially to Elias's youngest, "a little bitty boy" she told the patrollers she planned to marry after the harvest. She grabbed the patrollers' crotches and begged them to dance away with her because her intended was forever pretending he didn't know who she was. She called the white men by made-up names and gave them the day and time God would take them to heaven, would drag each and every member of their families across the sky and toss them into hell with no more thought than a woman dropping strawberries into a cup of cream.

In those first days after Henry bought Alice, the patrollers would haul her back to Henry's plantation, waking him and Caldonia as one of them rode up on the porch and pounded on the black man's front door with the butt of a pistol. "Your property out here loose and you just sleepin like everything's fine and dandy," they shouted to him, a giggling Alice sprawled before them in the dirt after they had run her back. "Come down here and find out about your property." Henry would come down and explain again that no one, not even his overseer, had been able to keep her from roaming. Moses had suggested tying her down at night, but Caldonia would not have it. Alice was nothing to worry about, Henry said to the patrollers, coming down the steps in his nightclothes and helping Alice up from the ground. She just had half a mind, he said, but other than that she was a good worker, never saying to the two or three white patrollers who owned no slaves that a woman of half a mind had been so much cheaper to buy than one with a whole mind: $228 and two bushels of apples not good enough to eat and only so-so enough for a cider that was bound to set someone's teeth on edge. The patrollers would soon ride away. "This is what happens," they said among themselves back on the road, "when you give niggers the same rights as a white man."

Toward the middle of her third week as Henry and Caldonia's property, the patrollers got used to seeing Alice wander about and she became just another fixture in the patrollers' night, worthy of no more attention than a hooting owl or a rabbit hopping across the road.

Sometimes, when the patrollers had tired of their own banter or when they anticipated getting their pay from Sheriff John Skiffington, they would sit their horses and make fun of her as she sang darky songs in the road. This show was best when the moon was at its brightest, shining down on them andeasing their fear of the night and of a mad slave woman and lighting up Alice as she danced to the songs. The moon gave more life to her shadow, and the shadow would bounce about with her from one side of the road to other, calming the horses and quieting the crickets. But when they suffered ill humor, or the rain poured down and wetted them and their threadbare clothes, and their horses were skittish and the skin down to their feet itched, then they heaped curse words upon her. Over time, over those six months after Henry bought Alice, the patrollers heard from other white people that a crazy Negro slave in the night was akin to a two-headed chicken, or a crowing hen. Bad luck. Very bad luck, so it was best to try to keep the cussing to themselves.

The rainy evening her master Henry died Alice again stepped out of the cabin she shared with Delphie and Delphie's daughter, Cassandra. Delphie was nearing forty-four years old and believed that God had greater dangers in store for everybody than a colored woman gone insane, which was what she told her daughter, who was at first afraid of Alice. Alice came out that evening and saw Elias standing at his door with the whittling knife and the pinewood in his hands, waiting for the rain to end. "Come on with me," she sang to Elias. "You just come on with me now. Come on, boy." Elias ignored her.

After she came back from watching Moses in the patch of woods, Alice went back down the lane and out to the road. The muddy road gave her a hard way but she kept on. Once on the road, she veered away from Henry's place and began to chant, even more loudly than when she was on her master's land.

Lifting the front of her frock for the moon and all to see, she shimmied in the road and chanted with all her might:

> *I met a dead man layin in Massa lane*
> *Ask that dead man what his name*
> *He raised he bony head and took off his hat*
> *He told me this, he told me that.*

Augustus Townsend, Henry's father, finally bought himself out of slavery when he was twenty-two. He was a carpenter, a wood-carver whose work people said could bring sinners to tears. His master, William Robbins, a white man with 113 slaves to his name, had long permitted Augustus to hire himself out, and Robbins kept part of what he earned. The rest Augustus used to pay for himself. Once free, he continued to hire himself out. He could make a four-poster bed of oak in three weeks, chairs he could do in two days, chiffoniers in seventeen days, give or take the time it took to get the mirrors. He built a shack—and later a proper house—on land he rented and then bought from a poor white man who needed money more than he needed land. The land was at the western end of Manchester County, a fairly large slip of land where the county, as if tired of pushing west, dipped abruptly to the south, toward Amherst County. Moses, "world stupid" as Elias was to call him, would get lost there in about two months, thinking that he was headed north. Augustus Townsend liked it because it was at the farthest end of the county and the nearest white man with slaves was a half a mile away.

Augustus made the last payment for his wife, Mildred, when she was twenty-six and he was twenty-five, some three years after he bought his own freedom. An 1806 act of the Virginia House of Delegates required that former slaves leave the Commonwealth within twelve months of getting their freedom; freed Negroes might give slaves too many "unnatural notions," a delegate from Northampton County had noted before the act was passed, and, added another delegate from Gloucester, freed Negroes lacked "the natural controls" put on a slave. The delegates decreed that any freed person who had not left Virginia after one year could be brought back into slavery. That happened to thirteen people the year of Augustus's petition—five men, seven women, and one child, a girl named Lucinda, whose parents died before the family could get out of Virginia. Based primarily on his skills, Augustus had managed to get William Robbins and a number of other white citizens to petition the state assembly to permit him to stay. "Our County— Indeed, our beloved Commonwealth—would be all the poorer without the talents of Augustus Townsend," the petition read in part. His and two other petitions for former slaves were the only ones out of twenty-three granted that year; a Norfolk City woman who made elaborate cakes and pies for parties and a Richmond barber, both with more white customers than black, were also permitted to stay in Virginia after freedom. Augustus did not seek a petition for Mildred his wife when he bought her freedom because the law allowed freed slaves to stay on in the state in cases where they lived as someone's property, and relatives and friends often took advantage of the law to keep loved ones close by. Augustus would also not seek a petition for Henry, his son, and over time, because of how well William Robbins, their former owner, treated Henry, people in Manchester County just failed to remember that Henry, in fact, was listed forever in the records of Manchester as his father's property.

Henry was nine when his mother, Mildred, came to freedom. That day she left, a mild day two weeks after harvest, she walked holding her son's hand down to the road where Augustus and his wagon and two mules were waiting. Rita, Mildred's cabin mate, was holding the boy's other hand.

At the wagon, Mildred sank to her knees and held on to Henry, who, at last realizing that he was to be separated from her, began crying. Augustus knelt beside his wife and promised Henry that they would be back for him. "Before you can turn around good," he said, "you be comin home with us." Augustus repeated himself, and the boy tried to make sense of the word *home*. He knew the word, knew the cabin with him and his mother and Rita that the word represented. He could no longer remember when his father was a part of that home. Augustus kept talking and Henry pulled at Mildred, wanting her to go back onto William Robbins's land, back to the cabin where the fireplace smoked when it was first lit. "Please," the boy said, "please, les go back."

Along about then William Robbins came slowly out to the road, heading into the town of Manchester on his prized bay, Sir Guilderham. Patting the horse's black mane, he asked Henry why was he crying and the boy said, "For nothin, Massa." Augustus stood up and took off his hat. Mildred continued holding on to her son. The boy knew his master only from a distance; this was the closest they had been in a very long time. Robbins sat high on his horse, a mountain separating the boy from the fullness of the sun. "Well don't do it anymore," Robbins said. He nodded at Augustus. "Counting off the days, are you, Augustus?" He looked to Rita. "You see things go right," Robbins said. He meant for her not to let the boy go too many steps beyond his property. He would have called Rita by name but she had not distinguished herself enough in his life for him to remember the name he had given her at birth. It was enough that the name was written somewhere in his large book of births and deaths, the comings and goings of slaves. "Noticeable mole on left cheek," he had written five days after Rita's birth. "Eyes grey." Years later, after Rita disappeared, Robbins would put those facts on the poster offering a reward for her return, along with her age.

Robbins gave a last look at Henry, whose name he also did not know, and set off at a gallop, his horse's black tail flipping first one pretty way and then another, as if the tail were separate and so had a life all its own. Henry stopped crying. In the end, Augustus had to pull his wife from the child. He turned Henry over to Rita, who had been friends with Mildred all her life. He lifted his wife up onto the wagon that sagged and creaked with her weight. The wagon and the mules were not as high as Robbins's horse. Before he got up, Augustus told his son that he would see him on Sunday, the day Robbins was now allowing for visits. Then Augustus said, "I'll be back for you," meaning the day he would ultimately free the boy. But it took far longer to buy Henry's freedom than his father had thought; Robbins would come to know what a smart boy Henry was. The cost of intelligence was not fixed and because it was fluid, it was whatever the market would bear and all of that burden would fall upon Mildred and Augustus.

Mildred fixed Henry as many of the things she knew he would enjoy to take with them on Sundays. Before freedom she had known only slave food, plenty of fatback and ash cakes and the occasional mouthful of rape or kale. But freedom and the money from their labors spread a better table before them. Still, she could not enjoy even one good morsel in her new place when she thought of what Henry had to eat. So she prepared him a little feast before each visit. Little meat pies, cakes that he could share with his friends through the week, the odd rabbit caught by Augustus, which she salted to last for days. The mother and the father would ride over in the wagon pulled by the mules and call onto Robbins's land for their boy, enticing him with what they had brought. They would wait in the road until Henry on his stick legs came up from the quarters and out to the lane, Robbins's mansion giant and eternal behind him.

He was growing quickly, eager to show them the little things he had carved. The horses in full stride, the mules loaded down, the bull with his head turned just so to look behind him. The three would settle on a quilt on a piece of no-man's-land across from Robbins's plantation. Behind them and way off to the left, there was a creek that had never seen a fish, but slaves fished in it nevertheless, practicing for the day when there would be better water. When the three had eaten, Mildred would sit between them as Augustus and Henry fished. She always wanted to know how he was treated and his answer was almost always the same—that Massa Robbins and his overseer were treating him well, that Rita was always good to him.

The fall that year, 1834, just dropped away one day and suddenly it was winter. Mildred and Augustus came every Sunday even when it turned cold and then even colder than that. They built a fire on no-man's-land and ate with few words. Robbins had told them not to take the boy beyond where his overseer could see them from the entrance to his property. The winter visits were short ones because the boy often complained of the cold. Sometimes Henry did not show up, even if the cold was bearable for a visit of a few minutes. Mildred and Augustus would wait hour after hour, huddled in the wagon under quilts and blankets, or walking hopefully up and down the road, for Robbins had forbidden them to come onto his land except when Augustus was making a payment on the second and fourth Tuesdays of the month. They would hope some slave would venture out, going to or from the mansion, so they could holler to him or her to go get their boy Henry. But even when they managed to see someone and tell them about Henry, they would wait in vain for the boy to show up.

"I just forgot," Henry would say the next time they saw him. Augustus had often been chastised as a boy but though Henry was his son, he was not yet his property and so beyond his reach.

"Try harder to remember, son. To know the right way," Augustus said, only to have Henry do right the next Sunday or two and then not show up the one after that.

Then, in mid-February, after they had waited two hours beyond when he was supposed to appear on the road, Augustus grabbed the boy when he shuffled up and shook him, then he pushed him to the ground. Henry covered his face and began to cry. "Augustus!" Mildred shouted and helped her son up. "Everything's good," she said to him as she cradled him in her arms. "Everything's good."

Augustus turned and walked across the road to the wagon. The wagon had a thick burlap covering, something he had come up with not long after the first cold visit. The mother and her child soon followed him across the road and the three settled into the wagon under the covering and around the stones Augustus and Mildred had boiled. They were quite large stones, which they would boil for many hours at home on Sunday mornings before setting out to see Henry. Then, just before they left home, the stones were wrapped in blankets and placed in the center of the wagon. When the stones stopped giving warmth and the boy began complaining of the cold, they knew it was time to go.

That Sunday Augustus pushed Henry, the three of them ate, once again, in silence. The next Sunday Robbins was waiting. "I heard you did something to my boy, to my property," he said before Augustus and Mildred were down from the wagon.

"No, Mr. Robbins. I did nothin," Augustus said, having forgotten the push.

"We wouldn't," Mildred said. "We wouldn't hurt him for the world. He our son."

Robbins looked at her as if she had told him the day was Wednesday. "I won't have you touching my boy, my property." His horse, Sir Guilderham, was idling two or so paces behind his master. And just as the horse began to wander away, Robbins turned and picked up the reins, mounted. "No more visits for a month," he said, picking one piece of lint from the horse's ear.

"Please, Mr. Robbins," Mildred said. Freedom had allowed her not to call him "Master" anymore. "We come all this way."

"I don't care,"Robbins said. "It'll take all of a month for him to heal from what you did, Augustus."

Robbins set off. Henry had not told his parents that he had become Robbins's groom. An older boy, Toby, had been the groom but Henry had bribed the boy with Mildred's food and the boy had commenced telling the overseer that he was not up to the task of grooming. "Henry be better," Toby said to the overseer so many times that it became a truth in the white man's head. Now all the food Mildred brought for her son each Sunday had already been promised to Toby.

"We wouldn't hurt him to save the world," Mildred said to Robbins's back. She began crying because she saw a month of days spread out before her and they added up to more than a thousand. Augustus held her and kissed her bonneted head and then helped her up on to the wagon. The journey home to southwest Manchester County always took about an hour or so, depending upon the bitterness or kindness of the weather.

Henry was indeed better as a groom, far more eager than Toby had been, not at all afraid to rise long before the sun to do his duties. He was always waiting for Robbins when he returned from town, from Philomena, a black woman, and the two children he had with her. Henry would, in those early days when he was trying to prove himself to Robbins, stand in front of the mansion and watch as Robbins and Sir Guilderham emerged from the winter fog of the road, the boy's heart beating faster and faster as the man and the horse became larger and larger. "Mornin, Massa," he would say and raise both hands to take the reins. "Good morning, Henry. Are you well?" "Yes, Massa." "Then stay that way." "Yes, Massa, I plan to."

Robbins would go into his mansion, to face a white wife who had not yet resigned herself to having lost her place in his heart to Philomena. The wife knew about the first child her husband had with Philomena, about Dora, but she would not know about the second, Louis, until the boy was three years old. This was in the days before Robbins's wife turned beastly sour and began to spend most of her time in a part of the mansion her daughter had named the East when the daughter was very young and didn't know what she was doing. When the wife did turn beastly sour, she took it out on the people nearest her that she could not love. It got to be, the slaves said, as if she hated the very ground they had to walk on.

Henry would take Sir Guilderham to the stable, the one reserved for the animals Robbins thought the most of, and rub him down until the animal was at peace and the sweat was gone, until he began to close his eyes and wanted to be left alone. Then Henry made sure the horse had enough hay and water. Sometimes, if he thought he could escape the other tasks of the day, he would stand on a stool and comb the mane until his hands tired. If the horse recognized the boy from all the work he did, it never showed.

Henry waited eagerly at one end of the road Robbins took at least three times a week, and at the other end of the road, at the very edge of the town of Manchester, the county seat, was another boy, Louis, who was eight in 1840 when Henry was sixteen and an accomplished groom. Louis, the son, was also Robbins's slave, which was how the U.S. census that year listed him. The census noted that the house on Shenandoah Road where the boy lived in Manchester was headed by Philomena, his mother, and that the boy had a sister, Dora, three years his senior. The census did not say that the children were Robbins's flesh and blood and that he traveled into Manchester because he loved their mother far more than anything he could name and that, in his quieter moments, after the storms in his head, he feared that he was losing his mind because of that love. Robbins's grandfather, who had stowed away as a boy on the HMS *Claxton*'s maiden voyage to America, would not have not approved—not of Robbins's having lost himself to a black but of having lost himself at all. Having given away so much to love, the grandfather would have told his grandson, where would Robbins get the fortitude to make his way back to Bristol, England, back to their home?

The 1840 U.S. census contained an enormous amount of facts, far more than the one done by the alcoholic state delegate in 1830, and all of the 1840 facts pointed to the one big fact that Manchester was then the largest county in Virginia, a place of 2,191 slaves, 142 free Negroes, 939 whites, and 136 Indians, most of them Cherokee but with a sprinkling of Choctaw. A well-liked and fastidious tanner, who doubled as the U.S. marshal and who had lost three fingers to frostbite, carried out the 1840 census in seven and a half summer weeks. It should have taken him less time but he had plenty of trouble, starting with people like Harvey Travis who wanted to make sure his own children were counted as white, though all the world knew his wife was a full-blooded Cherokee. Travis even called his children niggers and filthy half-breeds when they and that world got to be too much for him. The census taker/tanner/U.S. marshal told Travis he would count the children as white but he actually wrote in his report to the federal government in Washington, D.C., that they were slaves, the property of their father, which, in the eyes of the law, they truly were; the census taker had never seen the children before the day he rode out to Travis's place on one of two mules the American government had bought for him so he could do his census job. He thought the children were too dark for him and the federal government to consider them as anything else but black. He told his government the children were slaves and he let it go at that, not saying anything about their white blood or their Indian blood. The census taker had a great belief that his government could read between the lines. And though he came away with suspicions about Travis's wife being a full Indian, he gave Travis the benefit of the doubt and listed her as "American Indian/Full Cherokee." The census taker also had trouble trying to calculate how many square miles the county was, and in the end he sent in figures that were far short of the mark. The mountains, he told a confidant, threw him off because he was unable to take the measure of the land with the damn mountains in the way. Even with the mountains taken out of all the arithmetic, Manchester was still half as large as the next biggest county in the Commonwealth.

The boy Louis, by 1840, could not be contained on the days when he thought Robbins was coming to see them. He bounced around the house Robbins had had built when Philomena was pregnant with Dora and he did not want her to be on the plantation near a wife who early on had suspected she was losing her husband of ten years. The boy would run up the stairs and look out the second-floor windows that faced the road, but when he saw no sign of the dust from Sir Guilderham, he would run back down and look out the parlor window. "I must be not lookin in the right place for him," he would say to whoever was in the room before flying back up the stairs. The teacher Fern Elston had already reprimanded Louis about leaving out the g's on all his *ing* words.

There was no one else in the county who could have gotten away with putting a Negro and her two children in a house on the same block with white people. On one page of the census report to the federal government in Washington, D. C., the census taker put a check by William Robbins's name and footnoted on page 113 that he was the county's wealthiest man. He was a distant cousin of Robbins's and was quite proud that his kin had done so well in America.

Dora and Louis never called Robbins "Father." They addressed him as "Mr. William," and when he was not around he was referred to as "him." Louis liked for Robbins to set him on his knee and raise his knee up and down rapidly. "My horsey Mr. William" was what he sometimes called him. Robbins called him "my little prince. My little princely prince."

The boy had what people in that part of Virginia termed a traveling eye. As he looked directly at someone, his left eye would often follow some extraneous moving object that might be just to the side—a spot of dust in the near distance or a bird on the wing in the far distance. Follow it as the object or body moved a few feet. Then the eye would return to the person in front of the boy. The right eye, and his mind, never left the person Louis was talking to. Robbins was aware that a traveling eye in a boy he would have had with his white wife would have meant some kind of failing in the white boy, that he had a questionable future and could receive only so much fatherly love. But in the child whose mother was black and who had Robbins's heart, the traveling eye served only to endear him even more to his father. It was a cruel thing God had done to his son, he told himself many a time on the road back home.

Louis, over time, would learn how not to let the eye become his destiny, for people in that part of Virginia thought a traveling eye a sign of an inattentive and dishonest man. By the time he became friends with Caldonia and Calvin, her brother, at Fern Elston's tiny academy for free Negro children just behind her parlor, Louis would be able to tell the moment when the eye was wandering off just by the look on a person's face. He would blink and the eye would come back. This meant looking full and long into someone's eyes, and people came to see that as a sign of a man who cared about what was being said. He became an honest man in many people's eyes, honest enough for Caldonia Townsend to say yes when he asked her to marry him. "I never thought I was worthy of you," he said, thinking of the dead Henry, when he asked her to marry him. She said, "We are all worthy of one another."

Robbins was forty-one when Henry became his groom. The trips into town were not easy. It would have been best if he had traveled by buggy, but he was not a man for that. Sir Guilderham was expensive and grand horseflesh, meant to be paraded before the world. In 1840, when there were still many more payments to be made for Henry's freedom, Robbins had been thinking for a long time that he was losing his mind. On the way to town or on the way back, he would suffer what he called small storms, thunder and lightning, in the brain. The lightning would streak from the front of his head and explode with thunder at the base of his skull. Then there was a kind of calming rain throughout his head that he associated with the return of normalcy. He lost whole bits of time with some storms. Sir Guilderham sometimes sensed the coming of the storms, and when it did, the horse would slow and then stop altogether until the storm had passed. If the horse sensed nothing, a storm would hit Robbins, and he would emerge from the storm miles closer to his destination, with no memory of how he got there.

He saw the storms as the price to be paid for Philomena and their children. In 1841, awaking from a storm, he found a white man on the road back to the plantation asking if he was ill. Robbins's nose was bleeding and the man was pointing to the nose and the blood. Robbins rubbed his nose with the sleeve of his coat. The blood stopped. "Lemme see you home," the man said. Robbins pointed up the road to where he lived and they rode side by side, the man telling him who he was and what he did and Robbins not caring but just grateful for the company.

Robbins felt compelled to repay the kindness when two slaves caught the man's eye the second day he stayed with Robbins. The Bible said guests should be treated like royalty lest a host entertain angels unaware. The man had stepped out onto the verandah to smoke one of Robbins's cigars and saw Toby, the former groom, and his sister. Mildred's food had done things for the boy and his sister, marvelous things to their bones that Robbins's poor food could never have done. The man came inside and offered $233 for the pair, claiming that was all he had.

The three, the two children and the man who could have been an angel, had been gone four days when Robbins realized what a bad sale he had made, even if he took something off the price to express his gratitude to an angel. He soon got it into his head that the man had actually been a kind of abolitionist, no more than a thief, the devil in disguise. The idea of the slave patrols began with that bitter sale, with the idea that the storms made him vulnerable and that abolitionists could insinuate themselves and cheat him out of all that he and his father and his father's father had worked for. But the idea would take root and grow with the disappearance of Rita, the woman who became a kind of mother to Henry after Augustus Townsend bought his wife Mildred to freedom. Before the angel/man on the road and Rita's disappearance, Manchester County, Virginia, had not had much problem with the disappearance of slaves since 1837. In that year, a man named Jesse and four other slaves took off one night and were found two days later by a posse headed by Sheriff Gilly Patterson. The escape and the chase had put such bile in Jesse's master that he shot Jesse in the swamp where the posse found him. He had the four other escapees hobbled that night—sharp and swift knives back and forth through their Achilles' tendons—right after he cut off Jesse's head as a warning to his other fourteen slaves and stuck it on a post made from an apple-tree branch in front of the cabin Jesse had shared with three other men. The law ruled that Jesse's murder was justifiable homicide—though the escaped slaves were headed in a different direction from a white widow and her two teenage daughters, the five men were less than a mile from those women when they were caught. No white person wanted to imagine what would have happened if those five slaves had doubled back, heading south and away from freedom, and got to the place with the widow and the girls. Jesse got what was coming to him, Sheriff Patterson theorized as he thought of the widow and her daughters. He did not put it in those words in a report he made to the circuit judge, a man known for opposing the abuse of slaves. But Sheriff Patterson did write that Jesse's master was punished enough having to live with the knowledge that he had done away with property that was easily worth $500 in a seller's market.

In truth, the man William Robbins met on the road was not an abolitionist or an angel, and Toby and his sister never saw the north. The man on the road sold the children for $527 to a man who chewed his food with his mouth open. He met the openmouthed man in a very fancy Petersburg bar that closed down at night to become a brothel, and that openmouthed man sold the children to a rice planter from South Carolina for $619. The children's mother wasn't good for doing her job very much after that, after her children were sold, even with the overseer flaying the skin on her back with whippings meant to make her do what was right and proper. The mother wasted away to skin and bones. Robbins sold her to a man in Tennessee for $257 and a three-year-old mule, a profitless sale, considering all the potential the mother had if she had pulled herself together and considering what Robbins had already spent for her upkeep, food and clothes and a leakproof roof over her head and whatnot. In his big book about the comings and goings of slaves, Robbins put a line through the name of the children's mother, something he always did with people who died before old age or who were sold for no profit.

Robbins usually spent the night at Philomena's, braving all her talk about wanting to go and live in Richmond. He would set out for his plantation just after dawn, weather permitting. There was almost always a storm in his head on the way back. He would have preferred to suffer one going into town, so as to enjoy Philomena and their children knowing the worst was behind him. No matter what weather God gave Manchester County, Henry would be waiting. That first winter after seeing the boy shivering in the rags he tied around his feet, Robbins had his slave shoemaker make the boy something good for his feet. He told the servants who ran his mansion that Henry was to eat in the kitchen with them and forever be clothed the right way just the same as they were clothed. Robbins came to depend on seeing the boy waving from his place in front of the mansion, came to know that the sight of Henry meant the storm was over and that he was safe from bad men disguised as angels, came to develop a kind of love for the boy, and that love, built up morning after morning, was another reason to up the selling price Mildred and Augustus Townsend would have to pay for their boy.

2003

Questions for Discussion

1. What is the "known world" and the unknown world in the novel?
2. How to understand the statement that "It was already a strange world that made him a slave to a white man, but God had indeed set it twirling and twisting every which way when he put black people to owning their own kind. Was God even up there attending to business anymore?"
3. Is Master Robbins twisted in mind about family, love, and honesty? And how can he handle it?

African American Autobiography
非裔美国自传简介

非裔美国文学源于奴隶叙事,非裔美国自传更是奴隶叙事的自然发展与演变。反对奴役、争取自由、自我书写与自我塑造及反思等成为奴隶叙事以及非裔美国自传的主旋律。本教材选取 19 世纪具有代表性的奴隶叙事与 20 世纪的非裔美国自传,尝试比较全面地介绍这一文类。

艾奎亚诺的奴隶叙事不仅叙述了作为奴隶的艾奎亚诺在美洲特别是北美的旅程,更加注重描写他获得自由后的各种英勇行为,堪称第一阶段奴隶叙事的代表;道格拉斯的《自述》在内容与形式两个方面都成为奴隶叙事的典范:在内容方面突出反抗奴役,争取自由的主题,在形式方面,确定了由南方逃往北方追求自由新生活的路线,成为非裔美国文学中的母题;而雅各布斯的《女奴生平》则以关注黑人女奴的悲惨境遇,特别是奴隶主的性压迫与性剥削而独树一帜。安德鲁斯的研究表明,从 1760 年至 1865 年,大约有 70 部以书或小册子出版的奴隶叙事,1865—1930 年,至少有 50 部奴隶叙事著作;福斯特则认为,这些创作或口述的长短不一的奴隶叙事作品估计有 6 000 部。这些奴隶叙事的代表性文本不仅书写自我,更加注重外在社会因素对自我形成的影响,其通过书写自我从而创造自我的文化范式,成为非裔美国文学的显著特征,并持续反映在内战以后的非裔美国自传中。

20 世纪上半叶,最具代表性的非裔美国自传包括布克·华盛顿的《从奴役中奋起》(1901)、皮肯斯的《打破束缚》(1923)、杜波伊斯的《破晓时分》(1940)、休斯的《大海》(1940)、赫斯顿的《道路上的尘迹》(1942)以及赖特的《黑孩子》(1945)等,其中奴隶叙事的影响清晰可见,特别是在结构方面。20 世纪下半叶阅读最广泛的三部自传分别是《马尔科姆·艾克斯自传》(1965)、安吉洛的《我知道笼中鸟为何歌唱》(1970)以及德莱尼的《我们有话要说:德莱尼姐妹的前 100 年》(1993)。另外,反映民权运动时期黑人自我与文化的重要自传包括克里夫的《冰上的灵魂》(1967)、穆迪的《成长于密西西比》(1968)、金夫人的《我与马丁·路德·金在一起的日子》(1969)、威尔斯的《为正义而战》(1970)、帕克斯的《帕克斯:我的故事》(1992)以及比尔斯的《勇士不哭》(1994)等;20 世纪 80—90 年代,非裔美国作家、批评家、社会活动家所贡献的自传作品主要有怀德曼的《兄弟与看护人》(1984)、盖茨的《有色人民》(1994)、麦考尔的《让我真想吼》(1994)、奥巴马的《我父辈的梦想》(1995)以及鲍威尔的《我的美国之路》(1995)等,此外,体育明星与电影明星等也有大量自传面世,他们的"成功故事"让"美国梦"的光芒更加耀眼。

非裔美国自传全方位地记录了殖民地时期以来的美国黑人生活,传记家以美国理想为参照,反思非裔美国民族遭受的剥削、压迫与不公正对待,他们尝试精确描绘非裔美国族裔,渴望通过书写自我,发明自我,进而反思主流美国文化,作品具有极高的历史意义与文化价值。

1. Interesting Narrative of the Life of Olaudah Equiano

作家简介

奥拉达·艾奎亚诺(Olaudah Equiano)(1745—1797),又名古斯塔夫斯·瓦萨,是18世纪最著名的非洲人之一。作为一个大致位于现今尼日利亚内陆村落村长最小的儿子,他深受家人和村民们的疼爱,并将继承父业。不幸的是,他在11岁时与姐姐一起被奴隶贩子绑架,成为奴隶,并因此与姐姐永远分散。几个月后,他几经转手来到大西洋沿岸的海边,与其他黑奴一起被装上一艘贩奴船运送到美洲。经过生不如死的海上航行,包括在加勒比海岛屿上度过的数周,他最终抵达北美洲的英属弗吉尼亚殖民地。也就是在那里,他被卖给了英国皇家海军的迈克尔·帕斯卡尔中尉。作为帕斯卡尔的奴隶,他在皇家海军的舰船上待了六年。在此期间,他学会了识字、写作、算术以及航海等技能。1763年,他被卖给了一个爱尔兰商人。后来他又被带回加勒比海,被蒙塞拉特岛的商人罗伯特·金买下。不过,由于他识字并具有海上船员经历,他没有遭受更加严酷的奴役,而是在罗伯特的船上干活。他通过从事小额贸易和勤俭节约,终于攒够了足够的钱,于1766年从罗伯特手中赎回自己的自由。

获得自由后,艾奎亚诺大部分时间都居住在伦敦。18世纪80年代,有组织的废奴运动在伦敦兴起,他很快积极参与其中。早在1774年,他就已经与废奴运动的倡导者,英国学者和教会领袖格兰维尔·夏普建立联系。1785年,他开始写信给英国报纸、政坛要人和废奴运动倡导者。自传《奥拉达·艾奎亚诺生平奇事》(1789)就是他参与此项运动的产物,也是他唯一的一部正式出版的作品,十分畅销。这本自传集政论、游记和宗教皈依叙事于一体,详细记述了他为奴的艰难岁月和最终获得自由的漫长过程,引起广泛的社会关注。出版仅仅两周之后,英国国会就展开了是否要终止奴隶贸易的争论,而此前这桩从非洲向英国输送奴隶的罪恶贸易已经持续了近两个世纪。此后,他在英国和爱尔兰不遗余力地推广该书,成为知名公众人物。1791年,该书首次在美国发行。虽然英国国会直到艾奎亚诺过世十年后的1807年才最终宣布奴隶贸易为非法,但《奥拉达·艾奎亚诺生平奇事》依然是促成当时的政客们决心修改法律终止此项贸易的重要推动力量。作者通过亲身经历揭露奴隶贸易的黑暗与罪恶,并以自己获得自由的经历来激励其他黑人奴隶争取自由。因此,在当时的那场事关千百万黑人奴隶命运的辩论中,该书作为第一手的证词起到了十分重要的作用。

作品简介与赏析

在《奥拉达·艾奎亚诺生平奇事》中,作者以平实易懂的语言介绍了他原本在非洲安详与宁静的生活、他被绑架为奴之后的惨痛经历以及他如何通过个人的努力、优秀的品格以及上帝的眷顾而成为自由人的漫长旅程。虽然被多次转卖,他也曾多次产生自杀念头,却从未放弃自由的梦想。通过自强不息地学习知识、掌握技能,勤俭节约,他最终获得自由,并走上为其他奴隶争取自由的道路。这种百折不挠的精神令人感动,激励大量的黑人和白人积极投身废奴运动。作者的叙述既是殖民前的非洲生活景况的珍贵的第一手资料,也是当时罪恶奴隶贸易的直接见证,增进了人们对当时非洲奴隶历史的了解。①

---

① Sonya Ramsey, "Equiano, the African: Biography of a Self-Made Man by Vincent Carretta", *The North Carolina Historical Review*, Vol. 83, No. 2 (April 2006), p. 273.

尽管艾奎亚诺获得自由后的生活和工作地主要是在英国,但他却对非裔美国文学做出了重大贡献。他被公认为非裔美国文学在18世纪的先驱之一,开创了日后兴起的"奴隶叙事"(Slave Narrative)的自传体风格,对之后的非裔美国文学产生了重要的影响,并持续至今。《美国黑人作家综合选集》(1972)将艾奎亚诺作为第一个美国黑人作家列入其中。可以说,该书与道格拉斯的《自述》(1845)和雅各布斯的《女奴生平》(1861)等一起构成非裔美国作家第一人称叙述的自传文学传统。与《独立宣言》和美国《宪法》一起,这些叙述指出了自由、民主和普遍人权的真正含义,而这些思想也被后来的非裔美国作家所继承。

　　不过,他的叙述并非无懈可击。随着该自传的流传,人们开始对作者的非洲身份和自传的真实性产生了怀疑。文森特·加瑞塔认为作者并非如书中所言出生于非洲,而是北美的英属南卡罗来纳殖民地,这意味着他生来就是奴隶。在加瑞塔看来,艾奎亚诺也许从未造访过非洲,该著的前面部分可能只是口述史中所采用的修辞手法,而不是他个人的真实历史。加瑞塔还举证认为,在出版该著之前,作者一直都声称自己出生在南卡。同时,他还提供了艾奎亚诺的基督教洗礼记录和教堂名册以供佐证。[①] 尽管如此,加瑞塔仍然高度赞赏艾奎亚诺的成就,[②]许多读者仍然相信作品中的叙述,甚至这些争论和怀疑反过来也使作者和该作品受到人们更为广泛的关注。作者的出生地和早期的生活经历真相也许无从得知,但有一点是可以肯定的,那就是他的这本自传在殖民政治和非裔美国文学史上都产生了重大影响。

　　在19世纪中期欧美地区全面废除奴隶制后,艾奎亚诺逐渐被人遗忘。但20世纪60年代该书得以重印以来,依然被认为是非裔美国文学18世纪以来最重要的成果之一。如今,它已被译成多种语言,被全球各地的读者所研读。

　　选篇为该书第一章和第二章。作者回忆自己在非洲生活的方方面面,语言平实,娓娓道来,并将这种宁静、简朴、有序的非洲生活与欧洲所谓的"文明"生活进行对照,突出了非洲生活的优越性,以增加人们对非洲黑奴不幸遭遇的同情。[③] 虽然作者也讲述了当地存在的奴隶制度,但他强调指出当地的奴隶制度与美洲奴隶制度的不同,从而道出了美洲奴隶制度的惨无人道。总之,在他的笔下,这段田园牧歌式的童年生活是美好而值得怀念的。然而,这一切都在他11岁的某一天被无情地终止——他和姐姐被潜入村庄的奴隶贩子绑架带走,从此飘零异乡,沦落为奴。在前往西印度群岛的途中,他和其他黑人奴隶遭受了非人的对待,作者以这种方式控诉了奴隶贸易的罪恶。

　　1759年,他在伦敦接受洗礼,成为一名基督徒。因此,纵观全书,作者始终站在基督徒的立场上来回顾和审视自己的生活。他在第一章中试图证明非洲同胞也是犹太人亚伯拉罕的后裔,以事实说明他们与犹太人之间在风俗和习惯上的共同之处,而他们的黝黑皮肤只不过是因为长期生活在热带地区而已,因此不能因为肤色的不同而对他们怀有歧视,因为他们与其他白人一样都是上帝的子民。他们在欧洲人中间所表现出来的无知也只不过是没有学习和熟悉欧洲的"知识"而已。据此,作者在第一章结尾时呼吁欧洲白人要对黑人给予同情,要以兄弟之情对待他们;要在心中对上帝充满感激,因为"上帝使得居住在地球各个国家的人具有同样的血液。上帝的智慧是我们所不能及的,而我们的所作所为也不是上帝的所作所为"。同样,在第

---

　　① Brycchan Carey, "Equiano, Olaudah", in Wilfred Samuels, et al., eds., *Encyclopedia of African-American Literature*, New York: Facts On File, Inc., 2007, p.170.

　　② The JBHE Foundation, Inc., "Equiano, the African: Biography of a Self-Made Man by Vincent Carretta", *The Journal of Blacks in Higher Education*, No. 49 (Autumn, 2005), p.102.

　　③ Sonya Ramsey, "Equiano, the African: Biography of a Self-Made Man by Vincent Carretta", *The North Carolina Historical Review*, Vol. 83, No. 2 (April 2006), p.273.

二章结尾处,作者指责那些贪婪残忍的奴隶贩子只是"名义上的基督徒",因为他们没有遵守基督教"己所不欲,勿施于人"的训诫。由此可见,作者主张黑人和白人之间的平等和博爱的立场是十分鲜明的,这种强烈的种族平等意识对于一个 18 世纪曾经为奴者而言是难能可贵的。因为在当时,黑人无论在身体、智力还是情感和道德上,都被西方社会普遍认为低于白人。

当然,作者通过考证,认为非洲人和犹太人同属一个上帝的子民还具有其他含义:作者试图通过此举将黑人纳入白人主流文明之中,因为作为在白人社会和文化环境中成长起来的黑人作家,艾奎亚诺在内心深处认同白人文化,渴望成为白人社会的一员。与此同时,他也试图激励非洲同胞在奴役和压迫的苦难中通过信仰上帝来寻求精神寄托,他认为,正如《旧约》中的以色列人在埃及经受了漫长的奴役之后而最终获得自由一样,非洲的同胞也终将通过信仰上帝获得自己的自由。为此,作者在书中多次提及自己在经受奴役与欺凌的绝望时刻通过仰望上帝来寻求精神慰藉。而且他相信,作为上帝的子民,只要通过个人的诚实和努力的劳作,最终必将获得回报。作者讲述了自己如何通过个人的努力和优秀的品格获得了自由,诸如通过学习识字和计算等技能受到主人善待,为日后从事贸易打下良好基础;通过努力工作与节省开支攒够钱赎得自由,等等。但是需要当代读者警醒的是,他将这一切都看作是上帝的仁慈和眷顾,不能不说是白人文化深刻影响的结果。

总之,虽然这部作品名义上是一部自传,但它更是一部废奴主义文本,既具有服务于废奴运动的政治目的,也具有传播基督教的宗教目的,[1]因为在当时的废奴主义者看来,废奴运动应该与福音传播同步进行。可以说,艾奎亚诺的这部作品完全回应了这种时代需求。[2]

Chapter 1

The Author's account of his country, and their manners and customs—Administration of justice—Embrenche—Marriage ceremony, and public entertainments—Mode of living—Dress-Manufactures—Buildings—Commerce—Agriculture—War and Religion—Superstition of the natives—Funeral ceremonies of the priests or magicians—Curious mode of discovering poison—Some hints concerning the origin of the Author's countrymen, with the opinions of different writers on that subject.

I BELIEVE it is difficult for those who publish their own memoirs to escape the imputation of vanity; nor is this the only disadvantage under which they labour; it is also their misfortune, that whatever is uncommon is rarely, if ever, believed; and what is obvious we are apt to turn from with disgust, and to charge the writer with impertinence. People generally think those memoirs only worthy to be read or remembered which abound in great or striking events; those, in short, which in a high degree excite either admiration or pity: all others they consign to contempt and oblivion. It is, therefore, I confess, not a little hazardous, in a private and obscure individual, and a stranger too, thus to solicit the indulgent attention of the public; especially when I own I offer here the history of neither a saint, a hero, nor a tyrant. I believe there are a few events in my life which have not happened to many; it is true the incidents of it are numerous; and, did I consider myself an

① Vincent Carretta, "Response to Paul Lovejoy's 'Autobiography and Memory: Gustavus Vassa, alias Olaudah Equiano, the African'", *Slavery and Abolition*, Vol. 28, No. 1(April 2007), p. 116.

② Brycchan Carey, "Equiano, Olaudah", in Wilfred Samuels, et al., eds., *Encyclopedia of African-American Literature*, New York: Facts On File, Inc., 2007, p. 171.

European, I might say my sufferings were great; but, when I compare my lot with that of most of my countrymen, I regard myself as a *particular favourite of Heaven*, and acknowledge the mercies of Providence in every occurrence of my life. If, then, the following narrative does not appear sufficiently interesting to engage general attention, let my motive be some excuse for its publication. I am not so foolishly vain as to expect from it either immortality or literary reputation. If it affords any satisfaction to my numerous friends, at whose request it has been written, or in the smallest degree promotes the interest of humanity, the ends for which it was undertaken will be fully attained, and every wish of my heart gratified. Let it therefore be remembered that, in wishing to avoid censure, I do not aspire to praise.

That part of Africa, known by the name of Guinea, to which the trade for slaves is carried on, extends along the coast above 3,400 miles, from Senegal to Angola, and includes a variety of kingdoms. Of these the most considerable is the kingdom of Benin, both as to extent and wealth, the richness and cultivation of the soil, the power of its king, and the number and warlike disposition of the inhabitants. It is situated nearly under the line and extends along the coast about 170 miles, but runs back into the interior part of Africa to a distance hitherto I believe unexplored by any traveller; and seems only terminated at length by the empire of Abyssinia, near 1,500 miles from its beginning. This kingdom is divided into many provinces or districts: in one of the most remote and fertile of which, called Eboe, I was born, in the year 1745, in a charming fruitful vale, named Essaka. The distance of this province from the capital of Benin and the sea coast must be very considerable; for I had never heard of white men or Europeans, nor of the sea; and our subjection to the king of Benin was little more than nominal; for every transaction of the government, as far as my slender observation extended, was conducted by the chiefs or elders of the place. The manners and government of a people who have little commerce with other countries are generally very simple; and the history of what passes in one family or village may serve as a specimen of the whole nation. My father was one of those elders or chiefs I have spoken of, and was styled Embrenche; a term, as I remember, importing the highest distinction, and signifying in our language a mark of grandeur. This mark is conferred on the person entitled to it, by cutting the skin across at the top of the forehead, and drawing it down to the eye-brows; and, while it is in this situation, applying a warm hand, and rubbing it until it shrinks up into a thick *weal* across the lower part of the forehead. Most of the judges and senators were thus marked; my father had long borne it: I had seen it conferred on one of my brothers, and I was also *destined* to receive it by my parents. Those Embrenche, or chief men, decided disputes and punished crimes; for which purpose they always assembled together. The proceedings were generally short; and in most cases the law of retaliation prevailed. I remember a man was brought before my father, and the other judges, for kidnapping a boy; and, although he was the son of a chief or senator, he was condemned to make recompense by a man or woman slave. Adultery, however, was sometimes punished with slavery or death; a punishment which I believe is inflicted on it throughout most of the nations of Africa; so sacred among them is the honour of the marriage bed, and so jealous are they of the fidelity of their wives. Of this I recollect an instance. A woman was convicted before the judges of adultery, and delivered over, as the custom was, to her husband to be punished. Accordingly he determined to put her to death; but it being found, just before her execution, that she had an infant at her breast; and no woman being prevailed on to perform the part of a nurse, she was spared on account of the child. The men, however, do not preserve the same constancy to their wives, which they expect from them; for they indulge in a plurality, though seldom in more than two. Their mode of marriage is thus; both parties are usually betrothed when young by their parents (though I have known the males to betroth themselves). On this occasion a feast is prepared, and the bride and bridegroom stand up in the midst of all their friends, who are assembled for the purpose, while he declares she is thenceforth to be looked upon as his wife, and that no other person is to pay any addresses to her. This is also immediately proclaimed in the vicinity, on which the bride retires from the assembly. Some time after, she is brought home to her husband, and then another feast is made, to which the relations of both parties are invited; her parents then deliver her to the bridegroom, accompanied with a number of blessings, and at the same time they tie round her waist a cotton string of the thickness of a goose-quill, which none but married women are permitted to wear; she is now considered as completely his wife; and at this time the dowry is given to the new married pair, which generally consists of portions of land, slaves, and cattle, household goods, and implements of husbandry. These are offered by the friends of both parties; besides which the parents of the bridegroom present gifts to those of the bride, whose property she is looked upon before marriage; but after it she is esteemed the sole property of her husband. The ceremony being now ended the festival begins, which is celebrated with bonfires, and loud acclamations of joy, accompanied with music and dancing.

We are almost a nation of dancers, musicians, and poets. Thus every great event, such as a triumphant return from battle, or other cause of public rejoicing is celebrated in public dances, which are accompanied with songs and music suited to the occasion. The assembly is separated into four divisions, which dance either apart or in succession, and each with a character peculiar to itself. The first division contains the married men, who in their dances frequently exhibit feats of arms, and the representation of a battle. To these succeed the married women, who dance in the second division. The young men occupy the third; and the maidens the fourth. Each represents some interesting scene of real life, such as a great achievement, domestic employment, a pathetic story, or some rural sport; and as the subject is generally founded on some recent event, it is therefore ever new. This gives our dances a spirit and variety which I have scarcely seen elsewhere. We have many musical instruments, particularly drums of different kinds, a piece of music which resembles a guitar, and another much like a stickado. These last are chiefly used by betrothed virgins, who play on them on all grand festivals.

As our manners are simple, our luxuries are few. The dress of both sexes is nearly the same. It generally consists of a long piece of calico, or muslin, wrapped loosely round the body, somewhat in the form of a highland plaid. This is usually dyed blue, which is our favourite colour. It is extracted from a berry, and is brighter and richer than any I have seen in Europe. Besides this, our women of distinction wear golden ornaments, which they dispose with some profusion on their arms and legs. When our women are not employed with the men in tillage, their usual occupation is spinning and weaving cotton, which they afterwards dye, and make into garments. They also manufacture earthen vessels, of which we have many kinds. Among the rest tobacco pipes, made after the same fashion, and used in the same manner, as those in Turkey.

Our manner of living is entirely plain; for as yet the natives are unacquainted with those refinements in cookery which debauch the taste: bullocks, goats, and poultry supply the greatest part of their food. These constitute likewise the principal wealth of the country, and the chief articles of its commerce. The flesh is usually stewed in a pan. To make it savory, we sometimes use also pepper, and other spices, and we have salt made of wood ashes. Our vegetables are mostly plantains, eadas, yams, beans, and Indian corn. The head of the family usually eats alone; his wives and slaves have also their separate tables. Before we taste food, we always wash our hands: indeed our cleanliness on all occasions is extreme; but on this it is an indispensable ceremony. After washing, libation is made, by pouring out a small portion of the drink on the floor, and tossing a small quantity of the food in a certain place, for the spirits of departed relations, which the natives suppose to preside over their conduct, and guard them from evil. They are totally unacquainted with strong or spiritous liquours; and their principal beverage is palm wine. This is got from a tree of that name, by tapping it at the top, and fastening a large gourd to it; and sometimes one tree will yield three or four gallons in a night. When just drawn it is of a most delicious sweetness; but in a few days it acquires a tartish and more spirituous flavour: though I never saw anyone intoxicated by it. The same tree also produces nuts and oil. Our principal luxury is in perfumes; one sort of these is an odoriferous wood of delicious fragrance: the other a kind of earth; a small portion of which thrown into the fire diffuses a most powerful odour. We beat this wood into powder, and mix it with palm-oil; with which both men and women perfume themselves.

In our buildings we study convenience rather than ornament. Each master of a family has a large square piece of ground, surrounded with a moat or fence, or enclosed with a wall made of red earth tempered, which, when dry, is as hard as brick. Within this are his houses to accommodate his family and slaves; which, if numerous, frequently present the appearance of a village. In the middle stands the principal building, appropriated to the sole use of the master, and consisting of two apartments; in one of which he sits in the day with his family, the other is left apart for the reception of his friends. He has besides these a distinct apartment in which he sleeps, together with his male children. On each side are the apartments of his wives, who have also their separate day and night houses. The habitations of the slaves and their families are distributed throughout the rest of the enclosure. These houses never exceed one story in height: they are always built of wood, or stakes driven into the ground, crossed with wattles, and neatly plastered within, and without. The roof is thatched with reeds. Our day houses are left open at the sides; but those in which we sleep are always covered, and plastered in the inside, with a composition mixed with cow-dung, to keep off the different insects which annoy us during the night. The walls and floors also of these are generally covered with mats. Our beds consist of a platform, raised three or four feet from the ground, on which are laid skins, and different parts of a spongy tree called plantain. Our covering is calico or muslin, the same as our dress. The usual seats are a few logs of wood; but we have benches, which are generally perfumed, to accommodate strangers; these compose the greater part of our household furniture. Houses so constructed and furnished require but little skill to erect them. Every man is a sufficient architect for the purpose. The whole neighbourhood afford their unanimous assistance in building them, and, in return, receive and expect no other recompense than a feast.

As we live in a country where nature is prodigal of her favours, our wants are few and easily supplied; of course we have few manufactures. They consist for the most part of calicoes, earthen ware, ornaments, and instruments of war and husbandry. But these make no part of our commerce, the principal articles of which, as I have observed, are provisions. In such a state money is of little use; however we have some small pieces of coin, if I may call them such. They are made something like an anchor; but I do not remember either their value or denomination. We have also markets, at which I have been frequently with my mother. These are sometimes visited by stout, mahogany-coloured men from the south west of us: we call them Oye-Eboe, which term signifies red men living at a distance. They generally bring us firearms, gunpowder, hats, beads, and dried fish. The last we esteemed a great rarity, as our waters were only brooks and springs. These articles they barter with us for odoriferous woods and earth, and our salt of wood-ashes. They always carry slaves through our land; but the strictest account is exacted of their manner of procuring them before they are suffered to pass. Sometimes indeed we sold slaves to them, but they were only prisoners of war, or such among us as had been convicted of kidnapping, or adultery, and some other crimes which we esteemed heinous. This practice of kidnapping induces me to think, that, notwithstanding all our strictness, their principal business among us was to trepan our people. I remember too they carried great sacks along with them, which, not long after, I had an opportunity of fatally seeing applied to that infamous purpose.

Our land is uncommonly rich and fruitful, and produces all kinds of vegetables in great abundance. We have plenty of Indian corn, and vast quantities of cotton and tobacco. Our pine apples grow without culture; they are about the size of the largest sugarloaf, and finely flavoured. We have also spices of different kinds, particularly pepper; and a variety of delicious fruits which I have never seen in Europe; together with gums of various kinds, and honey in abundance. All our industry is exerted to improve those blessings of nature. Agriculture is our chief employment; and everyone, even the children and women, are engaged in it. Thus we are all habituated to labour from our earliest years. Everyone contributes something to the common stock; and as we are unacquainted with idleness, we have no beggars. The benefits of such a mode of living are obvious. The West-India planters prefer the slaves of Benin or Eboe to those of any other part of Guinea, for their hardiness, intelligence, integrity, and zeal. Those benefits are felt by us in the general healthiness of the people, and in their vigour and activity; I might have added too in their comeliness. Deformity is indeed unknown amongst us, I mean that of shape. Numbers of the natives of Eboe now in London might be brought in support of this assertion; for, in regard to complexion, ideas of beauty are wholly relative. I remember while in Africa to have seen three negro children, who were tawny, and another quite white, who were universally regarded by myself and the natives in general, as far as related to their complexions, as deformed. Our women too were, in my eyes at least, uncommonly graceful, alert, and modest to a degree of bashfulness; nor do I remember to have ever heard of an instance of incontinence amongst them before marriage. They are also remarkably cheerful. Indeed cheerfulness and affability are two of the leading characteristics of our nation.

Our tillage is exercised in a large plain or common, some hours walk from our dwellings, and all the neighbours resort thither in a body. They use no beasts of husbandry; and their only instruments are hoes, axes, shovels, and beaks, or pointed iron to dig with. Sometimes we are visited by locusts, which come in large clouds, so as to darken the air, and destroy our harvest. This however happens rarely, but when it does, a famine is produced by it. I remember an instance or two wherein this happened. This common is ofttimes the theatre of war; and therefore when our people go out to till their land, they not only go in a body, but generally take their arms with them, for fear of a surprise; and when they apprehend an invasion they guard the avenues to their dwellings, by driving sticks into the ground, which are so sharp at one end as to pierce the foot, and are generally dipt in poison. From what I can recollect of these battles, they appear to have been irruptions of one little state or district on the other, to obtain prisoners or booty. Perhaps they were incited to this by those traders who brought the European goods I mentioned amongst us. Such mode of obtaining slaves in Africa is common; and I believe more are procured this way, and by kidnapping, than any other. When a trader wants slaves, he applies to a chief for them, and tempts him with his wares. It is not extraordinary, if on this occasion he yields to the temptation with as little firmness, and accepts the price of his fellow creature's liberty with as little reluctance, as the enlightened merchant. Accordingly, he falls on his neighbours, and a desperate battle ensues. If he prevails, and takes prisoners, he gratifies his avarice by selling them; but, if his party be vanquished, and he falls into the hands of the enemy, he is put to death: for, as he has been known to foment their quarrels, it is thought dangerous to let him survive, and no ransom can save him, though all other prisoners may be redeemed. We have firearms, bows and arrows, broad two-edged swords and javelins; we have shields also, which cover a man from head to foot. All are taught the use of the weapons. Even our women are warriors, and march boldly out to fight along with the men. Our whole district is a kind of militia: on a certain signal given, such as the firing of a gun at night, they all rise in arms and rush upon their enemy. It is perhaps something remarkable, that when our people march to the field, a red flag or banner is borne before them. I was once a witness to a battle in our common. We had been all at work in it one day as usual when our people were suddenly attacked. I climbed a tree at some distance, from which I beheld the fight. There were many women as well as men on both sides; among others my mother was there and armed with a broad sword. After fighting for a considerable time with great fury, and many had been killed, our people obtained the victory, and took their enemy's Chief prisoner. He was carried off in great triumph, and, though he offered a large ransom for his life, he was put to death. A virgin of note among our enemies had been slain in the battle, and her arm was exposed in our market-place, where our trophies were always exhibited. The spoils were divided according to the merit of the warriors. Those prisoners which were not sold or redeemed we kept as slaves: but how different was their condition from that of the slaves in the West-Indies! With us they do no more work than other members of the community, even their master. Their food, clothing, and lodging were nearly the same as theirs, except that they were not permitted to eat with those who were free born and there was scarce any other difference between them, than a superior degree of importance which the head of a family possesses in our state, and that authority which, as such, he exercises over every part of his household. Some of these slaves have even slaves under them, as their own property, and for their own use.

As to religion, the natives believe that there is one Creator of all things, and that he lives in the sun, and is girded round with a belt, that he may never eat or drink; but, according to some, he smokes a pipe, which is our own favourite luxury. They believe he governs events, especially our deaths or captivity; but, as for the doctrine of eternity, I do not remember to have ever heard of it: some however believe in the transmigration of souls in a certain degree. Those spirits, which are not transmigrated, such as our dear friends or relations, they believe always attend them, and guard them from the bad spirits of their foes. For this reason, they always, before eating, as I have observed, put some small portion of the meat, and pour some of their drink, on the ground for them; and they often make oblations of the blood of beasts or fowls at their graves. I was very fond of my mother, and almost constantly with her. When she went to make these oblations at her mother's tomb, which was a kind of small solitary thatched house, I sometimes attended her. There she made her libations, and spent most of the night in cries and lamentations. I have been often extremely terrified on these occasions. The loneliness of the place, the darkness of the night, and the ceremony of libation, naturally awful and gloomy, were heightened by my mother's lamentations; and these, concurring with the doleful cries of birds, by which these places were frequented, gave an inexpressible terror to the scene.

We compute the year from the day on which the sun crosses the line, and, on its setting that evening, there is a general shout throughout the land; at least I can speak from my own knowledge throughout our vicinity. The people at the same time make a great noise with rattles, not unlike the basket rattles used by children here, though much larger, and hold up their hands to heaven for a blessing. It is then the greatest offerings are made; and those children whom our wise men foretell will be fortunate are then presented to different people. I remember many used to come to see me, and I was carried about to others for that purpose. They have many offerings, particularly at full moons; generally two at harvest, before the fruits are taken out of the ground: and, when any young animals are killed, sometimes they offer up part of them as a sacrifice. These offerings, when made by one of the heads of a family, serve for the whole. I remember we often had them at my father's and my uncle's, and their families have been present. Some of our offerings are eaten with bitter herbs. We had a saying among us to anyone of a cross temper, "That if they were to be eaten, they should be eaten with bitter herbs."

We practised circumcision like the Jews, and made offerings and feasts on that occasion in the same manner as they did. Like them also, our children were named from some event, some circumstance, or fancied foreboding at the time of their birth. I was named *Olaudah*, which, in our language, signifies vicissitude, or fortunate also; one favoured, and having a loud voice and well spoken. I remember we never polluted the name of the object of our adoration; on the contrary, it was always mentioned with the greatest reverence; and we were totally unacquainted with swearing, and all those terms of abuse and reproach which find the way so readily and copiously into the languages of more civilized people. The only expressions of that kind I remember were "May you rot, or may you swell, or may a beast take you."

I have before remarked, that the natives of this part of Africa are extremely cleanly. This necessary habit of decency was with us a part of religion, and therefore we had many purifications and washings; indeed almost as many, and used on the same occasions, if my recollection does not fail me, as the Jews. Those that touched the dead at any time were obliged to wash and purify themselves before they could enter a dwelling-house. Every woman too, at certain times, was forbidden to come into a dwelling-house, or touch any person, or anything we ate. I was so fond of my mother I could not keep from her, or avoid touching her at some of those periods, in consequence of which I was obliged to be kept out with her, in a little house made for that purpose, till offering was made, and then we were purified.

Though we had no places of public worship, we had priests and magicians, or wise men. I do not remember whether they had different offices, or whether they were united in the same persons but they were held in great reverence by the people. They calculated our time, and foretold events, as their name imported, for we called them Ah-affoe-way-cah, which signifies calculators, or yearly men, our year being called Ah-affoe. They wore their beards; and, when they died, they were succeeded by their sons. Most of their implements and things of value were interred along with them. Pipes and tobacco were also put into the grave with the corpse, which was always perfumed and ornamented; and animals were offered in sacrifice to them. None accompanied their funerals but those of the same profession or tribe. These buried them after sunset, and always returned from the grave by a different way from that which they went.

These magicians were also our doctors or physicians. They practised bleeding by cupping, and were very successful in healing wounds and expelling poisons. They had likewise some extraordinary method of discovering jealousy, theft, and poisoning; the success of which no doubt they derived from their unbounded influence over the credulity and superstition of the people. I do not remember what those methods were, except that as to poisoning. I recollect an instance or two, which I hope it will not be deemed impertinent here to insert, as it may serve as a kind of specimen of the rest, and is still used by the negroes in the West Indies. A young woman had been poisoned, but it was not known by whom; the doctors ordered the corpse to be taken up by some persons, and carried to the grave. As soon as the bearers had raised it on their shoulders, they seemed seized with some sudden impulse, and ran to and fro, unable to stop themselves. At last, after having passed through a number of thorns and prickly bushes unhurt, the corpse fell from them close to a house, and defaced it in the fall; and the owner being taken up, he immediately confessed the poisoning.

The natives are extremely cautious about poison. When they buy any eatable the seller kisses it all round before the buyer, to shew him it is not poisoned; and the same is done when any meat or drink is presented, particularly to a stranger. We have serpents of different kinds, some of which are esteemed ominous when they appear in our houses, and these we never molest. I remember two of those ominous snakes, each of which was as thick as the calf of a man's leg, and in colour resembling a dolphin in the water, crept at different times into my mother's night-house, where I always lay with her, and coiled themselves into folds, and each time they crowed like a cock. I was desired by some of our wise men to touch these, that I might be interested in the good omens, which I did, for they were quite harmless, and would tamely suffer themselves to be handled; and then they were put into a large open earthen pan, and set on one side of the highway. Some of our snakes, however, were poisonous: one of them crossed the road one day when I was standing on it, and passed between my feet, without offering to touch me, to the great surprise of many who saw it; and these incidents were accounted by the wise men, and likewise by my mother and the rest of the people, as remarkable omens in my favour.

...

Chapter 2

I hope the reader will not think I have trespassed on his patience in introducing myself to him, with some account of the manners and customs of my country. They had been implanted in me with great care, and made an impression on my mind, which time could not erase, and which all the adversity and variety of fortune I have since experienced, served only to rivet and record; for, whether the love of one's country be real or imaginary, or a lesson of reason, or an instinct of nature, I still look back with pleasure on the first scenes of my life, though that pleasure has been for the most part mingled with sorrow.

I have already acquainted the reader with the time and place of my birth. My father, besides many slaves, had a numerous family, of which seven lived to grow up, including myself and a sister, who was the only daughter. As I was the youngest of the sons, I became, of course, the greatest favorite with my mother, and was always with her; and she used to take particular pains to form my mind. I was trained up from my earliest years in the art of war; my daily exercise was shooting and throwing javelins; and my mother adorned me with emblems, after the manner of our greatest warriors. In this way I grew up till I was turned the age of eleven, when an end was put to my happiness in the following manner: —generally when the grown people in the neighborhood were gone far in the fields to labor, the children assembled together in some of the neighboring premises to play; and commonly some of us used to get up a tree to look out for any assailant, or kidnapper, that might come upon us; for they sometimes took those opportunities of our parents' absence, to attack and carry off as many as they could seize. One day as I was watching at the top of a tree in our yard, I saw one of those people come into the yard of our next neighbor but one to kidnap, there being many stout young people in it. Immediately on this I gave the alarm of the rogue, and he was surrounded by the stoutest of them, who entangled him with cords, so that he could not escape till some of the grown people came and secured him. But, alas! ere long① it was my fate to be thus attacked, and to be carried off, when none of the grown people were nigh. One day, when all our people were gone out to their works as usual, and only I and my dear sister were left to mind the house, two men and a woman got over our walls, and in a moment seized us both, and, without giving us time to cry out, or make resistance, they stopped our mouths, and ran off with us into the nearest wood. Here they tied our hands, and continued to carry us as far as they could, till night came on, when we reached a small house, where the robbers halted for refreshment, and spent the night. We were then unbound, but were unable to take any food; and, being quite overpowered by fatigue and grief, our only relief was some sleep, which allayed our misfortune for a short time. The next morning we left the house, and continued traveling all the day. For a long time we had kept the woods, but at last we came into a road which I believed I knew. I had now some hopes of being delivered; for we had advanced but a little way before I discovered some people at a distance, on which I began to cry out for their assistance: but my cries had no other effect than to make them tie me faster and stop my mouth, and then they put me into a large sack. They also stopped my sister's mouth, and tied her hands; and in this manner we proceeded till we were out of sight of these people. When we went to rest the following night, they offered us some victuals, but we refused it; and the only comfort we had was in being in one another's arms all that night, and bathing each other with our tears. But alas! we were soon deprived of even the small comfort of weeping together. The next day proved a day of greater sorrow than I had yet experienced; for my sister and I were then separated, while we lay clasped in each other's arms. It was in vain that we besought them not to part us; she was torn from me, and immediately carried away, while I was left in a state of distraction not to be described. I cried and grieved continually; and for several days did not eat any thing but

---

① ere long：不久以后。

what they forced into my mouth. At length, after many days traveling, during which I had often changed masters, I got into the hands of a chieftain, in a very pleasant country. This man had two wives and some children, and they all used me extremely well, and did all they could to comfort me; particularly the first wife, who was something like my mother. Although I was a great many days' journey from my father's house, yet these people spoke exactly the same language with us. This first master of mine, as I may call him, was a smith, and my principal employment was working his bellows, which were the same kind as I had seen in my vicinity. They were in some respects not unlike the stoves here in gentlemen's kitchens, and were covered over with leather; and in the middle of that leather a stick was fixed, and a person stood up, and worked it in the same manner as is done to pump water out of a cask with a hand pump. I believe it was gold he worked, for it was of a lovely bright yellow color, and was worn by the women on their wrists and ankles. I was there I suppose about a month, and they at last used to trust me some little distance from the house. This liberty I used in embracing every opportunity to inquire the way to my own home; and I also sometimes, for the same purpose, went with the maidens, in the cool of the evenings, to bring pitchers of water from the springs for the use of the house. I had also remarked where the sun rose in the morning, and set in the evening, as I had traveled along; and I had observed that my father's house was towards the rising of the sun. I therefore determined to seize the first opportunity of making my escape, and to shape my course for that quarter; for I was quite oppressed and weighed down by grief after my mother and friends; and my love of liberty, ever great, was strengthened by the mortifying circumstance of not daring to eat with the free-born children, although I was mostly their companion. While I was projecting my escape one day, an unlucky event happened, which quite disconcerted my plan, and put an end to my hopes. I used to be sometimes employed in assisting an elderly slave to cook and take care of the poultry; and one morning, while I was feeding some chickens, I happened to toss a small pebble at one of them, which hit it on the middle, and directly killed it. The old slave, having soon after missed the chicken, inquired after it; and on my relating the accident (for I told her the truth, for my mother would never suffer me to tell a lie), she flew into a violent passion, and threatened that I should suffer for it; and, my master being out, she immediately went and told her mistress what I had done. This alarmed me very much, and I expected an instant flogging, which to me was uncommonly dreadful, for I had seldom been beaten at home. I therefore resolved to fly; and accordingly I ran into a thicket that was hard by, and hid myself in the bushes. Soon afterwards my mistress and the slave returned, and, not seeing me, they searched all the house, but not finding me, and I not making answer when they called to me, they thought I had run away, and the whole neighborhood was raised in the pursuit of me. In that part of the country, as in ours, the houses and villages were skirted with woods, or shrubberies, and the bushes were so thick that a man could readily conceal himself in them, so as to elude the strictest search. The neighbors continued the whole day looking for me, and several times many of them came within a few yards of the place where I lay hid. I expected every moment, when I heard a rustling among the trees, to be found out, and punished by my master; but they never discovered me, though they were often so near that I even heard their conjectures as they were looking about for me; and I now learned from them that any attempts to return home would be hopeless. Most of them supposed I had fled towards home; but the distance was so great, and the way so intricate, that they thought I could never reach it, and that I should be lost in the woods. When I heard this I was seized with a violent panic, and abandoned myself to despair. Night, too, began to approach, and aggravated all my fears. I had before entertained hopes of getting home, and had determined when it should be dark to make the attempt; but I was now convinced it was fruitless, and began to consider that, if possibly I could escape all other animals, I could not those of the human kind; and that, not knowing the way, I must perish in the woods. Thus was I like the hunted deer:

—"Every leaf and every whisp'ring breath,
Convey'd a foe, and every foe a death."

I heard frequent rustlings among the leaves, and being pretty sure they were snakes, I expected every instant to be stung by them. This increased my anguish, and the horror of my situation became now quite insupportable. I at length quitted the thicket, very faint and hungry, for I had not eaten or drank any thing all the day, and crept to my master's kitchen, from whence I set out at first, which was an open shed, and laid myself down in the ashes with an anxious wish for death, to relieve me from all my pains. I was scarcely awake in the morning, when the old woman slave, who was the first up, came to light the fire, and saw me in the fire place. She was very much surprised to see me, and could scarcely believe her own eyes. She now promised to intercede forme, and went for her master, who soon after came, and, having slightly reprimanded me, ordered me to be taken care of, and not ill-treated.

Soon after this, my master's only daughter, and child by his first wife, sickened and died, which affected him so much that for some time he was almost frantic, and really would have killed himself, had he not been watched and prevented. However, in short time afterwards he recovered, and I was again sold. I was now carried to the left of the sun's rising, through many dreary wastes and dismal woods, amidst the hideous roarings of wild beasts. The people I was sold to used to carry me very often, when I was tired, either on their shoulders or on their backs. I saw many convenient well built sheds along the road, at proper distances, to accommodate the merchants and travelers, who lay in those buildings along with their wives, who often accompany them; and they always go well armed.

From the time I left my own nation, I always found somebody that understood me till I came to the sea coast. The languages of different nations did not totally differ, nor were they so copious as those of the Europeans, particularly the English. They were therefore, easily learned; and, while I was journeying thus through Africa, I acquired two or three different tongues. In this manner I had been traveling for a considerable time, when, one evening, to my great surprise, whom should I see brought to the house where I was but my dear sister! As soon as she saw me, she gave a loud shriek, and ran into my arms—I was quite overpowered: neither of us could speak; but, for a considerable time, clung to each other in mutual embraces, unable to do any thing but weep. Our meeting affected all who saw us; and, indeed, I must acknowledge, in honor of those sable destroyers of human rights, that I never met with any ill treatment, or saw any offered to their slaves, except tying them, when necessary, to keep them from running away. When these people knew we were brother and sister, they indulged us to be together; and the man, to whom I supposed we belonged, lay with us, he in the middle, while she and I held one another by the hands across his breast all night; and thus for a while we forgot our misfortunes, in the joy of being together; but even this small comfort was soon to have an end; for scarcely had the fatal morning appeared when she was again torn from me forever! I was now more miserable, if possible, than before. The small relief which her presence gave me from pain was gone, and the wretchedness of my situation was redoubled by my anxiety after her fate, and my apprehensions lest her sufferings should be greater than mine, when I could not be with her to alleviate them. Yes, thou dear partner of all my childish sports! thou sharer of my joys and sorrows! happy should I have ever esteemed myself to encounter every misery for you and to procure your freedom by the sacrifice of my own.—Though you were early forced from my arms, your image has been always riveted in my heart, from which neither time nor fortune have been able to remove it; so that, while the thoughts of your sufferings have damped my prosperity, they have mingled with adversity and increased its bitterness. To that Heaven which protects the weak from the strong, I commit the care of your innocence and virtues, if they have not already received their full reward, and if your youth and delicacy have not long since fallen victims to the violence of the African trader, the pestilential stench of a Guinea ship the seasoning in the European colonies, or the lash and lust of a brutal and unrelenting overseer.

I did not long remain after my sister. I was again sold, and carried through a number of places, till after traveling a considerable time, I came to a town called Tinmah, in the most beautiful country I had yet seen in Africa. It was extremely rich, and there were many rivulets which flowed through it, and supplied a large pond in the center of the town, where the people washed. Here I first saw and tasted cocoa nuts, which I thought superior to any nuts I had ever tasted before; and the trees which were loaded, were also interspersed among the houses, which had commodious shades adjoining, and were in the same manner as ours, the insides being neatly plastered and whitewashed. Here I also saw and tasted for the first time, sugar cane. Their money consisted of little white shells, the size of the finger nail. I was sold here for one hundred and seventy-two of them, by a merchant who lived and brought me there. I had been about two or three days at his house, when a wealthy widow, a neighbor of his, came there one evening, and brought with her an only son, a young gentleman about my own age and size. Here they saw me; and, having taken a fancy to me, I was bought of the merchant, and went home with them. Her house and premises were situated close to one of those rivulets I have mentioned, and were the finest I ever saw in Africa: they were very extensive, and she had a number of slaves to attend her. The next day I was washed and perfumed, and when mealtime came, I was led into the presence of my mistress, and ate and drank before her with her son. This filled me with astonishment; and I could scarce help expressing my surprise that the young gentleman should suffer me, who was bound, to eat with him who was free; and not only so, but that he would not at any time either eat or drink till I had taken first, because I was the eldest, which was agreeable to our custom. Indeed, every thing here, and all their treatment of me, made me forget that I was a slave. The language of these people resembled ours so nearly, that we understood each other perfectly. They had also the very same customs as we. There were likewise slaves daily to attend us, while my young master and I, with other boys, sported with our darts and bows and arrows, as I had been used to do at home. In this resemblance to my former happy state, I passed about two months; and I now began to think I was to be adopted into the family, and was beginning to be reconciled to my situation, and to forget by degrees my misfortunes, when all at once the delusion vanished; for, without the least previous knowledge, one morning early, while my dear master and companion was still asleep, I was awakened out of my reverie to fresh sorrow, and hurried away even amongst the uncircumcised.

Thus, at the very moment I dreamed of the greatest happiness, I found myself most miserable; and it seemed as if fortune wished to give me this taste of joy only to render the reverse more poignant.—The change I now experienced, was as painful as it was sudden and unexpected. It was a change indeed, from a state of bliss to a scene which is inexpressible by me, as it discovered to me an element I had never before beheld, and till then had no idea of, and wherein such instances of hardship and cruelty continually occurred, as I can never reflect on but with horror.

All the nations and people I had hitherto passed through resembled our own in their manners, customs, and language: but I came at length to a country, the inhabitants of which differed from us in all those particulars. I was very much struck with this difference, especially when I came among a people who did not circumcise, and ate without washing their hands. They cooked also in iron pots, and had European cutlasses and cross bows, which were unknown to us, and fought with their fists among themselves. Their women were not so modest as ours, for they ate, and drank, and slept with their men. But above all, I was amazed to see no sacrifices or offerings among them. In some of those places the people ornamented themselves with scars, and likewise filed their teeth very sharp. They wanted sometimes to ornament me in the same manner, but I would not suffer them; hoping that I might some time be among a people who did not thus disfigure themselves, as I thought they did. At last I came to the banks of a large river which was covered with canoes, in which the people appeared to live with their household utensils, and provisions of all kinds. I was beyond measure astonished at this, as I had never before seen any water larger than a pond or a rivulet: and my surprise was mingled with no small fear when I was put into one of these canoes, and we began to paddle and move along the river. We continued going on thus till night, and when we came to land, and made fires on the banks, each family by themselves; some dragged their canoes on shore, others stayed and cooked in theirs, and laid in them all night. Those on the land had mats, of which they made tents, some in the shape of little houses; in these we slept; and after the morning meal, we embarked again and proceeded as before. I was often very much astonished to see some of the women, as well as the men, jump into the water, dive to the bottom, come up again, and swim about.—Thus I continued to travel, sometimes by land, sometimes by water, through different countries and various nations, till, at the end of six or seven months after I had been kidnapped, I arrived at the sea coast. It would be tedious and uninteresting to relate all the incidents which befell me during this journey, and which I have not yet forgotten; of the various hands I passed through, and the manners and customs of all the different people among whom I lived—I shall therefore only observe, that in all the places where I was, the soil was exceedingly rich; the pumpkins, eadas, plaintains, yams, &c. &c. were in great abundance, and of incredible size. There were also vast quantities of different gums, though not used for any purpose, and every where a great deal of tobacco. The cotton even grew quite wild, and there was plenty of red-wood. I saw no mechanics whatever in all the way, except such as I have mentioned. The chief employment in all these countries was agriculture, and both the males and females, as with us, were brought up to it, and trained in the arts of war.

The first object which saluted my eyes when I arrived on the coast, was the sea, and a slave ship, which was then riding at anchor, and waiting for its cargo. These filled me with astonishment, which was soon converted into terror, when I was carried on board. I was immediately handled, and tossed up to see if I were sound, by some of the crew; and I was now persuaded that I had gotten into a world of bad spirits, and that they were going to kill me. Their complexions, too, differing so much from ours, their long hair, and the language they spoke (which was very different from any I had ever heard), united to confirm me in this belief. Indeed, such were the horrors of my views and fears at the moment, that, if ten thousand worlds had been my own, I would have freely parted with them all to have exchanged my condition with that of the meanest slave in my own country. When I looked round the ship too, and saw a large furnace of copper boiling, and a multitude of black people of every description chained together, every one of their countenances expressing dejection and sorrow, I no longer doubted of my fate; and, quite overpowered with horror and anguish, I fell motionless on the deck and fainted. When I recovered a little, I found some black people about me, who I believed were some of those who had brought me on board, and had been receiving their pay; they talked to me in order to cheer me, but all in vain. I asked them if we were not to be eaten by those white men with horrible looks, red faces, and long hair. They told me I was not: and one of the crew brought me a small portion of spirituous liquor in a wine glass, but, being afraid of him, I would not take it out of his hand. One of the blacks, therefore, took it from him and gave it to me, and I took a little down my palate, which, instead of reviving me, as they thought it would, threw me into the greatest consternation at the strange feeling it produced, having never tasted any such liquor before. Soon after this, the blacks who brought me on board went off, and left me abandoned to despair.

I now saw myself deprived of all chance of returning to my native country, or even the least glimpse of hope of gaining the shore, which I now considered as friendly; and I even wished for my former slavery in preference to my present situation, which was filled with horrors of everykind, still heightened by my ignorance of what I was to undergo. I was not long suffered to indulge my grief; I was soon put down under the decks, and there I received such a salutation in my nostrils as I had never experienced in my life: so that, with the loathsomeness of the stench, and crying together, I became so sick and low that I was not able to eat, nor had I the least desire to taste anything. I now wished for the last friend, death, to relieve me; but soon, to my grief, two of the white men offered me eatables; and, on my refusing to eat, one of them held me fast by the hands, and laid me across, I think the windlass, and tied my feet, while the other flogged me severely. I had never experienced anything of this kind before, and although not being used to the water, I naturally feared that element the first time I saw it, yet, nevertheless, could I have got over the nettings, I would have jumped over the side, but I could not; and besides, the crew used to watch us very closely who were not chained down to the decks, lest we should leap into the water; and I have seen some of these poor African prisoners most severely cut, for attempting to do so, and hourly whipped for not eating. This indeed was often the case with myself. In a little time after, amongst the poor chained men, I found some of my own nation, which in a small degree gave ease to my mind. I inquired of these what was to be done with us; They gave me to understand we were to be carried to these white people's country to work for them. I then was a little revived, and thought, if it were no worse than working, my situation was not so desperate; but still I feared I should be put to death, the white people looked and acted, as I thought, in so savage a manner; for I had never seen among any people such instances of brutal cruelty; and this not only shown towards us blacks, but also to some of the whites themselves. One white man in particular I saw, when we were permitted to be on deck, flogged so unmercifully with a large rope near the foremast, that he died in consequence of it; and they tossed him over the side as they would have done a brute. This made me fear these people the more; and I expected nothing less than to be treated in the same manner. I could not help expressing my fears and apprehensions to some of my countrymen; I asked them if these people had no country, but lived in this hollow place (the ship): they told me they did not, but came from a distant one. "Then," said I, "how comes it in all our country we never heard of them?" They told me because they lived so very far off. I then asked where were their women? had they any like themselves? I was told they had. "And why," said I, "do we not see them?" They answered, because they were left behind. I asked how the vessel could go? they told me they could not tell; but that there was cloth put upon the masts by the help of the ropes I saw, and then the vessel went on; and the white men had some spell or magic they put in the water when they liked, in order to stop the vessel. I was exceedingly amazed at this account, and really thought they were spirits. I therefore wished much to be from amongst them, for I expected they would sacrifice me; but my wishes were vain—for we were so quartered that it was impossible for any of us to make our escape.

While we stayed on the coast I was mostly on deck; and one day, to my great astonishment, I saw one of these vessels coming in with the sails up. As soon as the whites saw it, they gave a great shout, at which we were amazed; and the more so, as the vessel appeared larger by approaching nearer. At last, she came to an anchor in my sight, and when the anchor was let go, I and my countrymen who saw it, were lost in astonishment to observe the vessel stop and were now convinced it was done by magic. Soon after this the other ship got her boats out, and they came on board of us, and the people of both ships seemed very glad to see each other. Several of the strangers also shook hands with us black people, and made motions with their hands, signifying I suppose, we were to go to their country, but we did not understand them.

At last, when the ship we were in had got in all her cargo, they made ready with many fearful noises, and we were all put under deck, so that we could not see how they managed the vessel. But this disappointment was the least of my sorrow. The stench of the hold while we were on the coast was so intolerably loathsome, that it was dangerous to remain there for any time, and some of us had been permitted to stay on the deck for the fresh air; but now that the whole ship's cargo were confined together, it became absolutely pestilential. The closeness of the place, and the heat of the climate, added to the number in the ship, which was so crowded that each had scarcely room to turn himself, almost suffocated us. This produced copious perspirations, so that the air soon became unfit for respiration, from a variety of loathsome smells, and brought on a sickness among the slaves, of which many died—thus falling victims to the improvident avarice, as I may call it, of their purchasers. This wretched situation was again aggravated by the galling of the chains, now become insupportable, and the filth of the necessary tubs, into which the children often fell, and were almost suffocated. The shrieks of the women, and the groans of the dying, rendered the whole a scene of horror almost inconceivable. Happily perhaps, for myself, I was soon reduced so low here that it was thought necessary to keep me almost always on deck; and from my extreme youth I was not put in fetters. In this situation I expected every hour to share the fate of my companions, some of whom were almost daily brought upon deck at the point of death, which I began to hope would soon put an end to my miseries. Often did I think many of the inhabitants of the deep much more happy than myself. I envied them the freedom they enjoyed, and as often wished I could change my condition for theirs. Every circumstance I met with, served only to render my state more painful, and heightened my apprehensions, and my opinion of the cruelty of the whites.

Questions for Discussion

1. What do you think of the society in Eboe where the author was born regarding its gender relationship?
2. According to the author, what are the differences between the slaves in the author's hometown and those in the West Indies?
3. Equiano's *Interesting Narrative* contributes a lot to the development of *Slave Narrative*, please tell the similarity(ties) and difference(s) between this book and Frederick Douglass's *Narrative*.

2. Narrative of the Life of Frederick Douglass

作者简介

　　弗雷德里克·道格拉斯(Frederick Douglas)(1818—1895)是美国19世纪废奴主义的倡导者,在美国黑人解放运动中发挥了主导作用,被后世誉为"所有被压迫者的英雄典范"。道格拉斯还是一位杰出的作家,他的三部自传奠定了他在美国文学史上的重要地位。

　　1818年2月,道格拉斯诞生于美国马里兰州塔尔波特县吐卡霍地方的一个由奴隶主艾伦·安东尼经营的种植场。他的母亲是安东尼家的黑人女奴哈丽特·贝利,父亲是一个身份无从知悉的白人。道格拉斯生为奴隶,不知生父是谁,婴儿时期就与母亲分开,早年与外祖母柏西·贝利一起度过。道格拉斯于1824年夏被带到东海岸最大的种植园——劳埃种植园当家奴,18个月后被安东尼女婿的兄弟、居于巴尔的摩的休·奥德要去与其儿子汤姆做伴。在巴尔的摩的七年间,女主人索菲亚将道格拉斯视如己出,教他识字、读写《圣经》。道格拉斯也善于利用一切机会学习拼写与基本算术,并在获取新知中强化了争取个人自由的迫切愿望。

　　1833年3月,道格拉斯结束其家庭奴仆的生活,被转卖至位于东海岸圣米切尔的一处由奴隶主托马斯管理的种植园。特立独行的道格拉斯在此创办了一所主日学校,教有色人孩子识字,这让托马斯大为恼火,遂将其送往有着"驯奴师"之称的爱德华·柯维那里接受"调教"。在柯维手下,道格拉斯每天超负荷地劳作,忍受着非人的折磨,这一段痛苦经历更坚定了他争取自由的决心。

　　1835年1月,道格拉斯被雇佣给临近一个名叫威廉·弗里兰的奴隶主,生活条件有所改善,但与此同时他萌生了逃亡计划。1836年,道格拉斯计划带上四位同胞逃奔自由,但行动遭到泄密。道格拉斯作为密谋组织者被关进塔波特县监狱,最后因证据缺失被释放。1836年夏至1838年,道格拉斯在巴尔的摩的船厂工作,同时参加自由黑人组织——东巴尔的摩协进会的活动,在那里结识了他未来的妻子安·默里。

　　1838年9月,道格拉斯在友人帮助下,化装成水手,通过"地下铁道"逃到马萨诸塞州的新贝德福,终于挣脱了奴隶身份的枷锁。获得自由的道格拉斯没有忘记仍在奴隶主压迫下的南方同胞们的苦难,1841年他参加新贝德福的废奴运动,成为加里森派的演讲员;1845年至1847年他到访过英国,其间他从休·奥德那里赎买了人身自由;1848年成为美国黑人大会主席;1851年后又成为政治废奴派领袖。1877年至1881年,他担任哥伦比亚区联邦法院执行官;1881年至1886年,又担任哥伦比亚特区联邦法院书记官;1889年至1891年任美国驻圣多明各代办和驻海地公使。道格拉斯一生竭其所能为美国黑人寻求一条通往解放的光明大道,他成为那个时代黑人群体最重要的发言人。

作品简介与赏析

　　《弗雷德里克·道格拉斯:一个美国奴隶的生平自述》(以下简称《自述》)是19世纪美国著名黑人领袖、作家、演说家和政治家道格拉斯所著的三部自传中最广为流传、影响最为深远的一部。该作品涌动着苦难、压迫、挣扎和反抗,弥漫着血腥之味,充斥着暴力、摧残和戕害的黑色乐章,是沉重枷锁下黑人奴隶灵魂的一曲悲歌。作品从控诉黑奴交易、追求自由平等和弘扬人道主义精神等几个层面形成了一代美国黑奴反压迫、反暴力的历史叙事,成为叙述美国种植园奴隶制及其丑恶形态的经典之作,并将自传作为政治革新使命书的诠释方式推向极致。

《自述》于1845年问世,此时道格拉斯逃离南方种植园已有7年。自1841年起,道格拉斯就作为废奴运动的先锋开始了成功的演讲生涯,他的演讲在深受欢迎的同时也招来了一些白人的质疑,他们猜测道格拉斯是受雇于废奴主义领袖的职业演说家,而非逃自南方的黑奴。为了消除这些怀疑和敌意,道格拉斯决定详尽地写出个人经历,进一步摧垮黑奴制度,同时对那些怀疑和敌对者进行有力反击。此书一经出版即在北方引起轰动,后多次再版,并被翻译成多种文字畅销海外,在当时堪称奇迹。彼得·戈麦斯在该书引言中称:"此作品对于废奴进程的重要意义和作用,堪比早期福音传播之于基督教。"

《自述》共11章,总体呈现了道格拉斯作为被奴隶制暴力践踏的边缘者的文化身份,同时凸显其与奴隶制誓死抗争的自由斗士形象。道格拉斯从小目睹白人阶层小到贫苦农民,中到监管工、小奴隶主,大到大奴隶主对其亲人与其他众多黑人同胞的残暴蹂躏和非人性践踏;充斥其周围的是血腥的暴力和地狱般的生存状态。在这种极端生活状态下,接受知识启蒙的道格拉斯找到了逃脱黑暗魔爪的钥匙。他勤奋努力,学习新知、阅读进步书籍,逐渐走向通往自由之路。在废奴人士的帮助下,道格拉斯挣脱了捆绑在黑人祖先和同胞身上的罪恶奴隶枷锁,到达自由的北方,终结了自己的奴隶身份。自此,他的生命迎来重大转机,由一位黑奴成功转型为废奴勇士,自传到此画上了一个句号。

作为一名杰出的黑人作家与政治家,道格拉斯在《自述》中将黑人个体与集体的声音泯合于文本之中,使得黑人逐渐开始被认可为言说者主体,从而证明他们是文明之人而非生而为奴。该自传是道格拉斯争取黑人同胞自由之路的里程碑之作,有力控诉了蓄奴制度的罪恶,白人阶层的嗜血如狂、暴虐成性,在根本上动摇了美国奴隶制的根基。

自我意识的觉醒使道格拉斯意识到奴隶制的残暴。在《自述》第一章中,道格拉斯追忆的第一件事就是他七八岁时亲眼目睹奴隶主鞭打姨母海丝特的凶残行径,之前,他一直在"种植园的外围"和他的外婆生活在一起,并未亲历过种植园的暴力,更不知道暴力鞭笞实际上是种植园成年奴隶们生活的常态。虽然其后也目睹了许多类似的暴行,但姨母的受刑给他留下了极为痛苦且永生难忘的印象。"它以一种强大的力量击打着我",道格拉斯回忆道,似乎接受鞭刑的是他自己。他倏然意识到掌握在他人手中的身体之脆弱和卑贱,也意识到他与身处苦难中的奴隶同胞们心手相连。"这粗野的奴隶制特征"及此次的鞭打使他开始"探究奴隶制的本质和历史"。"它是一扇浸满鲜血的大门,一个通往地狱般奴隶制的入口,而我即将通过这一入口"。小道格拉斯对自己的未来充满了恐惧,同时也对剥夺了黑人基本人权的奴隶制极度憎恶。

奴隶主错误地认为可以通过鞭打把黑人变成没有思想的劳役机器。《自述》第十章中,道格拉斯被奴隶主送往有着"驯奴师"之称的爱德华·柯维手下接受"调教",在那里他遭受了非人的折磨。满腔悲愤的道格拉斯经常登临种植园附近切萨皮克湾高高的堤岸,对着浩瀚海洋中往来如织的商船大声抒发他内心的苦闷和渴望:"上帝啊,救救我吧!让我自由吧!为什么我是奴隶?我要逃跑。我受不了了!我一定要试一试,即使被抓住!反正我只能丧生一次……我不可能生而为奴死亦为奴。我要下水去!就在这个港湾里,我将获得自由!"道格拉斯向上帝呐喊、诉说着自己灵魂深处的痛苦与愤懑,字里行间是对奴隶制的强烈反叛,是乞求上帝把他们从奴役中解救出来的虔敬祷告。道格拉斯对奴隶制的憎恨和对自由的热切渴望在此处得到了淋漓尽致的展现,同时也为其日后逃亡成功并走上废奴运动的历史舞台埋下伏笔。

Narrative of the Life of Frederick Douglass

Chapter 1

I was born in Tuckahoe, near Hillsborough, and about twelve miles from Easton, in Talbot county[①], Maryland. I have no accurate knowledge of my age, never having seen any authentic record containing it. By far the larger part of the slaves know as little of their ages as horses know of theirs, and it is the wish of most masters within my knowledge to keep their slaves thus ignorant. I do not remember to have ever met a slave who could tell of his birthday. They seldom come nearer to it than planting-time, harvest-time, cherry-time, springtime, or fall-time. A want of information concerning my own was a source of unhappiness to me even during childhood. The white children could tell their ages. I could not tell why I ought to be deprived of the same privilege. I was not allowed to make any inquiries of my master concerning it. He deemed all such inquiries on the part of a slave improper and impertinent, and evidence of a restless spirit. The nearest estimate I can give makes me now between twenty-seven and twenty-eight years of age. I come to this, from hearing my master say, sometime during 1835, I was about seventeen years old.

My mother was named Harriet Bailey. She was the daughter of Isaac and Betsey Bailey, both colored, and quite dark. My mother was of a darker complexion than either my grandmother or grandfather.

My father was a white man. He was admitted to be such by all I ever heard speak of my parentage. The opinion was also whispered that my master was my father; but of the correctness of this opinion, I know nothing; the means of knowing was withheld from me. My mother and I were separated when I was but an infant—before I knew her as my mother. It is a common custom, in the part of Maryland from which I ran away, to part children from their mothers at a very early age. Frequently, before the child has reached its twelfth month, its mother is taken from it, and hired out on some farm a considerable distance off, and the child is placed under the care of an old woman, too old for field labor. For what this separation is done, I do not know, unless it be to hinder the development of the child's affection toward its mother, and to blunt and destroy the natural affection of the mother for the child. This is the inevitable result.

I never saw my mother, to know her as such, more than four or five times in my life; and each of these times was very short in duration, and at night. She was hired by a Mr. Stewart, who lived about twelve miles from my home. She made her journeys to see me in the night, travelling the whole distance on foot, after the performance of her day's work. She was a field hand, and a whipping is the penalty of not being in the field at sunrise, unless a slave has special permission from his or her master to the contrary—a permission which they seldom get, and one that gives to him that gives it the proud name of being a kind master. I do not recollect of ever seeing my mother by the light of day. She was with me in the night. She would lie down with me, and get me to sleep, but long before I waked

---

① Talbot county：塔尔博特县,位于马里兰州东海岸的核心地带。始建于 1661 年,以马里兰州的第一位州长巴尔的摩勋爵的妹妹格雷丝·塔尔博特夫人的名字命名。

she was gone. Very little communication ever took place between us. Death soon ended what little we could have while she lived, and with it her hardships and suffering. She died when I was about seven years old, on one of my master's farms, near Lee's Mill. I was not allowed to be present during her illness, at her death, or burial. She was gone long before I knew anything about it. Never having enjoyed, to any considerable extent, her soothing presence, her tender and watchful care, I received the tidings of her death with much the same emotions I should have probably felt at the death of a stranger.

Called thus suddenly away, she left me without the slightest intimation of who my father was. The whisper that my master was my father, may or may not be true; and, true or false, it is of but little consequence to my purpose whilst the fact remains, in all its glaring odiousness, that slaveholders have ordained, and by law established, that the children of slave women shall in all cases follow the condition of their mothers; and this is done too obviously to administer to their own lusts, and make a gratification of their wicked desires profitable as well as pleasurable; for by this cunning arrangement, the slaveholder, in cases not a few, sustains to his slaves the double relation of master and father.

I know of such cases; and it is worthy of remark that such slaves invariably suffer greater hardships, and have more to contend with, than others. They are, in the first place, a constant offence to their mistress. She is ever disposed to find fault with them; they can seldom do anything to please her; she is never better pleased than when she sees them under the lash, especially when she suspects her husband of showing to his mulatto children favors which he withholds from his black slaves. The master is frequently compelled to sell this class of his slaves, out of deference to the feelings of his white wife; and, cruel as the deed may strike anyone to be, for a man to sell his own children to human flesh-mongers, it is often the dictate of humanity for him to do so; for, unless he does this, he must not only whip them himself, but must stand by and see one white son tie up his brother, of but few shades darker complexion than himself, and ply the gory lash to his naked back; and if he lisp one word of disapproval, it is set down to his parental partiality, and only makes a bad matter worse, both for himself and the slave whom he would protect and defend.

Every year brings with it multitudes of this class of slaves. It was doubtless in consequence of a knowledge of this fact, that one great statesman of the south predicted the downfall of slavery by the inevitable laws of population. Whether this prophecy is ever fulfilled or not, it is nevertheless plain that a very different-looking class of people are springing up at the south, and are now held in slavery, from those originally brought to this country from Africa; and if their increase will do no other good, it will do away the force of the argument, that God cursed Ham, and therefore American slavery is right. If the lineal descendants of Ham are alone to be scripturally enslaved, it is certain that slavery at the south must soon become unscriptural; for thousands are ushered into the world, annually, who, like myself, owe their existence to white fathers, and those fathers most frequently their own masters.

I have had two masters. My first master's name was Anthony. I do not remember his first name. He was generally called Captain Anthony—a title which, I presume, he acquired by sailing a craft on the Chesapeake Bay. He was not considered a rich slaveholder. He owned two or three farms, and about thirty slaves. His farms and slaves were under the care of an overseer. The overseer's name was Plummer. Mr. Plummer was a miserable drunkard, a profane swearer, and a savage monster. He always went armed with a cowskin and a heavy cudgel. I have known him to cut and slash the women's heads so horribly, that even master would be enraged at his cruelty, and would threaten to whip him if he did not mind himself. Master, however, was not a humane slaveholder. It required extraordinary barbarity on the part of an overseer to affect him. He was a cruel man, hardened by a long life of slaveholding. He would at times seem to take great pleasure in whipping a slave. I have often been awakened at the dawn of day by the most heart-rending shrieks of an own aunt of mine, whom he used to tie up to a joist, and whip upon her naked back till she was literally covered with blood. No words, no tears, no prayers, from his gory victim, seemed to move his iron heart from its bloody purpose. The louder she screamed, the harder he whipped; and where the blood ran fastest, there he whipped longest. He would whip her to make her scream, and whip her to make her hush; and not until overcome by fatigue, would he cease to swing the blood-clotted cowskin. I remember the first time I ever witnessed this horrible exhibition. I was quite a child, but I well remember it. I never shall forget it whilst I remember anything. It was the first of a long series of such outrages, of which I was doomed to be a witness and a participant. It struck me with awful force. It was the blood-stained gate, the entrance to the hell of slavery, through which I was about to pass. It was a most terrible spectacle. I wish I could commit to paper the feelings with which I beheld it.

This occurrence took place very soon after I went to live with my old master, and under the following circumstances. Aunt Hester went out one night—where or for what I do not know—and happened to be absent when my master desired her presence. He had ordered her not to go out evenings, and warned her that she must never let him catch her in company with a young man, who was paying attention to her, belonging to Colonel Lloyd. The young man's name was Ned Roberts, generally called Lloyd's Ned. Why master was so careful of her, may be safely left to conjecture. She was a woman of noble form, and of graceful proportions, having very few equals, and fewer superiors, in personal appearance among the colored or white women of our neighborhood.

Aunt Hester had not only disobeyed his orders in going out, but had been found in company with Lloyd's Ned; which circumstance, I found, from what he said while whipping her, was the chief offence. Had he been a man of pure morals himself, he might have been thought interested in protecting the innocence of my aunt; but those who knew him will not suspect him of any such virtue. Before he commenced whipping Aunt Hester, he took her into the kitchen, and stripped her from neck to waist, leaving her neck, shoulders, and back entirely naked. He then told her to cross her hands, calling her at the same time a d—d b—h. After crossing her hands, he tied them with a strong rope, and led her to a stool under a large hook in the joist, put in for the purpose. He made her get upon the stool, and tied her hands to the hook. She now stood fair for his infernal purpose. Her arms were stretched up at their full length, so that she stood upon the ends of her toes. He then said to her, "Now, you d—d b—h, I'll learn you how to disobey my orders!" and after rolling up his sleeves, he commenced to lay on the heavy cowskin, and soon the warm, red blood (amid heartrending shrieks from her, and horrid oaths from him) came dripping to the floor. I was so terrified and horror-stricken at the sight, that I hid myself in a closet, and dared not venture out till long after the bloody transaction was over. I expected it would be my turn next. It was all new to me. I had never seen anything like it before. I had always lived with my grandmother on the outskirts of the plantation, where she was put to raise the children of the younger women. I had therefore been, until now, out of the way of the bloody scenes that often occurred on the plantation.

Chapter 10

I left Master Thomas's house, and went to live with Mr. Covey, on the 1st of January, 1833. I was now, for the first time in my life, a field hand. In my new employment, I found myself even more awkward than a country boy appeared to be in a large city. I had been at my new home but one week before Mr. Covey gave me a very severe whipping, cutting my back, causing the blood to run, and raising ridges on my flesh as large as my little finger. The details of this affair are as follows: Mr. Covey sent me, very early in the morning of one of our coldest days in the month of January, to the woods, to get a load of wood. He gave me a team of unbroken oxen. He told me which was the in-hand ox, and which the off-hand one. He then tied the end of a large rope around the horns of the in-hand ox, and gave me the other end of it, and told me, if the oxen started to run, that I must hold on upon the rope. I had never driven oxen before, and of course I was very awkward. I, however, succeeded in getting to the edge of the woods with little difficulty; but I had got a very few rods into the woods, when the oxen took fright, and started full tilt, carrying the cart against trees, and over stumps, in the most frightful manner. I expected every moment that my brains would be dashed out against the trees. After running thus for a considerable distance, they finally upset the cart, dashing it with great force against a tree, and threw themselves into a dense thicket. How I escaped death, I do not know. There I was, entirely alone, in a thick wood, in a place new to me. My cart was upset and shattered, my oxen were entangled among the young trees, and there was none to help me. After a long spell of effort, I succeeded in getting my cart righted, my oxen disentangled, and again yoked to the cart. I now proceeded with my team to the place where I had, the day before, been chopping wood, and loaded my cart pretty heavily, thinking in this way to tame my oxen. I then proceeded on my way home. I had now consumed one half of the day. I got out of the woods safely, and now felt out of danger. I stopped my oxen to open the woods gate; and just as I did so, before I could get hold of my ox-rope, the oxen again started, rushed through the gate, catching it between the wheel and the body of the cart, tearing it to pieces, and coming within a few inches of crushing me against the gate-post. Thus twice, in one short day, I escaped death by the merest chance. On my return, I told Mr. Covey what had happened, and how it happened. He ordered me to return to the woods again immediately. I did so, and he followed on after me. Just as I got into the woods, he came up and told me to stop my cart, and that he would teach me how to trifle away my time, and break gates. He then went to a large gum-tree, and with his axe cut three large switches, and, after trimming them up neatly with his pocket-knife, he ordered me to take off my clothes. I made him no answer, but stood with my clothes on. He repeated his order. I still made him no answer, nor did I move to strip myself. Upon this he rushed at me with the fierceness of a tiger, tore off my clothes, and lashed me till he had worn out his switches, cutting me so savagely as to leave the marks visible for a long time after. This whipping was the first of a number just like it, and for similar offences.

I lived with Mr. Covey one year. During the first six months, of that year, scarce a week passed without his whipping me. I was seldom free from a sore back. My awkwardness was almost always his excuse for whipping me. We were worked fully up to the point of endurance. Long before day we were up, our horses fed, and by the first approach of day we were off to the field with our hoes and ploughing teams. Mr. Covey gave us enough to eat, but scarce time to eat it. We were often less than five minutes taking our meals. We were often in the field from the first approach of day till its last lingering ray had left us; and at saving-fodder time, midnight often caught us in the field binding blades.

Covey would be out with us. The way he used to stand it, was this. He would spend the most of his afternoons in bed. He would then come out fresh in the evening, ready to urge us on with his words, example, and frequently with the whip. Mr. Covey was one of the few slaveholders who could and did work with his hands. He was a hardworking man. He knew by himself just what a man or a boy could do. There was no deceiving him. His work went on in his absence almost as well as in his presence; and he had the faculty of making us feel that he was ever present with us. This he did by surprising us. He seldom approached the spot where we were at work openly, if he could do it secretly. He always aimed at taking us by surprise. Such was his cunning, that we used to call him, among ourselves, "the snake." When we were at work in the cornfield, he would sometimes crawl on his hands and knees to avoid detection, and all at once he would rise nearly in our midst, and scream out, "Ha, ha! Come, come! Dash on, dash on!" This being his mode of attack, it was never safe to stop a single minute. His comings were like a thief in the night. He appeared to us as being ever at hand. He was under every tree, behind every stump, in every bush, and at every window, on the plantation. He would sometimes mount his horse, as if bound to St. Michael's①, a distance of seven miles, and in half an hour afterwards you would see him coiled up in the corner of the wood-fence, watching every motion of the slaves. He would, for this purpose, leave his horse tied up in the woods.

---

① St. Michael: 圣迈克尔,位于马里兰州东海岸,毗邻伊士顿县。

Again, he would sometimes walk up to us, and give us orders as though he was upon the point of starting on a long journey, turn his back upon us, and make as though he was going to the house to get ready; and, before he would get half way thither, he would turn short and crawl into a fence-corner, or behind some tree, and there watch us till the going down of the sun.

Mr. Covey's *forte* consisted in his power to deceive. His life was devoted to planning and perpetrating the grossest deceptions. Everything he possessed in the shape of learning or religion, he made conform to his disposition to deceive. He seemed to think himself equal to deceiving the Almighty. He would make a short prayer in the morning, and a long prayer at night; and, strange as it may seem, few men would at times appear more devotional than he. The exercises of his family devotions were always commenced with singing; and, as he was a very poor singer himself, the duty of raising the hymn generally came upon me. He would read his hymn, and nod at me to commence. I would at times do so; at others, I would not. My non-compliance would almost always produce much confusion. To show himself independent of me, he would start and stagger through with his hymn in the most discordant manner. In this state of mind, he prayed with more than ordinary spirit. Poor man! such was his disposition, and success at deceiving, I do verily believe that he sometimes deceived himself into the solemn belief, that he was a sincere worshipper of the most high God; and this, too, at a time when he may be said to have been guilty of compelling his woman slave to commit the sin of adultery. The facts in the case are these: Mr. Covey was a poor man; he was just commencing in life; he was only able to buy one slave; and, shocking as is the fact, he bought her, as he said, for *a breeder*. This woman was named Caroline. Mr. Covey bought her from Mr. Thomas Lowe, about six miles from St. Michael's. She was a large, able-bodied woman, about twenty years old. She had already given birth to one child, which proved her to be just what he wanted. After buying her, he hired a married man of Mr. Samuel Harrison, to live with him one year; and him he used to fasten up with her every night! The result was, that, at the end of the year, the miserable woman gave birth to twins. At this result Mr. Covey seemed to be highly pleased, both with the man and the wretched woman. Such was his joy, and that of his wife, that nothing they could do for Caroline during her confinement was too good, or too hard, to be done. The children were regarded as being quite an addition to his wealth.

If at any one time of my life more than another, I was made to drink the bitterest dregs of slavery, that time was during the first six months of my stay with Mr. Covey. We were worked in all weathers. It was never too hot or too cold; it could never rain, blow, hail, or snow, too hard for us to work in the field. Work, work, work, was scarcely more the order of the day than of the night. The longest days were too short for him, and the shortest nights too long for him. I was somewhat unmanageable when I first went there, but a few months of this discipline tamed me. Mr. Covey succeeded in breaking me. I was broken in body, soul, and spirit. My natural elasticity was crushed, my intellect languished, the disposition to read departed, the cheerful spark that lingered about my eye died; the dark night of slavery closed in upon me; and behold a man transformed into a brute!

Sunday was my only leisure time. I spent this in a sort of beast-like stupor, between sleep and wake, under some large tree. At times I would rise up, a flash of energetic freedom would dart through my soul, accompanied with a faint beam of hope, that flickered for a moment, and then vanished. I sank down again, mourning over my wretched condition. I was sometimes prompted to take my life, and that of Covey, but was prevented by a combination of hope and fear. My sufferings on this plantation seem now like a dream rather than a stern reality.

Our house stood within a few rods of the Chesapeake Bay, whose broad bosom was ever white with sails from every quarter of the habitable globe. Those beautiful vessels, robed in purest white, so delightful to the eye of freemen, were to me so many shrouded ghosts, to terrify and torment me with thoughts of my wretched condition. I have often, in the deep stillness of a summer's Sabbath, stood all alone upon the lofty banks of that noble bay, and traced, with saddened heart and tearful eye, the countless number of sails moving off to the mighty ocean. The sight of these always affected me powerfully. My thoughts would compel utterance; and there, with no audience but the Almighty, I would pour out my soul's complaint, in my rude way, with an apostrophe to the moving multitude of ships: —

"You are loosed from your moorings, and are free; I am fast in my chains, and am a slave! You move merrily before the gentle gale, and I sadly before the bloody whip! You are freedom's swift-winged angels, that fly round the world; I am confined in bands of iron! O that I were free! O, that I were on one of your gallant decks, and under your protecting wing! Alas! betwixt me and you, the turbid waters roll. Go on, go on. O that I could also go! Could I but swim! If I could fly! O, why was I born a man, of whom to make a brute! The glad ship is gone; she hides in the dim distance. I am left in the hottest hell of unending slavery. O God, save me! God, deliver me! Let me be free! Is there any God? Why am I a slave? I will run away. I will not stand it. Get caught, or get clear, I'll try it. I had as well die with ague as the fever. I have only one life to lose. I had as well be killed running as die standing. Only think of it; one hundred miles straight north, and I am free! Try it? Yes! God helping me, I will. It cannot be that I shall live and die a slave. I will take to the water. This very bay shall yet bear me into freedom. The steamboats steered in a north-east course from North Point. I will do the same; and when I get to the head of the bay, I will turn my canoe adrift, and walk straight through Delaware into Pennsylvania. When I get there, I shall not be required to have a pass; I can travel without being disturbed. Let but the first opportunity offer, and, come what will, I am off. Meanwhile, I will try to bear up under the yoke. I am not the only slave in the world. Why should I fret? I can bear as much as any of them. Besides, I am but a boy, and all boys are bound to someone. It may be that my misery in slavery will only increase my happiness when I get free. There is a better day coming."

Thus I used to think, and thus I used to speak to myself; goaded almost to madness at one moment, and at the next reconciling myself to my wretched lot.

I have already intimated that my condition was much worse, during the first six months of my stay at Mr. Covey's, than in the last six. The circumstances leading to the change in Mr. Covey's course toward me form an epoch in my humble history. You have seen how a man was made a slave; you shall see how a slave was made a man. On one of the hottest days of the month of August, 1833, Bill Smith, William Hughes, a slave named Eli, and myself, were engaged in fanning wheat. Hughes was clearing the fanned wheat from before the fan, Eli was turning, Smith was feeding, and I was carrying wheat to the fan. The work was simple, requiring strength rather than intellect; yet, to one entirely unused to such work, it came very hard. About three o'clock of that day, I broke down; my strength failed me; I was seized with a violent aching of the head, attended with extreme dizziness; I trembled in every limb. Finding what was coming, I nerved myself up, feeling it would never do to stop work. I stood as long as I could stagger to the hopper with grain. When I could stand no longer, I fell, and felt as if held down by an immense weight. The fan of course stopped; everyone had his own work to do; and no one could do the work of the other, and have his own go on at the same time.

Mr. Covey was at the house, about one hundred yards from the treading-yard where we were fanning. On hearing the fan stop, he left immediately, and came to the spot where we were. He hastily inquired what the matter was. Bill answered that I was sick, and there was no one to bring wheat to the fan. I had by this time crawled away under the side of the post and rail-fence by which the yard was enclosed, hoping to find relief by getting out of the sun. He then asked where I was. He was told by one of the hands. He came to the spot, and, after looking at me awhile, asked me what was the matter. I told him as well as I could, for I scarce had strength to speak. He then gave me a savage kick in the side, and told me to get up. I tried to do so, but fell back in the attempt. He gave me another kick, and again told me to rise. I again tried, and succeeded in gaining my feet; but, stooping to get the tub with which I was feeding the fan, I again staggered and fell. While down in this situation, Mr. Covey took up the hickory slat with which Hughes had been striking off the half-bushel measure, and with it gave me a heavy blow upon the head, making a large wound, and the blood ran freely; and with this again told me to get up. I made no effort to comply, having now made up my mind to let him do his worst. In a short time after receiving this blow, my head grew better. Mr. Covey had now left me to my fate. At this moment I resolved, for the first time, to go to my master, enter a complaint, and ask his protection. In order to do this, I must that afternoon walk seven miles; and this, under the circumstances, was truly a severe undertaking. I was exceedingly feeble; made so as much by the kicks and blows which I received, as by the severe fit of sickness to which I had been subjected. I, however, watched my chance, while Covey was looking in an opposite direction, and started for St. Michael's. I succeeded in getting a considerable distance on my way to the woods, when Covey discovered me, and called after me to come back, threatening what he would do if I did not come. I disregarded both his calls and his threats, and made my way to the woods as fast as my feeble state would allow; and thinking I might be overhauled by him if I kept the road, I walked through the woods, keeping far enough from the road to avoid detection, and near enough to prevent losing my way. I had not gone far before my little strength again failed me. I could go no farther. I fell down, and lay for a considerable time. The blood was yet oozing from the wound on my head. For a time I thought I should bleed to death; and think now that I should have done so, but that the blood so matted my hair as to stop the wound. After lying there about three quarters of an hour, I nerved myself up again, and started on my way, through bogs and briers, barefooted and bareheaded, tearing my feet sometimes at nearly every step; and after a journey of about seven miles, occupying some five hours to perform it, I arrived at master's store. I then presented an appearance enough to affect any but a heart of iron. From the crown of my head to my feet, I was covered with blood. My hair was all clotted with dust and blood; my shirt was stiff with blood. My legs and feet were torn in sundry places with briers and thorns, and were also covered with blood. I suppose I looked like a man who had escaped a den of wild beasts, and barely escaped them. In this state I appeared before my master, humbly entreating him to interpose his authority for my protection. I told him all the circumstances as well as I could, and it seemed, as I spoke, at times to affect him. He would then walk the floor, and seek to justify Covey by saying he expected I deserved it. He asked me what I wanted. I told him, to let me get a new home; that as sure as I lived with Mr. Covey again, I should live with but to die with him; that Covey would surely kill me; he was in a fair way for it. Master Thomas ridiculed the idea that there was any danger of Mr. Covey's killing me, and said that he knew Mr. Covey; that he was a good man, and that he could not think of taking me from him; that, should he do so, he would lose the whole year's wages; that I belonged to Mr. Covey for one year, and that I must go back to him, come what might; and that I must not trouble him with any more stories, or that he would himself *get hold of me*. After threatening me thus, he gave me a very large dose of salts, telling me that I might remain in St. Michael's that night, (it being quite late,) but that I must be off back to Mr. Covey's early in the morning; and that if I did not, he would *get hold of me*, which meant that he would whip me. I remained all night, and, according to his orders, I started off to Covey's in the morning, (Saturday morning,) wearied in body and broken in spirit. I got no supper that night, or breakfast that morning. I reached Covey's about nine o'clock; and just as I was getting over the fence that divided Mrs. Kemp's fields from ours, out ran Covey with his cowskin, to give me another whipping. Before he could reach me, I succeeded in getting to the cornfield; and as the corn was very high, it afforded me the means of hiding. He seemed very angry, and searched for me a long time. My behavior was altogether unaccountable. He finally gave up the chase, thinking, I suppose, that I must come home for something to eat; he would give himself no further trouble in looking for me. I spent that day mostly in the woods, having the alternative before me—to go home and be whipped to death, or stay in the woods and be starved to death. That night, I fell in with Sandy Jenkins, a slave with whom I was somewhat acquainted. Sandy had a free wife, who lived about four miles from

Mr. Covey's; and it being Saturday, he was on his way to see her. I told him my circumstances, and he very kindly invited me to go home with him. I went home with him, and talked this whole matter over, and got his advice as to what course it was best for me to pursue. I found Sandy an old adviser. He told me, with great solemnity, I must go back to Covey; but that before I went, I must go with him into another part of the woods, where there was a certain *root*, which, if I would take some of it with me, carrying it *always on my right side*, would render it impossible for Mr. Covey, or any other white man, to whip me. He said he had carried it for years; and since he had done so, he had never received a blow, and never expected to while he carried it. I at first rejected the idea, that the simple carrying of a root in my pocket would have any such effect as he had said, and was not disposed to take it; but Sandy impressed the necessity with much earnestness, telling me it could do no harm, if it did no good. To please him, I at length took the root, and, according to his direction, carried it upon my right side. This was Sunday morning. I immediately started for home; and upon entering the yard gate, out came Mr. Covey on his way to a meeting. He spoke to me very kindly, bade me drive the pigs from a lot nearby, and passed on towards the church. Now, this singular conduct of Mr. Covey really made me begin to think that there was something in the root which Sandy had given me; and had it been on any other day than Sunday, I could have attributed the conduct to no other cause than the influence of that root; and as it was, I was half inclined to think the *root* to be something more than I at first had taken it to be. All went well till Monday morning. On this morning, the virtue of the *root* was fully tested. Long before daylight, I was called to go and rub, curry, and feed, the horses. I obeyed, and was glad to obey. But whilst thus engaged, whilst in the act of throwing down some blades from the loft, Mr. Covey entered the stable with a long rope; and just as I was half out of the loft, he caught hold of my legs, and was about tying me. As soon as I found what he was up to, I gave a sudden spring, and as I did so, he holding to my legs, I was brought sprawling on the stable floor. Mr. Covey seemed now to think he had me, and could do what he pleased; but at this moment—from whence came the spirit I don't know—I resolved to fight; and, suiting my action to the resolution, I seized Covey hard by the throat; and as I did so, I rose. He held on to me, and I to him. My resistance was so entirely unexpected, that Covey seemed taken all aback. He trembled like a leaf. This gave me assurance, and I held him uneasy, causing the blood to run where I touched him with the ends of my fingers. Mr. Covey soon called out to Hughes for help. Hughes came, and, while Covey held me, attempted to tie my right hand. While he was in the act of doing so, I watched my chance, and gave him a heavy kick close under the ribs. This kick fairly sickened Hughes, so that he left me in the hands of Mr. Covey. This kick had the effect of not only weakening Hughes, but Covey also. When he saw Hughes bending over with pain, his courage quailed. He asked me if I meant to persist in my resistance. I told him I did, come what might; that he had used me like a brute for six months, and that I was determined to be used so no longer. With that, he strove to drag me to a stick that was lying just out of the stable door. He meant to knock me down. But just as he was leaning over to get the stick, I seized him with both hands by his collar, and brought him by a sudden snatch to the ground. By this time, Bill came. Covey called upon him for assistance. Bill wanted to know what he could do. Covey said, "Take hold of him, take hold of him!" Bill said his master hired him out to work, and not to help to whip me; so he left Covey and me to fight our own battle out. We were at it for nearly two hours. Covey at length let me go, puffing and blowing at a great rate, saying that if I had not resisted, he would not have whipped me half so much. The truth was, that he had not whipped me at all. I considered him as getting entirely the worst end of the bargain; for he had drawn no blood from me, but I had from him. The whole six months afterwards, that I spent with Mr. Covey, he never laid the weight of his finger upon me in anger. He would occasionally say, he didn't want to get hold of me again. "No," thought I, "you need not; for you will come off worse than you did before."

This battle with Mr. Covey was the turning-point in my career as a slave. It rekindled the few expiring embers of freedom, and revived within me a sense of my own manhood. It recalled the departed self-confidence, and inspired me again with a determination to be free. The gratification afforded by the triumph was a full compensation for whatever else might follow, even death itself. He only can understand the deep satisfaction which I experienced, who has himself repelled by force the bloody arm of slavery. I felt as I never felt before. It was a glorious resurrection, from the tomb of slavery, to the heaven of freedom. My long-crushed spirit rose, cowardice departed, bold defiance took its place; and I now resolved that, however long I might remain a slave in form, the day had passed forever when I could be a slave in fact. I did not hesitate to let it be known of me, that the white man who expected to succeed in whipping, must also succeed in killing me.

From this time I was never again what might be called fairly whipped, though I remained a slave four years afterwards. I had several fights, but was never whipped.

It was for a long time a matter of surprise to me why Mr. Covey did not immediately have me taken by the constable to the whipping-post, and there regularly whipped for the crime of raising my hand against a white man in defence of myself. And the only explanation I can now think of does not entirely satisfy me; but such as it is, I will give it. Mr. Covey enjoyed the most unbounded reputation for being a first-rate overseer and negro-breaker. It was of considerable importance to him. That reputation was at stake; and had he sent me—a boy about sixteen years old—to the public whipping-post, his reputation would have been lost; so, to save his reputation, he suffered me to go unpunished.

My term of actual service to Mr. Edward Covey ended on Christmas day, 1833. The days between Christmas and New Year's Day are allowed as holidays; and, accordingly, we were not required to perform any labor, more than to feed and take care of the stock. This time we regarded as our own, by the grace of our masters; and we therefore used or abused it nearly as we pleased. Those of us who had families at a distance, were generally allowed to spend the whole six days in their society. This time, however, was spent in various ways. The staid, sober, thinking and industrious ones of our number would employ themselves in making corn-brooms, mats, horse-collars, and baskets; and another class of us would spend the time in hunting opossums, hares, and coons. But by far the larger part engaged in such sports and merriments as playing ball, wrestling, running foot-races, fiddling, dancing, and drinking whisky; and this latter mode of spending the time was by far the most agreeable to the feelings of our masters. A slave who would work during the holidays was considered by our masters as scarcely deserving them. He was regarded as one who rejected the favor of his master. It was deemed a disgrace not to get drunk at Christmas; and he was regarded as lazy indeed, who had not provided himself with the necessary means, during the year, to get whisky enough to last him through Christmas.

From what I know of the effect of these holidays upon the slave, I believe them to be among the most effective means in the hands of the slaveholder in keeping down the spirit of insurrection. Were the slaveholders at once to abandon this practice, I have not the slightest doubt it would lead to an immediate insurrection among the slaves. These holidays serve as conductors, or safety-valves, to carry off the rebellious spirit of enslaved humanity. But for these, the slave would be forced up to the wildest desperation; and woe betide the slaveholder, the day he ventures to remove or hinder the operation of those conductors! I warn him that, in such an event, a spirit will go forth in their midst, more to be dreaded than the most appalling earthquake.

The holidays are part and parcel of the gross fraud, wrong, and inhumanity of slavery. They are professedly a custom established by the benevolence of the slaveholders; but I undertake to say, it is the result of selfishness, and one of the grossest frauds committed upon the down-trodden slave. They do not give the slaves this time because they would not like to have their work during its continuance, but because they know it would be unsafe to deprive them of it. This will be seen by the fact, that the slaveholders like to have their slaves spend those days just in such a manner as to make them as glad of their ending as of their beginning. Their object seems to be, to disgust their slaves with freedom, by plunging them into the lowest depths of dissipation. For instance, the slaveholders not only like to see the slave drink of his own accord, but will adopt various plans to make him drunk. One plan is, to make bets on their slaves, as to who can drink the most whisky without getting drunk; and in this way they succeed in getting whole multitudes to drink to excess. Thus, when the slave asks for virtuous freedom, the cunning slaveholder, knowing his ignorance, cheats him with a dose of vicious dissipation, artfully labelled with the name of liberty. The most of us used to drink it down, and the result was just what might be supposed: many of us were led to think that there was little to choose between liberty and slavery. We felt, and very properly too, that we had almost as well be slaves to man as to rum. So, when the holidays ended, we staggered up from the filth of our wallowing, took a long breath, and marched to the field—feeling, upon the whole, rather glad to go, from what our master had deceived us into a belief was freedom, back to the arms of slavery.

I have said that this mode of treatment is a part of the whole system of fraud and inhumanity of slavery. It is so. The mode here adopted to disgust the slave with freedom, by allowing him to see only the abuse of it, is carried out in other things. For instance, a slave loves molasses; he steals some. His master, in many cases, goes off to town, and buys a large quantity; he returns, takes his whip, and commands the slave to eat the molasses, until the poor fellow is made sick at the very mention of it. The same mode is sometimes adopted to make the slaves refrain from asking for more food than their regular allowance. A slave runs through his allowance, and applies for more. His master is enraged at him; but, not willing to send him off without food, gives him more than is necessary, and compels him to eat it within a given time. Then, if he complains that he cannot eat it, he is said to be satisfied neither full nor fasting, and is whipped for being hard to please! I have an abundance of such illustrations of the same principle, drawn from my own observation, but think the cases I have cited sufficient. The practice is a very common one.

On the first of January, 1834, I left Mr. Covey, and went to live with Mr. William Freeland, who lived about three miles from St. Michael's. I soon found Mr. Freeland a very different man from Mr. Covey. Though not rich, he was what would be called an educated southern gentleman. Mr. Covey, as I have shown, was a well-trained negro-breaker and slave-driver. The former (slaveholder though he was) seemed to possess some regard for honor, some reverence for justice, and some respect for humanity. The latter seemed totally insensible to all such sentiments. Mr. Freeland had many of the faults peculiar to slaveholders, such as being very passionate and fretful; but I must do him the justice to say, that he was exceedingly free from those degrading vices to which Mr. Covey was constantly addicted. The one was open and frank, and we always knew where to find him. The other was a most artful deceiver, and could be understood only by such as were skilful enough to detect his cunningly-devised frauds. Another advantage I gained in my new master was, he made no pretensions to, or profession of, religion; and this, in my opinion, was truly a great advantage. I assert most unhesitatingly, that the religion of the south is a mere covering for the most horrid crimes—a justifier of the most appalling barbarity—a sanctifier of the most hateful frauds—and a dark shelter under which the darkest, foulest, grossest, and most infernal deeds of slaveholders find the strongest protection. Were I to be again reduced to the chains of slavery, next to that enslavement, I should regard being the slave of a religious master the greatest calamity that could befall me. For of all slaveholders with whom I have ever met, religious slaveholders are the worst. I have ever found them the meanest and basest, the most cruel and cowardly, of all others. It was my unhappy lot not only to belong to a religious slaveholder, but to live in a community of such religionists. Very near Mr. Freeland lived the Rev. Daniel Weeden, and in the same neighborhood lived the Rev. Rigby Hopkins. These were members and ministers in the Reformed Methodist Church. Mr. Weeden owned, among others, a woman slave, whose name I have forgotten. This woman's back, for weeks, was kept literally raw, made so by the lash of this merciless, *religious* wretch. He used to hire hands. His maxim was, Behave well or behave ill, it is the duty of a master occasionally to whip a slave, to remind him of his master's authority. Such was his theory, and such his practice.

Mr. Hopkins was even worse than Mr. Weeden. His chief boast was his ability to manage slaves. The peculiar feature of his government was that of whipping slaves in advance of deserving it. He always managed to have one or more of his slaves to whip every Monday morning. He did this to alarm their fears, and strike terror into those who escaped. His plan was to whip for the smallest offences, to prevent the commission of large ones. Mr. Hopkins could always find some excuse for whipping a slave. It would astonish one, unaccustomed to a slaveholding life, to see with what wonderful ease a slaveholder can find things, of which to make occasion to whip a slave. A mere look, word, or motion—a mistake, accident, or want of power—are all matters for which a slave may be whipped at any time. Does a slave look dissatisfied? It is said, he has the devil in him, and it must be whipped out. Does he speak loudly when spoken to by his master? Then he is getting high-minded, and should be taken down a buttonhole lower. Does he forget to pull off his hat at the approach of a white person? Then he is wanting in reverence, and should be whipped for it. Does he ever venture to vindicate his conduct, when censured for it? Then he is guilty of impudence—one of the greatest crimes of which a slave can be guilty. Does he ever venture to suggest a different mode of doing things from that pointed out by his master? He is indeed presumptuous, and getting above himself; and nothing less than a flogging will do for him. Does he, while ploughing, break a plough— or, while hoeing, break a hoe? It is owing to his carelessness, and for it a slave must always be whipped. Mr. Hopkins could always find something of this sort to justify the use of the lash, and he seldom failed to embrace such opportunities. There was not a man in the whole county, with whom the slaves who had the getting their own home, would not prefer to live, rather than with this Rev. Mr. Hopkins. And yet there was not a mananywhere round, who made higher professions of religion, or was more active in revivals—more attentive to the class, love-feast, prayer and preaching meetings, or more devotional in his family—that prayed earlier, later, louder, and longer—than this same reverend slave-driver, Rigby Hopkins.

But to return to Mr. Freeland, and to my experience while in his employment. He, like Mr. Covey, gave us enough to eat; but, unlike Mr. Covey, he also gave us sufficient time to take our meals. He worked us hard, but always between sunrise and sunset. He required a good deal of work to be done, but gave us good tools with which to work. His farm was large, but he employed hands enough to work it, and with ease, compared with many of his neighbors. My treatment, while in his employment, was heavenly, compared with what I experienced at the hands of Mr. Edward Covey.

Mr. Freeland was himself the owner of but two slaves. Their names were Henry Harris and John Harris. The rest of his hands he hired. These consisted of myself, Sandy Jenkins, and Handy Caldwell. Henry and John were quite intelligent, and in a very little while after I went there, I succeeded in creating in them a strong desire to learn how to read. This desire soon sprang up in the others also. They very soon mustered up some old spelling-books, and nothing would do but that I must keep a Sabbath school[①]. I agreed to do so, and accordingly devoted my Sundays to teaching these my loved fellow-slaves how to read. Neither of them knew his letters when I went there. Some of the slaves of the neighboring farms found what was going on, and also availed themselves of this little opportunity to learn to read. It was understood, among all who came, that there must be as little display about it as possible. It was necessary to keep our religious masters at St. Michael's unacquainted with the fact, that, instead of spending the Sabbath in wrestling, boxing, and drinking whisky, we were trying to learn how to read the will of God; for they had much rather see us engaged in those degrading sports, than to see us behaving like intellectual, moral, and accountable beings. My blood boils as I think of the bloody manner in which Messrs. Wright Fairbanks and Garrison West, both class-leaders, in connection with many others, rushed in upon us with sticks and stones, and broke up our virtuous little Sabbath school, at St. Michael's—all calling themselves Christians! humble followers of the Lord Jesus Christ! But I am again digressing.

I held my Sabbath school at the house of a free colored man, whose name I deem it imprudent to mention; for, should it be known, it might embarrass him greatly, though the crime of holding the school was committed ten years ago. I had at one time over forty scholars, and those of the right sort, ardently desiring to learn. They were of all ages, though mostly men and women. I look back to those Sundays with an amount of pleasure not to be expressed. They were great days to my soul. The work of instructing my dear fellow-slaves was the sweetest engagement with which I was ever blessed. We loved each other, and to leave them at the close of the Sabbath was a severe cross indeed. When I think that these precious souls are to-day shut up in the prison-house of slavery, my feelings overcome me, and I am almost ready to ask, "Does a righteous God govern the universe? and for what does he hold the thunders in his right hand, if not to smite the oppressor, and deliver the spoiled out of the hand of the spoiler?" These dear souls came not to Sabbath school because it was popular to do so, nor did I teach them because it was reputable to be thus engaged. Every moment they spent in that school, they were liable to be taken up, and given thirty-nine lashes. They came because they wished to learn. Their minds had been starved by their cruel masters. They had been shut up in mental darkness. I taught them, because it was the delight of my soul to be doing something that looked like bettering the condition of my race. I kept up my school nearly the whole year I lived with Mr. Freeland; and, besides my Sabbath school, I devoted three evenings in the week, during the winter, to teaching the slaves at home. And I have the happiness to know, that several of those who came to Sabbath school learned how to read; and that one, at least, is now free through my agency.

The year passed off smoothly. It seemed only about half as long as the year which preceded it. I went through it without receiving a single blow. I will give Mr. Freeland the

---

① Sabbath school：主日学校，在星期日开设的为青少年进行宗教教育和识字教育的免费学校，兴起于 18 世纪末，盛行于 19 世纪上半期。

credit of being the best master I ever had, *till I became my own master*. For the ease with which I passed the year, I was, however, somewhat indebted to the society of my fellow-slaves. They were noble souls; they not only possessed loving hearts, but brave ones. We were linked and interlinked with each other. I loved them with a love stronger than anything I have experienced since. It is sometimes said that we slaves do not love and confide in each other. In answer to this assertion, I can say, I never loved any or confided in any people more than my fellow-slaves, and especially those with whom I lived at Mr. Freeland's. I believe we would have died for each other. We never undertook to do anything, of any importance, without a mutual consultation. We never moved separately. We were one; and as much so by our tempers and dispositions, as by the mutual hardships to which we were necessarily subjected by our condition as slaves.

At the close of the year 1834, Mr. Freeland again hired me of my master, for the year 1835. But, by this time, I began to want to live *upon free land* as well as *with Freeland*; and I was no longer content, therefore, to live with him or any other slaveholder. I began, with the commencement of the year, to prepare myself for a final struggle, which should decide my fate one way or the other. My tendency was upward. I was fast approaching manhood, and year after year had passed, and I was still a slave. These thoughts roused me—I must do something. I therefore resolved that 1835 should not pass without witnessing an attempt, on my part, to secure my liberty. But I was not willing to cherish this determination alone. My fellow-slaves were dear to me. I was anxious to have them participate with me in this, my life-giving determination. I therefore, though with great prudence, commenced early to ascertain their views and feelings in regard to their condition, and to imbue their minds with thoughts of freedom. I bent myself to devising ways and means for our escape, and meanwhile strove, on all fitting occasions, to impress them with the gross fraud and inhumanity of slavery. I went first to Henry, next to John, then to the others. I found, in them all, warm hearts and noble spirits. They were ready to hear, and ready to act when a feasible plan should be proposed. This was what I wanted. I talked to them of our want of manhood, if we submitted to our enslavement without at least one noble effort to be free. We met often, and consulted frequently, and told our hopes and fears, recounted the difficulties, real and imagined, which we should be called on to meet. At times we were almost disposed to give up, and try to content ourselves with our wretched lot; at others, we were firm and unbending in our determination to go. Whenever we suggested any plan, there was shrinking—the odds were fearful. Our path was beset with the greatest obstacles; and if we succeeded in gaining the end of it, our right to be free was yet questionable—we were yet liable to be returned to bondage. We could see no spot, this side of the ocean, where we could be free. We knew nothing about Canada. Our knowledge of the north did not extend farther than New York; and to go there, and be forever harassed with the frightful liability of being returned to slavery—with the certainty of being treated tenfold worse than before—the thought was truly a horrible one, and one which it was not easy to overcome. The case sometimes stood thus: At every gate through which we were to pass, we saw a watchman—at every ferry a guard—on every bridge a sentinel—and in every wood a patrol. We were hemmed in upon every side. Here were the difficulties, real or imagined—the good to be sought, and the evil to be shunned. On the one hand, there stood slavery, a stern reality, glaring frightfully upon us—its robes already crimsoned with the blood of millions, and even now feasting itself greedily upon our own flesh. On the other hand, away back in the dim distance, under the flickering light of the north star, behind some craggy hill or snow-covered mountain, stood a doubtful freedom—half frozen—beckoning us to come and share its hospitality. This in itself was sometimes enough to stagger us; but when we permitted ourselves to survey the road, we were frequently appalled. Upon either side we saw grim death, assuming the most horrid shapes. Now it was starvation, causing us to eat our own flesh; now we were contending with the waves, and were drowned; now we were overtaken, and torn to pieces by the fangs of the terrible bloodhound. We were stung by scorpions, chased by wild beasts, bitten by snakes, and finally, after having nearly reached the desired spot—after swimming rivers, encountering wild beasts, sleeping in the woods, suffering hunger and nakedness—we were overtaken by our pursuers, and, in our resistance, we were shot dead upon the spot! I say, this picture sometimes appalled us, and made us

"rather bear those ills we had,
Than fly to others, that we knew not of."

In coming to a fixed determination to run away, we did more than Patrick Henry, when he resolved upon liberty or death. With us it was a doubtful liberty at most, and almost certain death if we failed. For my part, I should prefer death to hopeless bondage.

Sandy, one of our number, gave up the notion, but still encouraged us. Our company then consisted of Henry Harris, John Harris, Henry Bailey, Charles Roberts, and myself. Henry Bailey was my uncle, and belonged to my master. Charles married my aunt: he belonged to my master's father-in-law, Mr. William Hamilton.

The plan we finally concluded upon was, to get a large canoe belonging to Mr. Hamilton, and upon the Saturday night previous to Easter holidays, paddle directly up the Chesapeake Bay. On our arrival at the head of the bay, a distance of seventy or eighty miles from where we lived, it was our purpose to turn our canoe adrift, and follow the guidance of the north star till we got beyond the limits of Maryland. Our reason for taking the water route was, that we were less liable to be suspected as runaways; we hoped to be regarded as fishermen; whereas, if we should take the land route, we should be subjected to interruptions of almost every kind. Anyone having a white face, and being so disposed, could stop us, and subject us to examination.

The week before our intended start, I wrote several protections, one for each of us. As well as I can remember, they were in the following words, to wit: —

"This is to certify that I, the undersigned, have given the bearer, my servant, full liberty to go to Baltimore, and spend the Easter holidays. Written with mine own hand, &c., 1835.

William Hamilton,
"Near St. Michael's, in Talbot county, Maryland."

We were not going to Baltimore; but, in going up the bay, we went toward Baltimore, and these protections were only intended to protect us while on the bay.

As the time drew near for our departure, our anxiety became more and more intense. It was truly a matter of life and death with us. The strength of our determination was about to be fully tested. At this time, I was very active in explaining every difficulty, removing every doubt, dispelling every fear, and inspiring all with the firmness indispensable to success in our undertaking; assuring them that half was gained the instant we made the move; we had talked long enough; we were now ready to move; if not now, we never should be; and if we did not intend to move now, we had as well fold our arms, sit down, and acknowledge ourselves fit only to be slaves. This, none of us were prepared to acknowledge. Every man stood firm; and at our last meeting, we pledged ourselves afresh, in the most solemn manner, that, at the time appointed, we would certainly start in pursuit of freedom. This was in the middle of the week, at the end of which we were to be off. We went, as usual, to our several fields of labor, but with bosoms highly agitated with thoughts of our truly hazardous undertaking. We tried to conceal our feelings as much as possible; and I think we succeeded very well.

After a painful waiting, the Saturday morning, whose night was to witness our departure, came. I hailed it with joy, bring what of sadness it might. Friday night was a sleepless one for me. I probably felt more anxious than the rest, because I was, by common consent, at the head of the whole affair. The responsibility of success or failure lay heavily upon me. The glory of the one, and the confusion of the other, were alike mine. The first two hours of that morning were such as I never experienced before, and hope never to again. Early in the morning, we went, as usual, to the field. We were spreading manure; and all at once, while thus engaged, I was overwhelmed with an indescribable feeling, in the fulness of which I turned to Sandy, who was nearby, and said, "We are betrayed!" "Well," said he, "that thought has this moment struck me." We said no more. I was never more certain of anything.

The horn was blown as usual, and we went up from the field to the house for breakfast. I went for the form, more than for want of anything to eat that morning. Just as I got to the house, in looking out at the lane gate, I saw four white men, with two colored men. The white men were on horseback, and the colored ones were walking behind, as if tied. I watched them a few moments till they got up to our lane gate. Here they halted, and tied the colored men to the gatepost. I was not yet certain as to what the matter was. In a few moments, in rode Mr. Hamilton, with a speed betokening great excitement. He came to the door, and inquired if Master William was in. He was told he was at the barn. Mr. Hamilton, without dismounting, rode up to the barn with extraordinary speed. In a few moments, he and Mr. Freeland returned to the house. By this time, the three constables rode up, and in great haste dismounted, tied their horses, and met Master William and Mr. Hamilton returning from the barn; and after talking awhile, they all walked up to the kitchen door. There was no one in the kitchen but myself and John. Henry and Sandy were up at the barn. Mr. Freeland put his head in at the door, and called me by name, saying, there were some gentlemen at the door who wished to see me. I stepped to the door, and inquired what they wanted. They at once seized me, and, without giving me any satisfaction, tied me—lashing my hands closely together. I insisted upon knowing what the matter was. They at length said, that they had learned I had been in a "scrape," and that I was to be examined before my master; and if their information proved false, I should not be hurt.

In a few moments, they succeeded in tying John. They then turned to Henry, who had by this time returned, and commanded him to cross his hands. "I won't!" said Henry, in a firm tone, indicating his readiness to meet the consequences of his refusal. "Won't you?" said Tom Graham, the constable. "No, I won't!" said Henry, in a still stronger tone. With this, two of the constables pulled out their shining pistols, and swore, by their Creator, that they would make him cross his hands or kill him. Each cocked his pistol, and, with fingers on the trigger, walked up to Henry, saying, at the same time, if he did not cross his hands, they would blow his damned heart out. "Shoot me, shoot me!" said Henry; "you can't kill me but once. Shoot, shoot—and be damned! *I won't be tied*!" This he said in a tone of loud defiance; and at the same time, with a motion as quick as lightning, he with one single stroke dashed the pistols from the hand of each constable. As he did this, all hands fell upon him, and, after beating him some time, they finally overpowered him, and got him tied.

During the scuffle, I managed, I know not how, to get my pass out, and, without being discovered, put it into the fire. We were all now tied; and just as we were to leave for Easton jail, Betsy Freeland, mother of William Freeland, came to the door with her hands full of biscuits, and divided them between Henry and John. She then delivered herself of a speech, to the following effect: —addressing herself to me, she said, "*You devil*! *You yellow devil*! it was you that put it into the heads of Henry and John to run away. But for you, you long-legged mulatto devil! Henry nor John would never have thought of such a thing." I made no reply, and was immediately hurried off towards St. Michael's. Just a moment previous to the scuffle with Henry, Mr. Hamilton suggested the propriety of making a search for the protections which he had understood Frederick had written for himself and the rest. But, just at the moment he was about carrying his proposal into effect, his aid was needed in helping to tie Henry; and the excitement attending the scuffle caused them either to forget, or to deem it unsafe, under the circumstances, to search. So we were not yet convicted of the intention to run away.

When we got about half way to St. Michael's, while the constables having us in charge were looking ahead, Henry inquired of me what he should do with his pass. I told him to eat it with his biscuit, and own nothing; and we passed the word around, "*Own nothing*;" and "*Own nothing*!" said we all. Our confidence in each other was unshaken. We were resolved to succeed or fail together, after the calamity had befallen us as much as before. We were now prepared for anything. We were to be dragged that morning fifteen miles behind horses, and then to be placed in the Easton jail. When we reached St. Michael's, we underwent a sort of examination. We all denied that we ever intended to run away. We did this more to bring out the evidence against us, than from any hope of getting clear of being sold; for, as I have said, we were ready for that. The fact was, we cared but little where we went, so we went together. Our greatest concern was about separation. We dreaded that more than anything this side of death. We found the evidence against us to be the testimony of one person; our master would not tell who it was; but we came to a unanimous decision among ourselves as to who their informant was. We were sent off to the jail at Easton. When we got there, we were delivered up to the sheriff, Mr. Joseph Graham, and by him placed in jail. Henry, John, and myself, were placed in one room together—Charles, and Henry Bailey, in another. Their object in separating us was to hinder concert.

We had been in jail scarcely twenty minutes, when a swarm of slave traders, and agents for slave traders, flocked into jail to look at us, and to ascertain if we were for sale. Such a set of beings I never saw before! I felt myself surrounded by so many fiends from perdition. A band of pirates never looked more like their father, the devil. They laughed and grinned over us, saying, "Ah, my boys! we have got you, haven't we?" And after taunting us in various ways, they one by one went into an examination of us, with intent to ascertain our value. They would impudently ask us if we would not like to have them for our masters. We would make them no answer, and leave them to find out as best they could. Then they would curse and swear at us, telling us that they could take the devil out of us in a very little while, if we were only in their hands.

While in jail, we found ourselves in much more comfortable quarters than we expected when we went there. We did not get much to eat, nor that which was very good; but we had a good clean room, from the windows of which we could see what was going on in the street, which was very much better than though we had been placed in one of the dark, damp cells. Upon the whole, we got along very well, so far as the jail and its keeper were concerned. Immediately after the holidays were over, contrary to all our expectations, Mr. Hamilton and Mr. Freeland came up to Easton, and took Charles, the two Henrys, and John, out of jail, and carried them home, leaving me alone. I regarded this separation as a final one. It caused me more pain than anything else in the whole transaction. I was ready for anything rather than separation. I supposed that they had consulted together, and had decided that, as I was the whole cause of the intention of the others to run away, it was hard to make the innocent suffer with the guilty; and that they had, therefore, concluded to take the others home, and sell me, as a warning to the others that remained. It is due to the noble Henry to say, he seemed almost as reluctant at leaving the prison as at leaving home to come to the prison. But we knew we should, in all probability, be separated, if we were sold; and since he was in their hands, he concluded to go peaceably home.

I was now left to my fate. I was all alone, and within the walls of a stone prison. But a few days before, and I was full of hope. I expected to have been safe in a land of freedom; but now I was covered with gloom, sunk down to the utmost despair. I thought the possibility of freedom was gone. I was kept in this way about one week, at the end of which, Captain Auld, my master, to my surprise and utter astonishment, came up, and took me out, with the intention of sending me, with a gentleman of his acquaintance, into Alabama. But, from some cause or other, he did not send me to Alabama, but concluded to send me back to Baltimore, to live again with his brother Hugh, and to learn a trade.

Questions for Discussion

1. How does Frederick Douglass describe his early life in the *Narrative*?
2. What insights do we gain from the *Narrative* into the life of a typical slave?
3. How does Frederick Douglass understand his identity as a male slave?
4. What is Frederick Douglass's attitude towards Christianity and its members?
5. How to change from a man to a slave and a slave to a man?

3. Incidents in the Life of a Slave Girl

作者简介

　　1813 年,哈丽雅特·雅各布斯(Harriet Jacobs)(1813—1897)出生于北卡罗来纳州的伊登顿镇,与同为奴隶的父亲、母亲和奶奶生活在一起。奶奶曾是北卡罗来纳州种植园里的一名农耕者,在独立战争期间被送往北方,并获得自由,但后来却阴差阳错地再次为奴,被送回南方。在伊登顿镇,她是一名备办宴席者,有些积蓄,镇上的居民对她充满敬意。

　　雅各布斯和哥哥约翰年幼时,父母均去世。1819 年母亲死后,她住在好心的女奴隶主玛格丽特·霍尼布洛家,玛格丽特去世后,她成为其年幼的侄女——詹姆斯·诺康博士的女儿——的财产。13 岁时,雅各布斯爱上一名黑人木匠,但遭到诺康的反对,为了摆脱好色的诺康肆无忌惮的骚扰,雅各布斯同意未婚律师萨缪尔·索耶的求爱,很快怀孕,被赶出家门,被迫和奶奶住在一起。

　　1829 年和 1833 年雅各布斯和索耶生下儿子约瑟夫和女儿路易莎。因局势动荡,南方对奴隶的控制加强,她试图带着儿女逃走。1842 年雅各布斯成功逃往纽约,在利顺德饭店为知名废奴人士纳撒尼尔·威利斯工作,成为一名住家婴儿保姆。

　　即便身在纽约,雅各布斯也没有安全感,感到被人"追捕",特别是 1850 年国会通过《逃奴法案》后更是如此,直到 1852 年纳撒尼尔·威利斯的第二任妻子赎买了她的自由。雅各布斯在为威利斯一家工作时,偷偷撰写自己的回忆录,1861 年,她用笔名琳达·布伦特出版了回忆录《女奴生平》,不过没有引起很大反响。

　　1862 年,雅各布斯搬到华盛顿特区,1863 年与女儿团聚。她们以贵格会教徒的身份,救助那些逃离奴隶制或者战争的黑人。1865 年和 1867 年,雅各布斯返回伊登顿镇,救济穷人,她也到过非洲的萨瓦纳和英格兰等地。随着南方重建的结束,她和女儿返回北方,经营一家为哈佛师生提供膳食和住宿的公司。雅各布斯卒于 1897 年 3 月 7 日,享年 84 岁,墓碑上刻着:为了上帝,忍受苦难,充满热情。

作品简介与赏析

　　雅各布斯的《女奴生平》与道格拉斯的《自述》(1845)一样享有盛誉,曾被误认为是编辑蔡尔德所著,直到 20 世纪 70 年代,才由让·耶林研究确认,发现它并非虚构,确实为雅各布斯本人所写。

　　雅各布斯在《女奴生平》中采取 19 世纪十分流行的言情小说笔调,描述女主人公与社会力量的对抗;这部作品中的女奴渴望过上有德行的生活,却在幼年就意识到女奴生活的艰难和辛酸;她与没有婚姻关系的男人生下两个小孩也属无奈的选择,因而恳请读者,不要把她与自由女性放置在同一道德框架里进行评判。

　　雅各布斯的《女奴生平》对 1831 年特纳领导的黑人起义,以及 1850 年通过的《逃奴法案》都有提及,揭露了北方一些人的虚伪,认为他们和某些南方人一样偏执,带着种族歧视的目光。她渴望能为那些被剥夺公民权的阶层发声,见证人性中黑暗的一面;为受奴役的姐妹呐喊,呼吁北方女性认识奴隶制的罪恶,并予以批判。

　　《女奴生平》不仅揭露了蓄奴制的丑恶,也探讨了黑人女性的身份构建问题。即便黑人女性积极参与废奴运动,但是她们的声音或被忽视、或流于伤感、或被轻描淡写一带而过,成为废奴文本的附属品。约翰尼·斯托弗认为,19世纪黑人女性传记作品利用她们独特的声音,在力图否定非洲女性身份的美国文化中诠释她们的不幸遭遇,利用自传体叙事模式,对企图把她们边缘化的文学、社会和政治体制进行无情的抨击。

雅各布斯在《女奴生平》中采用了多种叙事技巧:言情小说的感伤笔调,黑人方言的大量使用和"狡黠的抗争策略"。通过展示谦卑且贞洁的自我形象,渲染母亲和孩子之间的亲情纽带,她力图唤起白人女性的同情;此外,雅各布斯利用黑人方言,尝试重塑主流社会话语,从而达到误导、戏弄压迫者的目的;另外,雅各布斯通过"狡黠的抵抗"策略,使用"隐蔽、狡诈、犹豫、保密、沉默、喃喃自语、窃窃私语和视觉转换等手段",发表自己的见解,激发读者的情感体验。

和其他男性作者的奴隶叙事相比,《女奴生平》的艺术特点比较鲜明。首先,雅各布斯借助故事叙述者——琳达·布伦特的口吻直接和北方白人女性对话,呼吁她们加入废奴运动中来;其次,雅各布斯以一个基督徒的身份讲述自己的遭遇,因此共同的基督价值观增强了作者和读者之间的联系纽带,从某种程度上来说,《女奴生平》和《汤姆叔叔的小屋》颇为相似;最后,《女奴生平》聚焦主人公布伦特如何依靠黑人家庭、血亲关系和族群力量争取自由解放,这与男性作者的奴隶叙事,比如道格拉斯的《自述》相比差异很大,后者往往渲染男性黑奴孤独而英勇的抗争历程。

总之,自传文体是黑人妇女保持自己个人和文化记忆的方式,同时也对贬低她们的社会政治、经济和文学体制进行挑战。

Preface by the Author

READER,be assured this narrative is no fiction. I am aware that some of my adventures may seem incredible;but they are,nevertheless,strictly true. I have not exaggerated the wrongs inflicted by Slavery;on the contrary,my descriptions fall far short of the facts. I have concealed the names of places,and given persons fictitious names. I had no motive for secrecy on my own account,but I deemed it kind and considerate towards others to pursue this course.

I wish I were more competent to the task I have undertaken. But I trust my readers will excuse deficiencies in consideration of circumstances. I was born and reared in Slavery;and I remained in a Slave State twenty-seven years. Since I have been in the North,it has been necessary for me to work diligently for my own support,and the education of my children. This has not left me much leisure to make up for the loss of early opportunities to improve myself;and it has compelled me to write these pages at irregular intervals,whenever I could snatch an hour from household duties.

When I first arrived in Philadelphia,Bishop Paine1 advised me to publish a sketch of my life,but I told him I was altogether incompetent to complete such an undertaking. Though I have improved my mind somewhat since that time,I still remain of the same opinion;but I trust my motives will excuse what might otherwise seem presumptuous. I have not written my experiences in order to attract attention to myself;on the contrary,it would have been more pleasant to me to have been silent about my own history. Neither do I care to excite sympathy for my own sufferings. But I do earnestly desire to arouse the women of the North to a realizing sense of the condition of two millions of women in the

South, still in bondage, suffering what I suffered, and most of them far worse. I want to add my testimony to that of abler pens to convince the people of the Free States what Slavery really is. Only by experience can anyone realize how deep, and dark, and foul is that pit of abominations. May the blessing of God rest on this imperfect effort in behalf of my persecuted people!

Linda Brent

Introduction by the Editor

THE author of the following autobiography is personally known to me, and her conversation and manners inspire me with confidence. During the last seventeen years, she has lived the greater part of the time with a distinguished family in New York, and has so deported herself as to be highly esteemed by them. This fact is sufficient, without further credentials of her character. I believe those who know her will not be disposed to doubt her veracity, though some incidents in her story are more romantic than fiction.

At her request, I have revised her manuscript; but such changes as I have made have been mainly for purposes of condensation and orderly arrangement. I have not added anything to the incidents, or changed the import of her very pertinent remarks. With trifling exceptions, both the ideas and the language are her own. I pruned excrescences a little, but otherwise I had no reason for changing her lively and dramatic way of telling her own story. The names of both persons and places are known to me; but for good reasons I suppress them.

It will naturally excite surprise that a woman reared in Slavery should be able to write so well. But circumstances will explain this. In the first place, nature endowed her with quick perceptions. Secondly, the mistress, with whom she lived till she was twelve years old, was a kind, considerate friend, who taught her to read and spell. Thirdly, she was placed in favorable circumstances after she came to the North; having frequent intercourse with intelligent persons, who felt a friendly interest in her welfare, and were disposed to give her opportunities for self-improvement.

I am well aware that many will accuse me of indecorum for presenting these pages to the public; for the experiences of this intelligent and much-injured woman belong to a class which some call delicate subjects, and others indelicate. This peculiar phase of Slavery has generally been kept veiled; but the public ought to be made acquainted with its monstrous features, and I willingly take the responsibility of presenting them with the veil withdrawn. I do this for the sake of my sisters in bondage, who are suffering wrongs so foul, that our ears are too delicate to listen to them. I do it with the hope of arousing conscientious and reflecting women in the North to a sense of their duty in the exertion of moral influence on the question of Slavery, on all possible occasions. I do it with the hope that every man who reads this narrative will swear solemnly before God that, so far as he has power to prevent it, no fugitive from Slavery shall ever be sent back to suffer in that loathsome den of corruption and cruelty.

L. Maria Child

Incidents in the Life of a Slave Girl, Seven Years Concealed
Chapter 1
Childhood

I was born a slave; but I never knew it till six years of happy childhood had passed away. My father was a carpenter, and considered so intelligent and skilful in his trade, that, when buildings out of the common line were to be erected, he was sent for from long distances, to be head workman. On condition of paying his mistress two hundred dollars a year, and supporting himself, he was allowed to work at his trade, and manage his own affairs. His strongest wish was to purchase his children; but, though he several times offered his hard earnings for that purpose, he never succeeded. In complexion my parents were a light shade of brownish yellow, and were termed mulattoes. They lived together in a comfortable home; and, though we were all slaves, I was so fondly shielded that I never dreamed I was a piece of merchandise, trusted to them for safe keeping, and liable to be demanded of them at any moment. I had one brother, William, who was two years younger than myself—a bright, affectionate child. I had also a great treasure in my maternal grandmother, who was a remarkable woman in many respects. She was the daughter of a planter in South Carolina, who, at his death, left her mother and his three children free, with money to go to St. Augustine, where they had relatives. It was during the Revolutionary War; and they were captured on their passage, carried back, and sold to different purchasers. Such was the story my grandmother used to tell me; but I do not remember all the particulars. She was a little girl when she was captured and sold to the keeper of a large hotel. I have often heard her tell how hard she fared during childhood. But as she grew older she evinced so much intelligence, and was so faithful, that her master and mistress could not help seeing it was for their interest to take care of such a valuable piece of property. She became an indispensable personage in the household, officiating in all capacities, from cook and wet nurse to seamstress. She was much praised for her cooking; and her nice crackers became so famous in the neighborhood that many people were desirous of obtaining them. In consequence of numerous requests of this kind, she asked permission of her mistress to bake crackers at night, after all the household work was done; and she obtained leave to do it, provided she would clothe herself and her children from the profits. Upon these terms, after working hard all day for her mistress, she began her midnight bakings assisted by her two oldest children. The business proved profitable; and each year she laid by a little, which was saved for a fund to purchase her children. Her master died, and the property was divided among his heirs. The widow had her dower in the hotel, which she continued to keep open. My grandmother remained in her service as a slave; but her children were divided among her master's children. As she had five, Benjamin, the youngest one, was sold, in order that each heir might have an equal portion of dollars and cents. There was so little difference in our ages that he seemed more like my brother than my uncle. He was a bright, handsome lad, nearly white; for he inherited the complexion my grandmother had derived from Anglo-Saxon ancestors. Though only ten years old, seven hundred and twenty dollars were paid for him. His sale was a terrible blow to my grandmother; but she was naturally hopeful, and she went to work with renewed energy, trusting in time to be able to purchase some of her children. She had laid up three hundred dollars, which her mistress one day begged as a loan, promising to pay her soon. The reader probably knows that no promise or writing given to a slave is legally binding; for, according to Southern laws, a slave, *being* property, can *hold* no property. When my grandmother lent her hard earnings to her mistress, she trusted solely to her honor. The honor of a slaveholder to a slave!

To this good grandmother I was indebted for many comforts. My brother Willie and I often received portions of the crackers, cakes, and preserves she made to sell; and after we ceased to be children we were indebted to her for many more important services.

Such were the unusually fortunate circumstances of my early childhood. When I was six years old, my mother died; and then, for the first time, I learned, by the talk around me, that I was a slave. My mother's mistress was the daughter of my grandmother's mistress. She was the foster sister of my mother; they were both nourished at my grandmother's breast. In fact, my mother had been weaned at three months old, that the babe of the mistress might obtain sufficient food. They played together as children; and, when they became women, my mother was a most faithful servant to her whiter foster sister. On her death-bed her mistress promised that her children should never suffer for anything; and during her lifetime she kept her word. They all spoke kindly of my dead mother, who had been a slave merely in name, but in nature was noble and womanly. I grieved for her, and my young mind was troubled with the thought of who would now take care of me and my little brother. I was told that my home was now to be with her mistress; and I found it a happy one. No toilsome or disagreeable duties were imposed upon me. My mistress was so kind to me that I was always glad to do her bidding, and proud to labor for her as much as my young years would permit. I would sit by her side for hours, sewing diligently, with a heart as free from care as that of any free-born white child. When she thought I was tired, she would send me out to run and jump; and away I bounded, to gather berries or flowers to decorate her room. Those were happy days—too happy to last. The slave child had no thought for the morrow; but there came that blight, which too surely waits on every human being born to be a chattel.

When I was nearly twelve years old, my kind mistress sickened and died. As I saw the cheek grow paler, and the eye more glassy, how earnestly I prayed in my heart that she might live! I loved her; for she had been almost like a mother to me. My prayers were not answered. She died, and they buried her in the little churchyard, where, day after day, my tears fell upon her grave.

I was sent to spend a week with my grandmother. I was now old enough to begin to think of the future; and again and again I asked myself what they would do with me. I felt sure I should never find another mistress so kind as the one who was gone. She had promised my dying mother that her children should never suffer for anything; and when I, remembered that, and recalled her many proofs of attachment to me, I could not help having some hopes that she had left me free. My friends were almost certain it would be so. They thought she would be sure to do it, on account of my mother's love and faithful service. But, alas! we all know that the memory of a faithful slave does not avail much to save her children from the auction block.

After a brief period of suspense, the will of my mistress was read, and we learned that she had bequeathed me to her sister's daughter, a child of five years old. So vanished our hopes. My mistress had taught me the precepts of God's Word: "Thou shalt love thy neighbor as thyself."[①]"Whatsoever ye would that men should do unto you, do ye even so unto them." But I was her slave, and I suppose she did not recognize me as her neighbor. I would give much to blot out from my memory that one great wrong. As a child, I loved my mistress; and, looking back on the happy days I spent with her, I try to think with less bitterness of this act of injustice. While I was with her, she taught me to read and spell; and for this privilege, which so rarely falls to the lot of a slave, I bless her memory.

She possessed but few slaves; and at her death those were all distributed among her relatives. Five of them were my grandmother's children, and had shared the same milk that nourished her mother's children. Notwithstanding my grandmother's long and faithful service to her owners, not one of her children escaped the auction block. These God-breathing machines are no more, in the sight of their masters, than the cotton they plant, or the horses they tend.

Chapter 2
The New Master and Mistress

Dr. Flint, a physician in the neighborhood, had married the sister of my mistress, and I was now the property of their little daughter. It was not without murmuring that I prepared for my new home; and what added to my unhappiness, was the fact that my brother William was purchased by the same family. My father, by his nature, as well as by the habit of transacting business as a skilful mechanic, had more of the feelings of a freeman than is common among slaves. My brother was a spirited boy; and being brought up under such influences, he early detested the name of master and mistress. One day, when his father and his mistress both happened to call him at the same time, he hesitated between the two; being perplexed to know which had the strongest claim upon his obedience. He finally concluded to go to his mistress. When my father reproved him for it, he said, "You both called me, and I didn't know which I ought to go to first."

"You are *my* child," replied our father, "and when I call you, you should come immediately, if you have to pass through fire and water."

Poor Willie! He was now to learn his first lesson of obedience to a master. Grandmother tried to cheer us with hopeful words, and they found an echo in the credulous hearts of youth.

When we entered our new home we encountered cold looks, cold words, and cold treatment. We were glad when the night came. On my narrow bed I moaned and wept, I

---

① Thou shalt love thy neighbor as thyself: 爱人如己。

felt so desolate and alone.

I had been there nearly a year, when a dear little friend of mine was buried. I heard her mother sob, as the clods fell on the coffin of her only child, and I turned away from the grave, feeling thankful that I still had something left to love. I met my grandmother, who said, "Come with me, Linda;" and from her tone I knew that something sad had happened. She led me apart from the people, and then said, "My child, your father is dead." Dead! How could I believe it? He had died so suddenly I had not even heard that he was sick. I went home with my grandmother. My heart rebelled against God, who had taken from me mother, father, mistress, and friend. The good grandmother tried to comfort me. "Who knows the ways of God?" said she. "Perhaps they have been kindly taken from the evil days to come." Years afterwards I often thought of this. She promised to be a mother to her grandchildren, so far as she might be permitted to do so; and strengthened by her love, I returned to my master's. I thought I should be allowed to go to my father's house the next morning; but I was ordered to go for flowers, that my mistress's house might be decorated for an evening party. I spent the day gathering flowers and weaving them into festoons, while the dead body of my father was lying within a mile of me. What cared my owners for that? he was merely a piece of property. Moreover, they thought he had spoiled his children, by teaching them to feel that they were human beings. This was blasphemous doctrine for a slave to teach; presumptuous in him, and dangerous to the masters.

The next day I followed his remains to a humble grave beside that of my dear mother. There were those who knew my father's worth, and respected his memory.

My home now seemed more dreary than ever. The laugh of the little slave-children sounded harsh and cruel. It was selfish to feel so about the joy of others. My brother moved about with a very grave face. I tried to comfort him, by saying, "Take courage, Willie; brighter days will come by and by."

"You don't know anything about it, Linda," he replied. "We shall have to stay here all our days; we shall never be free."

I argued that we were growing older and stronger, and that perhaps we might, before long, be allowed to hire our own time, and then we could earn money to buy our freedom. William declared this was much easier to say than to do; moreover, he did not intend to *buy* his freedom. We held daily controversies upon this subject.

Little attention was paid to the slaves' meals in Dr. Flint's house. If they could catch a bit of food while it was going, well and good. I gave myself no trouble on that score, for on my various errands I passed my grandmother's house, where there was always something to spare for me. I was frequently threatened with punishment if I stopped there; and my grandmother, to avoid detaining me, often stood at the gate with something for my breakfast or dinner. I was indebted to *her* for all my comforts, spiritual or temporal. It was *her* labor that supplied my scanty wardrobe. I have a vivid recollection of the linsey-woolsey dress given me every winter by Mrs. Flint. How I hated it! It was one of the badges of slavery.

While my grandmother was thus helping to support me from her hard earnings, the three hundred dollars she had lent her mistress were never repaid. When her mistress died, her son-in-law, Dr. Flint, was appointed executor. When grandmother applied to him for payment, he said the estate was insolvent, and the law prohibited payment. It did not, however, prohibit him from retaining the silver candelabra, which had been purchased with that money. I presume they will be handed down in the family, from generation to generation.

My grandmother's mistress had always promised her that, at her death, she should be free; and it was said that in her will she made good the promise. But when the estate was settled, Dr. Flint told the faithful old servant that, under existing circumstances, it was necessary she should be sold.

On the appointed day, the customary advertisement was posted up, proclaiming that there would be a "public sale of negroes, horses, &c." Dr. Flint called to tell my grandmother that he was unwilling to wound her feelings by putting her up at auction, and that he would prefer to dispose of her at private sale. My grandmother saw through his hypocrisy; she understood very well that he was ashamed of the job. She was a very spirited woman, and if he was base enough to sell her, when her mistress intended she should be free, she was determined the public should know it. She had for a long time supplied many families with crackers and preserves; consequently, "Aunt Marthy," as she was called, was generally known, and everybody who knew her respected her intelligence and good character. Her long and faithful service in the family was also well known, and the intention of her mistress to leave her free. When the day of sale came, she took her place among the chattels, and at the first call she sprang upon the auction-block. Many voices called out, "Shame! Shame! Who is going to sell *you*, Aunt Marthy? Don't stand there! That is no place for *you*." Without saying a word, she quietly awaited her fate. No one bid for her. At last, a feeble voice said, "Fifty dollars." It came from a maiden lady, seventy years old, the sister of my grandmother's deceased mistress. She had lived forty years under the same roof with my grandmother; she knew how faithfully she had served her owners, and how cruelly she had been defrauded of her rights; and she resolved to protect her. The auctioneer waited for a higher bid; but her wishes were respected; no one bid above her. She could neither read nor write; and when the bill of sale was made out, she signed it with a cross. But of what consequence was that, when she had a big heart overflowing with human kindness? She gave the old servant her freedom.

At that time, my grandmother was just fifty years old. Laborious years had passed since then; and now my brother and I were slaves to the man who had defrauded her of her money, and tried to defraud her of her freedom. One of my mother's sisters, called Aunt Nancy, was also a slave in his family. She was a kind, good aunt to me; and supplied the place of both housekeeper and waiting maid to her mistress. She was, in fact, at the beginning and end of everything.

Mrs. Flint, like many southern women, was totally deficient in energy. She had not strength to superintend her household affairs; but her nerves were so strong that she could sit in her easy chair and see a woman whipped till the blood trickled from every stroke of the lash. She was a member of the church; but partaking of the Lord's supper did not seem to put her in a Christian frame of mind. If dinner was not served at the exact time on that particular Sunday, she would station herself in the kitchen, and wait till it was dished, and then spit in all the kettles and pans that had been used for cooking. She did this to prevent the cook and her children from eking out their meagre fare with the remains of the gravy and other scrapings. The slaves could get nothing to eat except what she chose to give them. Provisions were weighed out by the pound and ounce, three times a day. I can assure you she gave them no chance to eat wheat bread from her flour barrel. She knew how many biscuits a quart of flour would make, and exactly what size they ought to be.

Dr. Flint was an epicure. The cook never sent a dinner to his table without fear and trembling; for if there happened to be a dish not to his liking, he would either order her to be whipped, or compel her to eat every mouthful of it in his presence. The poor, hungry creature might not have objected to eating it; but she did object to having her master cram it down her throat till she choked.

They had a pet dog that was a nuisance in the house. The cook was ordered to make some Indian mush for him. He refused to eat, and when his head was held over it, the froth flowed from his mouth into the basin. He died a few minutes after. When Dr. Flint came in, he said the mush had not been well cooked, and that was the reason the animal would not eat it. He sent for the cook, and compelled her to eat it. He thought that the woman's stomach was stronger than the dog's; but her sufferings afterwards proved that he was mistaken. This poor woman endured many cruelties from her master and mistress; sometimes she was locked up, away from her nursing baby, for a whole day and night.

When I had been in the family a few weeks, one of the plantation slaves was brought to town, by order of his master. It was near night when he arrived, and Dr. Flint ordered him to be taken to the work house, and tied up to the joist, so that his feet would just escape the ground. In that situation he was to wait till the doctor had taken his tea. I shall never forget that night. Never before, in my life, had I heard hundreds of blows fall, in succession, on a human being. His piteous groans, and his "O, pray don't, massa," rang in my ear for months afterwards. There were many conjectures as to the cause of this terrible punishment. Some said master accused him of stealing corn; others said the slave had quarrelled with his wife, in presence of the overseer, and had accused his master of being the father of her child. They were both black, and the child was very fair.

I went into the work house next morning, and saw the cowhide still wet with blood, and the boards all covered with gore. The poor man lived, and continued to quarrel with his wife. A few months afterwards Dr. Flint handed them both over to a slave-trader. The guilty man put their value into his pocket, and had the satisfaction of knowing that they were out of sight and hearing. When the mother was delivered into the trader's hands, she said, "You *promised* to treat me well." To which he replied, "You have let your tongue run too far; damn you!" She had forgotten that it was a crime for a slave to tell who was the father of her child.

From others than the master persecution also comes in such cases. I once saw a young slave girl dying soon after the birth of a child nearly white. In her agony she cried out, "O Lord, come and take me!" Her mistress stood by, and mocked at her like an incarnate fiend. "You suffer, do you?" she exclaimed. "I am glad of it. You deserve it all, and more too."

The girl's mother said, "The baby is dead, thank God; and I hope my poor child will soon be in heaven, too."

"Heaven!" retorted the mistress. "There is no such place for the like of her and her bastard."

The poor mother turned away, sobbing. Her dying daughter called her, feebly, and as she bent over her, I heard her say, "Don't grieve so, mother; God knows all about it; and he will have mercy upon me."

Her sufferings, afterwards, became so intense, that her mistress felt unable to stay; but when she left the room, the scornful smile was still on her lips. Seven children called her mother. The poor black woman had but the one child, whose eyes she saw closing in death, while she thanked God for taking her away from the greater bitterness of life.

Chapter 3
The Slaves' New Year's Day

Dr. Flint owned a fine residence in town, several farms, and about fifty slaves, besides hiring a number by the year.

Hiring-day at the south takes place on the 1st of January. On the 2d, the slaves are expected to go to their new masters. On a farm, they work until the corn and cotton are laid. They then have two holidays. Some masters give them a good dinner under the trees. This over, they work until Christmas Eve. If no heavy charges are meantime brought against them, they are given four or five holidays, whichever the master or overseer may think proper. Then comes New Year's Eve; and they gather together their little alls, or more properly speaking, their little nothings, and wait anxiously for the dawning of day. At the appointed hour the grounds are thronged with men, women, and children, waiting, like criminals, to hear their doom pronounced. The slave is sure to know who is the most humane, or cruel master, within forty miles of him.

It is easy to find out, on that day, who clothes and feeds his slaves well; for he is surrounded by a crowd, begging, "Please, massa, hire me this year. I will work *very* hard, massa."

If a slave is unwilling to go with his new master, he is whipped, or locked up in jail, until he consents to go, and promises not to run away during the year. Should he chance to change his mind, thinking it justifiable to violate an extorted promise, woe unto him if he is caught! The whip is used till the blood flows at his feet; and his stiffened limbs are put in chains, to be dragged in the field for days and days!

If he lives until the next year, perhaps the same man will hire him again, without even giving him an opportunity of going to the hiring-ground. After those for hire are disposed of, those for sale are called up.

O, you happy free women, contrast *your* New Year's Day with that of the poor bond-woman! With you it is a pleasant season, and the light of the day is blessed. Friendly wishes meet you everywhere, and gifts are showered upon you. Even hearts that have been estranged from you soften at this season, and lips that have been silent echo back, "I wish you a happy New Year." Children bring their little offerings, and raise their rosy lips for a caress. They are your own, and no hand but that of death can take them from you.

But to the slave mother New Year's Day comes laden with peculiar sorrows. She sits on her cold cabin floor, watching the children who may all be torn from her the next morning; and often does she wish that she and they might die before the day dawns. She may be an ignorant creature, degraded by the system that has brutalized her from childhood; but she has a mother's instincts, and is capable of feeling a mother's agonies.

On one of these sale days, I saw a mother lead seven children to the auction-block. She knew that *some* of them would be taken from her; but they took *all*. The children were sold to a slave-trader, and their mother was bought by a man in her own town. Before night her children were all far away. She begged the trader to tell her where he intended to take them; this he refused to do. How *could* he, when he knew he would sell them, one by one, wherever he could command the highest price? I met that mother in the street, and her wild, haggard face lives to-day in my mind. She wrung her hands in anguish, and exclaimed, "Gone! All gone! Why *don't* God kill me?" I had no words wherewith to comfort her. Instances of this kind are of daily, yea, of hourly occurrence.

Slaveholders have a method, peculiar to their institution, of getting rid of *old* slaves, whose lives have been worn out in their service. I knew an old woman, who for seventy years faithfully served her master. She had become almost helpless, from hard labor and disease. Her owners moved to Alabama, and the old black woman was left to be sold to anybody who would give twenty dollars for her.

Chapter 5
The Trials of Girlhood

During the first years of my service in Dr. Flint's family, I was accustomed to share some indulgences with the children of my mistress. Though this seemed to me no more than right, I was grateful for it, and tried to merit the kindness by the faithful discharge of my duties. But I now entered on my fifteenth year—a sad epoch in the life of a slave girl. My master began to whisper foul words in my ear. Young as I was, I could not remain ignorant of their import. I tried to treat them with indifference or contempt. The master's age, my extreme youth, and the fear that his conduct would be reported to my grandmother, made him bear this treatment for many months. He was a crafty man, and resorted to many means to accomplish his purposes. Sometimes he had stormy, terrific ways that made his victims tremble; sometimes he assumed a gentleness that he thought must surely subdue. Of the two, I preferred his stormy moods, although they left me trembling. He tried his utmost to corrupt the pure principles my grandmother had instilled. He peopled my young mind with unclean images, such as only a vile monster could think of. I turned from him with disgust and hatred. But he was my master. I was compelled to live under the same roof with him—where I saw a man forty years my senior daily violating the most sacred commandments of nature. He told me I was his property; that I must be subject to his will in all things. My soul revolted against the mean tyranny. But where could I turn for protection? No matter whether the slave girl be as black as ebony or as fair as her mistress. In either case, there is no shadow of law to protect her from insult, from violence, or even from death; all these are inflicted by fiends who bear the shape of men. The mistress, who ought to protect the helpless victim, has no other feelings towards her but those of jealousy and rage. The degradation, the wrongs, the vices that grow out of slavery, are more than I can describe. They are greater than you would willingly believe. Surely, if you credited one half the truths that are told you concerning the helpless millions suffering in this cruel bondage, you at the north would not help to tighten the yoke. You surely would refuse to do for the master; on your own soil, the mean and cruel work which trained bloodhounds and the lowest class of whites to do for him at the south.

Everywhere the years bring to all enough of sin and sorrow; but in slavery the very dawn of life is darkened by these shadows. Even the little child, who is accustomed to wait on her mistress and her children, will learn, before she is twelve years old, why it is that her mistress hates such and such a one among the slaves. Perhaps the child's own mother is among those hated ones. She listens to violent outbreaks of jealous passion, and cannot help understanding what is the cause. She will become prematurely knowing in evil things. Soon she will learn to tremble when she hears her master's footfall. She will be compelled to realize that she is no longer a child. If God has bestowed beauty upon her, it will prove her greatest curse. That which commands admiration in the white woman only hastens the degradation of the female slave. I know that some are too much brutalized by slavery to feel the humiliation of their position; but many slaves feel it most acutely, and shrink from the memory of it. I cannot tell how much I suffered in the presence of these wrongs, nor how I am still pained by the retrospect. My master met me at every turn, reminding me that I belonged to him, and swearing by heaven and earth that he would compel me to submit to him. If I went out for a breath of fresh air, after a day of unwearied toil, his footsteps dogged me. If I knelt by my mother's grave, his dark shadow fell on me even there. The light heart which nature had given me became heavy with sad forebodings. The other slaves in my master's house noticed the change. Many of them pitied me; but none dared to ask the cause. They had no need to inquire. They knew too well the guilty practices under that roof; and they were aware that to speak of them was an offence that never went unpunished.

I longed for someone to confide in. I would have given the world to have laid my head on my grandmother's faithful bosom, and told her all my troubles. But Dr. Flint swore he would kill me, if I was not as silent as the grave. Then, although my grandmother was all in all to me, I feared her as well as loved her. I had been accustomed to look up to her with a respect bordering upon awe. I was very young, and felt shamefaced about telling her such impure things, especially as I knew her to be very strict on such subjects. Moreover, she was a woman of a high spirit. She was usually very quiet in her demeanor; but if her indignation was once roused, it was not very easily quelled. I had been told that she once chased a white gentleman with a loaded pistol, because he insulted one of her daughters. I dreaded the consequences of a violent outbreak; and both pride and fear kept me silent. But though I did not confide in my grandmother, and even evaded her vigilant watchfulness and inquiry, her presence in the neighborhood was some protection to me. Though she had been a slave, Dr. Flint was afraid of her. He dreaded her scorching rebukes. Moreover, she was known and patronized by many people; and he did not wish to have his villany made public. It was lucky for me that I did not live on a distant plantation, but in a town not so large that the inhabitants were ignorant of each other's affairs. Bad as are the laws and customs in a slaveholding community, the doctor, as a professional man, deemed it prudent to keep up some outward show of decency.

O, what days and nights of fear and sorrow that man caused me! Reader, it is not to awaken sympathy for myself that I am telling you truthfully what I suffered in slavery. I do it to kindle a flame of compassion in your hearts for my sisters who are still in bondage, suffering as I once suffered.

I once saw two beautiful children playing together. One was a fair white child; the other was her slave, and also her sister. When I saw them embracing each other, and heard their joyous laughter, I turned sadly away from the lovely sight. I foresaw the inevitable blight that would fall on the little slave's heart. I knew how soon her laughter would be changed to sighs. The fair child grew up to be a still fairer woman. From childhood to womanhood her pathway was blooming with flowers, and overarched by a sunny sky. Scarcely one day of her life had been clouded when the sun rose on her happy bridal morning.

How had those years dealt with her slave sister, the little playmate of her childhood? She, also, was very beautiful; but the flowers and sunshine of love were not for her. She drank the cup of sin, and shame, and misery, whereof her persecuted race are compelled to drink.

In view of these things, why are ye silent, ye free men and women of the north? Why do your tongues falter in maintenance of the right? Would that I had more ability! But my heart is so full, and my pen is so weak! There are noble men and women who plead for us, striving to help those who cannot help themselves. God bless them! God give them strength and courage to go on! God bless those, everywhere, who are laboring to advance the cause of humanity!

Chapter 6
The Jealous Mistress

I would ten thousand times rather that my children should be the half-starved paupers of Ireland than to be the most pampered among the slaves of America. I would rather drudge out my life on a cotton plantation, till the grave opened to give me rest, than to live with an unprincipled master and a jealous mistress. The felon's home in a penitentiary is preferable. He may repent, and turn from the error of his ways, and so find peace; but it is not so with a favorite slave. She is not allowed to have any pride of character. It is deemed a crime in her to wish to be virtuous.

Mrs. Flint possessed the key to her husband's character before I was born. She might have used this knowledge to counsel and to screen the young and the innocent among her slaves; but for them she had no sympathy. They were the objects of her constant suspicion and malevolence. She watched her husband with unceasing vigilance; but he was well practised in means to evade it. What he could not find opportunity to say in words he manifested in signs. He invented more than were ever thought of in a deaf and dumb asylum. I let them pass, as if I did not understand what he meant; and many were the curses and threats bestowed on me for my stupidity. One day he caught me teaching myself to write. He frowned, as if he was not well pleased; but I suppose he came to the conclusion that such an accomplishment might help to advance his favorite scheme. Before long, notes were often slipped into my hand. I would return them, saying, "I can't read them, sir." "Can't you?" he replied; "then I must read them to you." He always finished the reading by asking, "Do you understand?" Sometimes he would complain of the heat of the tea room, and order his supper to be placed on a small table in the piazza. He would seat himself there with a well-satisfied smile, and tell me to stand by and brush away the flies. He would eat very slowly, pausing between the mouthfuls. These intervals were employed in describing the happiness I was so foolishly throwing away, and in threatening me with the penalty that finally awaited my stubborn disobedience. He boasted much of the forbearance he had exercised towards me, and reminded me that there was a limit to his patience. When I succeeded in avoiding opportunities for him to talk to me at home, I was ordered to come to his office, to do some errand. When there, I was obliged to stand and listen to such language as he saw fit to address to me. Sometimes I so openly expressed my contempt for him that he would become violently enraged, and I wondered why he did not strike me. Circumstanced as he was, he probably thought it was better policy to be forbearing. But the state of things grew worse and worse daily. In desperation I told him that I must and would apply to my grandmother for protection. He threatened me with death, and worse than death, if I made any complaint to her. Strange to say, I did not despair. I was naturally of a buoyant disposition, and always I had a hope of somehow getting out of his clutches. Like many a poor, simple slave before me, I trusted that some threads of joy would yet be woven into my dark destiny.

I had entered my sixteenth year, and every day it became more apparent that my presence was intolerable to Mrs. Flint. Angry words frequently passed between her and her husband. He had never punished me himself, and he would not allow anybody else to punish me. In that respect, she was never satisfied; but, in her angry moods, no terms were too vile for her to bestow upon me. Yet I, whom she detested so bitterly, had far more pity for her than he had, whose duty it was to make her life happy. I never wronged her, or wished to wrong her; and one word of kindness from her would have brought me to her feet.

After repeated quarrels between the doctor and his wife, he announced his intention to take his youngest daughter, then four years old, to sleep in his apartment. It was necessary that a servant should sleep in the same room, to be on hand if the child stirred. I was selected for that office, and informed for what purpose that arrangement had been made. By managing to keep within sight of people, as much as possible, during the daytime, I had hitherto succeeded in eluding my master, though a razor was often held to my throat to force me to change this line of policy. At night I slept by the side of my great aunt, where I felt safe. He was too prudent to come into her room. She was an old woman, and had been in the family many years. Moreover, as a married man, and a professional man, he deemed it necessary to save appearances in some degree. But he resolved to remove the obstacle in the way of his scheme; and he thought he had planned it so that he should evade suspicion. He was well aware how much I prized my refuge by the side of my old aunt, and he determined to dispossess me of it. The first night the doctor had the little child in his room alone. The next morning, I was ordered to take my station as nurse the following night. A kind Providence interposed in my favor. During the day, Mrs. Flint heard of this new arrangement, and a storm followed. I rejoiced to hear it rage.

After a while my mistress sent for me to come to her room. Her first question was, "Did you know you were to sleep in the doctor's room?"

"Yes, ma'am."

"Who told you?"

"My master."

"Will you answer truly all the questions I ask?"

"Yes, ma'am."

"Tell me, then, as you hope to be forgiven, are you innocent of what I have accused you?"

"I am."

She handed me a Bible, and said, "Lay your hand on your heart, kiss this holy book, and swear before God that you tell me the truth."

I took the oath she required, and I did it with a clear conscience.

"You have taken God's holy word to testify your innocence," said she. "If you have deceived me, beware! Now take this stool, sit down, look me directly in the face, and tell me all that has passed between your master and you."

I did as she ordered. As I went on with my account her color changed frequently, she wept, and sometimes groaned. She spoke in tones so sad, that I was touched by her grief. The tears came to my eyes; but I was soon convinced that her emotions arose from anger and wounded pride. She felt that her marriage vows were desecrated, her dignity insulted; but she had no compassion for the poor victim of her husband's perfidy. She pitied herself as a martyr; but she was incapable of feeling for the condition of shame and misery in which her unfortunate, helpless slave was placed.

Yet perhaps she had some touch of feeling for me; for when the conference was ended, she spoke kindly, and promised to protect me. I should have been much comforted by this assurance if I could have had confidence in it; but my experiences in slavery had filled me with distrust. She was not a very refined woman, and had not much control over her passions. I was an object of her jealousy, and, consequently, of her hatred; and I knew I could not expect kindness or confidence from her under the circumstances in which I was placed. I could not blame her. Slaveholders' wives feel as other women would under similar circumstances. The fire of her temper kindled from small sparks, and now the flame became so intense that the doctor was obliged to give up his intended arrangement.

I knew I had ignited the torch, and I expected to suffer for it afterwards; but I felt too thankful to my mistress for the timely aid she rendered me to care much about that. She now took me to sleep in a room adjoining her own. There I was an object of her especial care, though not of her especial comfort, for she spent many a sleepless night to watch over me. Sometimes I woke up, and found her bending over me. At other times she whispered in my ear, as though it was her husband who was speaking to me, and listened to hear what I would answer. If she startled me, on such occasions, she would glide stealthily away; and the next morning she would tell me I had been talking in my sleep, and ask who I was talking to. At last, I began to be fearful for my life. It had been often threatened; and you can imagine, better than I can describe, what an unpleasant sensation it must produce to wake up in the dead of night and find a jealous woman bending over you. Terrible as this experience was, I had fears that it would give place to one more terrible.

My mistress grew weary of her vigils; they did not prove satisfactory. She changed her tactics. She now tried the trick of accusing my master of crime, in my presence, and gave my name as the author of the accusation. To my utter astonishment, he replied, "I don't believe it; but if she did acknowledge it, you tortured her into exposing me." Tortured into exposing him! Truly, Satan had no difficulty in distinguishing the color of his soul! I understood his object in making this false representation. It was to show me that I gained nothing by seeking the protection of my mistress; that the power was still all in his own hands. I pitied Mrs. Flint. She was a second wife, many years the junior of her husband; and the hoary-headed miscreant was enough to try the patience of a wiser and better woman. She was completely foiled, and knew not how to proceed. She would gladly have had me flogged for my supposed false oath; but, as I have already stated, the doctor never allowed anyone to whip me. The old sinner was politic. The application of the lash might have led to remarks that would have exposed him in the eyes of his children and grandchildren. How often did I rejoice that I lived in a town where all the inhabitants knew each other! If I had been on a remote plantation, or lost among the multitude of a crowded city, I should not be a living woman at this day.

The secrets of slavery are concealed like those of the Inquisition. My master was, to my knowledge, the father of eleven slaves. But did the mothers dare to tell who was the father of their children? Did the other slaves dare to allude to it, except in whispers among themselves? No, indeed! They knew too well the terrible consequences.

My grandmother could not avoid seeing things which excited her suspicions. She was uneasy about me, and tried various ways to buy me; but the never-changing answer was always repeated: "Linda does not belong to *me*. She is my daughter's property, and I have no legal right to sell her." The conscientious man! He was too scrupulous to *sell* me; but he had no scruples whatever about committing a much greater wrong against the helpless young girl placed under his guardianship, as his daughter's property. Sometimes my persecutor would ask me whether I would like to be sold. I told him I would rather be sold to anybody than to lead such a life as I did. On such occasions he would assume the air of a very injured individual, and reproach me for my ingratitude. "Did I not take you into the house, and make you the companion of my own children?" he would say. "Have I ever treated you like a negro? I have never allowed you to be punished, not even to please your mistress. And this is the recompense I get, you ungrateful girl!" I answered that he had reasons of his own for screening me from punishment, and that the course he pursued made my mistress hate me and persecute me. If I wept, he would say, "Poor child! Don't cry! don't cry! I will make peace for you with your mistress. Only let me arrange matters in my own way. Poor, foolish girl! you don't know what is for your own good. I would cherish you. I would make a lady of you. Now go, and think of all I have promised you."

I did think of it.

Reader, I draw no imaginary pictures of southern homes. I am telling you the plain truth. Yet when victims make their escape from this wild beast of Slavery, northerners consent to act the part of bloodhounds, and hunt the poor fugitive back into his den, "full of dead men's bones, and all uncleanness." Nay, more, they are not only willing, but proud, to give their daughters in marriage to slaveholders. The poor girls have romantic notions of a sunny clime, and of the flowering vines that all the year round shade a happy home. To what disappointments are they destined! The young wife soon learns that the husband in whose hands she has placed her happiness pays no regard to his marriage vows. Children of every shade of complexion play with her own fair babies, and too well she knows that they are born unto him of his own household. Jealousy and hatred enter the flowery home, and it is ravaged of its loveliness.

Southern women often marry a man knowing that he is the father of many little slaves. They do not trouble themselves about it. They regard such children as property, as marketable as the pigs on the plantation; and it is seldom that they do not make them aware of this by passing them into the slave-trader's hands as soon as possible, and thus getting them out of their sight. I am glad to say there are some honorable exceptions.

I have myself known two southern wives who exhorted their husbands to free those slaves towards whom they stood in a "parental relation"; and their request was granted. These husbands blushed before the superior nobleness of their wives' natures. Though they had only counselled them to do that which it was their duty to do, it commanded their respect, and rendered their conduct more exemplary. Concealment was at an end, and confidence took the place of distrust.

Though this bad institution deadens the moral sense, even in white women, to a fearful extent, it is not altogether extinct. I have heard southern ladies say of Mr. Such a one, "He not only thinks it no disgrace to be the father of those little niggers, but he is not ashamed to call himself their master. I declare, such things ought not to be tolerated in any decent society!"

Chapter 41

Free at Last

Mrs. Bruce, and every member of her family, were exceedingly kind to me. I was thankful for the blessings of my lot, yet I could not always wear a cheerful countenance. I was doing harm to no one; on the contrary, I was doing all the good I could in my small way; yet I could never go out to breathe God's free air without trepidation at my heart. This seemed hard; and I could not think it was a right state of things in any civilized country.

From time to time I received news from my good old grandmother. She could not write; but she employed others to write for her. The following is an extract from one of her last letters: —

"Dear Daughter: I cannot hope to see you again on earth; but I pray to God to unite us above, where pain will no more rack this feeble body of mine; where sorrow and parting from my children will be no more. God has promised these things if we are faithful unto the end. My age and feeble health deprive me of going to church now; but God is with me here at home. Thank your brother for his kindness. Give much love to him, and tell him to remember the Creator in the days of his youth, and strive to meet me in the Father's kingdom. Love to Ellen and Benjamin. Don't neglect him. Tell him for me, to be a good boy. Strive, my child, to train them for God's children. May he protect and provide for you, is the prayer of your loving old mother."

These letters both cheered and saddened me. I was always glad to have tidings from the kind, faithful old friend of my unhappy youth; but her messages of love made my heart yearn to see her before she died, and I mourned over the fact that it was impossible. Some months after I returned from my flight to New England, I received a letter from her, in which she wrote, "Dr. Flint is dead. He has left a distressed family. Poor old man! I hope he made his peace with God."

I remembered how he had defrauded my grandmother of the hard earnings she had loaned; how he had tried to cheat her out of the freedom her mistress had promised her, and how he had persecuted her children; and I thought to myself that she was a better Christian than I was, if she could entirely forgive him. I cannot say, with truth, that the news of my old master's death softened my feelings towards him. There are wrongs which even the grave does not bury. The man was odious to me while he lived, and his memory is odious now.

His departure from this world did not diminish my danger. He had threatened my grandmother that his heirs should hold me in slavery after he was gone; that I never should be free so long as a child of his survived. As for Mrs. Flint, I had seen her in deeper afflictions than I supposed the loss of her husband would be, for she had buried several children; yet I never saw any signs of softening in her heart. The doctor had died in embarrassed circumstances, and had little to will to his heirs, except such property as he was unable to grasp. I was well aware what I had to expect from the family of Flints; and my fears were confirmed by a letter from the south, warning me to be on my guard, because Mrs. Flint openly declared that her daughter could not afford to lose so valuable a slave as I was.

I kept close watch of the newspapers for arrivals; but one Saturday night, being much occupied, I forgot to examine the Evening Express as usual. I went down into the parlor for it, early in the morning, and found the boy about to kindle a fire with it. I took it from him and examined the list of arrivals. Reader, if you have never been a slave, you cannot imagine the acute sensation of suffering at my heart, when I read the names of Mr. and Mrs. Dodge, at a hotel in Courtland Street. It was a third-rate hotel, and that circumstance convinced me of the truth of what I had heard, that they were short of funds and had need of my value, as they valued me; and that was by dollars and cents. I hastened with the paper to Mrs. Bruce. Her heart and hand were always open to every one in distress, and she always warmly sympathized with mine. It was impossible to tell how near the enemy was. He might have passed and repassed the house while we were sleeping. He might at that moment be waiting to pounce upon me if I ventured out of doors. I had never seen the husband of my young mistress, and therefore I could not distinguish him from any other stranger. A carriage was hastily ordered; and, closely veiled, I followed Mrs. Bruce, taking the baby again with me into exile. After various turnings and crossings, and returnings, the carriage stopped at the house of one of Mrs. Bruce's friends, where I was kindly received. Mrs. Bruce returned immediately, to instruct the domestics what to say if any one came to inquire for me.

It was lucky for me that the evening paper was not burned up before I had a chance to examine the list of arrivals. It was not long after Mrs. Bruce's return to her house, before several people came to inquire for me. One inquired for me, another asked for my daughter Ellen, and another said he had a letter from my grandmother, which he was requested to deliver in person.

They were told, "She has lived here, but she has left."

"How long ago?"

"I don't know, sir."

"Do you know where she went?"

"I do not, sir." And the door was closed.

This Mr. Dodge, who claimed me as his property, was originally a Yankee pedler in the south; then he became a merchant, and finally a slaveholder. He managed to get introduced into what was called the first society, and married Miss Emily Flint. A quarrel arose between him and her brother, and the brother cowhided him. This led to a family feud, and he proposed to remove to Virginia. Dr. Flint left him no property, and his own means had become circumscribed, while a wife and children depended upon him for support. Under these circumstances, it was very natural that he should make an effort to put me into his pocket.

I had a colored friend, a man from my native place, in whom I had the most implicit confidence. I sent for him, and told him that Mr. and Mrs. Dodge had arrived in New York. I proposed that he should call upon them to make inquiries about his friends at the south, with whom Dr. Flint's family were well acquainted. He thought there was no impropriety in his doing so, and he consented. He went to the hotel, and knocked at the door of Mr. Dodge's room, which was opened by the gentleman himself, who gruffly inquired, "What brought you here? How came you to know I was in the city?"

"Your arrival was published in the evening papers, sir; and I called to ask Mrs. Dodge about my friends at home. I didn't suppose it would give any offence."

"Where's that negro girl, that belongs to my wife?"

"What girl, sir?"

"You know well enough. I mean Linda, that ran away from Dr. Flint's plantation, some years ago. I dare say you've seen her, and know where she is."

"Yes, sir, I've seen her, and know where she is. She is out of your reach, sir."

"Tell me where she is, or bring her to me, and I will give her a chance to buy her freedom."

" I don't think it would be of any use, sir. I have heard her say she would go to the ends of the earth, rather than pay any man or woman for her freedom, because she thinks she has a right to it. Besides, she couldn't do it, if she would, for she has spent her earnings to educate her children."

This made Mr. Dodge very angry, and some high words passed between them. My friend was afraid to come where I was; but in the course of the day I received a note from him. I supposed they had not come from the south, in the winter, for a pleasure excursion; and now the nature of their business was very plain.

Mrs. Bruce came to me and entreated me to leave the city the next morning. She said her house was watched, and it was possible that some clew to me might be obtained. I refused to take her advice. She pleaded with an earnest tenderness, that ought to have moved me; but I was in a bitter, disheartened mood. I was weary of flying from pillar to post. I had been chased during half my life, and it seemed as if the chase was never to end. There I sat, in that great city, guiltless of crime, yet not daring to worship God in any of the churches. I heard the bells ringing for afternoon service, and, with contemptuous sarcasm, I said, "Will the preachers take for their text, 'Proclaim liberty to the captive, and the opening of prison doors to them that are bound'? or will they preach from the text, 'Do unto others as ye would they should do unto you'?" Oppressed Poles and Hungarians could find a safe refuge in that city; John Mitchell' was free to proclaim in the City Hall his desire for "a plantation well stocked with slaves;" but there I sat, an oppressed American, not daring to show my face. God forgive the black and bitter thoughts I indulged on that Sabbath day! The Scripture says, "Oppression makes even a wise man mad;" and I was not wise.

I had been told that Mr. Dodge said his wife had never signed away her right to my children, and if he could not get me, he would take them. This it was, more than any thing else, that roused such a tempest in my soul. Benjamin was with his uncle William in California, but my innocent young daughter had come to spend a vacation with me. I thought of what I had suffered in slavery at her age, and my heart was like a tiger's when a hunter tries to seize her young.

Dear Mrs. Bruce! I seem to see the expression of her face, as she turned away discouraged by my obstinate mood. Finding her expostulations unavailing, she sent Ellen to entreat me. When ten o'clock in the evening arrived and Ellen had not returned, this watchful and unwearied friend became anxious. She came to us in a carriage, bringing a well-filled trunk for my journey—trusting that by this time I would listen to reason. I yielded to her, as I ought to have done before.

The next day, baby and I set out in a heavy snow storm, bound for New England again. I received letters from the City of Iniquity, addressed to me under an assumed name. In a few days one came from Mrs. Bruce, informing me that my new master was still searching for me, and that she intended to put an end to this persecution by buying my freedom. I felt grateful for the kindness that prompted this offer, but the idea was not so pleasant to me as might have been expected. The more my mind had become enlightened, the more difficult it was for me to consider myself an article of property; and to pay money to those who had so grievously oppressed me seemed like taking from my sufferings the glory of triumph. I wrote to Mrs. Bruce, thanking her, but saying that being sold from one owner to another seemed too much like slavery; that such a great obligation could not be easily cancelled; and that I preferred to go to my brother in California.

Without my knowledge, Mrs. Bruce employed a gentleman in New York to enter into negotiations with Mr. Dodge. He proposed to pay three hundred dollars down, if Mr. Dodge would sell me, and enter into obligations to relinquish all claim to me or my children forever after. He who called himself my master said he scorned so small an offer for such a valuable servant. The gentleman replied, "You can do as you choose, sir. If you reject this offer you will never get any thing; for the woman has friends who will convey her and her children out of the country."

Mr. Dodge concluded that "half a loaf was better than no bread," and he agreed to the proffered terms. By the next mail I received this brief letter from Mrs. Bruce: "I am rejoiced to tell you that the money for your freedom has been paid to Mr. Dodge. Come home to-morrow. I long to see you and my sweet babe."

My brain reeled as I read these lines. A gentleman near me said, "It's true; I have seen the bill of sale." "The bill of sale!" Those words struck me like a blow. So I was sold at last! A human being sold in the free city of New York! The bill of sale is on record, and future generations will learn from it that women were articles of traffic in New York, late in the nineteenth century of the Christian religion. It may hereafter prove a useful document to antiquaries, who are seeking to measure the progress of civilization in the United States. I well know the value of that bit of paper; but much as I love freedom, I do not like to look upon it. I am deeply grateful to the generous friend who procured it, but I despise the miscreant who demanded payment for what never rightfully belonged to him or his.

I had objected to having my freedom bought, yet I must confess that when it was done I felt as if a heavy load had been lifted from my weary shoulders. When I rode home in the cars I was no longer afraid to unveil my face and look at people as they passed. I should have been glad to have met Daniel Dodge himself; to have had him seen me and known me, that he might have mourned over the untoward circumstances which compelled him to sell me for three hundred dollars.

When I reached home, the arms of my benefactress were thrown round me, and our tears mingled. As soon as she could speak, she said, "O Linda, I'm so glad it's all over! You wrote to me as if you thought you were going to be transferred from one owner to another. But I did not buy you for your services. I should have done just the same, if you had been going to sail for California tomorrow. I should, at least, have the satisfaction of knowing that you left me a free woman."

My heart was exceedingly full. I remembered how my poor father had tried to buy me, when I was a small child, and how he had been disappointed. I hoped his spirit was rejoicing over me now. I remembered how my good old grandmother had laid up her earnings to purchase me in later years, and how often her plans had been frustrated. How that faithful, loving old heart would leap for joy, if she could look on me and my children now that we were free! My relatives had been foiled in all their efforts, but God had raised me up a friend among strangers, who had bestowed on me the precious, long-desired boon. Friend! It is a common word, often lightly used. Like other good and beautiful things, it may be tarnished by careless handling; but when I speak of Mrs. Bruce as my friend, the word is sacred.

My grandmother lived to rejoice in my freedom; but not long after, a letter came with a black seal. She had gone "where the wicked cease from troubling, and the weary are at rest."

Time passed on, and a paper came to me from the south, containing an obituary notice of my uncle Phillip. It was the only case I ever knew of such an honor conferred upon a colored person. It was written by one of his friends, and contained these words: "Now that death has laid him low, they call him a good man and a useful citizen; but what are eulogies to the black man, when the world has faded from his vision? It does not require man's praise to obtain rest in God's kingdom." So they called a colored man a citizen! Strange words to be uttered in that region!

Reader, my story ends with freedom; not in the usual way, with marriage. I and my children are now free! We are as free from the power of slaveholders as are the white people of the north; and though that, according to my ideas, is not saying a great deal, it is a vast improvement in my condition. The dream of my life is not yet realized. I do not sit with my children in a home of my own. I still long for a hearthstone of my own, however humble. I wish it for my children's sake far more than for my own. But God so orders circumstances as to keep me with my friend Mrs. Rruce. Love, duty, gratitude, also bind me to her side. It is a privilege to serve her who pities my oppressed people, and who has bestowed the inestimable boon of freedom on me and my children.

It has been painful to me, in many ways, to recall the dreary years I passed in bondage. I would gladly forget them if I could. Yet the retrospection is not altogether without solace; for with those gloomy recollections come tender memories of my good old grandmother, like light, fleecy clouds floating over a dark and troubled sea.

1861

Questions for discussion

1. Who was Aunt Marthy? What happened to her when she was brought to auction block and why?
2. In what way were those masters hypocritical in the eyes of the slaves?
3. Why is family so important to slaves?
4. How does *Incidents* show religion being used to justify slavery? And how is it used to condemn slavery?

4. Up from Slavery

布克·华盛顿(Booker Taliaferro Washington)(1856—1915)是美国最著名也最具争议的黑人领袖之一。他所持的准种族隔离主义论调,他作为依靠自身努力和意志力实现自我的典范,以及他在亚特兰大博览会发表演说后的声名鹊起,因而成为继道格拉斯之后美国黑人代言人的经历,都让人们,无论是他的同代人,还是后世之人,对他众说纷纭,褒贬不一,其身后名也随之起起伏伏。

华盛顿出生于弗吉尼亚(现西弗吉尼亚)州弗兰克林县,母亲是奴隶,父亲是白人。9岁那年华盛顿和其他黑奴一起获得解放。他边在煤矿等地做苦工,边上夜校勤奋学习,16岁考上弗吉尼亚汉普顿师范农业学校。毕业后边工作边进修,于1877年回到母校任教。该校创始人阿姆斯特朗上校提倡黑人应学习谋生手段自立自救,受其影响,华盛顿于1881年在亚拉巴马创立的塔斯克基师范工业学院照搬了阿姆斯特朗的教育理念和办学模式。从1882年起华盛顿为给学校募集资金开始去北方大城市做巡回演讲,其中最著名的一次是1895年他在亚特兰大博览会代表黑人所做的演讲。他温和的种族主义观念——黑人白人团结合作,黑人在打下经济基础之前不应急于争取政治权利——的观点,使得这次演讲深受赞誉,尤其深受白人听众的欢迎。他的声誉由此达到顶点,1895至1915年被称为"华盛顿时代"。1900年华盛顿发表了第一部自传《我的生活和工作》,1901年3月出版的第二部自传《从奴役中奋起》引起轰动。主流刊物如《大西洋月刊》《民族》《北美评论》等纷纷撰文,将它与富兰克林的《自传》媲美。《从奴役中奋起》被翻译成20多种语言,其影响持续了一个世纪。但华盛顿的社会同化主义立场让大部分人视他为以牺牲政治权利换取经济利益的妥协者。1915年华盛顿去世后,大多数美国黑人转而投向他的反对者杜波依斯。当代批评界则主张应避免对他进行简单化的批评。尽管遭人诟病,他的观点却在无形中影响着数代黑人,尤其是各种黑人改革运动。他提倡的自力更生、提高道德修养的理想则鼓舞着全世界的黑人。

华盛顿的第二部自传《从奴役中奋起》与第一部有所不同,它的读者不再是黑人,而是白人有产阶级。因而对黑人悲惨生活的描写没有上升到种族的高度,尽可能不涉及种族冲突和种族暴行,避免刺激南方。他把奴隶制比作一所学校,教会黑人成长并珍视未来。奴隶主则与黑人一样成为奴隶制的牺牲品。同时他指责黑人民权运动妨碍民族和解及黑人自身的利益。

这部自传的时间跨度从19世纪60年代直到20世纪初。华盛顿在该书的前言中提到,《从奴役中奋起》是上一年"在《了望》杂志上连续发表的、有关我一生中重要事件的一系列文章的集大成者"。作者所讲述的主要故事大都围绕这样几件事情展开:1) 早年在奴隶制压迫下遭受的苦难和为上学而做的种种努力;2) 在汉普顿学院的求学经历;3) 塔斯克基师范工业学院的筹建过程;4) 在亚特兰大博览会上所做的演讲;5) 在哈佛大学接受荣誉学位;6) 去欧洲度假等。概言之,这部自传主要讲述华盛顿的个人奋斗史及最终的成功。杜波依斯认为华盛顿的崛起"是自1876年以来美国黑人历史上最引人注目的事件"。自传《从奴役中奋起》也成为早期美国黑人的代表性文本。它延续了美国黑人文学的奴隶自传传统,突出事实和事件,风格上直接简洁,避免情感化和政治说教。传统的批评主要关注的是该书的政治意义以及它在美国和非裔美国人自传历史上的地位,近期则注重意识形态批评与形式研究的有机结合。

他在亚特兰大博览会上的演说开宗明义,明确指出演说主旨在于"加强黑白种族之间的友谊,推进双方的诚挚合作"。他呼吁黑人抓住博览会带来的商业发展机会,脚踏实地从事农业、机械、商业、家政服务等行业,从底层而非顶层开始自己的新生活。对种族关系的阐发则强调合作互惠、共同进步:"共同发展是唯一确保我们中任何人安全无虞的方式"。在演说中和演说后,华盛顿都一再重申自己的观点:政治权利的获得对黑人而言是一个缓慢而渐进的过程,黑人应等待时机成熟,做好在财产、智力和人品上的充分准备。人们对此次演说反应不一。有人认为它出卖了美国黑人民权,其中最具代表性的是杜波依斯,他把华盛顿的演说称为"亚特兰大妥协";也有人认为它是为今后种族间合作做准备的务实演说。华盛顿的传记作家路易斯·哈兰就认为它是"及时的",因为它表述的正是美国白人想听的话。

美国学术界普遍认为,华盛顿是世纪之交最重要的美国黑人公众人物,与杜波依斯齐名。人们也往往把二者相提并论。两人都致力于黑人种族自身的进步与发展,但采取的方法判然有别。华盛顿提倡发展经济、自我提升、由下而上、依靠大众,这与杜波依斯坚持争取黑人政治权利、由上而下、基于精英的想法相左。有论者认为他是讲求实际的道德理想主义者,寄希望于调和民主和种族隔离之间冲突的价值观来解决黑人问题,达成自己对美国种族关系的美好设想。

《从奴役中奋起》,特别是在亚特兰大博览会上的演说这一片段,集中体现了华盛顿对美国黑人未来和美国种族关系的思考。

Chapter 14　The Atlanta Exposition Address

The Atlanta Exposition, at which I had been asked to make an address as a representative of the Negro race, as stated in the last chapter, was opened with a short address from Governor Bullock. After other interesting exercises, including an invocation from Bishop Nelson, of Georgia, a dedicatory ode by Albert Howell, Jr., and addresses by the President of the Exposition and Mrs. Joseph Thompson, the President of the Woman's Board, Governor Bullock introduced me with the words, "We have with us to-day a representative of Negro enterprise and Negro civilization."

When I arose to speak, there was considerable cheering, especially from the coloured people. As I remember it now, the thing that was uppermost in my mind was the desire to say something that would cement the friendship of the races and bring about hearty cooperation between them. So far as my outward surroundings were concerned, the only thing that I recall distinctly now is that when I got up, I saw thousands of eyes looking intently into my face. The following is the address which I delivered: —

Mr. President and Gentlemen of the Board of Directors and Citizens.

One-third of the population of the South is of the Negro race. No enterprise seeking the material, civil, or moral welfare of this section can disregard this element of our population and reach the highest success. I but convey to you, Mr. President and Directors, the sentiment of the masses of my race when I say that in no way have the value and manhood of the American Negro been more fittingly and generously recognized than by the managers of this magnificent Exposition at every stage of its progress. It is a recognition that will do more to cement the friendship of the two races than any occurrence since the dawn of our freedom.

Not only this, but the opportunity here afforded will awaken among us a new era of industrial progress. Ignorant and inexperienced, it is not strange that in the first years of our new life we began at the top instead of at the bottom; that a seat in Congress or the state legislature was more sought than real estate or industrial skill; that the political convention or stump speaking[①] had more attractions than starting a dairy farm or truck garden.

A ship lost at sea for many days suddenly sighted a friendly vessel. From the mast of the unfortunate vessel was seen a signal, "Water, water; we die of thirst!" The answer from the friendly vessel at once came back, "Cast down your bucket where you are." A second time the signal, "Water, water; send us water!" ran up from the distressed vessel, and was answered, "Cast down your bucket where you are." And a third and fourth signal for water was answered, "Cast down your bucket where you are." The captain of the distressed vessel, at last heeding the injunction, cast down his bucket, and it came up full of fresh, sparkling water from the mouth of the Amazon River. To those of my race who depend on bettering their condition in a foreign land or who underestimate the importance of cultivating friendly relations with the Southern white man, who is their next-door neighbour, I would say: "Cast down your bucket where you are"—cast it down in making friends in every manly way of the people of all races by whom we are surrounded.

Cast it down in agriculture, mechanics, in commerce, in domestic service, and in the professions. And in this connection it is well to bear in mind that whatever other sins the South may be called to bear, when it comes to business, pure and simple, it is in the South that the Negro is given a man's chance in the commercial world, and in nothing is this Exposition more eloquent than in emphasizing this chance. Our greatest danger is that in the great leap from slavery to freedom we may overlook the fact that the masses of us are to live by the productions of our hands, and fail to keep in mind that we shall prosper in proportion as we learn to dignify and glorify common labour and put brains and skill into the common occupations of life; shall prosper in proportion as we learn to draw the line between the superficial and the substantial, the ornamental gewgaws of life and the useful. No race can prosper till it learns that there is as much dignity in tilling a field as in writing a poem. It is at the bottom of life we must begin, and not at the top. Nor should we permit our grievances to overshadow our opportunities.

To those of the white race who look to the incoming of those of foreign birth and strange tongue and habits for the prosperity of the South, were I permitted I would repeat what I say to my own race, "Cast down your bucket where you are." Cast it down among the eight millions of Negroes whose habits you know, whose fidelity and love you have tested in days when to have proved treacherous meant the ruin of your firesides. Cast down your bucket among these people who have, without strikes and labour wars, tilled your

---

① stump speaking: 巡回演说。

fields, cleared your forests, builded your railroads and cities, and brought forth treasures from the bowels of the earth, and helped make possible this magnificent representation of the progress of the South. Casting down your bucket among my people, helping and encouraging them as you are doing on these grounds, and to education of head, hand, and heart, you will find that they will buy your surplus land, make blossom the waste places in your fields, and run your factories. While doing this, you can be sure in the future, as in the past, that you and your families will be surrounded by the most patient, faithful, law-abiding, and unresentful people that the world has seen. As we have proved our loyalty to you in the past, in nursing your children, watching by the sick-bed of your mothers and fathers, and often following them with tear-dimmed eyes to their graves, so in the future, in our humble way, we shall stand by you with a devotion that no foreigner can approach, ready to lay down our lives, if need be, in defence of yours, interlacing our industrial, commercial, civil, and religious life with yours in a way that shall make the interests of both races one. In all things that are purely social we can be as separate as the fingers, yet one as the hand in all things essential to mutual progress.

There is no defence or security for any of us except in the highest intelligence and development of all. If anywhere there are efforts tending to curtail the fullest growth of the Negro, let these efforts be turned into stimulating, encouraging, and making him the most useful and intelligent citizen. Effort or means so invested will pay a thousand per cent interest. These efforts will be twice blessed—"blessing him that gives and him that takes."①

There is no escape through law of man or God from the inevitable: —

> The laws of changeless justice bind
> Oppressor with oppressed;
> And close as sin and suffering joined
> We march to fate abreast.②

Nearly sixteen millions of hands will aid you in pulling the load upward, or they will pull against you the load downward. We shall constitute one-third and more of the ignorance and crime of the South, or one-third its intelligence and progress; we shall contribute one-third to the business and industrial prosperity of the South, or we shall prove a veritable body of death, stagnating, depressing, retarding every effort to advance the body politic.

Gentlemen of the Exposition, as we present to you our humble effort at an exhibition of our progress, you must not expect overmuch. Starting thirty years ago with ownership here and there in a few quilts and pumpkins and chickens (gathered from miscellaneous sources), remember the path that has led from these to the inventions and production of agricultural implements, buggies, steam-engines, newspapers, books, statuary, carving,

_____

① These efforts will be twice blessed—"blessing him that gives and him that takes":这种努力将为双方造福,既有利于提供帮助的一方,也有利于被帮助的一方。

② 这几句诗歌出自美国诗人约翰·格林利夫·惠蒂尔的《黑人船夫之歌》。

paintings, the management of drug-stores and banks, has not been trodden without contact with thorns and thistles. While we take pride in what we exhibit as a result of our independent efforts, we do not for a moment forget that our part in this exhibition would fall far short of your expectations but for the constant help that has come to our educational life, not only from the Southern states, but especially from Northern philanthropists, who have made their gifts a constant stream of blessing and encouragement.

The wisest among my race understand that the agitation of questions of social equality is the extremest folly, and that progress in the enjoyment of all the privileges that will come to us must be the result of severe and constant struggle rather than of artificial forcing. No race that has anything to contribute to the markets of the world is long in any degree ostracized. It is important and right that all privileges of the law be ours, but it is vastly more important that we be prepared for the exercises of these privileges. The opportunity to earn a dollar in a factory just now is worth infinitely more than the opportunity to spend a dollar in an opera-house.

In conclusion, may I repeat that nothing in thirty years has given us more hope and encouragement, and drawn us so near to you of the white race, as this opportunity offered by the Exposition; and here bending, as it were, over the altar that represents the results of the struggles of your race and mine, both starting practically empty-handed three decades ago, I pledge that in your effort to work out the great and intricate problem which God has laid at the doors of the South, you shall have at all times the patient, sympathetic help of my race; only let this be constantly in mind, that, while from representations in these buildings of the product of field, of forest, of mine, of factory, letters, and art, much good will come, yet far above and beyond material benefits will be that higher good, that, let us pray God, will come, in a blotting out of sectional differences and racial animosities and suspicions, in a determination to administer absolute justice, in a willing obedience among all classes to the mandates of law. This, this, coupled with our material prosperity, will bring into our beloved South a new heaven and a new earth.

The first thing that I remember, after I had finished speaking, was that Governor Bullock rushed across the platform and took me by the hand, and that others did the same. I received so many and such hearty congratulations that I found it difficult to get out of the building. I did not appreciate to any degree, however, the impression which my address seemed to have made, until the next morning, when I went into the business part of the city. As soon as I was recognized, I was surprised to find myself pointed out and surrounded by a crowd of men who wished to shake hands with me. This was kept up on every street on to which I went, to an extent which embarrassed me so much that I went back to my boarding-place. The next morning I returned to Tuskegee. At the station in Atlanta, and at almost all of the stations at which the train stopped between that city and Tuskegee, I found a crowd of people anxious to shake hands with me.

The papers in all parts of the United States published the address in full, and for months afterward there were complimentary editorial references to it. Mr. Clark Howell, the editor of the Atlanta *Constitution*, telegraphed to a New York paper, among other words, the following, "I do not exaggerate when I say that Professor Booker T. Washington's address yesterday was one of the most notable speeches, both as to character and as to the warmth of its reception, ever delivered to a Southern audience. The address was a revelation. The whole speech is a platform upon which blacks and whites can stand with full justice to each other."

The Boston *Transcript* said editorially: "The speech of Booker T. Washington at the Atlanta Exposition, this week, seems to have dwarfed all the other proceedings and the Exposition itself. The sensation that it has caused in the press has never been equalled."

I very soon began receiving all kinds of propositions from lecture bureaus, and editors of magazines and papers, to take the lecture platform, and to write articles. One lecture bureau offered me fifty thousand dollars, or two hundred dollars a night and expenses, if I would place my services at its disposal for a given period. To all these communications I replied that my life-work was at Tuskegee; and that whenever I spoke it must be in the interests of the Tuskegee school and my race, and that I would enter into no arrangements that seemed to place a mere commercial value upon my services.

Some days after its delivery I sent a copy of my address to the President of the United States, the Hon. Grover Cleveland.[1] I received from him the following autograph reply: —

Gray Gables, Buzzard's Bay, Mass.,
October 6, 1895.

Booker T. Washington, Esq.[2]:
My Dear Sir: I thank you for sending me a copy of your address delivered at the Atlanta Exposition.

I thank you with much enthusiasm for making the address. I have read it with intense interest, and I think the Exposition would be fully justified if it did not do more than furnish the opportunity for its delivery. Your words cannot fail to delight and encourage all who wish well for your race; and if our coloured fellow-citizens do not from your utterances gather new hope and form new determinations to gain every valuable advantage offered them by their citizenship, it will be strange indeed.

Yours very truly,
Grover Cleveland.

Later I met Mr. Cleveland, for the first time, when, as President, he visited the Atlanta Exposition. At the request of myself and others he consented to spend an hour in the Negro Building, for the purpose of inspecting the Negro exhibit and of giving the coloured people in attendance an opportunity to shake hands with him. As soon as I met

---

① Hon. : Honorable, 阁下。
② Esq. : Esquire, 先生。

Mr. Cleveland I became impressed with his simplicity, greatness, and rugged honesty. I have met him many times since then, both at public functions and at his private residence in Princeton, and the more I see of him the more I admire him. When he visited the Negro Building in Atlanta he seemed to give himself up wholly, for that hour, to the coloured people. He seemed to be as careful to shake hands with some old coloured "auntie" clad partially in rags, and to take as much pleasure in doing so, as if he were greeting some millionaire. Many of the coloured people took advantage of the occasion to get him to write his name in a book or on a slip of paper. He was as careful and patient in doing this as if he were putting his signature to some great state document.

Mr. Cleveland has not only shown his friendship for me in many personal ways, but has always consented to do anything I have asked of him for our school. This he has done, whether it was to make a personal donation or to use his influence in securing the donations of others. Judging from my personal acquaintance with Mr. Cleveland, I do not believe that he is conscious of possessing any colour prejudice. He is too great for that. In my contact with people I find that, as a rule, it is only the little, narrow people who live for themselves, who never read good books, who do not travel, who never open up their souls in a way to permit them to come into contact with other souls—with the great outside world. No man whose vision is bounded by colour can come into contact with what is highest and best in the world. In meeting men, in many places, I have found that the happiest people are those who do the most for others; the most miserable are those who do the least. I have also found that few things, if any, are capable of making one so blind and narrow as race prejudice. I often say to our students, in the course of my talks to them on Sunday evenings in the chapel, that the longer I live and the more experience I have of the world, the more I am convinced that, after all, the one thing that is most worth living for—and dying for, if need be—is the opportunity of making someone else more happy and more useful.

The coloured people and the coloured newspapers at first seemed to be greatly pleased with the character of my Atlanta address, as well as with its reception. But after the first burst of enthusiasm began to die away, and the coloured people began reading the speech in cold type, some of them seemed to feel that they had been hypnotized. They seemed to feel that I had been too liberal in my remarks toward the Southern whites, and that I had not spoken out strongly enough for what they termed the "rights" of the race. For a while there was a reaction, so far as a certain element of my own race was concerned, but later these reactionary ones seemed to have been won over to my way of believing and acting.

While speaking of changes in public sentiment, I recall that about ten years after the school at Tuskegee was established, I had an experience that I shall never forget. Dr. Lyman Abbott, then the pastor of Plymouth Church, and also editor of the *Outlook* (then the *Christian Union*), asked me to write a letter for his paper giving my opinion of the exact condition, mental and moral, of the coloured ministers in the South, as based upon my observations. I wrote the letter, giving the exact facts as I conceived them to be. The picture painted was a rather black one—or, since I am black, shall I say "white"? It could not be otherwise with a race but a few years out of slavery, a race which had not had time or opportunity to produce a competent ministry.

What I said soon reached every Negro minister in the country, I think, and the letters of condemnation which I received from them were not few. I think that for a year after the publication of this article every association and every conference or religious body of any kind, of my race, that met, did not fail before adjourning to pass a resolution condemning me, or calling upon me to retract or modify what I had said. Many of these organizations went so far in their resolutions as to advise parents to cease sending their children to Tuskegee. One association even appointed a "missionary" whose duty it was to warn the people against sending their children to Tuskegee. This missionary had a son in the school, and I noticed that, whatever the "missionary" might have said or done with regard to others, he was careful not to take his son away from the institution. Many of the coloured papers, especially those that were the organs of religious bodies, joined in the general chorus of condemnation or demands for retraction.

During the whole time of the excitement, and through all the criticism, I did not utter a word of explanation or retraction. I knew that I was right, and that time and the sober second thought of the people would vindicate me. It was not long before the bishops and other church leaders began to make a careful investigation of the conditions of the ministry, and they found out that I was right. In fact, the oldest and most influential bishop in one branch of the Methodist Church said that my words were far too mild. Very soon public sentiment began making itself felt, in demanding a purifying of the ministry. While this is not yet complete by any means, I think I may say, without egotism, and I have been told by many of our most influential ministers, that my words had much to do with starting a demand for the placing of a higher type of men in the pulpit. I have had the satisfaction of having many who once condemned me thank me heartily for my frank words.

The change of the attitude of the Negro ministry, so far as regards myself, is so complete that at the present time I have no warmer friends among any class than I have among the clergymen. The improvement in the character and life of the Negro ministers is one of the most gratifying evidences of the progress of the race. My experience with them, as well as other events in my life, convinces me that the thing to do, when one feels sure that he has said or done the right thing, and is condemned, is to stand still and keep quiet. If he is right, time will show it.

In the midst of the discussion which was going on concerning my Atlanta speech, I received the letter which I give below, from Dr. Gilman, the President of Johns Hopkins University, who had been made chairman of the judges of award in connection with the Atlanta Exposition: —

Johns Hopkins University, Baltimore,
President's Office, September 30, 1895.

Dear Mr. Washington:

Would it be agreeable to you to be one of the Judges of Award in the Department of Education at Atlanta? If so, I shall be glad to place your name upon the list. A line by telegraph will be welcomed.

Yours very truly,
D. C. Gilman.

I think I was even more surprised to receive this invitation than I had been to receive the invitation to speak at the opening of the Exposition. It was to be a part of my duty, as one of the jurors, to pass not only upon the exhibits of the coloured schools, but also upon those of the white schools. I accepted the position, and spent a month in Atlanta in performance of the duties which it entailed. The board of jurors was a large one, consisting in all of sixty members. It was about equally divided between Southern white people and Northern white people. Among them were college presidents, leading scientists and men of letters, and specialists in many subjects. When the group of jurors to which I was assigned met for organization, Mr. Thomas Nelson Page, who was one of the number, moved that I be made secretary of that division, and the motion was unanimously adopted. Nearly half of our division were Southern people. In performing my duties in the inspection of the exhibits of white schools I was in every case treated with respect, and at the close of our labours I parted from my associates with regret.

I am often asked to express myself more freely than I do upon the political condition and the political future of my race. These recollections of my experience in Atlanta give me the opportunity to do so briefly. My own belief is, although I have never before said so in so many words, that the time will come when the Negro in the South will be accorded all the political rights which his ability, character, and material possessions entitle him to. I think, though, that the opportunity to freely exercise such political rights will not come in any large degree through outside or artificial forcing, but will be accorded to the Negro by the Southern white people themselves, and that they will protect him in the exercise of those rights. Just as soon as the South gets over the old feeling that it is being forced by "foreigners," or "aliens," to do something which it does not want to do, I believe that the change in the direction that I have indicated is going to begin. In fact, there are indications that it is already beginning in a slight degree.

Let me illustrate my meaning. Suppose that some months before the opening of the Atlanta Exposition there had been a general demand from the press and public platform outside the South that a Negro be given a place on the opening programme, and that a Negro be placed upon the board of jurors of award. Would any such recognition of the race have taken place? I do not think so. The Atlanta officials went as far as they did because they felt it to be a pleasure, as well as a duty, to reward what they considered merit in the Negro race. Say what we will, there is something in human nature which we cannot blot out, which makes one man, in the end, recognize and reward merit in another, regardless of colour or race.

I believe it is the duty of the Negro—as the greater part of the race is already doing—to deport himself modestly in regard to political claims, depending upon the slow but sure influences that proceed from the possession of property, intelligence, and high character for the full recognition of his political rights. I think that the according of the full exercise of political rights is going to be a matter of natural, slow growth, not an over-night, gourd-vine affair. I do not believe that the Negro should cease voting, for a man cannot learn the exercise of self-government by ceasing to vote, any more than a boy can learn to swim by keeping out of the water, but I do believe that in his voting he should more and more be influenced by those of intelligence and character who are his next-door neighbours.

I know coloured men who, through the encouragement, help, and advice of Southern white people, have accumulated thousands of dollars' worth of property, but who, at the same time, would never think of going to those same persons for advice concerning the casting of their ballots. This, it seems to me, is unwise and unreasonable, and should cease. In saying this I do not mean that the Negro should truckle, or not vote from principle, for the instant he ceases to vote from principle he loses the confidence and respect of the Southern white man even.

I do not believe that any state should make a law that permits an ignorant and poverty-stricken white man to vote, and prevents a black man in the same condition from voting. Such a law is not only unjust, but it will react, as all unjust laws do, in time; for the effect of such a law is to encourage the Negro to secure education and property, and at the same time it encourages the white man to remain in ignorance and poverty. I believe that in time, through the operation of intelligence and friendly race relations, all cheating at the ballot-box in the South will cease. It will become apparent that the white man who begins by cheating a Negro out of his ballot soon learns to cheat a white man out of his, and that the man who does this ends his career of dishonesty by the theft of property or by some equally serious crime. In my opinion, the time will come when the South will encourage all of its citizens to vote. It will see that it pays better, from every standpoint, to have healthy, vigorous life than to have that political stagnation which always results when one-half of the population has no share and no interest in the Government.

As a rule, I believe in universal, free suffrage, but I believe that in the South we are confronted with peculiar conditions that justify the protection of the ballot in many of the states, for a while at least, either by an educational test, a property test, or by both combined; but whatever tests are required, they should be made to apply with equal and exact justice to both races.

1901

Questions for Discussion

1. Booker T. Washington's most famous speech, the Atlanta Exposition address, came to be called his "Atlanta Compromise" address. In what way do you think it is a compromise?
2. What does Washington mean when he repeats the statement "cast down your bucket where you are"?
3. What does Washington mean by stating that both races could "be as separate as the fingers, yet one as the hand in all things essential to mutual progress"?

5. The Big Sea

作者简介

休斯(Langston Hughes)(1902—1967),著名非裔美国诗人、剧作家、传记家与小说家,一生共创作了50多部作品,涵盖诗歌、小说、戏剧、儿童文学、传记与自传等文类,是哈莱姆文艺复兴运动中的重要人物,是与惠特曼齐名的美国著名诗人,其成名作《黑人说河》(1921)发表在杜波伊斯主编的重要黑人刊物《危机》上。

休斯初中二年级就开始写诗,1922年到位于纽约市的哥伦比亚大学读书,虽然因为囊中羞涩,未能读完大学,但是他在哈莱姆的经历对他非裔美国身份意识的塑造,以及用诗歌表达黑人的经历的表现手法,产生了重要影响;其间,他结识当时著名非裔美国学者、作家,如杜波伊斯、洛克、福赛特、卡伦及赫斯顿等人,进一步丰富了自己的文学世界。1922—1926年间,他打过很多零工,利用在船上打工的机会游历非洲与巴黎,形成了很强的泛非意识,这反映在1926年出版的诗集《疲惫的布鲁斯》中,该诗集不仅体现了美国著名诗人惠特曼与桑德堡对他的影响,更显示出哈莱姆街头生活与夜总会的影响。

休斯以诗歌见长,注重借鉴非裔美国民间文化,如布鲁斯音乐的韵律与节奏,同时他利用诗歌直接抨击资本主义美国的种族歧视与经济剥削。20世纪30年代,他为黑人左翼刊物《新大众》与《黑人工人》供稿;50年代冷战时期,他与杜波伊斯等人一道被指责为同情共产主义。他的《三首关于私刑的诗歌》、《三K党》等诗歌直接揭露美国社会对黑人的不公正,他的第二部诗集《犹太人的好衣服》(1927)被誉为黑人世界的《草叶集》,《单程车票》(1949)描绘美国南方的吉姆·克劳种族隔离与歧视,以及对远离故土、另谋新生的渴望,《延误了的梦的蒙太奇》(1951)在主题与形式方面,反映了爵士乐时代哈莱姆的生活;1961年出版的诗集《问你妈去》则运用非裔美国民俗中的"骂娘"修辞,极具实验色彩,显示出作者高超的语言驾驭能力。

无论在诗歌、戏剧还是小说创作中,休斯始终关注非裔美国民族承受的苦难,以及他们秉持乐观心态,对梦想的追寻和对美好生活的向往;作为多产作家,他对美国理想的坚持及其对美国种族歧视的反思,很好地反映在他的两部回忆录《大海》(1940)与《我漂泊,我彷徨》(1956)中,为我们全面认识(非裔)美国社会与文化提供了第一手的资料。

作品简介与赏析

休斯共创作两部自传:《大海》与《我漂泊,我彷徨》,涵盖了他前35年的人生岁月,讲述了他1902年出生于密苏里州的乔普林到作为西班牙内战时期的战地记者回到美国的生活。《大海》的第一部分"21岁"讲述了他从出生到离开纽约港的一些重要事件;第二部分"大海"描绘了他的非洲与欧洲之旅;第三部分"黑人文艺复兴"重点介绍了1925—1930年间与哈莱姆文艺复兴有关的事件与人物,及其对哈莱姆文艺复兴的认识与反思,为我们更加客观地认识这次重要的黑人文艺运动提供了第一手的资料。

休斯的《大海》没有采取普通自传中平铺直叙的套路,没有从他的出生开始讲起,而是从他的"新生"开始介绍:他把在"哥伦比亚大学学习时买的书"扔进大海,准备作为商船餐室的侍应生离开纽约港去非洲,开启新的生活。休斯以倒叙的方式,补叙了因父母离异,外婆把自己抚养到12岁的成长经历,也提到自己早在初中二年级就显露诗才与诗情,为高中杂志撰稿的故事。此外，第一部分也讲到他去墨西哥与生父相处的一段时间，以及到哥伦比亚大学读书的经历，因为害怕会沦落于平庸的生活、需要从事繁重的体力劳动谋生，他登上开往非洲的商船，远离故土。

第二部分"大海"主要讲述1923—1924年休斯一边在去非洲与荷兰的船上工作，一边进行创作的经历，其间，他在法国巴黎的夜总会洗过碗，在意大利的海滩打过零工。回到美国后，他利用在旅馆打工的机会，把三首诗歌放在当时著名诗人林赛的桌上，得其赏识，成为所谓"餐馆诗人"的传奇经历。

第三部分"哈莱姆文艺复兴"记述了休斯1925—1930年间的四件重要大事。首先，他虽然住在华盛顿特区，但是经常去纽约，正逢哈莱姆文艺复兴繁荣鼎盛期，结识许多黑人作家，如图默、卡伦、赫斯顿等人。其次，他参加《机遇》杂志的文学竞赛，获得诗歌奖，在获奖宴会上，得遇维克腾，在他的帮助下，出版第一部诗集《疲惫的布鲁斯》。再次，他获得奖学金，得以在宾夕法尼亚州的林肯大学完成本科学业，1929年获得学士学位，而且有缘获得纽约的老夫人赏识。最后，他完成第一部小说《不是没有笑声》(1930)，获得哈蒙文学奖，虽然与"恩主"不和，但是休斯更加坚定了以写作为生的志向，所以才有了《大海》中"文学是一个满是鱼群的大海。我撒下网儿再用力拉"的比喻。

休斯的《大海》记述了作者的生平，为我们了解作者的创作与特定时期的美国社会与文化提供了丰富的史料，他对很多文化现象如"哈莱姆文艺复兴"运动的真实描绘与反思，如1929年开始的美国经济大萧条，客观上造成曾经风光无限的美国黑人文艺创作不再"时尚"等，为后人重新客观认识这一重要时段增添了许多翔实的资料。

When the Negro Was in Vogue

The 1920's were the years of Manhattan's black Renaissance[1]. It began with *Shuffle Along*, *Running Wild*, and the Charleston. Perhaps some people would say even with *The Emperor Jones*, Charles Gilpin, and the tom-toms at the Provincetown. But certainly it was the musical revue, *Shuffle Along*, that gave a scintillating send-off to that Negro vogue in Manhattan, which reached its peak just before the crash of 1929, the crash that sent Negroes, white folks, and all rolling down the hill toward the Works Progress Administration.

Shuffle Along was a honey of a show. Swift, bright, funny, rollicking, and gay, with a dozen danceable, singable tunes. Besides, look who were in it: The now famous choir director, Hall Johnson, and the composer, William Grant Still, were a part of the orchestra. Eubie Blake and Noble Sissle wrote the music and played and acted in the show. Miller and Lyles were the comics. Florence Mills skyrocketed to fame in the second act. Trixie Smith sang "He May Be Your Man But He Comes to See Me Sometimes." And Caterina Jarboro, now a European prima donna, and the internationally celebrated Josephine Baker were merely in the chorus. Everybody was in the audience—including me. People came back to see it innumerable times. It was always packed.

---

① 20世纪20年代，美国黑人文学出现第一次勃兴，史称哈莱姆文艺复兴。但是休斯以自己的个人经历，个性化地表明，哈莱姆文艺复兴对普通黑人民众没有产生太大影响，哈莱姆的酒吧、夜总会等仿佛也只是吸引外来好奇游客的所在。

To see *Shuffle Along* was the main reason I wanted to go to Columbia. When I saw it, I was thrilled and delighted. From then on I was in the gallery of the Cort Theatre every time I got a chance. That year, too, I saw Katharine Cornell in *A Bill of Divorcement*, Margaret Wycherly in *The Verge*, Maugham's *The Circle* with Mrs. Leslie Carter, and the Theatre Guild production of Kaiser's *From Morn Till Midnight*. But I remember *Shuffle Along* best of all. It gave just the proper push—a pre-Charleston kick—to that Negro vogue of the 20's, that spread to books, African sculpture, music, and dancing.

Put down the 1920's for the rise of Roland Hayes, who packed Carnegie Hall, the rise of Paul Robeson① in New York and London, of Florence Mills over two continents, of Rose McClendon in Broadway parts that never measured up to her, the booming voice of Bessie Smith and the low moan of Clara on thousands of records, and the rise of that grand comedienne of song, Ethel Waters, singing: "Charlie's elected now! He's in right for sure!" Put down the 1920's for Louis Armstrong and Gladys Bentley and Josephine Baker.

White people began to come to Harlem in droves. For several years they packed the expensive Cotton Club on Lenox Avenue. But I was never there, because the Cotton Club was a Jim Crow club for gangsters and monied whites. They were not cordial to Negro patronage, unless you were a celebrity like Bojangles. So Harlem Negroes did not like the Cotton Club and never appreciated its Jim Crow policy in the very heart of their dark community. Nor did ordinary Negroes like the growing influx of whites toward Harlem after sundown, flooding the little cabarets and bars where formerly only colored people laughed and sang, and where now the strangers were given the best ringside tables to sit and stare at the Negro customers—like amusing animals in a zoo.

The Negroes said: "We can't go downtown and sit and stare at you in your clubs. You won't even let us in your clubs." But they didn't say it out loud—for Negroes are practically never rude to white people. So thousands of whites came to Harlem night after night, thinking the Negroes loved to have them there, and firmly believing that all Harlemites left their houses at sundown to sing and dance in cabarets, because most of the whites saw nothing but the cabarets, not the houses.

Some of the owners of Harlem clubs, delighted at the flood of white patronage, made the grievous error of barring their own race, after the manner of the famous Cotton Club. But most of these quickly lost business and folded up, because they failed to realize that a large part of the Harlem attraction for downtown New Yorkers lay in simply watching the colored customers amuse themselves. And the smaller clubs, of course, had no big floor shows or a name band like the Cotton Club, where Duke Ellington usually held forth, so, without black patronage, they were not amusing at all.

Some of the small clubs, however, had people like Gladys Bentley, who was something worth discovering in those days, before she got famous, acquired an accompanist, specially written material, and conscious vulgarity. But for two or three amazing years, Miss Bentley sat, and played a big piano all night long, literally all night,

---

① Paul Robeson:著名美国黑人。

without stopping—singing songs like "The St. James Infirmary," from ten in the evening until dawn, with scarcely a break between the notes, sliding from one song to another, with a powerful and continuous underbeat of jungle rhythm. Miss Bentley was an amazing exhibition of musical energy—a large, dark, masculine lady, whose feet pounded the floor while her fingers pounded the keyboard—a perfect piece of African sculpture, animated by her own rhythm.

But when the place where she played became too well known, she began to sing with an accompanist, became a star, moved to a larger place, then downtown, and is now in Hollywood. The old magic of the woman and the piano and the night and the rhythm being one is gone. But everything goes, one way or another. The '20's are gone and lots of fine things in Harlem night life have disappeared like snow in the sun—since it became utterly commercial, planned for the downtown tourist trade, and therefore dull.

The lindy-hoppers at the Savoy even began to practise acrobatic routines, and to do absurd things for the entertainment of the whites, that probably never would have entered their heads to attempt merely for their own effortless amusement. Some of the lindy-hoppers had cards printed with their names on them and became dance professors teaching the tourists. Then Harlem nights became show nights for the Nordics.

Some critics say that that is what happened to certain Negro writers, too—that they ceased to write to amuse themselves and began to write to amuse and entertain white people, and in so doing distorted and overcolored their material, and left out a great many things they thought would offend their American brothers of a lighter complexion. Maybe—since Negroes have writer-racketeers, as has any other race. But I have known almost all of them, and most of the good ones have tried to be honest, write honestly, and express their world as they saw it.

All of us know that the gay and sparkling life of the so-called Negro Renaissance of the '20's was not so gay and sparkling beneath the surface as it looked. Carl Van Vechten[①], in the character of Byron in *Nigger Heaven*, captured some of the bitterness and frustration of literary Harlem that Wallace Thurman later so effectively poured into his *Infants of the Spring*—the only novel by a Negro about that fantastic period when Harlem was in vogue.

It was a period when, at almost every Harlem upper-crust dance or party, one would be introduced to various distinguished white celebrities there as guests. It was a period when almost any Harlem Negro of any social importance at all would be likely to say casually: "As I was remarking the other day to Heywood—," meaning Heywood Broun. Or: "As I said to George—," referring to George Gershwin. It was a period when local and visiting royalty were not at all uncommon in Harlem. And when the parties of A'Lelia Walker, the Negro heiress, were filled with guests whose names would turn any Nordic social climber green with envy. It was a period when Harold Jackman, a handsome young Harlem school teacher of modest means, calmly announced one day that he was sailing for

---

① Carl Van Vechten：哈莱姆文艺复兴时期著名白人作家，非常欣赏当时的很多年轻黑人作家。

the Riviera for a fortnight, to attend Princess Murat's yachting party. It was a period when Charleston preachers opened up shouting churches as sideshows for white tourists. It was a period when at least one charming colored chorus girl, amber enough to pass for a Latin American, was living in a pent house, with all her bills paid by a gentleman whose name was banker's magic on Wall Street. It was a period when every season there was at least one hit play on Broadway acted by a Negro cast. And when books by Negro authors were being published with much greater frequency and much more publicity than ever before or since in history. It was a period when white writers wrote about Negroes more successfully (commercially speaking) than Negroes did about themselves. It was the period (God help us!) when Ethel Barrymore appeared in blackface in *Scarlet Sister Mary*! It was the period when the Negro was in vogue.

I was there. I had a swell time while it lasted. But I thought it wouldn't last long. (I remember the vogue for things Russian, the season the Chauve-Souris first came to town.) For how could a large and enthusiastic number of people be crazy about Negroes forever? But some Harlemites thought the millennium had come. They thought the race problem had at last been solved through Art plus Gladys Bentley. They were sure the New Negro would lead a new life from then on in green pastures of tolerance created by Countee Cullen, Ethel Waters, Claude McKay, Duke Ellington, Bojangles, and Alain Locke[①].

I don't know what made any Negroes think that—except that they were mostly intellectuals doing the thinking. The ordinary Negroes hadn't heard of the Negro Renaissance. And if they had, it hadn't raised their wages any. As for all those white folks in the speakeasies and night clubs of Harlem—well, maybe a colored man could find *some* place to have a drink that the tourists hadn't yet discovered.

Then it was that house-rent parties began to flourish—and not always to raise the rent either. But, as often as not, to have a get-together of one's own, where you could do the black-bottom with no stranger behind you trying to do it, too. Non-theatrical, non-intellectual Harlem was an unwilling victim of its own vogue. It didn't like to be stared at by white folks. But perhaps the downtowners never knew this—for the cabaret owners, the entertainers, and the speakeasy proprietors treated them fine—as long as they paid.

The Saturday night rent parties that I attended were often more amusing than any night club, in small apartments where God knows who lived—because the guests seldom did—but where the piano would often be augmented by a guitar, or an odd cornet, or somebody with a pair of drums walking in off the street. And where awful bootleg whiskey and good fried fish or steaming chitterling were sold at very low prices. And the dancing and singing and impromptu entertaining went on until dawn came in at the windows.

These parties, often termed whist parties or dances, were usually announced by brightly colored cards stuck in the grille of apartment house elevators. Some of the cards were highly entertaining in themselves:

Almost every Saturday night when I was in Harlem I went to a house-rent party. I

---

① Alain Locke：有哈莱姆文艺复兴助产士之称，他所主编的《新黑人》(1925)开启"新黑人"的文化模式。

wrote lots of poems about house-rent parties, and ate thereat many a fried fish and pig's foot—with liquid refreshments on the side. I met ladies' maids and truck drivers, laundry workers and shoe shine boys, seamstresses and porters. I can still hear their laughter in my ears, hear the soft slow music, and feel the floor shaking as the dancers danced.

Harlem Literati [①]

The summer of 1926, I lived in a rooming house on 137th Street, where Wallace Thurman and Harcourt Tynes also lived. Thurman was then managing editor of the *Messenger*, a Negro magazine that had a curious career. It began by being very radical, racial, and socialistic, just after the war. I believe it received a grant from the Garland Fund in its early days. Then it later became a kind of Negro society magazine and a plugger for Negro business, with photographs of prominent colored ladies and their nice homes in it. A. Philip Randolph, now President of the Brotherhood of Sleeping Car Porters, Chandler Owen, and George S. Schuyler were connected with it. Schuyler's editorials, a la Mencken, were the most interesting things in the magazine, verbal brickbats that said sometimes one thing, sometimes another, but always vigorously. I asked Thurman what kind of magazine the *Messenger* was, and he said it reflected the policy of whoever paid off best at the time.

Anyway, the *Messenger* bought my first short stories. They paid me ten dollars a story. Wallace Thurman wrote me that they were very bad stories, but better than any others they could find, so he published them.

Thurman had recently come from California to New York. He was a strangely brilliant black boy, who had read everything, and whose critical mind could find something wrong with everything he read. I have no critical mind, so I usually either like a book or don't. But I am not capable of liking a book and then finding a million things wrong with it, too—as Thurman was capable of doing.

Thurman had read so many books because he could read eleven lines at a time. He would get from the library a great pile of volumes that would have taken me a year to read. But he would go through them in less than a week, and be able to discuss each one at great length with anybody. That was why, I suppose, he was later given a job as a reader at Macaulay's—the only Negro reader, so far as I know, to be employed by any of the larger publishing firms.

Later Thurman became a ghost writer for *True Story*, and other publications, writing under all sorts of fantastic names, like Ethel Belle Mandrake or Patrick Casey. He did Irish and Jewish and Catholic "true confessions." He collaborated with William Jordan Rapp on plays and novels. Later he ghosted books. In fact, this quite dark young Negro is said to have written *Men, Women, and Checks*.

Wallace Thurman wanted to be a great writer, but none of his own work ever made him happy. *The Blacker the Berry*, his first book, was an important novel on a subject little

---

① 休斯介绍了很多黑人艺术家,为我们全面、深入地了解那个时代提供了第一手的信息。

dwelt upon in Negro fiction—the plight of the very dark Negro woman, who encounters in some communities a double wall of color prejudice within and without the race. His play *Harlem*, considerably distorted for box office purposes, was, nevertheless, a compelling study—and the only one in the theater—of the impact of Harlem on a Negro family fresh from the South. And his *Infants of the Spring*, a superb and bitter study of the bohemian fringe of Harlem's literary and artistic life, is a compelling book.

But none of these things pleased Wallace Thurman. He wanted to be a *very* great writer, like Gorki or Thomas Mann, and he felt that he was merely a journalistic writer. His critical mind, comparing his pages to the thousands of other pages he had read, by Proust, Melville, Tolstoy, Galsworthy, Dostoyevski, Henry James, Sainte-Beauve, Taine, Anatole France, found his own pages vastly wanting. So he contented himself by writing a great deal for money, laughing bitterly at his fabulously concocted "true stories," creating two bad motion pictures of the "Adults Only" type for Hollywood, drinking more and more gin, and then threatening to jump out of windows at people's parties and kill himself.

During the summer of 1926, Wallace Thurman, Zora Neale Hurston, Aaron Douglas, John P. Davis, Bruce Nugent, Gwendolyn Bennett, and I decided to publish "a Negro quarterly of the arts" to be called *Fire*—the idea being that it would burn up a lot of the old, dead conventional Negro-white ideas of the past, *épater le bourgeois* into a realization of the existence of the younger Negro writers and artists, and provide us with an outlet for publication not available in the limited pages of the small Negro magazines then existing, the *Crisis*, *Opportunity*, and the *Messenger*①—the first two being house organs of inter-racial organizations, and the latter being God knows what.

Sweltering summer evenings we met to plan *Fire*. Each of the seven of us agreed to give fifty dollars to finance the first issue. Thurman was to edit it, John P. Davis to handle the business end, and Bruce Nugent to take charge of distribution. The rest of us were to serve as an editorial board to collect material, contribute our own work, and act in any useful way that we could. For artists and writers, we got along fine and there were no quarrels. But October came before we were ready to go to press. I had to return to Lincoln, John Davis to Law School at Harvard, Zora Hurston to her studies at Barnard, from whence she went about Harlem with an anthropologist's ruler, measuring heads for Franz Boas.

Only three of the seven had contributed their fifty dollars, but the others faithfully promised to send theirs out of tuition checks, wages, or begging. Thurman went on with the work of preparing the magazine. He got a printer. He planned the layout. It had to be on good paper, he said, worthy of the drawings of Aaron Douglas. It had to have beautiful type, worthy of the first Negro art quarterly. It had to be what we seven young Negroes dreamed our magazine would be—so in the end it cost almost a thousand dollars, and nobody could pay the bills.

---

① 哈莱姆文艺复兴时期的重要黑人杂志,特别是《危机》和《机遇》杂志,发表了很多年轻黑人作者的诗歌、短篇小说等,成为促成哈莱姆文艺复兴产生的直接媒介。

I don't know how Thurman persuaded the printer to let us have all the copies to distribute, but he did. I think Alain Locke, among others, signed notes guaranteeing payments. But since Thurman was the only one of the seven of us with a regular job, for the next three or four years his checks were constantly being attached and his income seized to pay for *Fire*. And whenever I sold a poem, mine went there, too—to *Fire*.

None of the older Negro intellectuals would have anything to do with *Fire*. Dr. Du Bois in the *Crisis* roasted it. The Negro press called it all sorts of bad names, largely because of a green and purple story by Bruce Nugent, in the Oscar Wilde tradition, which we had included. Rean Graves, the critic for the *Baltimore Afro-American*, began his review by saying: "I have just tossed the first issue of *Fire* into the fire." Commenting upon various of our contributors, he said: "Aaron Douglas who, in spite of himself and the meaningless grotesqueness of his creations, has gained a reputation as an artist, is permitted to spoil three perfectly good pages and a cover with his pen and ink hudge pudge. Countee Cullen has written a beautiful poem in his 'From a Dark Tower,' but tries his best to obscure the thought in superfluous sentences. Langston Hughes displays his usual ability to say nothing in many words."

So *Fire* had plenty of cold water thrown on it by the colored critics. The white critics (except for an excellent editorial in the *Bookman* for November, 1926) scarcely noticed it at all. We had no way of getting it distributed to bookstands or news stands. Bruce Nugent took it around New York on foot and some of the Greenwich Village bookshops put it on display, and sold it for us. But then Bruce, who had no job, would collect the money and, on account of salary, eat it up before he got back to Harlem.

Finally, irony of ironies, several hundred copies of *Fire* were stored in the basement of an apartment where an actual fire occurred and the bulk of the whole issue was burned up. Even after that Thurman had to go on paying the printer.

Now *Fire* is a collector's item, and very difficult to get, being mostly ashes.

That taught me a lesson about little magazines. But since white folks had them, we Negroes thought we could have one, too. But we didn't have the money.

Wallace Thurman laughed a long bitter laugh. He was a strange kind of fellow, who liked to drink gin, but *didn't* like to drink gin; who liked being a Negro, but felt it a great handicap; who adored bohemianism, but thought it wrong to be a bohemian. He liked to waste a lot of time, but he always felt guilty wasting time. He loathed crowds, yet he hated to be alone. He almost always felt bad, yet he didn't write poetry.

Once I told him if I could feel as bad as he did *all* the time, I would surely produce wonderful books. But he said you had to know how to *write*, as well as how to feel bad. I said I didn't have to know how to feel bad, because, every so often, the blues just naturally overtook me, like a blind beggar with an old guitar:

> *You don't know,*
> *You don't know my mind—*
> *When you see me laughin',*
> *I'm laughin' to keep from cryin'.*

About the future of Negro literature Thurman was very pessimistic. He thought the Negro vogue had made us all too conscious of ourselves, had flattered and spoiled us, and had provided too many easy opportunities for some of us to drink gin and more gin, on which he thought we would always be drunk. With his bitter sense of humor he called the Harlem literati the "niggerati."

Of this "niggerati," Zora Neale Hurston was certainly the most amusing. Only to reach a wider audience, need she ever write books—because she is a perfect book of entertainment in herself. In her youth she was always getting scholarships and things from wealthy white people, some of whom simply paid her just to sit around and represent the Negro race for them, she did it in such a racy fashion. She was full of side-splitting anecdotes, humorous tales, and tragicomic stories, remembered out of her life in the South as a daughter of a travelling minister of God. She could make you laugh one minute and cry the next. To many of her white friends, no doubt, she was a perfect "darkie," in the nice meaning they give the term—that is a naive, childlike, sweet, humorous, and highly colored Negro.

But Miss Hurston was clever, too—a student who didn't let college give her a broad *a* and who had great scorn for all pretensions, academic or otherwise. That is why she was such a fine folk-lore collector, able to go among the people and never act as if she had been to school at all. Almost nobody else could stop the average Harlemite on Lenox Avenue and measure his head with a strange looking, anthropological device and not get bawled out for the attempt, except Zora, who used to stop anyone whose head looked interesting, and measure it.

When Miss Hurston graduated from Barnard she took an apartment In West 66th Street near the park, in that row of Negro houses there. She moved in with no furniture at all and no money, but in a few days friends had given her everything, from decorative silver birds, perched atop the linen cabinet, down to a footstool. And on Saturday night, to christen the place, she had a *hand*-chicken dinner, since she had forgotten to say she needed forks.

She seemed to know almost everybody in New York. She had been a secretary to Fannie Hurst, and had met dozens of celebrities whose friendship she retained. Yet she was always having terrific ups-and-downs about money. She tells this story on herself, about needing a nickel to go downtown one day and wondering where on earth she would get it. As she approached the subway, she was stopped by a blind beggar holding out his cup.

"Please help the blind! Help the blind! A nickel for the blind!"

"I need money worse than you today," said Miss Hurston, taking five cents out of his cup. "Lend me this! Next time, I'll give it back." And she went on downtown.

Harlem was like a great magnet for the Negro intellectual, pulling him from everywhere. Or perhaps the magnet was New York—but once in New York, he had to live in Harlem, for rooms were hardly to be found elsewhere unless one could pass for white or Mexican or Eurasian and perhaps live in the Village—which always seemed to me a very arty locale, in spite of the many real artists and writers who lived there. Only a few of the New Negroes lived in the Village, Harlem being their real stamping ground.

The wittiest of these New Negroes of Harlem, whose tongue was flavored with the sharpest and saltiest humor, was Rudolph Fisher, whose stories appeared in the *Atlantic Monthly*. His novel *Walls of Jericho* captures but slightly the raciness of his own conversation. He was a young medical doctor and X-ray specialist, who always frightened me a little, because he could think of the most incisively clever things to say—and I could never think of anything to answer. He and Alain Locke together were great for intellectual wise-cracking. The two would fling big and witty words about with such swift and punning innuendo that an ordinary mortal just sat and looked wary for fear of being caught in a net of witticisms beyond his cultural ken. I used to wish I could talk like Rudolph Fisher. Besides being a good writer, he was an excellent singer, and had sung with Paul Robeson during their college days. But I guess Fisher was too brilliant and too talented to stay long on this earth. During the same week, in December, 1934, he and Wallace Thurman both died.

Thurman died of tuberculosis in the charity ward at Bellevue Hospital, having just flown back to New York from Hollywood.

Questions for Discussion

1. Please comment on Langston Hughes' views of the 1920s and the Harlem Renaissance.
2. White people flooded to Harlem's cabarets, and believed that all Harlemites left their houses at sundown to sing and dance in cabarets, what does this suggest?
3. There are many young black artists and writers mentioned in *The Big Sea*, and in the selection of "Harlem Literati", among which Wallace Thurman was given detailed descriptions, do you think that Wallace Thurman is a typical character in the Harlem Renaissance? And how?

6. Black Boy

作者简介

赖特（Richard Wright）（1908—1960）是 20 世纪美国著名黑人小说家、剧作家，也是一位自传作者。1940 年出版的《土生子》为他赢得广泛赞誉，奠定了他在美国文学史上的重要地位。著名批评家欧文·豪甚至有所谓"《土生子》出版之日，即美国文化从此改变之时"之说。而其自传《黑孩子》（1945）的出版，进一步巩固了他在美国文坛的地位。

1908 年，赖特出生于美国密西西比州的纳其兹——密西西比州属于种族歧视与种族隔离比较严重的地方。6 岁时父亲弃家出走，他与母亲相依为命，后因母亲多病，不得不与笃信宗教的外婆生活，赖特的童年生活非常凄苦。因为经常搬家，他无法完成正规学业，但是他阅读兴趣广泛，深受美国作家门肯、德莱塞、安德森以及俄国作家陀思妥耶夫斯基等人的影响。

为改善自己的处境，他 1927 年离开南方，来到芝加哥谋生，打过很多零工。美国经济大萧条时期，他参与美国联邦作家项目，得以结识美国左翼作家，为左翼刊物撰稿，继而加入美国共产党；但是因不满其他人的偏颇、狭隘，他 1944 年退出美共，但是这段"激情燃烧的岁月"成为他创作的底色与背景，深刻地影响着他的思想与创作。

1938 年，赖特的第一部短篇小说集《汤姆叔叔的孩子》问世，该书重点关注美国南方黑人遭受的种族歧视与暴力；1940 年出版的小说《土生子》主要聚焦芝加哥南岸黑人区的黑人生活，塑造了新的黑人形象——与美国主流社会熟悉的汤姆叔叔形象截然相反的黑人主人公别格·托马斯，挑战了美国社会的种族主义，以及自由主义者的"伪善"，但是其不加修饰的残忍与赤裸裸的暴力也引发很多人的反感。赖特 1945 出版的自传《黑孩子》进一步巩固了他在美国文坛的地位，把他的声誉推至顶峰。应出版社要求，本书只保留了赖特在南方生活的部分，直到 1992 年，他来到芝加哥以后的岁月才被收录在美国图书馆新出版的《黑孩子》自传中。

赖特不仅是位小说家，也具有明确的批评意识，他的论文"黑人文学的蓝图"（1937）和"美国的黑人文学"（1957）等反映了 20 世纪 30 年代美国文坛的左翼倾向以及 50 年代的融合诗学，体现了他对（非裔）美国文学传统及其发展趋势的准确把握与认识，成为非裔美国文学批评中的重要文献。

因为无法忍受美国社会对黑人的种族歧视与偏见，1947 年，赖特举家迁居法国，他与萨特、波伏娃、加缪等法国著名作家为友，创作了存在主义小说《局外人》（1953），以及注重心理探索的《野蛮的假日》（1954）与《伟大的梦想》（1958）等作品，但是遗憾的是，这些作品都未能达到他早期作品的社会影响力与接受度。此外，赖特还出版了多部游记类作品，如《黑人权力》（1954）、《有色窗帘》（1956）、《异教的西班牙》（1957）和《听着，白人！》（1957）等，其中《黑人权力》描绘了 1953 年加纳的独立及其反殖民政策，《听着，白人！》则表达了赖特尝试打破帝国主义话语，重点书写西方的黑人历史的愿望。

赖特的创作旨在解构美国的种族主义意识形态，揭露其对美国黑人族群的歧视与压迫，尝试消除其对黑人心灵的腐蚀作用，至今仍有不容忽视的现实意义。

作品简介与赏析

饱受饥饿之苦的赖特，在其成名作《土生子》中重点描绘了北方城市黑人青年别格的愤怒、恐惧与逃亡;在其自传《黑孩子》中,他详细描绘了自己悲惨的童年经历,以及穷苦的黑人家庭成员相依为命的艰难,以具体的事例,揭露美国南方的种族歧视,特别是白人对黑人政治上的压迫、经济上的剥削,以及文化上的偏见,成为与道格拉斯的《自述》(1845)、布克·华盛顿的《力争上游》(1901)、马尔科姆·艾克斯的《马尔科姆·艾克斯自传》(1965)以及安吉洛的《我知道笼中鸟为何歌唱》(1970)等齐名的非裔美国自传杰作,对非裔美国自传创作以及非裔美国文学均产生了比较大的影响。

《黑孩子》第一版以4岁的赖特放火烧自己家的帘子开始,以他勇敢地离开南方到芝加哥谋生结束,比较详细地描绘了敏感、孤独的黑人少年的成长历程。如果自传开始部分叙述自己烧家里帘子的破坏举动预示了他的反叛性格与抗争精神,那么他长大后北上寻找新生活的举动则不仅是其个人选择,也反映了许多南方黑人迁徙北方寻求自由的历史,与传统奴隶叙事的承继关系一目了然。更为重要的是,像许多杰出的奴隶叙事作品一样,赖特的《黑孩子》虽然讲述的是其个人的成长经历,但是却反映黑人族群在美国的社会经历与生命状态,具有比较普适的意义。

读罢此书,读者不仅了解了其父亲的佃农身份及其悲苦处境,更意识到内战后被解放的黑人与内战前的奴隶并没有本质上的区别,寻求自由依然是他们生活中的最高目标;此外,他观察到自己父母对外界的粗暴反应,他们漫无目的地发泄自己的愤怒,表明某些黑人已经内化对他们受到的压迫,并施加到自己的孩子或其他弱小者身上。对孩子的心灵伤害预示着孩子们长大成人后的愤怒与反叛——这种恶性循环的毒素始终在黑人社区弥漫,造成更多的黑人之间的相互伤害。

作为传主,赖特非常真诚,在这部自传中对自己外婆近乎迂腐的虔信宗教不无调侃,对自己小姨的莫名愤怒既反映了青春期少年的敏感多疑,也反映了寄人篱下者的心理上的不平衡及其极端表现,但是,这种对美国黑人家庭的"病理性"描绘也遭到杜波伊斯等杰出黑人学者的批判,认为这有违黑人文艺应该正面"宣传"的功能。

当然,《黑孩子》中揭示最多的还是赖特面临或遭遇的种族歧视。他描绘了白人因觊觎姨父霍斯金利润可观的酒水生意,就对其处以私刑,害得他们家人连夜逃亡的经历;以及他们无论在南方的哪个地方生活,都几乎随处可见黑人遭遇的各种不公与歧视,几乎随处可见白人警察的残暴,白人的强奸、私刑、羞辱与无端指责。在此环境下,他被迫学会了保护自己的策略,压低自己的声音,不让白人感到受到挑衅或冒犯。

《黑孩子》的力量在于,赖特不仅发现了文学的世界,也以文学的方式向世界呈现美国黑人族群的生活,让黑人自传见证美国社会的不公与歧视,让美国文学感受一种新的来自黑人族群的声音。

Chapter 13 [①]

One morning I arrived early at work and went into the bank lobby where the Negro porter was mopping. I stood at a counter and picked up the *Memphis Commercial Appeal* and began my free reading of the press. I came finally to the editorial page and saw an article dealing with one H. L. Mencken. [②] I knew by hearsay that he was the editor of the

---

① 本章重点叙述赖特通过借阅门肯等人的著作,进一步扩大眼界,并认识到文字的解放力量,预示着他后来的创作之路。

② H. L. Mencken:门肯(1880—1956),20世纪初美国著名文化批评家。

American Mercury, but aside from that I knew nothing about him. The article was a furious denunciation of Mencken, concluding with one, hot, short sentence: Mencken is a fool.

I wondered what on earth this Mencken had done to call down upon him the scorn of the South. The only people I had ever heard denounced in the South were Negroes, and this man was not a Negro. Then what ideas did Mencken hold that made a newspaper like the *Commercial Appeal* castigate him publicly? Undoubtedly he must be advocating ideas that the South did not like. Were there, then, people other than Negroes who criticized the South? I knew that during the Civil War the South had hated northern whites, but I had not encountered such hate during my life. Knowing no more of Mencken than I did at that moment, I felt a vague sympathy for him. Had not the South, which had assigned me the role of a non-man, cast at him its hardest words.

Now, how could I find out about this Mencken? There was a huge library near the riverfront, but I knew that Negroes were not allowed to patronize its shelves any more than they were the parks and playgrounds of the city. I had gone into the library several times to get books for the white men on the job. Which of them would now help me to get books? And how could I read them without causing concern to the white men with whom I worked? I had so far been success in hiding my thoughts and feelings from them, but I knew that I would create hostility if I went about this business of reading in a clumsy way.

I weighed the personalities of the men on the job. There was Don, a Jew; but I distrusted him. His position was not much better than mine and I knew that he was uneasy and insecure; he had always treated me in an offhand, bantering way that barely concealed his contempt. I was afraid to ask him to help me to get books; his frantic desire to demonstrate a racial solidarity with the whites against Negroes might make him betray me.

Then how about the boss? No, he was a Baptist and I had the suspicion that he would not be quite able to comprehend why a black boy would want to read Mencken. There were other white men on the job whose attitudes showed clearly that they were Kluxers or sympathizers, and they were out of the question.

There remained only one man whose attitude did not fit into an anti-Negro category, for I had heard the white men refer to him as a "Pope lover." He was an Irish Catholic and was hated by the white Southerners. I knew that he read books, because I had got him volumes from the library several times. Since he, too, was an object of hatred, I felt that he might refuse me but would hardly betray me. I hesitated, weighing and balancing the imponderable realities.

One morning I paused before the Catholic fellow's desk.

"I want to ask you a favor," I whispered to him.

"What is it?"

"I want to read. I can't get books from the library. I wonder if you'd let me use your card?"

He looked at me suspiciously.

"My card is full most of the time," he said.

"I see," I said and waited, posing my question silently.

"You're not trying to get me into trouble, are you, boy?" he asked, staring at me.

"Oh, no, sir."

"What book do you want?"

"A book by H. L. Mencken."

"Which one?"

"I don't know. Has he written more than one?"

"He has written several."

"I didn't know that."

"What makes you want to read Mencken?"

"Oh, I just saw his name in the newspaper," I said.

"It's good of you to want to read," he said. "But you ought to read the right things."

I said nothing. Would he want to supervise my reading?

"Let me think," he said. "I'll figure out something."

I turned from him and he called me back. He stared at me quizzically.

"Richard, don't mention this to the other white men," he said.

"I understand," I said. "I won't say a word."

A few days later he called me to him.

"I've got a card in my wife's name," he said. "Here's mine."

"Thank you, sir."

"Do you think you can manage it?"

"I'll manage fine," I said.

"If they suspect you, you'll get in trouble," he said.

"I'll write the same kind of notes to the library that you wrote when you sent me for books," I told him. "I'll sign your name."

He laughed.

"Go ahead. Let me see what you get," he said.

That afternoon I addressed myself to forging a note. Now, what were the names of books written by H. L. Mencken? I did not know any of them. I finally wrote what I thought would be a fool-proof note: Dear Madam: Will you please let this nigger boy—I used the word "nigger" to make the librarian feel that I could not possibly be the author of the note—have some books by H. L. Mencken? I forged the white man's name.

I entered the library as I had always done when on errands for whites, but I felt that I would somehow slip up and betray myself. I doffed my hat, stood a respectful distance from the desk, looked as unbookish as possible, and waited for the white patrons to be taken care of. When the desk was clear of people, I still waited. The white librarian looked at me.

"What do you want, boy?"

As though I did not possess the power of speech, I stepped forward and simply handed her the forged note, not parting my lips.

"What books by Mencken does he want?" she asked.

"I don't know, ma'am," I said, avoiding her eyes.

"Who gave you this card?"

"Mr. Falk," I said.

"Where is he?"

"He's at work, at the M—Optical Company," I said. "I've been in here for him before."

"I remember," the woman said. "But he never wrote notes like this."

Oh, God, she's suspicious. Perhaps she would not let me have the books? If she had turned her back at that moment, I would have ducked out the door and never gone back. Then I thought of a bold idea.

"You can call him up, ma'am," I said, my heart pounding.

"You're not using these books, are you?" she asked pointedly.

"Oh, no, ma'am. I can't read."

"I don't know what he wants by Mencken," she said under her breath.

I knew now that I had won; she was thinking of other things and the race question had gone out of her mind. She went to the shelves. Once or twice she looked over her shoulder at me, as though she was still doubtful. Finally she came forward with two books in her hand.

"I'm sending him two books," she said. "But tell Mr. Falk to come in next time, or send me the names of the books he wants. I don't know what he wants to read."

I said nothing. She stamped the card and handed me the books. Not daring to glance at them, I went out of the library, fearing that the woman would call me back for further questioning. A block away from the library I opened one of the books and read a title: *A Book of Prefaces*. I was nearing my nineteenth birthday and I did not know how to pronounce the word "preface." I thumbed the pages and saw strange words and strange names. I shook my head, disappointed. I looked at the other book; it was called *Prejudices*. I knew what that word meant; I had heard it all my life. And right off I was on guard against Mencken's books. Why would a man want to call a book Prejudices? The word was so stained with all my memories of racial hate that I could not conceive of anybody using it for a title. Perhaps I had made a mistake about Mencken? A man who had prejudices must be wrong.

When I showed the books to Mr. Falk, he looked at me and frowned.

"That librarian might telephone you," I warned him.

"That's all right," he said. "But when you're through reading those books, I want you to tell me what you get out of them."

That night in my rented room, while letting the hot water run over my can of pork and beans in the sink, I opened *A Book of Prefaces* and began to read. I was jarred and shocked by the style, the clear, clean, sweeping sentences. Why did he write like that? And how did one write like that? I pictured the man as a raging demon, slashing with his pen, consumed with hate, denouncing everything American, extolling everything European or German, laughing at the weaknesses of people, mocking God, authority.

What was this? I stood up, trying to realize what reality lay behind the meaning of the words ... Yes, this man was fighting, fighting with words. He was using words as a weapon, using them as one would use a club. Could words be weapons? Well, yes, for here they were. Then, maybe, perhaps, I could use them as a weapon? No. It frightened me. I read on and what amazed me was not what he said, but how on earth anybody had the courage to say it.

Occasionally I glanced up to reassure myself that I was alone in the room. Who were these men about whom Mencken was talking so passionately? Who was Anatole France? Joseph Conrad? Sinclair Lewis, Sherwood Anderson, Dostoevski, George Moor, Gustave Flaubert, Maupassant, Tolstoy, Frank Harris, Mark Twain, Thomas Hardy, Arnold Bennett, Stephen Crane, Zola, Norris, Gorky, Bergson, Ibsen, Balzac, Bernard Shaw, Dumas, Poe, Thomas Mann, O. Henry, Dreiser, H. G. Wells, Gogol, T. S. Eliot, Gide, Baudelaire, Edgar Lee Masters, Stendhal, Turgenev, Huneker, Nietzsche, and scores of others? Were these men real? Did they exist or had they existed? And how did one pronounce their names?

I ran across many words whose meanings I did not know, and I either looked them up in a dictionary or, before I had a chance to do that, encountered the word in a context that made its meaning clear. But what strange world was this? I concluded the book with the conviction that I had somehow overlooked something terribly important in life. I had once tried to write, had once reveled in feeling, had let my crude imagination roam, but the impulse to dream had been slowly beaten out of me by experience. Now it surged up again and I hungered for books, new ways of looking and seeing. It was not a matter of believing or disbelieving what I read, but of feeling something new, of being affected by something that made the look of the world different.

As dawn broke I ate my pork and beans, feeling dopey, sleepy. I went to work, but the mood of the book would not die; it lingered, coloring everything I saw, heard, did. I now felt that I knew what the white men were feeling. Merely because I had read a book that had spoken of how they lived and thought, I identified myself with that book. I felt vaguely guilty. Would I, filled with bookish notions, act in a manner that would make the whites dislike me?

I forged more notes and my trips to the library became frequent. Reading grew into a passion. My first serious novel was Sinclair Lewis's *Main Street*. [1]It made me see my boss, Mr. Gerald, and identify him as an American type. I would smile when I saw him lugging his golf bags into the office. I had always felt a vast distance separating me from the boss, and now I felt closer to him, though still distant. I felt now that I knew him, that I could feel the very limits of his narrow life. And this had happened because I had read a novel about a mythical man called George F. Babbitt.

The plots and stories in the novels did not interest me so much as the point of view

---

① Sinclair Lewis：辛克莱·刘易斯(1885—1951)，美国第一位获得诺贝尔文学奖的小说家，对美国中产阶级生活的描绘入木三分，代表作品有《大街》和《巴比特》等。

revealed. I gave myself over to each novel without reserve, without trying to criticize it; it was enough for me to see and feel something different. And for me, everything was something different. Reading was like a drug, a dope. The novels created moods in which I lived for days. But I could not conquer my sense of guilt, my feeling that the white men around me knew that I was changing, that I had begun to regard them differently.

Whenever I brought a book to the job, I wrapped it in newspaper—a habit that was to persist for years in other cities and under other circumstances. But some of the white men pried into my packages when I was absent and they questioned me.

"Boy, what are you reading those books for?"

"Oh, I don't know, sir."

"That's deep stuff you're reading, boy."

"I'm just killing time, sir."

"You'll addle your brains if you don't watch out."

I read Dreiser's *Jennie Gerhardt* and *Sister Carrie*① and they revived in me a vivid sense of my mother's suffering; I was overwhelmed. I grew silent, wondering about the life around me. It would have been impossible for me to have told anyone what I derived from these novels, for it was nothing less than a sense of life itself. All my life had shaped me for the realism, the naturalism of the modern novel, and I could not read enough of them.

Steeped in new moods and ideas, I bought a ream of paper and tried to write; but nothing would come, or what did come was flat beyond telling. I discovered that more than desire and feeling were necessary to write and I dropped the idea. Yet I still wondered how it was possible to know people sufficiently to write about them? Could I ever learn about life and people? To me, with my vast ignorance, my Jim Crow station in life, it seemed a task impossible of achievement. I now knew what being a Negro meant. I could endure the hunger. I had learned to live with hate. But to feel that there were feelings denied me, that the very breath of life itself was beyond my reach, that more than anything else hurt, wounded me. I had a new hunger.

In buoying me up, reading also cast me down, made me see what was possible, what I had missed. My tension returned, new, terrible, bitter, surging, almost too great to be contained. I no longer felt that the world about me was hostile, killing; I knew it. A million times I asked myself what I could do to save myself, and there were no answers. I seemed forever condemned, ringed by walls.

I did not discuss my reading with Mr. Falk, who had lent me his library card; it would have meant talking about myself and that would have been too painful. I smiled each day, fighting desperately to maintain my old behavior, to keep my disposition seemingly sunny. But some of the white men discerned that I had begun to brood.

"Wake up there, boy!" Mr. Olin said one day.

"Sir!" I answered for the lack of a better word.

"You act like you've stolen something," he said.

---

① Dreiser：德莱塞(Theodore Dreiser)，美国著名自然主义作家，重要作品有《嘉莉妹妹》(1900)和《美国悲剧》(1925)等。

I laughed in the way I knew he expected me to laugh, but I resolved to be more conscious of myself, to watch my every act, to guard and hide the new knowledge that was dawning within me.

If I went north, would it be possible for me to build a new life then? But how could a man build a life upon vague, unformed yearnings? I wanted to write and I did not even know the English language. I bought English grammars and found them dull. I felt that I was getting a better sense of the language from novels than from grammars. I read hard, discarding a writer as soon as I felt that I had grasped his point of view. At night the printed page stood before my eyes in sleep.

Mrs. Moss, my landlady, asked me one Sunday morning:

"Son, what is this you keep on reading?"

"Oh, nothing. Just novels."

"What you get out of 'em?"

"I'm just killing time," I said.

"I hope you know your own mind," she said in a tone which implied that she doubted if I had a mind.

I knew of no Negroes who read the books I liked and I wondered if any Negroes ever thought of them. I knew that there were Negro doctors, lawyers, newspapermen, but I never saw any of them. When I read a Negro newspaper I never caught the faintest echo of my preoccupation in its pages. I felt trapped and occasionally, for a few days, I would stop reading. But a vague hunger would come over me for books, books that opened up new avenues of feeling and seeing, and again I would forge another note to the white librarian. Again I would read and wonder as only the naïve and unlettered can read and wonder, feeling that I carried a secret, criminal burden about with me each day.

That winter my mother and brother came and we set up house-keeping, buying furniture on the installment plan, being cheated and yet knowing no way to avoid it. I began to eat warm food and to my surprise found that regular meals enabled me to read faster. I may have lived through many illnesses and survived them, never suspecting that I was ill. My brother obtained a job and we began to save toward the trip north, plotting our time, setting tentative dates for departure. I told none of the white men on the job that I was planning to go north; I knew that the moment they felt I was thinking of the North they would change toward me. It would have made them feel that I did not like the life I was living, and because my life was completely conditioned by what they said or did, it would have been tantamount to challenging them.

I could calculate my chances for life in the South as a Negro fairly clearly now.

I could fight the southern whites by organizing with other Negroes, as my grandfather had done. But I knew that I could never win that way; there were many whites and there were but few blacks. They were strong and we were weak. Outright black rebellion could never win. If I fought openly I would die and I did not want to die. News of lynchings[①] were frequent.

I could submit and live the life of a genial slave, but that was impossible. All of my life had shaped me to live by my own feelings and thoughts. I could make up to Bess and marry her and inherit the house. But that, too, would be the life of a slave; if I did that, I would crush to death something within me, and I would hate myself as much as I knew the whites already hated those who had submitted. Neither could I ever willingly present myself to be kicked, as Shorty had done. I would rather have died than do that.

I could drain off my restlessness by fighting with Shorty and Harrison. I had seen many Negroes solve the problem of being black by transferring their hatred of themselves to others with a black skin and fighting them. I would have to be cold to do that, and I was not cold and I could never be.

I could, of course, forget what I had read, thrust the whites out of my mind, forget them; and find release from anxiety and longing in sex and alcohol. But the memory of how my father had conducted himself made that course repugnant. If I did not want others to violate my life, how could I voluntarily violate it myself?

I had no hope whatever of being a professional man. Not only had I been so conditioned that I did not desire it, but the fulfillment of such an ambition was beyond my capabilities. Well-to-do Negroes lived in a world that was almost as alien to me as the world inhabited by whites.

What, then, was there? I held my life in my mind, in my consciousness each day, feeling at times that I would stumble and drop it, spill it forever. My reading had created a vast sense of distance between me and the world in which I lived and tried to make a living, and that sense of distance was increasing each day. My days and nights were one long, quiet, continuously contained dream of terror, tension, and anxiety. I wondered how long I could bear it.

Chapter 16

In the spring I took the postal examination again. Time had somewhat repaired the ravages of hunger and I was able to meet the required physical weight. We moved to a larger apartment. My increased pay made better food possible. I was happy in my own way.

Working nights, I spent my days in experimental writing, filling endless pages with stream-of-consciousness Negro dialect, trying to depict the dwellers of the Black Belt as I felt and saw them. My reading in sociology had enabled me to discern many strange types of Negro characters, to identify many modes of Negro behavior; and what moved me above all was the frequency of mental illness, that tragic toll that the urban environment exacted of the black peasant. Perhaps my writing was more an attempt at understanding

---

① lynching：美国内战结束后，南方白人至上主义的信奉者，成立 3K 党，经常不经过法律程序，私自处死敢于反抗或有反抗精神的黑人。

than self-expression. A need that I did not comprehend made me use words to create religious types, criminal types, the warped, the lost, the baffled; my pages were full of tension, frantic poverty, and death.

But something was missing in my imaginative efforts; my flights of imagination were too subjective, too lacking in reference to social action. I hungered for a grasp of the framework of contemporary living, for a knowledge of the forms of life about me, for eyes to see the bony structures of personality, for theories to light up the shadows of conduct.

While sorting mail in the post office, I met a young Irish chap whose sensibilities amazed me. We would take a batch of mail in our fingers and, while talking in low monotones out of the sides of our mouths, toss them correctly into their designated holes and suddenly our hands would be empty and we would have no memory of having worked. Most of the clerks could work in this automatic manner. The Irish chap and I had read a lot in common and we laughed at the same sacred things. He was as cynical as I was regarding uplift and hope, and we were proud of having escaped what we called the "childhood disease of metaphysical fear." I was introduced to the Irish chap's friends and we formed a "gang" of Irish, Jewish, and Negro wits who poked fun at government, the masses, statesmen, and political parties. We assumed that all people were good to the degree to which they amused us, or to the extent to which we could make them objects of laughter. We ridiculed all ideas of protest, of organized rebellion or revolution. We felt that all businessmen were thoroughly stupid and that no other group was capable of rising to challenge them. We sneered at voting, for we felt that the choice between one political crook and another was too small for serious thought. We believed that man should live by hard facts alone, and we had so long ago put God out of our minds that we did not even discuss Him.

During this cynical period I met a Negro literary group on Chicago's South Side; it was composed of a dozen or more boys and girls, all of whom possessed academic learning, economic freedom, and vague ambitions to write. I found them more formal in manner than their white counterparts; they wore stylish clothes and were finicky about their personal appearance. I had naïvely supposed that I would have much in common with them, but I found them preoccupied with twisted sex problems. Coming from a station in life which they no doubt would have branded "lower class," I could not understand why they were so all-absorbed with sexual passion. I was encountering for the first time the full-fledged Negro Puritan invert—the emotionally sick—and I discovered that their ideas were but excuses for sex, leads to sex, hints at sex, substitutes for sex. In speech and action they strove to act as un-Negro as possible, denying the racial and material foundations of their lives, accepting their class and racial status in ways so oblique that one had the impression that no difficulties existed for them. Though I had never had any assignments from a college professor, I had made much harder and more prolonged attempts at self-expression than any of them. Swearing love for art, they hovered on the edge of Bohemian life. Always friendly, they could never be anybody's friend; always reading, they could really never learn; always boasting of their passions, they could never really feel and were afraid to live.

The one group I met during those exploring days whose lives enthralled me was the Garveyites, an organization of black men and women who were forlornly seeking to return to Africa. Theirs was a passionate rejection of America, for they sensed with that directness of which only the simple are capable that they had no chance to live a full human life in America. Their lives were not cluttered with ideas in which they could only half believe; they could not create illusions which made them think they were living when they were not; their daily lives were too nakedly harsh to permit of camouflage. I understood their emotions, for I partly shared them.

The Garveyites had embraced a totally racialistic outlook which endowed them with a dignity that I had never seen before in Negroes. On the walls of their dingy flats were maps of Africa and India and Japan, pictures of Japanese generals and admirals, portraits of Marcus Garvey in gaudy regalia, the faces of colored men and women from all parts of the world. I gave no credence to the ideology of Garveyism; it was, rather, the emotional dynamics of its adherents that evoked my admiration. Those Garveyites I knew could never understand why I liked them but would never follow them, and I pitied them too much to tell them that they could never achieve their goal, that Africa was owned by the imperial powers of Europe, that their lives were alien to the mores of the natives of Africa, that they were people of the West and would forever be so until they either merged with the West or perished. It was when the Garveyites spoke fervently of building their own country, of someday living within the boundaries of a culture of their own making, that I sensed the passionate hunger of their lives, that I caught a glimpse of the potential strength of the American Negro.

Rumors of unemployment came, but I did not listen to them. I heard of the organizational efforts of the Communist party among the Negroes of the South Side, but Communist activities were too remote to strike my mind with any degree of vividness. Whenever I met a person whom I suspected of being a Communist, I talked to him affably but from an emotional distance. I sensed that something terrible was beginning to happen in the world, but I tried to shut it out of my mind by reading and writing.

When the time came for my appointment as a regular clerk, I was told that no appointments would be made for the time being. The volume of mail dropped. My hours of work dwindled. My paychecks grew small. Food became scarce at home. The hunger I thought I had left behind returned. One winter afternoon, in 1929, en route to work from the library, I passed a newsstand on which papers blazed:

Stocks Crash—Billions Fade

Most of what I had seen in newspapers had never concerned me, so why should this? Newspapers reported the doings in a life I did not share. But the volume of mail fell so low that I worked but one or two nights a week. In the post-office canteen the boys stood about and talked.

"The cops beat up some demonstrators today."

"The Reds had a picket line around the City Hall."

"Wall Street's cracking down on the country."

"Surplus production's throwing millions out of work."

"There're more than two million unemployed."

"They don't count. They're always out of work."

"Read Karl Marx and get the answer, boys."

"There'll be a revolution if this keep up."

"Hell, naw. Americans are too dumb to make a revolution."

The post-office job ended and again I was out of work. I could no longer think that the tides of economics were not my concern. But how could I have had any possible say in how the world had been run? I had grown up in complete ignorance of what created jobs. Having been thrust out of the world because of my race, I had accepted my destiny by not being curious about what shaped it.

The following summer I was again called for temporary duty in the post office, and the work lasted into the winter. Aunt Cleo succumbed to a severe cardiac condition and, hard on the heels of her illness, my brother developed stomach ulcers. To rush my worries to a climax, my mother also became ill. I felt that I was maintaining a private hospital. Finally the post-office work ceased altogether and I haunted the city for jobs. But when I went into the streets in the morning I saw sights that killed my hope for the rest of the day. Unemployed men loitered in doorways with blank looks in their eyes, sat dejectedly on front steps in shabby clothing, congregated in sullen groups on street corners, and filled all the empty benches in the parks of Chicago's South Side.

Luck of a sort came when a distant cousin of mine, who was a superintendent in a Negro burial society, offered me a position on his staff as an agent. The thought of selling insurance policies to ignorant Negroes disgusted me.

"Well, if you don't sell them, somebody else will," my cousin told me. "You've got to eat, haven't you?"

During that year I worked for several burial and insurance societies that operated among Negroes, and I received a new kind of education. I found that the burial societies, with some exceptions, were mostly "rackets." Some of them conducted their businesses legitimately, but there were many that exploited the ignorance of their black customers.

I was paid under a system that netted me fifteen dollars for every dollar's worth of new premiums that I placed upon the company's books, and for every dollar's worth of old premiums that lapsed I was penalized fifteen dollars. In addition, I was paid a commission of ten per cent on total premiums collected, but during the depression it was extremely difficult to persuade a black family to buy a policy carrying even a dime premium. I considered myself lucky if, after subtracting lapses from new business, there remained fifteen dollars that I could call my own.

This "gambling" method of remuneration was practiced by some of the burial companies because of the tremendous "turnover" in policyholders, and the companies had to have a constant stream of new business to keep afloat. Whenever a black family moved or suffered a slight reverse in fortune, it usually let its policy lapse and later bought another policy from some other company.

Each day now I saw how the Negro in Chicago lived, for I visited hundreds of dingy flats filled with rickety furniture and ill-clad children. Most of the policyholders were illiterate and did not know that their policies carried clauses severely restricting their benefit payments, and, as an insurance agent, it was not my duty to tell them.

After tramping the streets and pounding on doors to collect premiums, I was dry, strained, too tired to read or write. I hungered for relief and, as a salesman of insurance to many young black girls, I found it. There were many comely black housewives who, trying desperately to keep up their insurance payments, were willing to make bargains to escape paying a ten-cent premium. I had a long, tortured affair with one girl by paying her ten-cent premium each week. She was an illiterate black child with a baby whose father she did not know. During the entire period of my relationship with her, she had but one demand to make of me: She wanted me to take her to a circus. Just what significance circuses had for her, I was never able to learn.

After I had been with her one morning—in exchange for the dime premium—I sat on the sofa in the front room and began to read a book I had with me. She came over shyly.

"Lemme see that," she said.

"What?" I asked.

"That book," she said.

I gave her the book; she looked at it intently. I saw that she was holding it upside down.

"What's in here you keep reading?" she asked.

"Can't you really read?" I asked.

"Naw," she giggled. "You know I can't read."

"You can read some," I said.

"Naw," she said.

I stared at her and wondered just what a life like hers meant in the scheme of things, and I came to the conclusion that it meant absolutely nothing. And neither did my life mean anything.

"How come you looking at me that way for?" she asked.

"Nothing."

"You don't talk much."

"There isn't much to say."

"I wished Jim was here," she sighed.

"Who's Jim?" I asked, jealous. I knew that she had other men, but I resented her mentioning them in my presence.

"Just a friend," she said.

I hated her then, then hated myself for coming to her.

"Do you like Jim better than you like me?" I asked.

"Naw. Jim just likes to talk."

"Then why do you be with me, if you like Jim better?" I asked, trying to make an issue and feeling a wave of disgust because I wanted to.

"You all right," she said, giggling. "I like you."

"I could kill you," I said.

"What?" she exclaimed.

"Nothing," I said, ashamed.

"Kill me, you said? You crazy, man," she said.

"Maybe I am," I muttered, angry that I was sitting beside a human being to whom I could not talk, angry with myself for coming to her, hating my wild and restless loneliness.

"You oughta go home and sleep," she said. "You tired."

"What do you ever think about?" I demanded harshly.

"Lotta things."

"What, for example?"

"You," she said, smiling.

"You know I mean just one dime to you each week," I said.

"Naw, I thinka lotta you."

"Then what do you think?"

"Bout how you talk when you talk. I wished I could talk like you," she said seriously.

"Why?" I taunted her.

"When you gonna take me to a circus?" she demanded suddenly.

"You ought to be in a circus," I said.

"I'd like it," she said, her eyes shining.

I wanted to laugh, but her words sounded so sincere that I could not laugh.

"There's no circus in town," I said.

"I bet there is and you won't tell me 'cause you don't wanna take me," she said, pouting.

"But there's no circus in town, I tell you!"

"When will one come?"

"I don't know."

"Can't you read it in the papers?" she asked.

"There's nothing in the papers about a circus."

"There is," she said. "If I could read, I'd find it."

I laughed and she was hurt.

"There *is* a circus in town," she said stoutly.

"There's no circus in town," I said. "But if you want to learn to read, then I'll teach you."

She nestled at my side, giggling.

"See that word?" I said, pointing.

"Yeah."

"That's an 'and,'" I said.

She doubled, giggling.

"What's the matter?" I asked.

She rolled on the floor, giggling.

"What's so funny?" I demanded.

"You," she giggled. "You so funny."

I rose.

"The hell with you," I said.

"Don't you go and cuss me now," she said. "I don't cuss you."

"I'm sorry," I said.

I got my hat and went to the door.

"I'll see you next week?" she asked.

"Maybe," I said.

When I was on the sidewalk, she called to me from a window.

"You promised to take me to a circus, remember?"

"Yes." I walked close to the window. "What is it you like about a circus?"

"The animals," she said simply.

I felt that there was a hidden meaning, perhaps, in what she had said; but I could not find it. She laughed and slammed the window shut.

Each time I left her I resolved not to visit her again. I could not talk to her; I merely listened to her passionate desire to see a circus. She was not calculating; if she liked a man, she just liked him. Sex relations were the only relations she had ever had; no others were possible with her, so limited was her intelligence.

Most of the other agents also had their bought girls and they were extremely anxious to keep other agents from tampering with them. One day a new section of the South Side was given to me as a part of my collection area and the agent from whom the territory had been taken suddenly became very friendly with me.

"Say, Wright," he asked, "did you collect from Ewing at Champlain Avenue yet?"

"Yes," I answered, after consulting my book.

"How did you like her?" he asked, staring at me.

"She's a good-looking number," I said.

"You had anything to do with her yet?" he asked.

"No, but I'd like to," I said, laughing.

"Look," he said. "I'm a friend of yours."

"Since when?" I countered.

"No, I'm really a friend," he said.

"What's on your mind?"

"Listen, that gal's sick," he said seriously.

"What do you mean?"

"She's got the clap," he said. "Keep away from her. She'll lay with anybody."

"Gee, I'm glad you told me," I said.

"You had your eye on her, didn't you?" he asked.

"Yes, I did," I said.

"Leave her alone," he said. "She'll get you down."

That night I told my cousin what the agent had said about Miss Ewing. My cousin laughed.

"That gal's all right," he said. "That agent's been fooling around with her. He told you she had a disease so that you'd be scared to bother her. He was protecting her from you."

That was the way the black women were regarded by the black agents. Some of the agents were vicious; if they had claims to pay to a sick black woman and if the woman was able to have sex relations with them, they would insist upon it, using the claim money as a bribe. If the woman refused, they would report to the office that the woman was a malingerer. The average black woman would submit because she needed the money badly.

As an insurance agent, it was necessary for me to take part in one swindle. It appears that the burial society had originally issued a policy that was—from their point of view—too liberal in its provisions, and the officials decided to exchange the policies then in the hands of their clients for other policies carrying stricter clauses; of course, this had to be done in a manner that would not allow the policyholder to know that his policy was being switched, that he was being swindled. I did not like it, but there was only one thing I could do to keep from being a party to it: I could quit and starve. But I did not feel that being honest was worth the price of starvation.

The swindle worked in this way. In my visits to the homes of policyholders to collect premiums, I was accompanied by the superintendent who claimed to the policyholder that he was making a routine inspection. The policyholder, usually an illiterate black woman, would dig up her policy from the bottom of a trunk or a chest and hand it to the superintendent. Meanwhile I would be marking the woman's premium book, an act which would distract her from what the superintendent was doing. The superintendent would exchange the old policy for a new one which was identical in color, serial number, and beneficiary, but which carried much smaller payments. It was dirty work and I wondered how I could stop it. And when I could think of no safe way I would curse myself and the victims and forget about it. (The black owners of the burial societies were leaders in the Negro communities and were respected by whites.)

As I went from house to house collecting money, I saw black men mounted upon soapboxes at street corners, bellowing about bread, rights, and revolution. I liked their courage, but I doubted their wisdom. The speakers claimed that Negroes were angry, that they were about to rise and join their white fellow workers to make a revolution. I was in and out of many Negro homes each day and I knew that the Negroes were lost, ignorant, sick in mind and body. I saw that a vast distance separated the agitators from the masses, a distance so vast that the agitators did not know how to appeal to the people they sought to lead.

Some mornings I found leaflets on my steps telling of China, Russia, and Germany; on some days I witnessed as many as five thousand jobless Negroes, led by Communists, surging through the streets. I would watch them with an aching heart, firmly convinced that they were being duped; but if I had been asked to give them another solution for their problems, I would not have known how.

It became a habit of mine to visit Washington Park of an afternoon after collecting a part of my premiums, and I would wander through crowds of unemployed Negroes, pausing here and there to sample the dialectic or indignation of Communist speakers. What I heard and saw baffled and angered me. The Negro Communists were deliberately careless in their personal appearance, wearing their shirt collars turned in to make V's at their throats, wearing their caps—they wore caps because Lenin had worn caps—with the visors turned backward, tilted upward at the nape of their necks. Many of their mannerisms, pronunciations, and turns of speech had been consciously copied from white Communists whom they had recently met. While engaged in conversation, they stuck their thumbs in their suspenders or put their left hands into their shirt bosoms or hooked their thumbs into their back pockets as they had seen Lenin or Stalin do in photographs. Though they did not know it, they were naïvely practicing magic; they thought that if they acted like the men who had overthrown the czar, then surely they ought to be able to win their freedom in America.

In speaking they rolled their "r's" in Continental style, pronouncing "party" as "parrrtee," stressing the last syllable, having picked up the habit from white Communists. "Comrades" became "cumrrrades," and "distribute," which they had known how to pronounce all their lives, was twisted into "distrrribuuute," with the accent on the last instead of the second syllable, a mannerism which they copied from Polish Communist immigrants who did not know how to pronounce the word. Many sensitive Negroes agreed with the Communist program but refused to join their ranks because of the shabby quality of those Negroes whom the Communists had already admitted to membership.

When speaking from the platform, the Negro Communists, eschewing the traditional gestures of the Negro preacher—as though they did not possess the strength to develop their own style of Communist preaching—stood straight, threw back their heads, brought the edge of the right palm down hammerlike into the outstretched left palm in a series of jerky motions to pound their points home, a mannerism that characterized Lenin's method of speaking. When they walked, their stride quickened; all the peasant hesitancy of their speech vanished as their voices became clipped, terse. In debate they interrupted their opponents in a tone of voice that was an octave higher, and if their opponents raised their voices to be heard, the Communists raised theirs still higher until shouts rang out over the park. Hence, the only truth that prevailed was that which could be shouted and quickly understood.

Their emotional certainty seemed buttressed by access to a fund of knowledge denied to ordinary men, but a day's observation of their activities was sufficient to reveal all their thought processes. An hour's listening disclosed the fanatical intolerance of minds sealed against new ideas, new facts, new feelings, new attitudes, new hints at ways to live. They denounced books they had never read, people they had never known, ideas they could never understand, and doctrines whose names they could not pronounce. Communism, instead of making them leap forward with fire in their hearts to become masters of ideas and life, had frozen them at an even lower level of ignorance than had been theirs before they met Communism.

When Hoover threatened to drive the bonus marchers from Washington, one Negro Communist speaker said:

"If he drives the bonus marchers out of Washington, the people will rise up and make a revolution!"

I went to him, determined to get at what he really meant.

"You know that even if the United States Army actually kills the bonus marchers, there'll be no revolution," I said.

"You don't know the indignation of the masses!" he exploded.

"But you don't seem to know what it takes to make a revolution," I explained. "Revolutions are rare occurrences."

"You underestimate the masses," he told me.

"No, I know the masses of Negroes very well," I said. "But I don't believe that a revolution is pending. Revolutions come through concrete historical processes ..."

"You're an intellectual," he said, smiling disdainfully.

A few days later, after Hoover had had the bonus marchers driven from Washington at the point of bayonets, I accosted him:

"What about that revolution you predicted if the bonus marchers were driven out?" I asked.

"The prerequisite conditions did not exist," he shrugged and muttered.

I left him, wondering why he felt it necessary to make so many ridiculous overstatements. I could not refute the general Communist analysis of the world; the only drawback was that their world was just too simple for belief. I liked their readiness to act, but they seemed lost in folly, wandering in a fantasy. For them there was no yesterday or tomorrow, only the living moment of today; their only task was to annihilate the enemy that confronted them in any manner possible.

At times their speeches, glowing with rebellion, were downright offensive to lowly, hungry Negroes. Once a Negro Communist speaker, inveighing against religion, said:

"There ain't no goddamn God! If there is, I hereby challenge Him to strike me dead!"

He paused dramatically before his vast black audience for God to act, but God declined. He then pulled out his watch.

"Maybe God didn't hear me!" he yelled. "I'll give Him two more minutes!" Then, with sarcasm: "Mister God, kill me!"

He waited, looking mockingly at his watch. The audience laughed uneasily.

"I'll tell you where to find God," the speaker went on in a hard, ranting voice. "When it rains at midnight, take your hat, turn it upside down on a floor in a dark room, and you'll have God!"

I had to admit that I had never heard atheism of so militant a nature; but the Communist speaker seemed to be amusing and frightening the people more than he was convincing them.

"If there is a God up there in that empty sky," the speaker roared on, "I'll reach up there and grab Him by His beard and jerk Him down here on this hungry earth and cut His throat!" He wagged his head. "Now, let God dare me!"

The audience was shocked into silence for a moment, then it yelled with delight. I shook my head and walked away. That was not the way to destroy people's outworn beliefs ... They were acting like irresponsible children ...

I was now convinced that they did not know the complex nature of Negro life, did not know how great was the task to which they had set themselves. They had rejected the state of things as they were, and that seemed to me to be the first step toward embracing a creative attitude toward life. I felt that it was not until one wanted the world to be different that one could look at the world with will and emotion. But these men had rejected what was before their eyes without quite knowing what they had rejected and why.

I felt that the Negro could not live a full, human life under the conditions imposed upon him by America; and I felt, too, that America, for different reasons, could not live a full, human life. It seemed to me, then, that if the Negro solved his problem, he would be solving infinitely more than his problem alone. I felt certain that the Negro could never solve his problem until the deeper problem of American civilization had been faced and solved. And because the Negro was the most cast-out of all the outcast people in America, I felt that no other group in America could tackle this problem of what our American lives meant so well as the Negro could.

But, as I listened to the Communist Negro speakers, I wondered if the Negro, blasted by three hundred years of oppression, could possibly cast off his fear and corruption and rise to the task. Could the Negro ever possess himself, learn to know what had happened to him in relation to the aspirations of Western society? It seemed to me that for the Negro to try to save himself he would have to forget himself and try to save a confused, materialistic nation from its own drift toward self-destruction. Could the Negro accomplish this miracle? Could he take up his bed and walk?

Election time was nearing and a Negro Republican precinct captain asked me to help him round up votes. I had no interest in the candidates, but I needed the money. I went from door to door with the precinct captain and discovered that the whole business was one long process of bribery, that people voted for three dollars, for the right to continue their illicit trade in sex or alcohol. On election day, I went into the polling booth and drew the curtain behind me and unfolded my ballots. As I stood there the sordid implications of politics flashed through my mind. "Big Bill" Thompson headed the local Republican machine and I knew that he was using the Negro vote to control the city hall; in turn, he was engaged in vast political deals of which the Negro voters, political innocents, had no notion. With my pencil I wrote in a determined scrawl across the face of the ballots:

I Protest This Fraud

I knew that my gesture was futile. But I wanted somebody to know that out of that vast sea of ignorance in the Black Belt there was at least one person who knew the game for what it was. I collected my ten dollars and went home.

The depression deepened and I could not sell insurance to hungry Negroes. I sold my watch and scouted for cheaper rooms; I found a rotting building and rented an apartment in it. The place was dismal; plaster was falling from the walls; the wooden stairs sagged. When my mother saw it, she wept. I felt bleak. I had not done what I had come to the city to do.

One morning I rose and my mother told me that there was no food for breakfast. I knew that the city had opened relief stations, but each time I thought of going into one of them I burned with shame. I sat for hours, fighting hunger, avoiding my mother's eyes. Then I rose, put on my hat and coat, and went out. As I walked toward the Cook County Bureau of Public Welfare to plead for bread, I knew that I had come to the end of something.

Questions for Discussion

1. Why do you think that Richard Wright wants to read H. L. Mencken? What has he got in reading Mencken's writings?
2. Richard Wright has a new hunger after his reading more books, what is he hungry for?
3. Knowing that he could fight but could not win, and he does not want to be indulged in sex and alcohol, Richard Wright plans to go to North. Do you think it is a good choice?
4. In Chapter 16, Richard Wright mentions "that the Negro could not live a full, human life under the conditions imposed upon him by America; and I felt, too, that America, for different reasons, could not live a full, human life." How to understand this, and is there any alternative to this situation?

7. Autobiography of Malcolm X

作者简介

马尔科姆·艾克斯(Malcolm X)(1925—1965),原名马尔科姆·里特(Malcolm Little),是演说家、美国黑人民权活动家,与马丁·路德·金齐名的美国黑人民权运动领袖。1925 年 5 月 19 日,马尔科姆出生于美国内布拉斯加州的奥马哈,是家中的第三个儿子,父母是马库斯·加维所创建的"全球黑人促进会"的积极成员,父母从事的事业最终帮助塑造了他的泛非主义的立场,体现在他对文化、人权、政治斗争以及世界历史的一系列观点之中。在奥马哈的家园被三K党烧毁之后,他们举家迁居到密歇根州的兰辛,里特夫妇关于黑人自豪、经济独立、文化完整性的种种言论触动了兰辛当地白人社会的敏感神经,终于招来杀身之祸,父亲 1931 年丧生于车轮之下,母亲悲愤不已,精神失常,在精神病院度过了 24 年。

遭遇这些家庭变故之后,几个孩子被法庭安置到不同的孤儿院,马尔科姆被一白人家庭领养,他非常聪明,学业优异,因不堪种族歧视,于 15 岁那年突然辍学,后彻底中断学业,次年年初,他前往底特律,开始一段新的人生。他先后打过各种零工,擦鞋、卖货、跟车、跑堂,不一而足;也到过不少地方,如波士顿、纽约等,最后堕入行窃、赌博、吸毒、拉皮条的行列,1946 年,他因盗窃罪(更因为与白人女性有染)被送进监狱服刑。

在入狱服刑的六年时间里,马尔科姆再次重塑了自己,也因此改变了他后半生的命运。他从美国"伊斯兰国"精神领袖伊莱贾·穆罕默德的教导中获得安慰,高度认同其关于家庭生活的重要性、黑人自豪、经济独立、掌握文化、节俭、自律等方面的思想,在"伊斯兰国"教士的影响下,他在狱中发愤学习,利用监狱图书馆阅读了大量经典书籍,他还在狱中磨练辩才,利用自己的才智帮助黑人狱友争取权利,最终完成了精神上的重塑。1950 年,他更名马尔科姆·艾克斯,表示遵从"伊斯兰国"的教义,成为坚定的穆斯林。出狱后,他追随穆罕默德,成为"伊斯兰国"的重要传教士。

1963 年 11 月,由于对美国总统约翰·肯尼迪遇刺身亡事件发表了违反组织原则的"政治不正确"言论,马尔克姆被"伊斯兰国"封口三个月。随后,他与"伊斯兰国"教主穆罕默德的矛盾公开化,终于翌年 4 月脱离该组织。不久,马尔克姆前往伊斯兰圣地麦加朝觐,宣布改奉逊尼派,并再次更名为艾尔-哈吉·马立克·艾尔-夏巴兹(El Hajj Malik El Shabazz),完成自己一生中的第三次也是最后一次重塑。他抛弃之前激烈的黑白分离主张,成立穆斯林清真寺社团,以及非裔美国人团结组织,寻求与不同宗教、种族的民权运动人士合作。1965 年 2 月 21 日,已多次领略人身安全威胁的马尔克姆遇刺身亡。

批评他的人认为,他集煽动、传播暴力、仇恨、黑人优越主义、种族主义、反犹太主义于一身;肯定者则认为,他是非裔美国人权利的提倡者,也是美国种族暴行的有力批判者。

作品简介与赏析

《马尔科姆·艾克斯自传》是由传主马尔科姆在 1963 至 1965 年间本人口述,著名作家阿列克斯·黑利记录整理,并于 1965 年出版的传记文学名作,1988 年被《时代周刊》评为"十大必读非虚构作品之一"。《自传》以其女儿的前言开始,以阿列克斯的后记结束,正文共 19 章,忠实地再现了传主从一个混迹街头的不羁少年成长为一位举世闻名的美国黑人民权运动领袖的励志传奇、充满奋斗、短暂而充实的一生。

他的一生可以说充满戏剧性的转折。马尔科姆在《自传》中将自己的人生历程划分成三个清晰可辨的阶段，每个阶段都有一个不同的名字，他分别从马尔科姆·里特变成马尔科姆·艾克斯，再到艾尔-哈吉·马立克·艾尔-夏巴兹，标志着每个成长阶段的心智发展和精神上的浴火重生。父辈几乎全部死于白人的迫害，母亲又由于受打击而被送进精神病院。年幼的他由于没有经济支持而被迫在当时黑人社会的底层成长。他做过擦鞋童、饭店侍者、火车服务生，最后在纽约做起了倒卖彩票的生意。由于和当时的合作伙伴关系恶化，他被迫又回到了原来所住的波士顿，在那里当起了毒品贩子，他不仅倒卖，自己也同时染上了各种不良恶习，每天处于"牲畜"般的生活之中。之后，他又开始行窃，最终自食恶果，被投进监狱，服刑十年。在狱中，他在自己兄弟的影响下，接受了穆斯林的思想，博览群书，开始自学历史、社会学、哲学，等等。

出狱之后，马尔科姆正式加入美国黑人穆斯林的行列，并努力把最初只有几百人规模的黑人穆斯林扩大到了全美几十个穆斯林教点。他要求黑人同胞们摆脱白人的统治，建立自己的社会和法律体系，认识到自己真正的根是在非洲大陆，美国并不是他们真正的国家。他反对白人社会中信奉的基督教，并提出所谓的金发碧眼的白人耶稣基督实际上只可能是除了白色以外的任何颜色。他指出黑人在膜拜这个白色皮肤耶稣的时候也被白人深深地毒害了。

马尔科姆能言善辩，领导能力卓众，声望日隆，在媒体大众面前声名鹊起，赢得了美国社会的广泛关注，但这也招致他自己的穆斯林弟兄的嫉妒，他们纷纷和他断绝了关系。马尔科姆承受了背叛、摈弃，失去了当时他唯一信赖的同教兄弟姐妹的支持，但是他没有倒下去，相反，他建立起自己独立的穆斯林组织，更远赴非洲等地，并特地赶去了穆斯林圣地麦加，参加全世界穆斯林的盛大集会。在那里，他声称自己感受到一生从未感受到的来自不同肤色的平等、团结和友爱。这次旅行改变了他的思想。

回到美国后，马尔科姆开始接受一些正直白人的友好帮助，同时也修正了自己的立场，他希望团结一切渴望平等、自由的兄弟姊妹，共同营造起一个真正民主和平的环境。

本节选是《马尔科姆·艾克斯自传》的第九章，主要叙述了马尔科姆在波士顿的浪荡不羁的街头生活及其被捕入狱的前因后果，可视为整部传记的转折点。波士顿开启了马尔科姆的人生道路上的一个重要篇章，在那里他开始亲身体验美国社会底层黑人的生活，并逐渐成长为一名游戏人生的街头小人物，几乎参与了当时美国社会底层黑人所经历的一切，贩毒吸毒，走私酒，赌博，拉皮条，入室行窃，混迹于舞厅酒吧、街头巷尾，春风得意，游刃有余。凡此种种，使他对当时社会的规则和人性的幽暗以及黑人与白人的关系谙熟于胸，银铛入狱后，对白人女性同伙的轻判与对他自己的重判更使得他对美国的司法制度的本质有了深刻的了解，打家劫舍偷盗财物算不上重罪，俘获漂亮白人女子芳心使她们与之沆瀣一气才是弥天大罪，冒天下之大不韪。另一方面，马尔科姆虽然浪荡不羁堕落不堪，但他仍不失赤子之心，对朋友的兄弟情义，对兄弟姐妹的同胞温情，在本章中也表现得淋漓尽致。

从叙事的角度来看，这部自传所采用的第一人称叙事使得传主马尔科姆将自己的亲身经历与所见所闻忠实地传递给读者，令读者感觉身临其境，极大地增强了传记中所叙述事件的即视性和现场感，本章前半部分叙事者对马尔科姆与约翰·休斯之间赌局的叙述堪称经典，其中对赌场紧张刺激的氛围的描述，对赌客心理的细致揣摩，对赌技的极致把握，无不曲尽其妙，读者仿佛置身于戏院欣赏一场惊心动魄的大戏，欲罢不能。本章中后半部分中传主与警方的直面交锋，与白人女友丈夫的战友的狭路相逢，以及最后在钟表修理店被警方布控围捕等一系列叙述都值得细读。不仅如此，细心的读者会发现传记文本中存在着双重声音，一个声音来自过去不断经事的年轻的传主,充当叙事者讲述发生的事件,另一个声音来自撰述自传的后来的传主,充当权威对过去发生的事件进行解释、评判和剖析。

就这部传记文学性而言,传主一生当中的三次重大改变所反映出来的心路历程可与早已成为经典的圣奥古斯丁的《忏悔录》媲美,传记作者黑利与传主之间的合作,传主的信任和坦诚,作者对于叙事距离的精心掌控,又让读者联想到英国文学史上鲍斯韦尔与约翰逊博士之间合作完成的经典之作《约翰逊传》。

Chapter 9
Caught

Ella couldn't believe how atheist①, how uncouth I had become. I believed that a man should do anything that he was slick enough, or bad and bold enough, to do and that a woman was nothing but another commodity. Every word I spoke was hip or profane. I would bet that my working vocabulary wasn't two hundred words.

Even Shorty, whose apartment I now again shared, wasn't prepared for how I lived and thought—like a predatory② animal. Sometimes I would catch him watching me.

At first, I slept a lot—even at night. I had slept mostly in the daytime during the preceding two years. When awake, I smoked reefers③. Shorty had originally introduced me to marijuana④, and my consumption of it now astounded him.

I didn't want to talk much, at first. When awake, I'd play records continuously. The reefers gave me a feeling of contentment. I would enjoy hours of floating, day dreaming, imaginary conversations with my New York musician friends.

Within two weeks, I'd had more sleep than during any two months when I had been in Harlem hustling day and night. When I finally went out in the Roxbury⑤ streets, it took me only a little while to locate a peddler of "snow"—cocaine. It was when I got back into that familiar snow feeling that I began to want to talk.

Cocaine produces, for those who sniff its powdery white crystals, an illusion of supreme well-being, and a soaring over-confidence in both physical and mental ability. You think you could whip the heavyweight champion, and that you are smarter than anybody. There was also that feeling of timelessness. And there were intervals of ability to recall and review things that had happened years back with an astonishing clarity.

Shorty's band played at spots around Boston three or four nights a week. After he left for work, Sophia would come over and I'd talk about my plans. She would be gone back to her husband by the time Shorty returned from work, and I'd bend his ear⑥ until daybreak.

Sophia's husband had gotten out of the military, and he was some sort of salesman. He was supposed to have a big deal going which soon would require his traveling a lot to the

---

① atheist:无神论的,不敬神的,不虔诚的。
② predatory:以捕食其他动物为生的,掠夺性的。
③ reefer:大麻烟卷。
④ marijuana:大麻毒品。
⑤ Roxbury:罗克斯伯里,波士顿一地名。
⑥ bend one's ear:与某人喋喋不休。

West Coast. I didn't ask questions, but Sophia often indicated they weren't doing too well. I know I had nothing to do with that. He never dreamed I existed. A white woman might blow up at her husband and scream and yell and call him every name she can think of, and say the most vicious things in an effort to hurt him, and talk about his mother and his grandmother, too, but one thing she never will tell him herself is that she is going with a black man. That's one automatic red murder flag to the white man, and his woman knows it.

Sophia always had given me money. Even when I had hundreds of dollars in my pocket, when she came to Harlem I would take everything she had short of her train fare back to Boston. It seems that some women love to be exploited. When they are not exploited, they exploit the man. Anyway, it was his money that she gave me, I guess, because she never had worked. But now my demands on her increased, and she came up with more; again, I don't know where she got it. Always, every now and then, I had given her a hard time, just to keep her in line. Every once in a while a woman seems to need, in fact wants this, too. But now, I would feel evil and slap her around worse than ever, some of the nights when Shorty was away. She would cry, curse me, and swear that she would never be back. But I knew she wasn't even thinking about not coming back.

Sophia's being around was one of Shorty's greatest pleasures about my homecoming. I have said it before, I never in my life have seen a black man that desired white women as sincerely as Shorty did. Since I had known him, he had had several. He had never been able to keep a white woman any length of time, though, because he was too good to them, and, as I have said, any woman, white or black, seems to get bored with that.

It happened that Shorty was between white women when one night Sophia brought to the house her seventeen-year-old sister. I never saw anything like the way that she and Shorty nearly jumped for each other. For him, she wasn't only a white girl, but a young white girl. For her, he wasn't only a Negro, but a Negro musician. In looks, she was a younger version of Sophia, who still turned heads. Sometimes I'd take the two girls to Negro places where Shorty played. Negroes showed thirty-two teeth apiece as soon as they saw the white girls. They would come over to your booth, or your table; they would stand there and drool. And Shorty was no better. He'd stand up there playing and watching that young girl waiting for him, and waving at him, and winking. As soon as the set was over, he'd practically run over people getting down to our table.

I didn't lindy-hop① any more now, I wouldn't even have thought of it now, just as I wouldn't have been caught in a zoot suit② now. All of my suits were conservative. A banker might have worn my shoes.

I met Laura again. We were really glad to see each other. She was a lot more like me now, a good-time girl. We talked and laughed. She looked a lot older than she really was. She had no one man, she free-lanced around. She had long since moved away from her

---

① lindy-hop:跳林迪舞,林迪舞是源于纽约哈勒姆区的一种黑人舞蹈,在 20 世纪 30 年代和 40 年代尤为流行。
② zoot suit:佐特套服,流行于 20 世纪 40 年代的一种男装,上衣肩宽而长,裤子高腰裤口狭窄。

grandmother. Laura told me she had finished school, but then she gave up the college idea. Laura was high whenever I saw her, now, too; we smoked some reefers together.

After about a month of "laying dead," as inactivity was called, I knew I had to get some kind of hustle going.

A hustler, broke, needs a stake. Some nights when Shorty was playing, I would take whatever Sophia had been able to get for me, and I'd try to run it up into something, playing stud poker① at John Hughes' gambling house.

When I had lived in Roxbury before, John Hughes had been a big gambler who wouldn't have spoken to me. But during the war the Roxbury "wire" had carried a lot about things I was doing in Harlem, and now the New York name magic was on me. That was the feeling that hustlers everywhere else had: if you could hustle and make it in New York, they were well off to know you; it gave them prestige. Anyway, through the same flush war years, John Hughes had hustled profitably enough to be able to open a pretty good gambling house.

John, one night, was playing in a game I was in. After the first two cards were dealt around the table, I had an ace showing. I looked beneath it at my hole card②; another ace—a pair, back-to-back.

My ace showing made it my turn to bet.

But I didn't rush. I sat there and studied.

Finally, I knocked my knuckles on the table, passing, leaving the betting to the next man. My action implied that beneath my ace was some "nothing" card that I didn't care to risk my money on.

The player sitting next to me took the bait. He bet pretty heavily. And the next man raised him. Possibly each of them had small pairs. Maybe they just wanted to scare me out before I drew another ace. Finally, the bet reached John, who had a queen showing; he raised everybody.

Now, there was no telling what John had. John truly was a clever gambler. He could gamble as well as anybody I had gambled with in New York.

So the bet came back to me. It was going to cost me a lot of money to call all the raises. Some of them obviously had good cards but I knew I had every one of them beat. But again I studied, and studied; I pretended perplexity. And finally I put in my money, calling the bets.

The same betting pattern went on, with each new card, right around to the last card. And when that last card went around, I hit another ace in sight. Three aces. And John hit another queen in sight.

He bet a pile. Now, everyone else studied a long time—and, one by one, all folded

---

① stud poker:明扑克,种马扑克,五张牌玩法发牌时第一张牌面朝下,随后 4 张牌面朝上,发牌后下注;七张牌玩法发牌时头两张和最后一张都是牌面朝下,中间 4 张牌面朝上。

② hole card:牌面朝下发出的牌。

their hands. Except me. All I could do was put what I had left on the table.

If I'd had the money, I could have raised five hundred dollars or more, and he'd have had to call me. John couldn't have gone the rest of his life wondering if I had bluffed[①] him out of a pot that big.

I showed my hole card ace; John had three queens. As I hauled in the pot, something over five hundred dollars—my first real stake in Boston—John got up from the table. He'd quit. He told his house man, "Anytime Red comes in here and wants anything, let him have it." He said, "I've never seen a young man play his hole card like he played."

John said "young man," being himself about fifty, I guess, although you can never be certain about a Negro's age. He thought, as most people would have, that I was about thirty. No one in Roxbury except my sisters Ella and Mary suspected my real age.

The story of that poker game helped my on-scene reputation among the other gamblers and hustlers around Roxbury. Another thing that happened in John's gambling house contributed: the incident that made it known that I carried not a gun, but some guns.

John had a standing rule that anyone who came into the place to gamble had to check his guns if he had any. I always checked two guns. Then, one night, when a gambler tried to pull something slick, I drew a third gun, from its shoulder holster. This added to the rest of my reputation the word that I was "trigger-happy" and "crazy."

Looking back, I think I really was at least slightly out of my mind. I viewed narcotics[②] as most people regard food. I wore my guns as today I wear my neckties. Deep down, I actually believed that after living as fully as humanly possible, one should then die violently. I expected then, as I still expect today, to die at any time. But then, I think I deliberately invited death in many, sometimes insane, way.

For instance, a merchant marine sailor who knew me and my reputation came into a bar carrying a package. He motioned me to follow him downstairs into the men's room. He unwrapped a stolen machine gun; he wanted to sell it. I said, "How do I know it works?" He loaded it with a cartridge clip[③], and told me that all I would have to do then was squeeze the trigger release. I took the gun, examined it, and the first thing he knew I had it jammed right up in his belly. I told him I would blow him wide open. He went backwards out of the restroom and up the stairs the way Bill "Bojangles" Robinson[④] used to dance going backwards. He knew I was crazy enough to kill him. I was insane enough not to consider that he might just wait his chance to kill me. For perhaps a month I kept the machine gun at Shorty's before I was broke and sold it.

When Reginald came to Roxbury visiting, he was shocked at what he'd found out upon returning to Harlem. I spent some time with him. He still was the kid brother whom I still felt more "family" toward than I felt now even for our sister Ella. Ella still liked me. I

---

① bluff: 虚张声势。

② narcotics: 麻醉剂，致幻毒品。

③ cartridge clip: 弹夹。

④ Bill "Bojangles" Robinson: 比尔·罗宾逊(1878—1949)，the most famous of all African American tap dancers in the twentieth century. 美国好莱坞和百老汇的舞蹈家，以和秀兰·邓波儿在30年代影片中合演的角色而出名。

would go to see her once in a while. But Ella had never been able to reconcile herself to the way I had changed. She has since told me that she had a steady foreboding that I was on my way into big trouble. But I always had the feeling that Ella somehow admired my rebellion against the world, because she, who had so much more drive and guts than most men, often felt stymied by having been born female.

Had I been thinking only in terms of myself, maybe I would have chosen steady gambling as a hustle. There were enough chump① gamblers that hung around John Hughes' for a good gambler to make a living off them; chumps that worked, usually. One would just have to never miss the games on their paydays. Besides, John Hughes had offered me a job dealing for games; I didn't want that.

But I had come around to thinking not only of myself. I wanted to get something going that could help Shorty, too. We had been talking; I really felt sorry for Shorty. The same old musician story. The so-called glamor of being a musician, earning just about enough money so that after he paid rent and bought his reefers and food and other routine things, he had nothing left. Plus debts. How could Shorty have anything? I'd spent years in Harlem and on the road around the most popular musicians, the "names," even, who really were making big money for musicians—and they had nothing.

For that matter, all the thousands of dollars I'd handled, and I had nothing. Just satisfying my cocaine habit alone cost me about twenty dollars a day. I guess another five dollars a day could have been added for reefers and plain tobacco cigarettes that I smoked; besides getting high on drugs, I chain-smoked as many as four packs a day. And, if you ask me today, I'll tell you that tobacco, in all its forms, is just as much an addiction as any narcotic.

When I opened the subject of a hustle with Shorty, I started by first bringing him to agree with my concept—of which he was a living proof—that only squares kept on believing they could ever get anything by slaving.

And when I mentioned what I had in mind—house burglary—Shorty, who always had been so relatively conservative, really surprised me by how quickly he agreed. He didn't even know anything about burglarizing.

When I began to explain how it was done, Shorty wanted to bring in this friend of his, whom I had met, and liked, called Rudy.

Rudy's mother was Italian, his father was a Negro. He was born right therein Boston, a short, light fellow, a pretty boy type. Rudy worked regularly for an employment agency that sent him to wait on tables at exclusive parties. He had a side deal going, a hustle that took me right back to the old steering days in Harlem. Once a week, Rudy went to the home of this old, rich Boston blueblood, pillar-of-society aristocrat. He paid Rudy to undress them both, then pick up the old man like a baby, lay him on his bed, then stand over him and sprinkle him all over with talcum powder②.

---

① chump:傻瓜,笨蛋。
② talcum powder:滑石粉。

Rudy said the old man would actually reach his climax from that.

I told him and Shorty about some of the things I'd seen. Rudy said that as far as he knew, Boston had no organized specialty sex houses, just individual rich whites who had their private specialty desires catered to by Negroes who came to their homes camouflaged① as chauffeurs, maids, waiters, or some other accepted image. Just as in New York, these were the rich, the highest society—the predominantly old men, past the age of ability to conduct any kind of ordinary sex, always hunting for new ways to be "sensitive."

Rudy, I remember, spoke of one old white man who paid a black couple to let him watch them have intercourse on his bed. Another was so "sensitive" that he paid to sit on a chair outside a room where a couple was—he got his satisfaction just from imagining what was going on inside.

A good burglary team includes, I knew, what is called a "finder." A finder is one who locates lucrative places to rob. Another principal need is someone able to "case" these places' physical layouts—to determine means of entry, the best getaway routes, and so forth. Rudy qualified on both counts. Being sent to work in rich homes, he wouldn't be suspected when he sized up their loot and cased the joint, just running around looking busy with a white coat on.

Rudy's reaction, when he was told what we had in mind, was something, I remember, like "Man, when do we start?"

But I wasn't rushing off half-cocked. I had learned from some of the pros, and from my own experience, how important it was to be careful and plan. Burglary, properly executed, though it had its dangers, offered the maximum chances of success with the minimum risk. If you did your job so that you never met any of your victims, it first lessened your chances of having to attack or perhaps kill someone. And if through some slip-up you were caught, later, by the police, there was never a positive eyewitness.

It is also important to select an area of burglary and stick to that. There are specific specialities (*sic*) among burglars. Some work apartments only, others houses only, others stores only, or warehouses; still others will go after only safes or strongboxes.

Within the residence burglary category, there are further specialty distinctions. There are the day burglars, the dinner and theater-time burglars, the night burglars. I think that any city's police will tell you that very rarely do they find one type who will work at another time. For instance Jumpsteady, in Harlem, was a nighttime apartment specialist. It would have been hard to persuade Jumpsteady to work in the daytime if a millionaire had gone out for lunch and left his front door wide open.

I had one very practical reason never to work in the daytime, aside from my inclinations. With my high visibility, I'd have been sunk in the daytime. I could just hear people: "A reddish-brown Negro over six feet tall." One glance would be enough.

---

① camouflage：伪装。

Setting up what I wanted to be the perfect operation, I thought about pulling the white girls into it for two reasons. One was that I realized we'd be too limited relying only upon places where Rudy worked as a waiter. He didn't get to work in too many places; it wouldn't be very long before we ran out of sources. And when other places had to be found and cased in the rich, white residential areas, Negroes hanging around would stick out like sore thumbs, but these white girls could get invited into the right places.

I disliked the idea of having too many people involved, all at the same time. But with Shorty and Sophia's sister so close now, and Sophia and me as though we had been together for fifty years, and Rudy as eager and cool as he was, nobody would be apt to spill, everybody would be under the same risk; we would be like a family unit.

I never doubted that Sophia would go along. Sophia would do anything I said. And her sister would do anything that Sophia said. They both went for it. Sophia's husband was away on one of his trips to the coast when I told her and her sister.

Most burglars, I knew, were caught not on the job, but trying to dispose of the loot①. Finding the fence② we used was a rare piece of luck. We agreed upon the plan for operations. The fence didn't work with us directly. He had a representative, an ex-con, who dealt with me, and no one else in my gang. Aside from his regular business, he owned around Boston several garages and small warehouses. The arrangement was that before a job, I would alert the representative, and give him a general idea of what we expected to get, and he'd tell me at which garage or warehouse we should make the drop. After we had made our drop, the representative would examine the stolen articles. He would remove all identifying marks from everything. Then he would call the fence, who would come and make a personal appraisal. The next day the representative would meet me at a prearranged place and would make the payment for what we had stolen—in cash.

One thing I remember. This fence always sent your money in crisp, brand-new bills. He was smart. Somehow that had a very definite psychological effect upon all of us, after we had pulled a job, walking around with that crisp green money in our pockets. He may have had other reasons.

We needed a base of operations—not in Roxbury. The girls rented an apartment in Harvard Square. Unlike Negroes, these white girls could go shopping for the locale and physical situation we wanted. It was on the ground floor, where, moving late at night, all of us could come and go without attracting notice.

In any organization, someone must be the boss. If it's even just one person, you've got to be the boss of yourself.

At our gang's first meeting in the apartment, we discussed how we were going to work. The girls would get into houses to case them by ringing bells and saying they were saleswomen, poll-takers, college girls making a survey, or anything else suitable. Once in

---

① loot:抢劫。
② fence:收受贼赃者,买卖赃物的人。

the houses, they would get around as much as they could without attracting attention. Then, back, they would report what special valuables they had seen, and where. They would draw the layout for Shorty, Rudy, and me. We agreed that the girls would actually burglarize only in special cases where there would be some advantage. But generally the three men would go, two of us to do the job while the third kept watch in the getaway car, with the motor running.

Talking to them, laying down the plans, I had deliberately sat on a bed away from them. All of a sudden, I pulled out my gun, shook out all five bullets, and then let them see me put back only one bullet. I twirled the cylinder①, and put the muzzle② to my head.

"Now, I'm going to see how much guts all of you have," I said.

I grinned at them. All of their mouths had flapped open. I pulled the trigger—we all heard it click.

"I'm going to do it again, now."

They begged me to stop. I could see in Shorty's and Rudy's eyes some idea of rushing me.

We all heard the hammer *click* on another empty cylinder.

The women were in hysterics. Rudy and Shorty were begging, "*Man ... Red ... cut it out, man! ... Freeze!*" I pulled the trigger once more.

"I'm doing this, showing you I'm not afraid to die," I told them. "Never cross a man not afraid to die ... now, let's get to work!"

I never had one moment's trouble with any of them after that. Sophia acted awed, her sister all but called me "Mr. Red." Shorty and Rudy were never again quite the same with me. Neither of them ever mentioned it. They thought I was crazy. They were afraid of me.

We pulled the first job that night—the place of the old man who hired Rudy to sprinkle him with talcum powder. A cleaner job couldn't have been asked for. Everything went like clockwork. The fence was full of praise; he proved he meant it with his crisp, new money. The old man later told Rudy how a small army of detectives had been there— and they decided that the job had the earmarks③ of some gang which had been operating around Boston for about a year.

We quickly got it down to a science. The girls would scout and case in wealthy neighborhoods. The burglary would be pulled; sometimes it took no more than ten minutes. Shorty and I did most of the actual burglary. Rudy generally had the getaway car.

If the people weren't at home, we'd use a passkey④ on a common door lock. On a patent lock, we'd use a jimmy⑤, as it's called, or a lockpick. Or, sometimes, we would enter by windows from a fire-escape, or a roof. Gullible women often took the girls all

---

① cylinder：（左轮手枪的）旋转弹膛。
② muzzle：枪口。
③ earmark：记号，特征。
④ passkey：万能钥匙。
⑤ jimmy：铁撬棍。

over their houses, just to hear them exclaiming over the finery. With the help of the girls'
drawings and a finger-beam searchlight, we went straight to the things we wanted.
Sometimes the victims were in their beds asleep. That may sound very daring. Actually, it
was almost easy. The first thing we had to do when people were in the house was to wait,
very still, and pick up the sounds of breathing. Snorers we loved; they made it real easy.
In stockinged feet, we'd go right into the bedrooms. Moving swiftly, like shadows, we
would lift clothes, watches, wallets, handbags, and jewelry boxes.

The Christmas season was Santa Claus for us; people had expensive presents lying all
over their houses. And they had taken more cash than usual out of their banks.
Sometimes, working earlier than we usually did, we even worked houses that we hadn't
cased. If the shades were drawn full, and no lights were on, and there was no answer when
one of the girls rang the bell, we would take the chance and go in.

I can give you a very good tip if you want to keep burglars out of your house. A light
on for the burglar to see is the very best single means of protection. One of the ideal things
is to leave a bathroom light on all night. The bathroom is one place where somebody could
be, for any length of time, at any time of the night, and he would be likely to hear the
slightest strange sound. The burglar, knowing this, won't try to enter. It's also the
cheapest possible protection. The kilowatts are a lot cheaper than your valuables.

We became efficient. The fence sometimes relayed tips as to where we could find good
loot. It was in this way that for one period, one of our best periods, I remember, we
specialized in Oriental rugs. I have always suspected that the fence himself sold the rugs to
the people we stole them from. But, anyway, you wouldn't imagine the value of those
things. I remember one small one that brought us a thousand dollars. There's no telling
what the fence got for it. Every burglar knew that fences robbed the burglars worse than
the burglars had robbed the victims.

Our only close brush with the law came once when we were making our getaway, three
of us in the front seat of the car, and the back seat loaded with stuff. Suddenly we saw a
police car round the corner, coming toward us, and it went on past us. They were just
cruising. But then in the rear-view mirror, we saw them make a U-turn, and we knew they
were going to flash us to stop. They had spotted us, in passing, as Negroes, and they knew
that Negroes had no business in the area at that hour.

It was a close situation. There was a lot of robbery going on; we weren't the only gang
working, we knew, not by any means. But I knew that the white man is rare who will ever
consider that a Negro can outsmart him. Before their light began flashing, I told Rudy to
stop. I did what I'd done once before—got out and flagged them, walking toward them.
When they stopped, I was at their car. I asked them, bumbling my words like a confused
Negro, if they could tell me how to get to a Roxbury address. They told me, and we, and
they, went on about our respective businesses.

We were going along fine. We'd make a good pile and then lay low awhile, living it
up. Shorty still played with his band, Rudy never missed attending his sensitive old man,
or the table-waiting at his exclusive parties, and the girls maintained their routine home

schedules.

Sometimes, I still took the girls out to places where Shorty played, and to other places, spending money as though it were going out of style, the girls dressed in jewelry and furs they had selected from our hauls. No one knew our hustle, but it was clear that we were doing fine. And sometimes, the girls would come over and we'd meet them either at Shorty's in Roxbury or in our Harvard Square place, and just smoke reefers, and play music. It's a shame to tell on a man, but Shorty was so obsessed with the white girl that even if the lights were out, he would pull up the shade to be able to see that white flesh by the street lamp from outside.

Early evenings when we were laying low between jobs, I often went to a Massachusetts Avenue night club called the Savoy. And Sophia would telephone me there punctually. Even when we pulled jobs, I would leave from this club, then rush back thereafter the job. The reason was so that if it was ever necessary, people could testify that they had seen me at just about the time the job was pulled. Negroes being questioned by policemen would be very hard to pin down on any exact time.

Boston at this time had two Negro detectives. Ever since I had come back on the Roxbury scene, one of these detectives, a dark brown fellow named Turner, had never been able to stand me, and it was mutual. He talked about what he would do to me, and I had promptly put an answer back on the wire. I knew from the way he began to act that he had heard it. Everyone knew that I carried guns. And he did have sense enough to know that I wouldn't hesitate to use them—and on him, detective or not.

This early evening I was in this place when at the usual time, the phone in the booth rang. It rang just as this detective Turner happened to walk in through the front door. He saw me start to get up, he knew the call was for me, but stepped inside the booth, and answered.

I heard him saying, looking straight at me, "Hello, hello, hello—" And I knew that Sophia, taking no chances with the strange voice, had hung up.

"Wasn't that call for me?" I asked Turner.

He said that it was.

I said, "Well, why didn't you say so?"

He gave me a rude answer. I knew he wanted me to make a move, first. We both were being cagey①. We both knew that we wanted to kill each other. Neither wanted to say the wrong thing. Turner didn't want to say anything that, repeated, would make him sound bad. I didn't want to say anything that could be interpreted as a threat to a cop.

But I remember exactly what I said to him anyway, purposely loud enough for some people at the bar to hear me. I said, "You know, Turner—you're trying to make history. Don't you know that if you play with me, you certainly will go down in history because you've got to kill me?"

---

① cagey:秘而不宣的，谨小慎微的。

Turner looked at me. Then he backed down. He walked on by me. I guess he wasn't ready to make history.

I had gotten to the point where I was walking on my own coffin.

It's a law of the rackets that every criminal expects to get caught. He tries to stave off^{①} the inevitable for as long as he can.

Drugs helped me push the thought to the back of my mind. They were the center of my life. I had gotten to the stage where every day I used enough drugs—reefers, cocaine, or both—so that I felt above any worries, any strains. If any worries did manage to push their way through to the surface of my consciousness, I could float them back where they came from until tomorrow, and then until the next day.

But where, always before, I had been able to smoke the reefers and to sniff the snow and rarely show it very much, by now it was not that easy.

One week when we weren't working—after a big haul—I was just staying high, and I was out nightclubbing. I came into this club, and from the bartender's face when he spoke, "Hello, Red," I knew that something was wrong. But I didn't ask him anything. I've always had this rule—never ask anybody in that kind of situation; they will tell you what they want you to know. But the bartender didn't get a chance to tell me, if he had meant to. When I sat down on a stool and ordered a drink, I saw them. Sophia and her sister sat at a table inside, near the dance floor, with a white man.

I don't know how I ever made such a mistake as I next did. I could have talked to her later. I didn't know, or care, who the white fellow was. My cocaine told me to get up.

It wasn't Sophia's husband. It was his closest friend. They had served in the war together. With her husband out of town, he had asked Sophia and her sister out to dinner, and they went. But then, later, after dinner, driving around, he had suddenly suggested going over to the black ghetto.

Every Negro who lives in a city has seen the type a thousand times, the Northern cracker who will go to visit "niggertown," to be amused at "the coons."

The girls, so well known in the Negro places in Roxbury, had tried to change his mind, but he had insisted. So they had just held their breaths coming into this club where they had been a hundred times. They walked in stiff-eyeing the bartenders and waiters who caught their message and acted as though they never had seen them before. And they were sitting there with drinks before them, praying that no Negro who knew them would barge up to their table.

Then up I came. I know I called them "Baby." They were chalky-white, he was beet-red.

That same night, back at the Harvard Square place, I really got sick. It was less of a physical sickness than it was all of the last five years catching up. I was in my pajamas in bed, half asleep, when I heard someone knock.

I knew that something was wrong. We all had keys. No one ever knocked at the door.

---

① stave off: 挡开或避开, 延迟。

I rolled off and under the bed; I was so groggy① it didn't cross my mind to grab for my gun on the dresser.

Under the bed, I heard the key turn, and I saw the shoes and pants cuffs walk in. I watched them walk around. I saw them stop. Every time they stopped, I knew what the eyes were looking at. And I knew, before he did, that he was going to get down and look under the bed. He did. It was Sophia's husband's friend. His face was about two feet from mine. It looked congealed.

"Ha, ha, ha, I fooled you, didn't I?" I said. It wasn't at all funny. I got out from under the bed, still fake-laughing. He didn't run, I'll say that for him. He stood back; he watched me as though I were a snake.

I didn't try to hide what he already knew. The girls had some things in the closets, and around; he had seen all of that. We even talked some. I told him the girls weren't there, and he left. What shook me the most was realizing that I had trapped myself under the bed without a gun. I really was slipping.

I had put a stolen watch into a jewelry shop to replace a broken crystal. It was about two days later, when I went to pick up the watch, that things fell apart.

As I have said, a gun was as much a part of my dress as a necktie. I had my gun in a shoulder holster, under my coat. The loser of the watch, the person from whom it had been stolen by us, I later found, had described the repair that it needed. It was a very expensive watch, that's why I had kept it for myself. And all of the jewelers in Boston had been alerted.

The Jew waited until I had paid him before he laid the watch on the counter. He gave his signal—and this other fellow suddenly appeared, from the back, walking toward me.

One hand was in his pocket. I knew he was a cop.

He said, quietly, "Step into the back."

Just as I started back there, an innocent Negro walked into the shop. I remember later hearing that he had just that day gotten out of the military. The detective, thinking he was with me, turned to him.

There I was, wearing my gun, and the detective talking to that Negro with his back to me. Today I believe that Allah② was with me even then. I didn't try to shoot him. And that saved my life.

I remember that his name was Detective Slack.

I raised my arm, and motioned to him, "Here, take my gun."

I saw his face when he took it. He was shocked. Because of the sudden appearance of the other Negro, he had never thought about a gun. It really moved him that I hadn't tried to kill him.

Then, holding my gun in his hand, he signaled. And out from where they had been

---

① groggy:虚弱的，眩晕的。
② Allah:安拉，真主。

concealed walked two other detectives. They'd had me covered. One false move, I'd have been dead.

I was going to have a long time in prison to think about that.

If I hadn't been arrested right when I was, I could have been dead another way. Sophia's husband's friend had told her husband about me. And the husband had arrived that morning, and had gone to the apartment with a gun, looking for me. He was at the apartment just about when they took me to the precinct. The detectives grilled me. They didn't beat me. They didn't even put a finger on me. And I knew it was because I hadn't tried to kill the detective.

They got my address from some papers they found on me. The girls soon were picked up. Shorty was pulled right off the bandstand that night. The girls also had implicated^① Rudy. To this day, I have always marveled at how Rudy, somehow, got the word, and I know he must have caught the first thing smoking out of Boston, and he got away. They never got him.

I have thought a thousand times, I guess, about how I so narrowly escaped death twice that day. That's why I believe that everything is written.

The cops found the apartment loaded with evidence—fur coats, some jewelry, other small stuff—plus the tools of our trade. A jimmy, a lockpick, glass cutters, screwdrivers, pencil-beam flashlights, false keys ... and my small arsenal of guns.

The girls got low bail. They were still white—burglars or not. Their worst crime was their involvement with Negroes. But Shorty and I had bail set at $10,000 each, which they knew we were nowhere near able to raise.

The social workers worked on us. White women in league with Negroes was their main obsession. The girls weren't so-called "tramps," or "trash," they were well-to-do upper-middle-class whites. That bothered the social workers and the forces of the law more than anything else.

How, where, when, had I met them? Did we sleep together? Nobody wanted to know anything at all about the robberies. All they could see was that we had taken the white man's women.

I just looked at the social workers: "Now, what do you think?"

Even the court clerks and the bailiffs: "Nice white girls ... goddam niggers—" It was the same even from our court-appointed lawyers as we sat down, under guard, at a table, as our hearing assembled. Before the judge entered, I said to one lawyer, "We seem to be getting sentenced because of those girls." He got red from the neck up and shuffled his papers: "You had no business with white girls!"

Later, when I had learned the full truth about the white man, I reflected many times that the average burglary sentence for a first offender, as we all were, was about two years. But we weren't going to get the average—not for *our* crime.

---

① implicate: 表明(某人)与(罪行)有牵连。

I want to say before I go on that I have never previously told anyone my sordid① past in detail. I haven't done it now to sound as though I might be proud of how bad, how evil, I was.

But people are always speculating—why am I as I am? To understand that of any person, his whole life, from birth, must be reviewed. All of our experiences fuse into our personality. Everything that ever happened to us is an ingredient.

Today, when everything that I do has an urgency, I would not spend one hour in the preparation of a book which had the ambition to perhaps titillate② some readers. But I am spending many hours because the full story is the best way that I know to have it seen, and understood, that I had sunk to the very bottom of the American white man's society when—soon now, in prison—I found Allah and the religion of Islam and it completely transformed my life.

Questions for Discussion

1. How had Malcolm's addiction to narcotics and abuse of drugs influenced the working of his mentality which had calamitous consequences?
2. How do you understand Malcolm X's critical remarks about the different treatments extended to the members of the gang of burglary?
3. What is the difference between Martin Luther King, Jr. and Malcolm X in the common struggle for civil rights of the Black people? Whose approach do you prefer? And why?

---

① sordid:卑鄙的,肮脏的。
② titillate:挑逗。

8. I Know Why the Caged Bird Sings

作者简介

玛雅·安吉洛(Maya Angelou)(1928—2014),原名玛格丽特·约翰逊,美国著名黑人女作家、诗人、编剧、歌手、演员,同时也是积极的民权活动家。她出生于密苏里州圣路易斯市,在阿肯色州和加利福尼亚州长大,写过很多诗歌、自传和剧本。她的自传作品给美国文学带来巨大影响,尤其是第一部《我知道笼中鸟为何歌唱》(1969)。之后她连续发表五部自传:《以我的名义重整旗鼓》(1974),《像过圣诞节般唱歌、跳舞、欢乐》(1976),《女人心》(1981),《所有上帝的孩子都需要旅游鞋》(1986),《掷向天堂的歌》(2002)。20 世纪 60 年代初,安吉洛侨居埃及和加纳,担任杂志编辑,1965 年回到美国。与此同时,安吉洛积极投身于黑人民权运动。她与马丁·路德·金会面,成为南方基督教领导大会的北方协调员。安吉洛的诗歌创作同样成果丰硕。自第一本诗集《我死前只要给我一杯冷饮》(1971)问世以来,至今已出版《我仍将升起》(1978)、《谢柯,为什么不歌唱》(1983)、《现在希巴唱歌》(1987)、《我绝不会动摇》(1990)等 10 部诗集。1993 年,在克林顿总统的就职典礼上,她应邀朗诵了她的诗歌《早晨的脉搏》(On the Pulse of Morning),成为家喻户晓的人物。1995 年,安吉洛在旧金山庆祝联合国成立 50 周年大会上朗诵了诗篇《一条勇敢而令人惊异的真理》。2011 年奥巴马总统授予她总统自由奖章。安吉洛已成为美国声音的代表。

作品简介与赏析

《我知道笼中鸟为何歌唱》这部自传的名字取自保罗·劳伦斯·邓巴的诗《同情》。自出版以来获得众多赞誉,被称为是民权运动结束之后最具艺术审美价值的传记。它曾获 1970 年美国图书奖的提名,连续两年荣登《纽约时代》最畅销的平装图书。1979 年被改编拍成电视剧在哥伦比亚广播公司电视台播放。

作品记录了作者从 3 岁到 16 岁的人生经历,再现了作者童年和少女时代的坎坷与不幸。她的讲述再现了作者遭遇的三重处境:男性的偏见、白人的仇恨和黑人的无权无势。故事从玛雅 3 岁时与哥哥一起被离异的父母送往南方的祖母家开始讲起。祖母住在阿肯色州的斯坦普镇,她性格坚韧,充满自尊,在当地开杂货铺为生。在那个种族隔离严重的南方小镇,玛雅一直认为自己是个丑陋的小女孩,永远也比不上那些白人女孩。而祖母教会了他们很多作为黑人的生存原则,并使他们成为聪明、懂礼貌的孩子。在斯坦普镇的这些难忘岁月构成了这部作品的主体。8 岁时,玛雅回到母亲身边,却被母亲的男友奸污,后者在玛雅说出实情后,被她的舅舅们殴打致死。这一段痛苦经历让玛雅此后五年除了和哥哥外不再开口说话,把情感寄托在读书和写作之中。其后玛雅和哥哥又被送回到祖母家。八年级时,他们被带到母亲所定居的加州旧金山市,在一所没有种族隔离制度的学校上学。她鼓足勇气去应聘,成为旧金山市第一位黑人公车售票员。16 岁时,处于青春期的玛雅因为担心自己是同性恋,而主动去接近一个白人男孩,成了未婚妈妈。

在这部作品中,安吉洛描述了身为一名黑人女孩,在阿肯色州这个很少为非裔美国文学所关注的地方意味着什么。其中一个生动的例子就是她在白人牙医林肯大夫那里的遭遇。因为她的黑人身份,医生拒绝为她看病。安吉洛回忆道:"忍受着牙痛、头痛,同时还得承受身为黑人的重负,这是多么可怕的不公!"早年经历的困苦多舛并没有击垮安吉洛,相反,她的作品处处都在歌颂美国黑人积极正面的价值观,尤其是面对困难的勇气和坚强。作者积极乐观的态度,充满激情的笔触使原本黯淡凄凉的黑人女性生活变成了一首激荡人心的生存颂歌,为人们研究黑人女性自传体文学提供了新的思路。作品问世后深受评论界好评,激发了作者创作系列自传的热情。在黑人自传传统中,安吉洛与道格拉斯、赖特、布克·华盛顿等齐名,被文学界誉为20世纪70年代美国黑人文学复兴的代表作家之一。

批评界多从女性主义和美国黑人研究的视角出发,讨论文本中的种族、性别、身份、背井离乡等话题。近年来则更多从成长小说、女性自传、物质文化、形式分析等角度切入作品。

本文节选自该书的第16章。作者讲述了自己10岁那年在卡利南太太家厨房帮佣的经历。她把这位白种女人的厨房比作自己的进修学校,期待能在那里学到别处学不到的优雅精致的生活方式和持家之道。初到此处的小玛雅对一切都感到新奇。"汤匙、船形肉汁盘、切黄油的刀、色拉叉子、用来盛放切好的菜的大浅盘,成了我的新增词汇,事实上几乎代表了一种新的语言。这种新鲜感,还有忙乱的卡利南太太和她爱丽丝梦游仙境般的家,都让我深深着迷。"白人的物质生活世界从小女孩细细罗列的各种眼花缭乱的厨房物件里呈现出来,笼罩上一层魔咒般的光彩。但很快小玛雅就从对白人的美好幻想中被迫清醒过来。太太嫌她的名字"玛格丽特"太长,改叫她为"玛丽"。名字是身份的象征,白人雇主对黑人女孩的随意更名是在否定她的身份和独特性。出于反抗,她故意摔碎了卡利南太太祖传的珍贵餐具。因为,"我认识的每一个人都对'不以本名相称'的做法怀有极端的恐惧。对黑人想叫什么就叫什么,这种做法很危险,会被简单地理解为侮辱,因为几个世纪以来他们一直被叫作黑鬼、脏鬼、黑鸟、乌鸦、擦鞋的、鬼怪,等等"。通过捍卫自己的名字,玛雅赢得了获取尊严的第一场战争。

Chapter 16

Recently a white woman from Texas, who would quickly describe herself as a liberal, asked me about my hometown. When I told her that in Stamps my grandmother had owned the only Negro general merchandise store since the turn of the century, she exclaimed, "Why, you were a debutante." Ridiculous and even ludicrous. But Negro girls in small Southern towns, whether poverty-stricken or just munching along on a few of life's necessities, were given as extensive and irrelevant preparations for adulthood as rich white girls shown in magazines. Admittedly the training was not the same. While white girls learned to waltz and sit gracefully with a tea cup balanced on their knees, we were lagging behind, learning the mid-Victorian values with very little money to indulge them. (Come and see Edna Lomax spending the money she made picking cotton on five balls of ecru tatting thread. Her fingers are bound to snag the work and she'll have to repeat the stitches time and time again. But she knows that when she buys the thread.)

We were required to embroider and I had trunkfuls of colored dishtowels, pillowcases, runners and handkerchiefs to my credit. I mastered the art of crocheting and tatting, and there was a lifetime's supply of dainty doilies that would never be used in sacheted dresser drawers. It went without saying that all girls could iron and wash, but the finer touches around the home, like setting a table with real silver, baking roasts and cooking vegetables without meat, had to be learned elsewhere. Usually at the source of those habits. During my tenth year, a white woman's kitchen became my finishing school.

Mrs. Viola Cullinan was a plump woman who lived in a three-bedroom house somewhere behind the post office. She was singularly unattractive until she smiled, and then the lines around her eyes and mouth which made her look perpetually dirty disappeared, and her face looked like the mask of an impish elf. She usually rested her smile until late afternoon when her women friends dropped in and Miss Glory, the cook, served them cold drinks on the closed-in porch.

The exactness of her house was inhuman. This glass went here and only here. That cup had its place and it was an act of impudent rebellion to place it anywhere else. At twelve o'clock the table was set. At 12:15 Mrs. Cullinan sat down to dinner (whether her husband had arrived or not). At 12:16 Miss Glory brought out the food.

It took me a week to learn the difference between a salad plate, a bread plate and a dessert plate.

Mrs. Cullinan kept up the tradition of her wealthy parents. She was from Virginia. Miss Glory, who was a descendant of slaves that had worked for the Cullinans, told me her history. She had married beneath her (according to Miss Glory). Her husband's family hadn't had their money very long and what they had "didn't 'mount to much."

As ugly as she was, I thought privately, she was lucky to get a husband above or beneath her station. But Miss Glory wouldn't let me say a thing against her mistress. She was very patient with me, however, over the housework. She explained the dishware, silverware and servants' bells.

The large round bowl in which soup was served wasn't a soup bowl, it was a tureen. There were goblets, sherbet glasses, ice-cream glasses, wine glasses, green glass coffee cups with matching saucers, and water glasses. I had a glass to drink from, and it sat with Miss Glory's on a separate shelf from the others. Soup spoons, gravy boat, butter knives, salad forks and carving platter were additions to my vocabulary and in fact almost represented a new language. I was fascinated with the novelty, with the fluttering Mrs. Cullinan and her Alice-in-Wonderland① house.

Her husband remains, in my memory, undefined. I lumped him with all the other white men that I had ever seen and tried not to see.

On our way home one evening, Miss Glory told me that Mrs. Cullinan couldn't have children. She said that she was too delicate-boned. It was hard to imagine bones at all under those layers of fat. Miss Glory went on to say that the doctor had taken out all her lady organs. I reasoned that a pig's organs included the lungs, heart and liver, so if Mrs. Cullinan was walking around without those essentials, it explained why she drank alcohol out of unmarked bottles. She was keeping herself embalmed.

When I spoke to Bailey about it, he agreed that I was right, but he also informed me that Mr. Cullinan had two daughters by a colored lady and that I knew them very well. He added that the girls were the spitting image of their father. I was unable to remember what

---

① Alice-in-Wonderland:《爱丽丝梦游仙境》(*Alice's Adventures in Wonderland*),英国作家路易斯·卡罗尔(Lewis Carroll)于 1865 年出版的儿童文学作品。

he looked like, although I had just left him a few hours before, but I thought of the Coleman girls. They were very light-skinned and certainly didn't look very much like their mother (no one ever mentioned Mr. Coleman).

My pity for Mrs. Cullinan preceded me the next morning like the Cheshire cat's smile[①]. Those girls, who could have been her daughters, were beautiful. They didn't have to straighten their hair. Even when they were caught in the rain, their braids still hung down straight like tamed snakes. Their mouths were pouty little cupid's bows. Mrs. Cullinan didn't know what she missed. Or maybe she did. Poor Mrs. Cullinan.

For weeks after, I arrived early, left late and tried very hard to make up for her barrenness. If she had had her own children, she wouldn't have had to ask me to run a thousand errands from her back door to the back door of her friends. Poor old Mrs. Cullinan.

Then one evening Miss Glory told me to serve the ladies on the porch. After I set the tray down and turned toward the kitchen, one of the women asked, "What's your name, girl?" It was the speckled-faced one. Mrs. Cullinan said, "She doesn't talk much. Her name's Margaret."

"Is she dumb?"

"No. As I understand it, she can talk when she wants to but she's usually quiet as a little mouse. Aren't you, Margaret."

I smiled at her. Poor thing. No organs and couldn't even pronounce my name correctly.

"She's a sweet little thing, though."

"Well, that may be, but the name's too long. I'd never bother myself. I'd call her Mary if I was you."

I fumed into the kitchen. That horrible woman would never have the chance to call me Mary because if I was starving I'd never work for her. I decided I wouldn't pee on her if her heart was on fire. Giggles drifted in off the porch and into Miss Glory's pots. I wondered what they could be laughing about.

White folks were so strange. Could they be talking about me? Everybody knew that they stuck together better than the Negroes did. It was possible that Mrs. Cullinan had friends in St. Louis who heard about a girl from Stamps being in court and wrote to tell her. Maybe she knew about Mr. Freeman.

My lunch was in my mouth a second time and I went outside and relieved myself on the bed of four-o'clocks. Miss Glory thought I might be coming down with something and told me to go on home, that Momma would give me some herb tea, and she'd explain to her mistress.

I realized how foolish I was being before I reached the pond. Of course Mrs. Cullinan didn't know. Otherwise she wouldn't have given me the two nice dresses that Momma cut down, and she certainly wouldn't have called me a "sweet little thing." My stomach felt

---

① the Cheshire cat:一只咧着大嘴笑的猫,是《爱丽丝梦游仙境》中的角色。

fine, and I didn't mention anything to Momma.

That evening I decided to write a poem on being white, fat, old and without children. It was going to be a tragic ballad. I would have to watch her carefully to capture the essence of her loneliness and pain.

The very next day, she called me by the wrong name. Miss Glory and I were washing up the lunch dishes when Mrs. Cullinan came to the doorway. "Mary?"

Miss Glory asked, "Who?"

Mrs. Cullinan, sagging a little, knew and I knew. "I want Mary to go down to Mrs. Randall's and take her some soup. She's not been feeling well for a few days."

Miss Glory's face was a wonder to see. "You mean Margaret, ma'am. Her name's Margaret."

"That's too long. She's Mary from now on. Heat that soup from last night and put it in the china tureen and, Mary, I want you to carry it carefully."

Every person I knew had a hellish horror of being "called out of his name." It was a dangerous practice to call a Negro anything that could be loosely construed as insulting because of the centuries of their having been called niggers, jigs, dinges, blackbirds, crows, boots and spooks.

Miss Glory had a fleeting second of feeling sorry for me. Then as she handed me the hot tureen she said, "Don't mind, don't pay that no mind. Sticks and stones may break your bones, but words ... You know, I been working for her for twenty years."

She held the back door open for me. "Twenty years. I wasn't much older than you. My name used to be Hallelujah. That's what Ma named me, but my mistress give me 'Glory,' and it stuck. I likes it better too."

I was in the little path that ran behind the houses when Miss Glory shouted, "It's shorter too."

For a few seconds it was a tossup over whether I would laugh (imagine being named Hallelujah) or cry (imagine letting some white woman rename you for her convenience). My anger saved me from either outburst. I had to quit the job, but the problem was going to be how to do it. Momma wouldn't allow me to quit for just any reason.

"She's a peach. That woman is a real peach." Mrs. Randall's maid was talking as she took the soup from me, and I wondered what her name used to be and what she answered to now.

For a week I looked into Mrs. Cullinan's face as she called me Mary. She ignored my coming late and leaving early. Miss Glory was a little annoyed because I had begun to leave egg yolk on the dishes and wasn't putting much heart in polishing the silver. I hoped that she would complain to our boss, but she didn't.

Then Bailey solved my dilemma. He had me describe the contents of the cupboard and the particular plates she liked best. Her favorite piece was a casserole shaped like a fish and the green glass coffee cups. I kept his instructions in mind, so on the next day when Miss Glory was hanging out clothes and I had again been told to serve the old biddies on the porch, I dropped the empty serving tray. When I heard Mrs. Cullinan scream, "Mary!" I picked up the casserole and two of the green glass cups in readiness. As she rounded the kitchen door I let them fall on the tiled floor.

I could never absolutely describe to Bailey what happened next, because each time I got to the part where she fell on the floor and screwed up her ugly face to cry, we burst out laughing. She actually wobbled around on the floor and picked up shards of the cups and cried, "Oh, Momma. Oh, dear Gawd. It's Momma's china from Virginia. Oh, Momma, I sorry."

Miss Glory came running in from the yard and the women from the porch crowded around. Miss Glory was almost as broken up as her mistress. "You mean to say she broke our Virginia dishes? What we gone do?"

Mrs. Cullinan cried louder, "That clumsy nigger. Clumsy little black nigger."

Old speckled-face leaned down and asked, "Who did it, Viola? Was it Mary? Who did it?"

Everything was happening so fast I can't remember whether her action preceded her words, but I know that Mrs. Cullinan said, "Her name's Margaret, goddamn it, her name's Margaret!" And she threw a wedge of the broken plate at me. It could have been the hysteria which put her aim oft, but the flying crockery caught Miss Glory right over her ear and she started screaming.

I left the front door wide open so all the neighbors could hear.

Mrs. Cullinan was right about one thing. My name wasn't Mary.

Questions for Discussion

1. What does she mean by her finishing school when Maya first mentions it at the beginning of her narrative? What else do you think she learns towards the end of it?
2. At what point does Maya's attitude towards Mrs. Cullinan change? Why?
3. By the end of the narrative, Mrs. Cullinan broke out, "her name's Margaret, goddamn it, her name's Margaret." In what sense is the quote important? What does it symbolize?

9. Brothers and Keepers

作者简介

约翰·埃德加·怀德曼(John Edgar Wideman)(1941—　)不仅是美国当代著名小说家,也是传记家与社会批评家,获得过多项殊荣,两次获得福克纳笔会文学奖、美国小说图书奖;两次进入美国国家图书奖和美国书评人协会奖的短名单,是 20 世纪美国最优秀的小说家之一,是一位堪与福克纳比肩的著名作家,因为他有黑人血统,所以一直被称为黑人小说家。

怀德曼出生于华盛顿特区,但是在匹兹堡布鲁斯彤山脚下长大,借助于富兰克林奖学金,他得以到宾夕法尼亚大学读书,并于 1963 年以优异成绩毕业,获得学士学位。他是第二位获得罗德奖学金的黑人(第一位获此殊荣的是 20 世纪初著名黑人学者洛克),赴英国牛津大学学习哲学,1966 年毕业。之后他在多所学校教书,如宾夕法尼亚大学、怀俄明大学以及马萨诸塞大学阿默斯特校区等。

1967 年,年仅 26 岁的怀德曼发表第一部小说《远眺》,虽然当时黑人民权运动如火如荼,但他刻意与黑人文学先锋派保持距离,截然不同于巴拉卡、尼尔以及盖尔等人当时把黑人艺术变成黑人权力的“精神姐妹”的主张,对他而言,离开匹兹堡去费城的宾夕法尼亚大学读书就是逃离故乡、逃离贫困、逃离自己的黑人身份、奔向自由。在 1976 年的访谈中,怀德曼指出,自己对小说形式实践非常着迷,特别欣赏 18 世纪英国作家,如笛福、菲尔丁,特别是《项笛传》的作者斯泰恩,对黑人作家,他比较喜欢赖特与埃里森,对图默更是情有独钟。

他的第二部小说《赶快回家》和第三部小说《私刑者》继续深入探讨非裔美国经历的独特品质,重点聚焦语言与种族问题,虽然他的文学世界中的主要人物既有黑人也有白人,重点关注的也是人类的普世经历,但是批评家依然把他归入当代黑人文学的谱系当中。20 世纪 80 年代以来,他在创作中有意模糊虚构、历史与自传的界限,把过去与现在紧密地联系在一起。

怀德曼作品多、质量高,他像个经验丰富的教练,魔术般地调适黑人历史与文化经验,不仅进行记录、评价,也对那些惨遭破坏的经历予以复原,庆祝新的文化形态的诞生,目的主要在于打破束缚非裔美国人的藩篱,如自我憎恨等;他作品中的主人公仿佛都在遗忘与记忆中挣扎,他们渴望创造足够的空间,重新创造过去,创新未来。许多批评家已经认识到,可与福克纳、乔伊斯、沃尔夫媲美的怀德曼通过融合非裔美国街头方言与传统文学语言,发展了一种独特的美国文学声音。

作品简介与赏析

有资料显示,15—45 岁的美国黑人男性入狱的比例非常高,虽然原因各异,但是主要因为贩毒、暴力、抢劫、杀人等罪行被监禁。怀德曼的《兄弟与看护人》采取自传的形式——类似于美国早期的囚房叙事,不仅描绘了弟弟鲁比的各种坏习惯及导致其入狱的暴力倾向,而且也开始严肃思考普遍存在的、与其弟弟类似的黑人男性的悲惨处境。但是,怀德曼没有在行文中袒护自己兄弟的犯罪事实,与人们常见的暴力犯罪及其惩罚的文学类型不同的是,怀德曼以细致的笔触进行分析,为我们更加深入、全面地认识美国当代社会的种族问题,特别是针对黑人男性的惩戒,提供了新的视角。此外,本书对两兄弟之间的关系所做的细致入微的分析也丰富了人们对复杂人性的认识:这个世界给了作家怀德曼足够的空间发展,但是却把作为“罪犯”的弟弟鲁比置于狭小的狱室里，为何会这样？其本质差异何在？

与弟弟鲁比相比，怀德曼可谓成功的黑人男性的代表：他因自己的努力，获得奖学金，得以顺利完成学业；文学创作方面，也获得社会的多方认可，收获很多荣誉，成为大学教授。但是怀德曼也在反思，自己取得这些成功的背后，是否放下了什么、牺牲了什么。如果说弟弟因不遵守社会规则而被监禁，那么自己这位成功的哥哥是否像个"逃奴"——逃离家庭、逃离黑人社区、逃离自我、"融入"美国社会的逃奴。更为遗憾的是，因为被监禁，鲁比原有的梦想、追求等全部被遮蔽，不为人所知。鲁比曾说："我们过去并没有那么坏，但是与那些白人孩子啥都有相比，我觉得好像自己啥也没有。"而怀德曼要做的，就是要仔细探究鲁比暴力犯罪背后的其他社会因素，特别是种族因素对黑人的负面影响。

怀德曼借助弟弟鲁比的被监禁，反思自己的所作所为，同时也让广大读者直面这样的问题，即在鲁比每天都面临各种公然的或微妙的种族歧视问题上，大家是否都有意无意地扮演了"同谋"的角色，在黑人男性追求进步的道路上，对他们怀揣的梦想视而不见，甚至都或隐或显地在为他们设置障碍。

作为本书所选的最后一篇自传，《兄弟与看护人》并非（非裔）美国文学史上孤立的个案，而是美国监狱文学的典范，也是非裔美国自传中的重要一环。上承马尔科姆·艾克斯自传中的监狱描写，下启麦考尔的《让我真想吼》中对黑人监禁及改造更为直观的再现，为我们认识当代美国的种族问题，特别是黑人男性犯罪及其监禁问题提供了真实的材料。

本节选自作品的第一部分"探访"。

Visits

Daddy's father, our grandfather, Harry Wideman, migrated from Greenwood, South Carolina, to Pittsburgh, Pennsylvania, in 1906. He found a raw, dirty, double-dealing city. He learned its hills and rivers, the strange names of Dagos and Hunkies and Polacks who's been drawn, as he had, by steel mills and coal mines, by the smoke and heat and dangerous work that meant any strong-backed, stubborn young man, even a black one, could earn pocketfuls of money. Grandpa's personal quest connected him with hordes of other displaced black men seeking a new day in the promised land of the North. Like so many others, he boarded in an overcrowded rooming house, working hard by day, partying hard at night against the keen edge of exhaustion. When his head finally hit the pillow, he didn't care that the sheets were still warm from the body of the man working nights who rented the bed ten hours a day while Harry pulled his shift at the mill.

Harry Wideman was a short, thick, dark man whose mahogany color passed on to Daddy, blended with the light, bright skin of John and Freeda French's daughter Bette to produce the brown we wear. Do you remember anything about him, or were you too young? Have you ever wondered how the city appeared through his eyes, the eyes of a rural black boy far from home, a stranger in a strange land? Have you ever been curious? Grandpa took giant steps forward in time. As a boy not quite old enough to be much help in the fields, his job was looking out for Charley Rackett, his ancient, crippled grandfather, an African, a former slave. Grandpa listened to Charley Rackett's African stories and African words, then lived to see white men on the moon. I think of grandpa high up on Bruston Hill looking over the broad vista spreading out below him. He's young and alone; he sees things with his loins as much as his eyes. Hills rolling to the horizon, toward the invisible rivers, are breasts and buttocks. Shadowed spaces, nestling between the rounded hills, summon him. Whatever happens to him in this city, whatever he accomplishes will be an answer to the soft, insinuating challenge thrown up at him as he stares over the teeming land. This city will measure his manhood. *Our Father Who art ...* I hear prayer words interrupting his dreaming, disturbing the woman shapes his glance fashions from the landscape. The earth turns. He plants his seed. In the blink of an eye he's an old man, close to death. He has watched the children of his children's children born in this city. Some of his children's children dead already. He ponders the wrinkled tar paper on the backs of his hands. Our father. A challenge still rises from the streets and rooftops the way it once floated up from long-gone, empty fields. And the old man's no nearer now to knowing, to understanding why the call digs so deeply at his heart.

Wagons once upon a time in the streets of Pittsburgh. Delivering ice and milk and coal. Sinking in the mud, trundling over cobblestones, echoing in the sleep of a man who works all day in the mouth of a fiery furnace, who dreams of green fish gliding along the clear, stony bottoms of a creek in South Carolina. In the twenty years between 1910 and 1930, the black population of Pittsburgh increased by nearly fifty thousand. Black music, blues and jazz, came to town in places like the Pythian Temple, the Ritz, the Savoy, the Showboat. In the bars on the North Side, Homewood, and the Hill you could get whatever you thought you wanted. Gambling women, a good pork chop. Hundreds of families took in boarders to earn a little extra change. A cot in a closet in somebody's real home seemed nicer, better than the dormitories with their barracks-style rows of beds, no privacy, one toilet for twenty men. Snores and funk, eternal coming and going because nobody wanted to remain in those kennels one second longer than he had to. Fights, thieves, people dragged in stinking drunk or bloody from the streets, people going straight to work after hanging out all night with some whore and you got to smell him and smell her beside you while you trying to pull your shift in all that heat. Lawd. Lawd. Got no money in the bank. Joints was rowdy and mean and like I'm telling you if some slickster don't hustle your money in the street or a party-time gal empty your pockets while you sleep and you don't nod off and fall in the fire, then maybe you earn you a few quarters to send home for that wife and them babies waiting down yonder for you if she's still waiting and you still sending. If you ain't got no woman to send for then maybe them few quarters buy you a new shirt and a bottle of whiskey so you can find you some trifling body give all your money to.

The strong survive. The ones who are strong and *lucky*. You can take that back as far as you want to go. Everybody needs one father, two grandfathers, four great-grandfathers, eight great-great-grandfathers, sixteen great-great-great-grandfathers, then thirty-two, then sixty-four, and that's only eight generations backward in time, eight generations linked directly, intimately with what you are. Less than 150 years ago, 128 men made love to 128 women, not all in the same hotel or on the same day but within a relatively short expanse of time, say twenty years, in places as distant as Igboland, New Amsterdam, and south Carolina. Unknown to each other, probably never even coming face to face in their lifetimes, each of these couples was part of the grand conspiracy to produce you. Think of a pyramid balanced on one of its points, a vast cone of light whose sides flare outward, vectors of force like the slanted lines kid draw to show a star's shining. You once were a pinprick of light, a spark whose radiance momentarily upheld the design, stabilized the ever-expanding V that opens to infinity. At some inconceivable distance the lights bends, curves back on itself like a ram's horn or conch shell, spiraling toward its greatest compass but simultaneously narrowing to that needle's eye it must enter in order to flow forth bounteously again. You hovered at that nexus, took your turn through that open door.

The old people died. Our grandfathers, Harry Wideman and John French, are both gone now. The greatest space and no space at all separates us from them. I see them staring, dreaming this ravaged city; and we are in the dream, it's our dream, enclosed, enclosing. We could walk down into that valley they saw from atop Bruston Hill and scoop up the houses, dismantle the bridges and tall buildings, pull cars and trucks off the streets, roll up roads and highways and stuff them all like toys into the cotton-picking sacks draped over our shoulders. We are that much larger than the things that happen to us. Accidents like the city poised at the meeting of these rivers, the city strewn like litter over precipitous hills.

Did our grandfathers run away from the South? Black Harry from Greenwood, South Carolina, mulatto white John from Culpepper, Virginia. How would they answer that question? Were they running from something or running to something? What did you figure you were doing when you started running? When did your flight begin? Was escape the reason or was there a destination, a promised land exerting its pull? Is freedom inextricably linked with both, running *from* and running *to*? Is freedom the motive and means and end and everything in between?

I wonder if the irony of a river beside the prison is intentional. The river was brown last time I saw it, mud-brown and sluggish in its broad channel. Nothing pretty about it, a working river, a place to dump things, to empty sewers. The Ohio's thick and filthy, stinking of coal, chemicals, offal, bitter with rust from the flaking hulls of iron-ore barges iching grayly to and from the steel mills. But viewed from barred windows, from tiered cages, the river must call to the prisoners' hearts, a natural symbol of flight and freedom. The river is a path, a gateway to the West, the frontier. Somewhere it meets the sea. Is it somebody's cruel joke, an architect's way of giving the knife an final twist, hanging this sign outside the walls, this river always visible but a million miles away between the spiked steel fence guarding its banks?

When I think of the distance between us in terms of miles or the height and thickness of walls or the length of your sentence or the deadly prison regimen, you're closer to me, more accessible than when I'm next to you in the prison visiting room trying to speak and find myself at the edge of a silence vaster than oceans. I turned forty-three in June and you'll be thirty-three in December. Not kids any longer by any stretch of the imagination. You're my little brother and maybe it's generally true that people never allow their little brothers and sisters to grow up, but something more seems at work here, something more damaging than vanity, than wishful thinking that inclines us to keep our pasts frozen, intact, keeps us calling our forty-year-old cronies "the boys" and a grown man "little brother." I think of you as little brother because I have no other handle. At a certain point a wall goes up and easy memories stop.

When I think back, I have plenty of recollections of you as a kid. How you looked. The funny things you said. Till about the time you turned a gangly, stilt-legged, stringbean thirteen, we're still family. Our lives connect in typical, family ways: holidays, picnics, births, deaths, the joking and teasing, the time you were a baby just home from the hospital and Daddy John French died and I was supposed to be watching you while the grown-ups cleaned and cooked, readying the house on Finance Street for visitors, for Daddy John to return and lie in his coffin downstairs. Baby-sitting you in Aunt Geraldine's room while death hovered in there with us and no way I could have stayed in that room alone. Needing you much more than you needed me. You just zzz'ed away in your baby sleep, your baby ignorance. You couldn't have cared less whether death or King Kong or a whole flock of those loose-feathered, giant birds haunting my sleep had gathered round your crib. If the folks downstairs were too quiet, my nerves would get jumpy and I'd snatch you up and walk the floor. Hold you pressed in my arms against my heart like a shield. Or if the night cracks and groans of the house got too loud, I'd poke you awake, worry you so your crying would keep me company.

After you turned thirteen, after you grew a mustache and fuzz on your chin and a voluminous Afro so nobody could call you "Beanhead" anymore, after girls and the move from Shadyside to Marchand Street so you started Westinghouse High instead of Peabody where the rest of us had done our time, you begin to get separate. I have to struggle to recall anything about you till you're real again in prison. It's as if I was asleep for fifteen years and when I awakened you were gone. I was out of the country for three years then lived in places like Iowa City and Philly and Laramie, so at best I couldn't have seen much of you, but the sense of distance I'm trying to describe had more to do with the way I related to you than with the amount of time we spent together. We had chances to talk, opportunities to grow beyond the childhood bonds linking us. The problem was that in order to be the person I thought I wanted to be, I believed I had to seal myself off you, construct a wall between us.

Your hands, your face became a man's. You accumulated scars, a deeper voice, lovers, but the changes taking place in you might as well have been occurring on a different planet. The scattered images I retain of you from the sixties through the middle seventies form no discernible pattern, are rooted in no vital substance like childhood or family. Your words and gestures belonged to a language I was teaching myself to unlearn. When we spoke, I was conscious of a third party short-circuiting our conversations. What I'd say to you came from the mouth of a translator who always talked down or up or around you, who didn't know you or me but pretended he knew everything.

Was I as much a stranger to you as you seemed to me? Because we were brothers, holidays, family celebrations, and troubles drew us to the same rooms at the same time, but I felt uncomfortable around you. Most of what I felt was guilt. I'd made my choices. I was running away from Pittsburgh, from poverty, from blackness. To get ahead, to make something of myself, college had seemed a logical, necessary step; my exile, my flight from home began with good grades, with good English, with setting myself apart long before I'd earned a scholarship and a train ticket over the mountains to Philadelphia. With that willed alienation behind me, between us, guilt was predictable. One measure of my success was the distance I'd put between us. Coming home was a kind of bragging, like the suntans people bring back from Hawaii in the middle of winter. It's sure fucked up around here, ain't it? But looked at me, I got away. I got mine. I didn't want to be caught looking back. I needed home to reassure myself of how far I'd come. If I ever doubted how good I had it away at school in that world of books, exams, pretty, rich white girls, a roommate from Long Island who unpacked more pairs of brand-new jockey shorts and T-shirts than they had in Kaufmann's department store, if I ever had any hesitations or reconsiderations about the path I'd chosen, you all were back home in the ghetto to remind me how lucky I was.

Fear marched along beside guilt. Fear of acknowledging in myself any traces of the poverty, ignorance, and danger I'd find surrounding me when I returned to Pittsburgh. Fear that I was contaminated and would carry the poison wherever I ran. Fear that the evil would be discovered in me and I'd be shunned like a leper.

I was scared stiff but at the same time I needed to prove I hadn't lost my roots. Needed to boogie and drink wine and chase pussy, need to prove I could still do it all. Fight, talk trash, hoop with the best playground players at Mellon Park. Claim the turf, wear it like a badge, yet keep my distance, be in the street but not of it.

Your world. The blackness that incriminated me. Easier to change the way I talked and walked, easier to be two people than to expose in either world the awkward mix of school and home I'd become. When in Rome. Different strokes for different folks. Nobody had pulled my coat and whispered the news about Third Worlds. Just two choices as far as I could tell: either/or. Rich or poor. White or black. Win or lose. I figured which side I wanted to be on when the Saints came marching in. Who the Saints, the rulers of the earth were, was clear. My mind was split by oppositions, by mutually exclusive categories. Manichaeism, as Frantz Fanon[①] would say. To succeed in the man's world you

---

① 法农(1925—1961),法国马提尼克作家,心理分析学家,主要代表作为《黑皮肤、白面具》与《地球上的苦难者》等。

must become like the man and the man sure didn't claim no bunch of nigger relatives in Pittsburgh.

Who, me? You must be kidding. You must be thinking of those other guys. They're the ones listen to the Midnighters, the Miracles, the Turbans, Louis Berry, the Spaniels, the Flamingos. My radio stays set on WFLN. They play that nigger stuff way down the dial, at the end, on WDAS, down where WAMO is at home. ①

Some of that mess so dumb, so unbelievable I can laugh now. Like when I was driving you up to Maine to work as a waiter in summer camp. Just you and me and Judy in the car for the long haul from Pittsburgh to Takajo on Long Lake. Nervous the whole time because you kept finding black music on the radio. Not only did you find it. You played it loud and sang along. Do wah diddy and ow bop she bop, having a good ole nigger ball like you'd seen me having with my cut buddies when we were the Commodores chirping tunes on the corner and in Mom's living room. The music we'd both grown up hearing and loving and learning to sing, but you were doing it in my new 1966 Dodge Dart, on the way to Martha's Vineyard and Maine with my new white wife in the backseat. Didn't you know we'd left Pittsburgh, didn't you understand that classical music volume moderate was preferred in these circumstances? Papa's got a brand-new bag. And you were gon act nigger and let the cat out.

Of course I was steady enjoying the music, too. James Brown. Baby Ray and the Raylettes. The Drifters. ② Missed it on the barren stretches of turnpike between cities. Having it both ways. Listening my ass off and patting my foot but in between times wondering how Judy was reacting, thinking about how I'd complain later about your monolithic fondness for rhythm and blues, your habit of turning the volume up full blast. In case she was annoyed, confused, or doubting me in any way, I'd reassure her by disassociating myself from your tastes, your style. Yeah, when I was a kid. Yes. Once upon a time I was like that but now ...

Laughing now to keep from crying when I think back to those days.

My first year at college when I was living in the dorms a white boy asked me if I liked the blues. Since I figured I *was* the blues I answered, Yeah, sure. We were in Darryl Dawson's room. Darryl and I comprised approximately one-third of the total number of black males in our class. About ten of the seventeen hundred men and women who entered the University of Pennsylvania as freshmen in 1959 were black. After a period of wariness and fencing, mutual embarrassment and resisting the inevitable, I'd buddied up with Darryl, even though he'd attended Putney Prep School in Vermont and spoke with an accent I considered phony. Since the fat white boy in work shirt, motorcycle boots, and dirty jeans was in Darryl's room, I figured maybe the guy was alright in spite of the fact he

---

① 地方性广播电台。
② 20 世纪 60 年代，美国蓝调音乐的歌手与音乐家。

asked dumb questions. I'd gotten used to answering or ignoring plenty of those in two months on campus. "Yeah, sure," should have closed the topic but the white boy wasn't finished. He said he had a big collection of blues records and that I ought to come by his room sometime with Darryl and dig, man.

Who do you like? Got everybody, man. Leadbelly and Big Bill Broonzy. Lightning and Lemon and Sonny Boy.① You dig Broonzy? Just copped a new side of his.

None of the names meant a thing to me. Maybe I'd heard Leadbelly at a party at a white girl's house in Shadyside but the other names were a mystery. What was this sloppy-looking white boy talking about? His blond hair, long and greasy, was combed back James Dean style. Skin pale and puffy like a Gerber baby. He wore a smartass, whole-lot-hipper-than-you expression on his face. His mouth is what did it. Pudgy, soft lips with just a hint of blond fuzz above them, pursed into a permanent sneer.

He stared at me, waiting for an answer. At home we didn't get in other people's faces like that. You talked toward a space and the other person had a choice of entering or not entering, but this guy's blue eyes bored directly into mine. Waiting, challenging, prepared to send a message to that sneering mouth. I wanted no part of him, his records, or his questions.

Blues. Well, that's all I listen to. I like different songs at different times. Midnighters. Drifters got one I like out now.

Not that R-and-B crap on the radio, man. Like the real blues. Down home country blues. The old guys picking and singing.

Ray Charles. I like Ray Charles.

Hey, that ain't blues. Tell him, Darryl.

Darryl don't need to tell me anything. Been listening to blues all my life. Ray Charles is great. He's the best there is. How you gon tell me what's good and not good? It's my music. I've been hearing it all my life.

You're still talking about rock 'n' roll②. Rhythm and blues. Most of it's junk. Here today and gone tomorrow crap. I'm talking about authentic blues. Big Bill Broonzy. The Classics.

When he talked, he twisted his mouth so the words slithered out of one corner of his face, like garbage dumped off one end of a cafeteria tray. He pulled a cigarette from a pack in his shirt pocket. Lit it without disturbing the sneer.

Bet you've never even heard Bill Broonzy.

Don't need to hear no Broonzy or Toonsy or whoever the fuck he is. I don't give a shit about him nor any of them other old-timey dudes you're talking about, man. I know what I like and you can call it rhythm and blues or rock 'n' roll, it's still the best music. It's what I like and don't need nobody telling me what's good.

What are you getting mad about, man? How can you put down something you know

---

① 布鲁斯音乐家。

② rock 'n' roll: 摇滚乐。

nothing about? Bill Broonzy is the greatest twelve-string guitar player who ever lived. Everybody knows that. You've never heard a note he's played but you're setting yourself up as an expert. This is silly. You obviously can't back up what you're saying. You have a lot to learn about music, my friend.

He's wagging his big head and looking over at Darryl like Darryl's supposed to back his action. You can imagine what's going through my mind. How many times I've already gone upside his fat jaw. Biff. Bam. My fists were burning. I could see blood running out both his nostrils. The sneer split at the seams, smeared all over his chin. Here's this white boy in this white world bad-mouthing me to one of the few black faces I get to see, messing with the little bit of understanding I'm beginning to have with Darryl. And worse, trespassing on the private turf of my music, the black sounds from home I carry round in my head as a saving grace against the pressures of the university.

Talk about uptight. I don't believe that pompous ass could have known, because even I didn't know at that moment, how much he was hurting me. What hurt most was the truth of what he was saying. His whiteness, his arrogance made me mad, but it was truth putting the real hurt on me.

I didn't hit him. I should have but never did. A nice forget-me-knot upside his jaw. I should have but didn't. Not that time. Not him. Smashing his mouth would have been too easy, so I hated him instead. Let anger and shame and humiliation fill me to overflowing so the hate is still there, today, over twenty years later. The dormitory room had pale green walls, a bare wooden floor, contained the skimpy desk and sagging cot allotted to each cubicle in the hall. Darryl's things scattered everywhere. A self-portrait he'd painted stared down from one dirt-speckled wall. The skin of the face in the portrait was wildly molded, violent bruises of color surrounding haunted jade eyes. Darryl's eyes were green like my brother David's, but I hadn't noticed their color until I dropped by his room one afternoon between classes and Darryl wasn't there and I didn't have anything better to do than sit and wait and study the eyes in his painting. Darryl's room had been a sanctuary but when the white boy started preaching there was no place to hide. Even before he spoke the room had begun to shrink. He sprawled, lounged, an exaggerated casualness announcing how comfortable he felt, how much he belonged. Lord of the manor wherever he happened to plant his boots.

Darryl cooled it. His green eyes didn't choose either of us when we looked toward him for approval. Dawson had to see what a miserable corner I was in. He had to feel that room clamped tight around my neck and the sneer tugging the noose tighter.

A black motorcycle jacket, carved from a lump of coal, studded with silver and rhinestones, was draped over the desk chair. I wanted to stomp it, chop it into little pieces.

Hey, you guys, knock it off. Let's talk about something else. Obviously you have different tastes in music.

Darryl knew damn well that wasn't the problem. Together we might have been able to say the right things. Put the white boy in his place. Recapture some breathing space. But

— 282 —

Darryl had his own ghosts to battle. His longing for his blonde, blue-eyed Putney girl friend whose parent had rushed her off to Europe when they learned of her romance with the colored boy who was Putney school president. His ambivalence toward his blackness that would explode one day and hurtle him into the quixotic campaign of the Black Revolutionary Army to secede from the United States. So Darryl cooled it that afternoon in his room and the choked feeling never left my throat. I can feel it now as I write.

Why did that smartass white son of a bitch have so much power over me? Why could he confuse me, turn me inside out, make me doubt myself? Waving just a tiny fragment of truth, he could back me into a corner. Who was I? What was I? Did I really fear the truth about myself that much? Four hundred years of oppression, of lies had empowered him to use the music of my people as a weapon against me. Twenty years ago I hadn't begun to comprehend the larger forces, the ironies, the obscenities that permitted such a reversal to occur. All I had sensed was his power, the raw, crude force mocking me, diminishing me. I should have smacked him. I should have affirmed another piece of the truth he knew about me, the nigger violence.

Darryl and I would ride buses across Philly searching for places like home. Like the corner of Frankstown and Bruston in Homewood. A poolroom, barbershop, rib joint, record store strip with bloods in peacock colors strolling up and down and hanging out on the corner. After a number of long, unsuccessful expeditions (how could you ask directions? Who in the island of University would know what you were asking, let alone be able to tell you how to get there?), we found South Street. Just over the bridge, walking distance if you weren't in a hurry, but as far from school, as close to home as we could get. Another country.

Coming home from the university, from people and situations that continually set me against them and against myself, I was a dangerous person. If I wanted to stay in one piece and stay in school, I was forced to pull my punches. To maintain any semblance of dignity and confidence I had to learn to construct a shell around myself. Be cool. Work on appearing dignified, confident. Fool people with appearances, surfaces, live my real life underground in a region where no one could touch me. The trouble with this survival mechanism was the time and energy expended on upkeep of the shell. The brighter, harder, more convincing and impenetrable the shell became, the more I lost touch with the inner sanctuary where I was supposed to be hiding. It was no more accessible to me than it was to the people I intended to keep out. Inside was a breeding ground for rage, hate, dreams of vengeance.

Nothing original in my tactics. I'd adopted the strategy of slaves, the oppressed, the powerless. I thought I was running but I was fashioning a cage. Working hand in hand with my enemies. Knowledge of my racial past, of the worldwide struggle of people of color against the domination of Europeans would have been invaluable. History could have been a tool, a support in the day-to-day confrontations I experienced in the alien university environment. History could have taught me I was not alone, my situation was not unique. Believing I was alone made me dangerous, to myself and others.

College was a time of precipitous ups and downs. I was losing contact with the truth of my own feelings. Not trusting, not confiding in anyone else, learning to mistrust and deny my own responses left me solid ground, nowhere to turn. I was an expert at going with the flow, protecting myself by taking on the emotional or intellectual coloring of whatever circumstances I found myself in. All of this would have been bad enough if I'd simply been camouflaging my feelings. Yet it was far worse. I had no feelings apart from the series of roles and masquerades I found myself playing. And my greatest concern at the time had nothing to do with reestablishing an authentic core. What I feared most and spent most of my energy avoiding, was being unmasked.

Away from school I worked hard at being the same old home boy everybody remembered, not because I identified with that mask but because I didn't want you all to discover I was a traitor. Even at home a part of me stood outside, watching me perform. Even within the family. The watching part was unnamable. I hated it and depended on it. It was fear and cunning and anger and alienation; it was chaos, a yawning emptiness at the center of my being.

Once, in Wyoming, I saw a gut-shot antelope. A bullet had dropped the animal abruptly to its knees. It waggled to its feet again, tipsy, dazed. Then it seemed to hear death, like a prairie fire crackling through the sagebrush at its heels. The antelope bolted, a flat-out, bounding sprint, trailing guts like streamers from its low-slung pot-belly. I was running that hard, that fast, but without the antelope's blessed ignorance. I knew I was coming apart.

I could get ugly, vicious with people real quick. They'd think they knew the person they were dealing with, then I'd turn on them. Get drunk or fed up or just perverse for perversity's sake. Exercise the dark side of my power. Become a stranger, a different person. I'd scare people, hurt them. What I did to others, I was doing to myself. I wasn't sure I cried real tears, bled real blood. Didn't know whose eyes stared back at me from the mirror.

Problem is, I'm not talking about ancient history. I've changed. We've all changed. A lot's happened in the last twenty years. But what I was, I still am. You have to know this. My motives remain suspect. A potential for treachery remains deep inside the core. I can blend with my surroundings, because invisible. An opaque curtain slides down between me and others, between the part of me that judges and weighs and is accountable for my actions and that part that acts. Then, as always, I'm capable of profound irresponsibility. No way of being accountable because there's no one, no place to turn to.

I try harder these days. Love, marriage, children, a degree of success in the world, leisure to reconsider, to reason with myself, to read and write have increased my insight and altered my perspective. But words like "insight" and "altered perspective" are bullshit. They don't tell you what you need to know. Am I willing to go all the way? Be with you?

Share the weight? Go down with you wherever you have to go? No way to know beforehand. Words can't do that. Words may help me find you. Then we'll have to see. ...

You've seen Jamila almost yearly. Since she was a baby she's accompanied us on our visits to the prison. One of the family. I date your time in prison by her age. She used to cry coming and going. Now she asks questions, the hard kind I can't answer. The kinds of questions few in this society bother to pose about the meaning, the intent, the utility of locking people behind bars.

How long will Robby be in cage?

In a book about the evolution of imprisonment during the Middle Ages I discovered the word "jail" does in fact derive from "cage." Prisons in medieval England were basically custodial *cages* where convicted felons awaited punishment or the accused were held till traveling magistrates arrived to pass judgment. At specified towns or villages within the circuit of his jurisdiction a justice would *sit* (old French *assise*, hence the modern "assizes"), and prisoners would be transported from gaol to have their fate determined. Jamila knew what she was talking about. We said "jail" and she heard "cage," heard steel doors clanking, iron locks rattling, remembered animals penned in the zoo. Kids use words in ways that release hidden meanings, reveal the history buried in sounds. They haven't forgotten that words can be more than signs, that words have magic, the power to be things, to point to themselves and materialize. With their back-formations, archaisms, their tendency to play the music in words—rhythm, rhyme, alliteration, repetition—children peel the skin from language. Words become incantatory. Open Sesame. Abracadabra. Perhaps a child will remember the word and will bring the walls tumbling down.

Maybe Jamila's a yardstick for you too. Years registering in terms of pounds and inches. The changes in her body are the reality of time passing, the reality less observable in your outward appearance. People ask, How's Robby? and I don't know what to answer. If I say he's okay, people take that to mean he's the same. He's still the person we knew when he was free. I don't want to give anyone that impression of you. I know you're changing, growing as fast as Jamila. No one does time outside of time.

A narrow sense of time as a material entity, as a commodity like money that can be spent, earned, lost, owed, or stolen is at the bottom of the twisted logic of incarceration. When a person is convicted of a crime, the state dispossesses that criminal of a given number of days, months, years. Time pays for crime. By surrendering a certain portion of his allotment of time on earth the malefactor pays his debt to society.

But how does anyone do time outside of time? Since a person can't be removed from time unless you kill him, what prison does to its inmates is make time as miserable, as unpleasant, as possible. Prison time must be hard time, a metaphorical death, a sustained, twilight condition of death-in-life. The prisoner's life is violently interrupted, enclosed within a parenthesis. The point is to create the fiction that he doesn't exist. Prison is an experience of death by inches, minutes, hours, days.

Yet the little death of a prison sentence doesn't quite kill the prisoner, because prisons, in spite of their ability to make the inmate's life unbearable, can't kill time. Incarceration as punishment always achieves less and more than its intent. No matter how drastically you deprive a prisoner of the benefits of society, abridge his civil and legal rights, unman and torture him, unless you take his life, you can't take away his time. Many inmates die violently in prisons, almost all suffer in ways beyond an outsider's comprehension, but life goes on and since it does, miracles occur. Bodies languish, spirits are broken, yet in some rare cases the prison cell becomes the monk's cell, exile a spiritual retreat, isolation the blessed solitude necessary for self-examination, self-discipline.

In spite of all the measures Western society employs to secularize time, time transcends the conventional social order. Prisoners can be snatched from that order but not from time. Time imprisons us all. When the prisoner returns to society after serving his time, in an important sense he's never been away. Prisoners cannot step into the same river twice—prison may have rendered them unfit to live in free society, prison may have radically altered the prisoner's sense of self, his relation to his family and friends—but the river never goes away; it breaches the walls, washes them, washes us. We only pretend the prisoner has gone away.

We visit you in prison. Here we come. The whole family. Judy, Dan, Jake, Jamila. Our nuclear unit and Mom and whoever else we can fit into the Volvo station wagon. We try to arrive at the prison as early as possible, but with five in our crew competing for time and space in Mom's tiny bathroom in the house on Tokay, and slow-as-molasses nieces Monique and Tameka to pick up in East Liberty after we're all ready, we're lucky if we set off before noon. But here we come. Getting ready as we'd get ready for any family outing. Baths, teeth brushed, feeding, coaxing, the moment somewhere at the height of the bustle, frustration, and confusion when I say to myself, Shit. Is it worth all this hassle? Let's just call it off. Let's muzzle these little beasts and go back to bed and forget the whole thing. But we persevere. We're on our way.

Questions for Discussion

1. In this part, the family history is briefly illustrated, do you think the narrator wants to create a link between the past and the present?
2. What is (are) the big difference(s) between the two brothers? What makes "I" so distinctive, and make "my" dream come true?
3. It is said, that "History could have taught me I was not alone, my situation was not unique. Believing I was alone made me dangerous, to myself and others." How to understand this loneness and danger of the loneness?
4. How can the modern prison system change its victim? And what is the real function of the system?

参考书目

1. Baym, Nina (general editor). *The Norton Anthology of American Literature* (shorter, sixth edition). New York • London: W. W. Norton & Company, 2003.

2. Bercovitch, Sacvan (general editor). *The Cambridge History of American Literature* (Vol. 1-8). New York: Cambridge University Press, 1996-2003.

3. Bigsby, C. W. E. *Modern American Drama*, *1945-1990*. New York: Cambridge University Press, 1992.

4. Gates, Henry Louis Jr. and Nellie Y. McKay (general editors). *The Norton Anthology of African American Literature* (second edition). New York • London: W. W. Norton & Company, 2004.

5. Graham, Maryemma and Jerry Ward (eds.). *The Cambridge History of African American Literature*. New York: Cambridge University Press, 2011.

6. Jarrett, Gene (ed.). *A Companion to African American Literature*. Malden: Wiley-Blackwell, 2010.

7. Nadel, Alan (ed.). *May All Your Fences Have Gates: Essays on the Drama of August Wilson*. Iowa City: University of Iowa Press, 1994.

8. Samuels, Wilfred. *Encyclopedia of African-American Literature*. New York: Facts on File, Inc., 2017.

9. 伯科维奇.剑桥美国文学史(第1—8卷).北京:中央编译出版社,2008—2012.

10. 程锡麟.赫斯顿研究.上海:上海外语教育出版社,2005.

11. 郭继德.当代美国戏剧发展趋势.济南:山东大学出版社,2009.

12. 刘海平,王守仁.新编美国文学史(第1—4卷).上海:上海外语教育出版社,2019.

13. 王家湘.20世纪美国黑人小说.南京:译林出版社,2006.

图书在版编目(CIP)数据

非裔美国文学作品选读 / 王玉括主编. — 南京：
南京大学出版社，2020.10
ISBN 978-7-305-23705-8

Ⅰ. ①非… Ⅱ. ①王… Ⅲ. ①美国黑人-文学作品研
究-高等学校-教材 Ⅳ. ①I712.06

中国版本图书馆 CIP 数据核字(2020)第 154817 号

出版发行　南京大学出版社
社　　址　南京市汉口路 22 号　　　　　邮　编　210093
出 版 人　金鑫荣

书　　名　非裔美国文学作品选读
主　　编　王玉括
责任编辑　董　颖　　　　　　　编辑热线　025-83596997

照　　排　南京南琳图文制作有限公司
印　　刷　江苏苏中印刷有限公司
开　　本　787×1092　1/16　印张 18.75　字数 308 千字
版　　次　2020 年 10 月第 1 版　2020 年 10 月第 1 次印刷
ISBN 978-7-305-23705-8
定　　价　55.00 元

网址：http://www.njupco.com
官方微博：http://weibo.com/njupco
官方微信号：njupress
销售咨询热线：(025) 83594756